LADIES OF
THE MANOR

The RELUCTANT DUCHESS

ROSEANNA M. WHITE

BETHANYHOUSE
a division of Baker Publishing Group
Minneapolis, Minnesota

Published by Bethany House Publishers
11400 Hampshire Avenue South
Bloomington, Minnesota 55438
www.bethanyhouse.com

Bethany House Publishers is a division of
Baker Publishing Group, Grand Rapids, Michigan

Printed in the United States of America

ISBN 978-0-7642-1351-9

Library of Congress Control Number: 2015956735

Scripture quotations are from the King James Version of the Bible.

This is a work of historical reconstruction; the appearances of certain historical figures are therefore inevitable. All other characters, however, are products of the author's imagination, and any resemblance to actual persons, living or dead, is coincidental.

Cover design by Jennifer Parker
Cover photography by Mike Habermann Photography, LLC

Author represented by The Steve Laube Agency

16 17 18 19 20 21 22 8 7 6 5 4 3 2

To my childhood friends,
Brittney, Jennifer, Melissa, Elisa, Christy, Lisa.

We traveled many years together, grew together,
became who we are together.
And though now we've drifted apart,
nothing can ever change the memories forged
in the innocence of childhood.
That's a magic no amount of time can ever erase.

Character List

Rowena's Family

Rowena Kinnaird	Daughter of Douglas and Nora Kinnaird.
The Earl of Lochaber and Chief of Clan Kinnaird	Rowena's father. Given name of Douglas Kinnaird, and though he should officially always be addressed as Lord Lochaber or Lochaber, he prefers his clan title to his peerage one and often answers to "the Kinnaird."
Nora	Rowena's mother, deceased. Called Lady Lochaber while she lived. American-born.
The Countess of Lochaber	Rowena's stepmother. Given name of Elspeth. Called Lady Lochaber.
Annie	Rowena's stepsister, daughter of Elspeth. Given name of Annys.
Lilias Cowan	Rowena's lady's maid and distant Kinnaird cousin.
Malcolm Kinnaird	Rowena's third cousin and the heir to the chiefdom of Clan Kinnaird.

Brice's Family

Brice Myerston	The Duke of Nottingham. Called Nottingham or Duke. Called Brice by family.
Charlotte, the (Dowager) Duchess of Nottingham	Brice's mother. Called Duchess or Duchess of Nottingham by peers, Your Grace by the public, Charlotte by friends. Her family (family name Brice) was from Scotland—Highland ancestral home, Gaoth Lodge.
Lady Ella Myerston	Brice's younger sister. Called Lady Ella.

Other Characters

Duke and Duchess of Stafford	Brice's closest friends. Brook and Justin from *The Lost Heiress*. Young son, William—usually referred to as Lord Abingdon.
The Earl of Whitby	Brook's father, called Lord Whitby, Whitby, or Whit.
The Earl of Cayton	Justin's cousin. Given name is James, called Cayton. A recent widower. Infant daughter, Addie. Deceased wife, Adelaide.
Lady Pratt	Widowed viscountess. Called Lady Pratt by most, Catherine or Kitty by friends.
Lord Rushworth	Catherine's brother, given name of Crispin. Called Lord Rushworth, Rushworth, or Rush.
Geoff Abbott	Brice's oldest friend; soon to be a vicar in Bristol. Called Mr. Abbott or Abbott by most, Geoff by his sister and father.
Stella Abbott	Ella's oldest friend; soon to be a governess in Hertfordshire. Called Miss Abbott by most, Stella by friends.
Old Abbott	Steward of Midwynd Park; father of Geoff and Stella.
Davis	Brice's valet.
Lewis	Ella's lady's maid.
Lapham	Charlotte's lady's maid.
Mr. Gordon	Butler at Gaoth Lodge.
Mr. Macnab	Jeweler in Lochaber.
Mr. Child	Butler at Midwynd Park.
Mrs. Granger	Housekeeper at Midwynd Park.
Mr. Morris	The constable in Brighton.

One

Aᴜɢᴜsᴛ 1912
Lᴏᴄʜᴀʙᴇʀ, Hɪɢʜʟᴀɴᴅs, Sᴄᴏᴛʟᴀɴᴅ

She could have been more than she was. Rowena dug her toes into the cold sand, wrapped her wool-clad arms around her tweed-clad knees, and stared out into the clear, fathomless waters of Loch Morar. Here, land gave way gently to loch. Not so a mile northward, where the crags tumbled down into waters too deep to plumb. Deep and cold and wind-wracked.

She was a lady, by rights. Daughter of Douglas Kinnaird, the Earl of Lochaber and chief of Clan Kinnaird. Lady Rowena they had called her at school in Edinburgh for those two blessed years she had gotten away.

She didn't feel like a lady. Hadn't since her father barged into the gymnasium when she was fifteen and dragged her out in full view of all the girls she'd thought were her friends—all the girls who laughed at her and tittered about barbarian Celts. She hadn't felt like a lady since he told her that Mother had plunged from one of those crags, into the loch.

To escape him, no doubt. Assuming he hadn't given her a helpful push.

Rowena tugged the heavy woolen sleeves farther down over her wrists. The bruising hadn't yet faded. Not from her father's fingers though—not this time. Father had learned not to leave marks when he punished her for saying the wrong thing. For not being strong enough to honor the clan.

For being too much like Mother.

The wind whipped around her, stinging her eyes. That was why tears blurred the image of the golden eagle soaring above the lake. The wind. Not the thought of her mother . . . or Malcolm. Certainly not a vain wish for those carefree days of childhood, before she realized what a monster her father was. Before his laughter had died and his hand had turned so heavy. Sometimes she thought she must have imagined those lovely years of ease in Castle Kynn. Created the memories of a loving father, for there had been no evidence of him for the last decade.

She sniffed and dashed the scratchy sleeve over her eyes. It was brown, like the weathered grass three feet back, where sandy shore turned to hilly trail. Brown, like the leaves of the dead tree the eagle settled onto. Brown, like she felt inside.

Dead. Withered. Done.

Were she brave enough, she would follow in her mother's footsteps and toss herself into the loch. Let the cold waters close over top of her and swallow her, erase it all. But, nay, the very thought sent her heart pounding and had her throat closing off. Ending it all would be so quick—but she couldn't.

She would just have to suffer whatever blow life dealt her next.

"There ye are, *mo muirnín.*"

The voice, dark and deep as the nightmares that had plagued her these weeks, sent her scrambling to her feet. Her eyes darted to and yon, but no path of escape lay open to her. The beach ran into too-steep banks, the water lapped, and *he* blocked the way back to the castle. She spun to face him and saw the centuries-old stone on Castle Kynn's promontory in the loch, out of reach.

But then, her home hadn't kept her safe before, had it? Why should she think it would now?

Clutching her jacket closed, she backed away until she nearly stumbled over her discarded shoes. "Dinna come any closer, Malcolm. And dinna be calling me your darling."

He smiled. Looked for all the world as if he hadn't a care, hadn't a worry, hadn't a side so black and cruel.

A year he'd fooled her. Made her think he was something different than her father, made her think him kind and charming. The sort of man she would be grateful to call husband, whom she could trust to protect her from the rages of her father, the Kinnaird. How could she not have seen it?

"What's got into you, Rowena?" He held out a hand as if expecting her to place her fingers in his. "I'm gone two weeks to attend business, and ye turn to a cowering shrew? Come. Greet me properly."

A shiver made her shoulders convulse. That was what he had said then. *Come. Say good-bye properly*. But he hadn't just wanted a kiss as she'd given him before. She could still feel the stone floor he'd shoved her to when she'd tried to pull away. Still saw—every time she closed her eyes—his sneer as she'd begged him to stop.

The bruises on her wrist throbbed, though they hadn't hurt for a week. "As if ye dinna ken what's 'got into' me." She took another step back, but her legs hit against the bank. "Go away, Malcolm, and dinna be coming back."

It flashed in his eyes, that storm she hadn't seen until recently. Lightning and thunder and deadly, driving wind. "Is that any way to talk to the man ye'll marry?"

She shook like a leaf in his gale. "I'll not marry you." It would be a slower death than drowning, but no less certain than if she waded into the loch with stones in her pockets. "Ye'll never touch me again, Malcolm Kinnaird."

Three large steps, and the hands he curled around her arms proved otherwise. Shackles, even though they were—now—gentle. To match the charming smile she'd been fooled by. "*Mo muirnín*. I'm sorry if I hurt you. I didna mean to."

If? If he'd hurt her? Did he not remember how he'd bloodied her lip, how he'd knocked her head to the stone floor so that the world went grey, how she'd cried out in agony as he—

"I love you." One of his hands stroked through her hair, which the wind had already pulled free of its chignon. A month ago, the soft touch would have sent shivers of delight down her back. A month ago, the words would have made her shout for joy. Today, her stomach threatened to heave. "It got the better of me, is all. I forgot m'self."

And she'd lose herself forever if she didn't get free of him. He'd devour her whole, leaving nothing but the empty shell her mother had become. She tried to shrug him off, to push at his chest. He didn't budge. "Let me go." Her voice came out strangled and tremulous. "Please, Malcolm. Please let me go."

"Why must ye fight me? If ye hadna fought me . . ."

Bile rose in her throat. "*Ye must have invited it, Rowena*"—that's what her father had said when he found her, bloodied and sobbing, in the tower. "*I ken young Kinnaird. He's a fine Highlander and will be a fine chief after me, and if ye're glaikit enough to anger him, then it's on yer own head. I'll see that he marries you, and ye'd best be wise enough to thank me for it.*"

Never. She wouldn't marry him—*that* would be the foolish thing, not daring to anger him. She wouldn't. He'd never take again what he stole from her in the tower, and she would sooner set herself outside for a winter night's freezing than thank her father for trying to force her to it.

"Rowena." Malcolm's hands slid from her arms to her back, pulling her closer. "Forgive me—I beg you. I'll never hurt you again. I swear it. I'll be a good husband." He sounded as he always had done. Charming, earnest. His dark hair still spilled onto his forehead in that way that made all the village lasses swoon. But she had no more blinders on her eyes.

She swallowed down the bile and put her arms up, against his chest. "No." She wanted it to sound strong—it didn't, but at least she managed to speak it. "I said I'll not marry you, and I mean it, ye ken? Now, let me go. My father'll be fashed if I'm not back in by tea."

"Ach." He grinned and trailed his fingers up her spine. "I was just in speaking with him, *mo muirnín*. He knows I've come out here to find you and make the betrothal official. He won't mind if we linger."

A stone sank deep in her stomach, churning rather than settling. She could fight them both. She could, and she would. But it would be an ugly business, and she was none too sure there was any way to win.

A flitter of movement dragged her gaze away from the monster's handsome mask and lit another flurry of panic in her stomach. Little Annie was galloping toward them, through the high grasses, happy oblivion on her face as she called out, "Wena! Mrs. MacPherson has made the cakes you like. Aren't you coming?"

The idea of cake, of any food, made the bile surge up again. But Malcolm's arms loosened as her eight-year-old stepsister loped their way, and Rowena seized the chance to step free of him. Her eyes scanned the space beyond Annie's fine dark head, spotting the child's mother walking at a more sedate pace, Lilias beside her.

No doubt it was Lilias who'd suggested they come fetch her. She must have seen, from Rowena's window, when Malcolm headed her way. Heaven knew Elspeth—Lady Lochaber for the last three years—never had aught but a sneer for Rowena.

Rowena summoned up a smile for her stepsister and bent to catch her in an embrace that felt warmer than anything else ever did. "Of course I'll come, Annie. I didna realize the time." The wee one had hair the same shade as the Kinnaird's, and the first time Rowena saw her sitting on his knee, the resemblance had been unmistakable—not just his coloring, but his nose, his chin. She was his daughter as sure as Rowena was, though the man Annie thought was her father hadn't died until she was three, and Rowena's mother just a year before that.

In that moment she had been able to imagine what some of her parents' arguments had been about. She had shot her father a look, and another to Elspeth.

The woman had despised her ever since.

Malcolm bent down to put his face on a level with Annie's, his face wreathed in the grin that was such a convincing lie. "A bonny day to you, wee one. I declare, ye get prettier each time I see you."

Annie tucked herself to Rowena's side and scowled at him. "I'm not a wee one anymore, Malcolm Kinnaird, and I'll thank you to remember it. I'm nearly nine."

Barely eight, but who wanted to quibble? Rowena smoothed back one of the dark locks that the wind tore free of Annie's ribbon. "And soon to be as tall as me."

Malcolm reached out, presumably to chuck the girl under the chin, but Rowena pulled her back a step, out of reach.

Thunder rumbled in his eyes as he straightened. "I could do with one of Mrs. MacPherson's cakes myself. We had better head in. We can finish our conversation later, *mo muirnín*."

Alone, he meant. He'd ask her father for a few minutes with her, and then he'd shut the door. Back her into a corner. Clamp his hand down over her mouth again and shove her to the stones.

Her fingers dug into her sister's shoulder, but Annie just wrapped an arm around Rowena's waist, making no complaint. The wee one lifted her chin. "I didna say ye were invited, did I?"

The older women had, by now, drawn near, and Elspeth drew in a shocked gasp. "Annys! How dare ye speak so to Malcolm! Ye know well he's always a welcome guest."

By the look on Annie's face, she was about to let loose and kick the monster in the shins. Rowena had done her best to shield the girl from the truth, but the bruises and swollen lip had been impossible to hide, and the little one was too good a spy not to have heard who inflicted them—though she prayed the girl had heard no whisper of *how*.

Rowena steered her a step away before Annie's boldness could get them all in trouble. Thus far her father had shown only fondness for the girl—like he had once done toward Rowena. That wouldn't change on her account. She scooped up her shoes and stockings and then headed for the grass, giving Malcolm wide berth.

She expected a scolding to be upon Elspeth's lips as they drew near—for Rowena's bare feet, if not for Annie's rudeness—but the countess's gaze had latched on to a distant point, her pretty brown brows drawn in. "I had hoped they wouldn't come this year, after the duke's death last autumn. Ach, now the Kinnaird's sure to be scunnered for a week."

Rowena turned with the others to see what had captured her stepmother's attention. But she knew what she would see. The line of fine carriages were pulled by proud horses, and a gleaming red automobile even bounced over the rutted road—one of only a few of those Rowena had ever seen, and no doubt by far the nicest. Though she couldn't make out details, she knew it would all bear the crest of the Duke of Nottingham. Gaoth Lodge would come alive, then, for a month or more. The duke's group would hunt and fish and invite all the Highland families of any note to dine and dance.

Not the Kinnairds, though. Never them.

Rowena rubbed a finger behind her ear. She could still feel the scar where the stone had bit that first time her father had lost his head with her and sent her reeling when she was ten. Her mother had gotten it worse, though, for daring to call on the duchess the first time they came to the Lodge.

Or, as it were, the first time they came *back*. Until that summer, the Duchess of Nottingham's Lowland parents had come to their second home often enough, but their daughter and her family had not. Apparently Father had known them though. And liked them none too well.

Malcolm grunted and altered his course away from the castle. "Let me know when it passes, eh, Lady Lochaber? No use trying to talk to him before."

"Aye. Though perhaps planning the wedding will distract him this year."

Annie's arm tightened around Rowena's waist. Her voice came at a murmur, barely audible over the wind. "Ye canna marry him, Wena. Ye canna. He hurt you."

Sweet girl. Rowena held her tight to her side and met Lilias's blue gaze. "I dinna mean to, Annie. It's just I havena yet worked out how to avoid it."

Lilias stepped to Rowena's other side as Malcolm strode to the horse hobbled near the road. "We'll find a way, lass. I promise."

Rowena leaned into the older woman's strength for a moment. But only one. Lilias Cowan may be a distant cousin, but hard times had forced her to a servant's post. She had first been her mother's lady's maid and was now hers. And much as Rowena loved her as a second mother, Lilias could do nothing Rowena herself couldn't.

She couldn't create hope where there was none.

Lilias leaned close. "We'll find one soon," she whispered directly into Rowena's ear, so Annie wouldn't hear. "We must. Lady Lochaber is with child, and the Kinnaird plans to wed you to Malcolm before it's known, fearing otherwise he won't be able to at all. If the babe's a boy . . ."

A shudder stole through Rowena. If her stepmother produced the long-awaited son, then Rowena would no longer be the heiress of Lochaber. And Malcolm's "love" for her would likely go the way of mist in the summer.

Perhaps hope existed after all. "Then if we can but put him off—or tell Malcolm."

"Maybe." Though the squeeze of Lilias's arm around Rowena's shoulder carried a warning. "But if you do that, yer father will be as angry as Malcolm is like to be—and if . . . if ye're in the same way . . ."

Nothing but pure determination kept Rowena on her feet. Other young ladies who found themselves so compromised would be sent away on tour, where they could deliver the child in anonymity and into the hands of a family who would raise it in secret.

But the Kinnaird would never do that. No, if she refused to wed Malcolm while carrying his child, her father would likely give her beating enough to guarantee a miscarriage. Quite possibly to kill her too, now that he had another heir on the way.

She ran a hand down Annie's arm to chafe some warmth into it and felt the strangest pang in her middle.

She didn't want to die. Much as it felt she had nothing to live for, there it was. She wanted a chance to make a life. To forge a path for herself.

But if the courses already a day late never came, if she were with child . . . She squeezed her eyes shut against a stinging gust of wind and sucked in a breath. If the Lord still heard her prayers, she would pray against such a thing. But what point was there to that? He had left her long ago. He must have, for her to have ended up here, like this. Hated by her father, violated by the man she had thought loved her.

Perhaps this was just fitting. The hated child bearing a hated child. Another link in the chain. A perpetuation of the cycle.

No! I willna. A sob nearly burst its way out of her throat. She subdued all but a gasp that had her little sister looking up at her with question in her eyes, and then she managed a tight smile that she doubted would convince her all was well.

But she wouldn't hate the bairn if she had one—she *wouldn't.* She knew how it felt to live knowing you were detested for who you were born to. Father despised her because she was Mother's daughter—how could she in turn hate a child for being Malcolm's? It was no fault of the babe's, if a babe there was.

No. If she was with child, then . . . then it meant she had some innocence inside her, despite being stripped of her own. And she would love it. She would. Despite everything, she would—she would be a better parent than either of hers had been.

"Annys! Come here."

With a sigh older than her eight years, Annie gave Rowena's waist one last squeeze and joined her mother.

Rowena turned to Lilias. "Maybe I should run away. I could go to Gasta Hall."

"It's the first place he'd look, given how ye once loved the place, before he let it go to rot." Lilias shook her head, looking back toward Gaoth Lodge, where the last of the duke's procession was disappearing from sight.

Rowena's shoulders slumped. Two homes—the one he had inherited from his mother, and the castle that came from the Kinnairds—and neither open to her. Not if she disobeyed her father. "I've my mother's people in America."

"Finding them could be a task, since the Kinnaird cut off all communication." Lilias sighed, her focus still locked on the Lodge. "Nay, lass. Ye need a more immediate means of escape."

Then why was she looking that direction? Rowena folded her arms over the shoes she had pressed to her middle. That summer a decade past, when Father had been in London for the Sessions and the duke's carriages had first rolled up the road alongside those belonging to the Brice family, she had made a friend. She and Lady Ella, two years her junior, had gotten on from the first and had played together most every day.

But Ella would be a society lady now, no doubt with a dozen suitors and the fanciest gowns and that way of walking and talking that Rowena hadn't mastered in her two years at school in Edinburgh. Ella would now be like all the other girls she'd once called friends—quick to laugh at her and declare her naught but the bumpkin daughter of a barbarian clinging to an age long dead.

Yet . . . yet if she could somehow renew the acquaintance. If she could somehow convince Ella to invite her south, down to England. If her father for some reason let her go. Things would surely look different away from here. Away from her father and Malcolm, from the ghosts of Loch Morar. Maybe in the south of England she could seize a stray wisp of freedom.

But it would take a true miracle to get her there—and the ghosts of Loch Morar were fonder of giving curses than blessings.

Two

Brice Myerston wasn't given to belief in curses, as a rule. But as he sat down at the massive desk in the locked study of Gaoth Lodge and set the box in front of him, he wondered. Wondered what powers people could harness that went beyond normal understanding. Wondered why God would forbid something, if it didn't exist. Wondered how much of the world he would never comprehend.

The wondering was more easily done in the Highlands, where one couldn't turn around without butting into a local eager to share a story about ghosts or fairies or water horses or charms. In past years, when they'd come up with his mother's kin for a few weeks of relaxation and sport, he had found the stories and superstitions nothing but that. This year, with this box before him, he was a little less certain that he knew where fact ended and fantasy began.

He stared at the box. It was nothing out of the ordinary—just a small wooden thing that he had pilfered from his rooms at Midwynd Park before they'd closed up house to head to London for the Season. But he hadn't opened the box in the four months since he closed it over the collection of gleaming red jewels—two gleaming more than the rest.

And he didn't want to open it now.

"Rubbish." Brice drew in a breath, shook off the doubt that cloaked him like the morning mist over the loch, and raised the hinged lid.

It required another deep breath to convince himself to reach inside and pull out one of the twin gems. He held it up and let the light from the lamp catch and play with the internal flames.

The Fire Eyes. He knew the story of the red diamonds, and of the tiger's curse they had supposedly carried with them from India. Were he to tell the tale of greed and death around the hearth one night, the Highlanders among them would no doubt sketch a cross from head to heart to ward off any evil attached to the things—assuming they didn't take them and toss them into the loch out of abject terror.

No, Brice Myerston wasn't given to belief in curses. But the fact remained that death followed the things, thanks to the greed they inspired. And in the year since he had accepted them from his friends' hands, death had visited his house too.

When he had put the gems in his pocket, he had been the Marquess of Worthing, free of any concerns that would hinder him from flushing out those hunting the gems so that Brook and Stafford, the rightful owners, could have a rest from it all and settle into married life.

A week later, his father had fallen on the steps of Gaoth Lodge, clutching at his chest. Brice had been coming outside to meet him, had seen him fall. Had been unable to do anything other than rush forward in time to hear the final breath wheeze from his father's lips.

Now Brice was the Duke of Nottingham. Not the fault of the curse—he would never say that. It had been happenstance, not greed. A defect in Father's heart. But his death was a fact. A fact that changed everything.

Heaving a sigh, he dropped the small, perfect jewel back into the unassuming box and closed the lid. He looked to the window. Dawn barely lightened the mist. The loch, though usually visible from this room, was nothing but a shrouded shadow in the predawn.

The expected tap came at the study door. Without a word, Brice stood, stepped to the solid oak panel, turned the key in the lock. With a silent nod to the butler, he ushered in the second man, as shrouded as the morning in a hat and coat.

He locked the door again behind the old man. "Thank you for coming, Mr. Macnab."

The fellow took off his hat, revealing smiling blue eyes. "Anything for yer family, Yer Grace. Sorry I was to hear of yer father's passing last year. Never did an autumn go by without him coming to my shop to buy a bauble for yer mother, though we both kent she needed none from my feeble hand."

Brice smiled and ushered the aging jeweler to a seat. "Father always delighted in showering Mother with gifts. And she especially loves the ones you crafted—she says you always bring a bit of Scotland to them, and it makes her feel at home."

To most Highlanders, his mother barely qualified as Scottish, being firstly from the Lowlands and secondly of a noble—which was to say, English—family. But Macnab had never made such a distinction.

The old man eased into the seat, as if it or he might shatter if he sat too quickly. "Yer words do me honor, Yer Grace. As much an honor as it is to ken that my work graces the throat and wrists of such a fine lady."

"She is, at that. And that's why I asked you to come here in secret. Were I to go to your shop, word of it would make its way back to her, and she would catch on too quickly to my scheme." Brice sat too—not behind the desk but beside the jeweler. He smiled and hoped the story—not strictly false but not entirely true—would not be too much questioned.

Light gleamed warm and steady in the old man's eyes. "Ye wish to make a surprise to yer matron, to ease the loss. A good son ye must be."

A better one probably wouldn't intend to give his mother this particular gift, but it was the only answer he could find when he prayed last year over what to do with the jewels. Hidden they had been in a necklace for nigh unto twenty years—hidden they needed to be again.

And he trusted no jeweler in England to be above bribery. But Macnab . . . Father had always trusted him implicitly. That was good enough for Brice.

He reached over, pulling forward not the small box but a larger one—more ornate and, when he opened it, with a pillowed interior made to display the heavy pieces within.

"The Nottingham rubies. Necklace and bracelet, as you can see, but the earbobs went missing some fifteen years ago—Mother's lady's maid was dismissed over it, but they were never recovered. Father gave the set to Mother to commemorate their wedding, and she has always been greatly distressed that part of it went missing on her watch, as it were. I thought to have the set completed while she is still wearing only jet and present it to her when she dons color again in a few weeks."

While Macnab nodded along, Brice pulled forward the smaller box, along with a framed photograph. "I've secured gems that match the others in clarity and color. Six of them—three for each side. And here is Mother's wedding portrait. As you can see, they were dangling affairs."

"Aye." The jeweler traced a finger over the ornate setting of the necklace, his eyes focused on the picture. No doubt envisioning the gleam of gold dripping down and around the jewels. He held out a steady, lined palm for the loose gems.

Brice shook them into the hand as if they were nothing. As if two of them hadn't brought his friends unimaginable grief. As if they were all the same, and scarcely worth counting.

Macnab turned them in his palm. Perhaps he was noting the cut, the size, or some other factor known best to the men of his trade. He wouldn't, Brice prayed, look at them too closely. The rubies were the best match he had been able to find for the diamonds—bright, clear, red as blood. But no ruby ever had such fire in its heart.

When the old man pulled out a loupe and held it to his eye, Brice nearly whimpered. But Macnab made no sharp inhalation of shock, no grunts of discovery, no sign whatsoever that he had noted the difference that must be obvious under magnification.

He just lowered the loupe again and looked over at Brice with calm, questioning blue eyes.

Well, he'd known this was likely. The average viewer wouldn't note the difference at a glance, but this was a man who had dealt with gems longer than Brice had been alive. He passed a hand through his hair and held the jeweler's gaze. "It's to help a friend. Discretion, you understand, is vital."

A smile drew deeper creases into the man's lined face. "Then allow me to exclaim now, just this once—I've only heard of such things as a possibility. Never thought to hold such rarity in my own hands. Where do they come from—do ye know? Africa?"

"India—these, anyway."

"India." Macnab echoed him reverently as he shook the gems together. "Ye must have searched for months looking for rubies so close a match. *Those* are rare enough too. Though the ones in the Nottingham pieces are nearly as clear and bright, I grant you."

He had shared his search with absolutely no one. Frustration had nearly bested him once or twice too. "Six months. I trust no jeweler in England enough to handle them and keep quiet about it."

Macnab let the jewels drip back into the box. Blinked, and blinked again as he now drew in that sharp breath. "I'm right honored, Yer Grace. Right honored. I'll ne'er breathe a word, nor will I put it to paper. And if by chance my Maggie asks why I've not recorded the work I've done, I'll tell her ye wanted no proof that the earbobs weren't original to the set. Family secrets, ye ken. Yer mother can claim to have found them, misplaced all this time."

A grin pulled at the corners of Brice's mouth. "I appreciate it. And I shall pay you—"

"The price of gold and labor, and not a pence more. Yer father, God rest his soul, helped me from a tough spot some years ago." He lowered the lid and clasped the box in his hands. "I'm only thankful for a chance to repay one of his own, in small part."

A bit of the weight on Brice's shoulders eased. He closed the more ornate box and handed it over as well, for comparison as Macnab worked. "It isn't so small to me. I'm grateful."

"Say no more of it." The old man levered himself to his feet with the same slow care he had used sitting down. "I'll take my leave before the house stirs and questions get asked. When I've finished, I'll send word as to when I'll stop by again, aye?"

"Thank you." Brice stood to see Macnab to the door, and he didn't bother locking it again after the man had gone. Instead he fetched his hat and a light overcoat and headed out into the mist himself.

Most mornings, Brice wouldn't be up quite this early, and he would usually call for a horse. But he had no desire to rouse the grooms from their breakfast, so he headed out on foot. He crossed the green where there would later be a football game with some of the neighbors, assuming the rain held off, and rounded the tennis courts that Father had put in for Ella a few years back, when she was—briefly—in love with the sport. Minutes later he stepped to the edge of the property, where they had the best view of the loch below.

There, a hunkering form rose from the waters, only slightly more mysterious in the fog than it ever looked. Castle Kynn was without question one of the most picturesque places he had ever seen. Built onto one of the many small islands just off the shore of the loch, it had naught but a stone bridge, arched and lovely, to connect it to the mainland. Every time he saw it, Brice imagined clans warring in their various tartans, or ill-fated Highlanders charging in the wake of Bonny Prince Charlie. It seemed a place preserved in time.

Or perhaps that was just because he had never seen anything but the never-changing stones of its walls. Surely inside it was more modern. They wouldn't have electricity—power had not yet made its way to Lochaber—and so no telephones either. But other improvements had no doubt been made by the dour-faced earl Brice had only glimpsed a time or two in town.

"You're up and about early, darling."

He jumped at his mother's voice, though it had been quiet, and spun with a grin. She wore a stylish black kimono jacket against the chill and a close-fitting hat, both trimmed in the crepe of mourning. But the highest of fashions couldn't disguise the pain that still shadowed her eyes. He held out an arm to welcome her to his side. "Taking advantage while it isn't raining. I thought you and Ella would rest until eight or nine this morning after the journey."

"Mm." She leaned into him, her weariness obvious. "I'm

afraid the journey left me too sore and achy to rest properly. When I saw you, I thought I would join you on your stroll—only, you seem to have stopped strolling."

He rubbed a hand over her silk-clad arm and nodded toward the castle. "Just admiring the view. Have you ever seen the inside?"

Mother cleared her throat and straightened. "Many, many years ago."

"Did they once offer tours? Or was the previous earl not quite so stern?"

Now his mother sighed. "Lord Lochaber's father was chief of the clan but not the earl—that came from his mother. I'm afraid the lady passed away when the earl was young, and his father raised him to despise the side of his heritage that came with English ties. Castle Kynn is, of course, the Kinnaird estate. They've another home twenty miles away or so that goes with the Lochaber title. So far as I know, the earl never goes there. Most of the time he isn't even called Lochaber, but 'the Kinnaird.' Like a chief of old."

That prejudice, Brice supposed, explained why Lord Lochaber never replied to any of their invitations and never issued any of his own. Brice had seen a veritable procession of Highlanders coming and going from the castle every year, but apparently, if one wasn't of the Clan Kinnaird, one wasn't fit for Lochaber's regard.

Only that didn't answer the question of how Mother had managed to see the interior. "How did you finagle an invitation, then?" He tipped his head toward the castle again.

Mother turned up her lips, though it was hardly a smile. Not compared to what she used to have done, before Father . . . "I was not always an English duchess, Brice. Always a Lowlander, but they were willing to forgive that much. At least long enough to invite us to dine with them once or twice. It's as lovely inside as you would think—positively medieval. Though I can't think I would ever want to live with cold stone surrounding me always."

"Well." In consideration of her aching muscles, he turned them both away, back toward the walking path. "I obviously should have come with you and Ella the summer the earl was away. So I could have seen it for myself."

His mother laughed. Not so bright, not so free, but a laugh nonetheless. He had heard precious few of them from her over the past months. "We never went there that summer. They always came here. And besides, you would have been bored senseless, with no boys your age about."

"Young men, you mean." He bit back a grin as he said it. He'd thought himself a man at seventeen, to be sure. Though praise to the Lord that he'd never had to prove it. He hadn't had to manage stewards and solicitors and tenants and rents and . . .

He missed his father. Missed walking through the village at Midwynd with him, cataloguing repairs that needed made, inquiring about the tenants' ailing mothers and wayward sons. Missed seeing the measured wisdom alight in his father's eyes. Missed knowing that he was there, always there, ready to answer questions and pat backs and smile encouragement.

Mother gripped his arm. "There are invitations awaiting us and replies to the ones we sent out. After breakfast, we should go through them. Plan our stay."

Brice nodded. His mother had still been in first mourning throughout the Season, so he and Ella had gone through his sister's debut summer on their own. Only now was Mother accepting and giving invitations—though it was other plans *he* felt most compelled to make. Plans about what he would do once they went back to England. How he would draw out Lady Pratt and prove—and thereby halt—her hunt for the Fire

Eyes. Put an end to that nonsense once and for all so he could focus on the estates.

Heaviness gripped his chest. It wouldn't be so simple. He knew that so clearly that words might as well have sounded audibly, so perfectly did they settle in his mind. Just like they had when Brook had been kidnapped last year. And like that dreadful day when the silent but echoing *Go* had sent him outside to meet his father, crumpled on the steps so near where they now walked.

Maybe one of these days, the Lord would send the warning when he could actually *do* something about it.

By the time Brice found his sister and their guests, they had all taken their separate breakfasts and the sun had burned the mist from the face of the loch. He followed the girls' laughter to what Mother had always called the morning room—east-facing, with golden sunshine spilling in, nearly as bright as his sister's laughter.

He paused outside the door just long enough to thank the Lord for hearing it again. Too long Ella had been nearly silent, all of her mirth dampened by grief. Bringing Geoff and Stella Abbott along to the Highlands had been a good idea, though. Their steward's children had grown up alongside them, knew how to brighten their moods. He rather wished they wouldn't both be heading off to far and sunder parts of England in the next few months.

Sucking in a fortifying breath, Brice fastened a smile onto his lips and strode in just in time to see Abbott balance himself on one foot, arms up and tugging back as if holding an imaginary fishing pole.

"And then the beast gave a mighty tug and sent him splashing into the river." Abbott flung himself onto the divan amidst another shout of laughter from the girls.

Brice's smile went more earnest. "You ought to include that tale in your first sermon, Abbott. Complete with reenactment."

His old friend laughed, too, and took a more proper seat upon the cushions. "Perhaps I shall, Your Grace. An altered account of how Jonah ended up in the belly of the great fish. My new parishioners will be on the edges of their pews."

"If you do, I'll be sure to travel all the way to Bristol to hear it." Aiming his steps for the larger couch on which the girls perched, Brice chose a seat in between them. "And how did the bells sleep?"

His sister tilted her head, putting it into the path of the sunlight that obligingly set fire to the locks she stubbornly denied were red. "Well enough, once we made it to our beds."

"Up talking half the night again, I suppose." To be expected—Miss Abbott had been away at school these past few years and was just back for a few months before accepting her new post. Much like her brother. Still, they would think him ill if he didn't tease. "Ella and Stella, the two little bellas—"

"Oh, Brice, *stop*." Ella groaned and clapped her hands over her ears, even while Miss Abbott chuckled.

As if he could leave his and Abbott's old rhyme unfinished. "Ding-donging their way through the day. They ring and they chime at any old time—"

"And oh, how very loudly they play," Abbott finished for him, grinning.

"Thank heavens you both have something besides poetry to fall back on." Ella leaned into Brice's arm, covering a yawn with her hand. "I may need a nap before the sport begins this afternoon. I hope Mother won't have scheduled us any evening engagements quite yet."

Miss Abbott grinned and reached for her needlework. "Oh, I don't know, El. I'm rather looking forward to the balls and fêtes."

"No doubt so she can put all the ladies to shame and set the peerage abuzz." Brice arched a brow at the girl, still not quite able to believe she was grown and would soon be instructing the children of some of those ladies in their schooling. "Admit it, Miss Abbott—you mean to be another Jane Eyre, using your position as governess to secure a favorable match with some rich widower."

"Never." But she knew how to grin at his teasing, and how to dismiss it with a stitch upon her sampler. "Miss Eyre didn't set her sights nearly high enough. If I'm going to be grubbing, it'll be for a title, not just riches—neither of which I'll find at my first post, so the peeresses are safe, for now, from my competition."

Brice winked at his old friend. "And lucky they are, for you will outshine them all."

"Always the flatterer." But she grinned. She may know when he exaggerated, but she knew him well enough to appreciate the good wishes behind it.

"There you all are." Mother bustled into the room, her hands full of envelopes and unfolded letters—that particular determination in her eyes that always struck when she was in a scheduling frenzy. "I've invitations from the Sutherlands, the Carnegies, the McIntoshes . . . I daresay no one expects us to accept them all this year, considering, but we must choose which to honor."

As the discussion began, Brice was for the most part content to leave the weighing of each invitation to Mother and Ella, putting in only a phrase here or there in agreement or disagreement. But when his mother paused and cleared her throat before lifting one of the last pieces of paper, he knew to pay attention.

"This is not pertaining to our time in Scotland, but rather

for our trip home next month. We've been invited to a house party in Yorkshire."

"Brook?" But Ella frowned even as she said it. "I cannot imagine she would be ambitious enough to host a house party with the babe still so young, and she still so determined to eschew the help of a nurse."

Brice chuckled. "I cannot imagine her father actually agreeing to another house party at Whitby Park."

"Oh, true." Ella toyed with one of the scarlet curls spilling over her shoulder. "I suppose I don't even know if they're visiting Whitby in Yorkshire now or are still in Gloucestershire at Ralin Castle."

"They are in fact in Yorkshire for the autumn." Mother waved a separate paper. "And invited us as usual to visit with them on our return from Scotland. But the house party is hosted by their neighbor."

Silence fell so quick and thick that Brice could not blame the Abbotts for the questioning glance that passed between them. He cleared his throat. "Lady Pratt, you mean?"

At Mother's nod, Ella huffed. "Well, I don't know why you even bothered bringing that one up, Mama. Of course we'll refuse it."

"No." Brice thought he deserved credit for saying it at a normal volume, when he'd wanted to leap to his feet and shout. "No, we must accept."

Ella looked at him as if he were a dunce. "Are you daft? It has barely been a year since Lord Pratt kidnapped Brook—his widow oughtn't to be hosting a party, much less inviting *us* to it, when she knows well we take our stand with the Staffords."

"Now, Ella, her first mourning has passed, and you know these things have relaxed in recent years." Mother ran a hand over the black of her frock. "Though as for the other . . . I do rather side with your sister, Brice. I feel no inclination to spend a week in her company, not at the very house where the lady's late husband held our Brook prisoner."

"You needn't. I'm certain Whitby would welcome you all to stay there instead, but I, at least, will go to Delmore." And since he didn't want to argue about it, he stood, tugging his waistcoat back into place. "Do excuse me, everyone. I have some correspondence of my own to go through now."

He ought to have known escape wouldn't be so simple. He barely made it into the hall before Ella came racing up behind him, grabbing his arm. "Brice, what in the world are you thinking?"

Darting a glance over his shoulder to see whether their guests or any servants lingered nearby, he pulled her a few more steps along before answering. "What do you mean?"

"What do I . . . ? You know very well what I mean! You were there when her husband was killed, right alongside Brook and Stafford. They are convinced she blames them for his death and will seek revenge—why would you not assume she'll do the same with you?"

"Shh! Do you want to worry Mother more?" He tucked Ella's ivory hand into the crook of his elbow and propelled her out the door at the end of the hall, into the autumnal garden.

"You can't think her innocent in all that. You *can't*."

"On the contrary." He was convinced she had been involved in each and every step of planning Brook's kidnapping and potential murder, was convinced she would do anything to get her hands on the diamonds she thought rightfully hers. "And I intend to prove it."

Ella tugged him to a halt, her brown eyes wide with outrage. "How? By flirting a confession from her? Even you aren't so charming, and if you think you are, then we need to have a serious conversation about your hubris."

Flirtation may play a role in his plan, but a confession did not. Catherine Pratt would never give one—he knew that. He would have to catch her in a new crime. Like attempting to steal the gems she well knew he had. The ones she had watched Brook drop into his hand a year ago.

He might as well provide her the opportunity. "If she intends revenge, I would rather she try to take it on me than on the Staffords—they've little Lord Abingdon to consider now. But you needn't fear, Ella-bell. I'll be prepared for anything she might try."

"You are not invincible. No one is." Her voice cracked, shook. No doubt her eyes were seeing their father, collapsed and broken when he had seemed so infinitely strong. "And you are in no better position to take such risks than are Brook and Stafford. Perhaps you've no infant son, but that is part of the point, isn't it? You are all we have. You are Nottingham."

All true . . . and if something went wrong, if something happened to him—worse, if something happened to Ella or Mother—he would never forgive himself. But the Lord had not released him. Every time he prayed about it, he received the self-same answer he had gotten *before* Father's death—that he must draw Lady Pratt's attention away from the Staffords. "The Lord will keep me safe."

"Brice . . ."

The cool autumn air swirled around them, and a golden eagle circled overhead. Brice gripped his sister's hands. "Trust me in this, Ella. Lady Pratt is vicious and is not above hiring thugs to do her dirty work—it is wiser to take the offensive than to wait for her to spring some trap on *me*."

He knew from the glint in Ella's eyes that his claim did nothing to put her at ease. But she pressed her lips together against further argument. For the moment.

He had no doubt she'd have more to say about it, though, once she'd had time to form her words.

He only hoped she kept Mother out of it. She had enough to suffer, with the loss of Father still so fresh in her heart. She didn't need to be worrying about losing her son too.

Three

Lilias Cowan paused outside the study door long enough to draw in a fortifying breath. To wipe her hands on her skirt and to roll back her shoulders. She had learned long ago that if one wanted the Kinnaird to listen, one had to be strong—a task not always so easy in the face of his tempers. But when her rap upon the door earned her a gruff "Enter," she strode in as if she planned to ask for no more than an afternoon off.

As if she weren't about to suggest that he go back on his own word, twice over.

Douglas Kinnaird glanced over at her, his brows still in the perpetual frown he had worn the past fortnight, ever since he found Rowena sobbing into the stones. Granted, he was never one for abundant smiles, but never in her life had Lilias seen him so grave for so long. What more proof did Rowena need that her father loved her, worried for her? Even Lady Lochaber's good news of a coming child had earned only a fleeting smile from him.

"What is it, Lilias? I've work to do."

Sometimes she searched his face looking for the boy she had grown up with. There was no hint of him today. There seldom was. But she believed he was still there, somewhere under the years of hurt and determination. She dredged up the same smile she used to give him when they were skipping rocks across the face of the loch. "Aye, I know ye have. But we need to speak o' Rowena."

He didn't just sigh, he hissed out his breath and flung his pen to his desk. "Is she with child, then?"

"It's too soon to say." With the Kinnaird, careful meant bold. She strode to the chair opposite his desk and sat, not upon the seat but on the wide arm of it, to keep herself higher. "But we all know it's a possibility."

He grunted.

She angled her head and prayed he couldn't see how she dreaded speaking of this. "How could ye take his side, Douglas? When he hurt what's yours?"

He spat out a Gaelic curse and shoved to his feet, paced to the window. At least this one offered no sight of Gaoth, so it wouldn't sour his mood more. Not like her proposal would. "It was a valid question, Lil—she'd been hanging on him for months. How was I to know she didna invite him and then regret it? I was scunnered, too blinded by the rage at first to see . . ."

"Oh, aye. And isna that a familiar refrain?"

He spun, but the fury died away quickly, as it always did when someone had the gumption to call him on it. "Ye think I *want* to promise her to him, when he would treat a Kinnaird in such a way? I've no choice, ye ken. He ruined her. Possibly got a child on her. The only security I can give her is marriage."

"Marriage to that monster is no security, Douglas. It's a death sentence, and she willna do it."

He snorted and turned back to the window. "She hasna backbone enough to refuse. Just like her mother, going where're the wind blows her, that one."

"Ye've the wrong of her." Lilias stood, fire burning away any weakness now. She'd been there from the day Rowena was born, even from before that day. She knew her better than anyone on Earth. Loved her like her own. "Ye just canna get it through that thick skull of yours that some people are made strong by a soft hand, not a heavy one."

"Like Nora? What did a soft hand get me with her, hmm? I tried it for a decade, and look what happened. And Rowena's just like her."

"No." Much as Rowena failed to realize it, it wasn't true. "She's half yer blood too."

He pivoted again and folded his arms across his chest. "What is it ye want, Lily? Other than to berate me for rearing my child as I saw fit?"

She took time enough to moisten her lips, to tuck back a greying curl that had slipped loose. "She willna marry Malcolm. If it's a stand ye want from her, ye'll get it on this. But he'll not let her go, not if he can help it. Especially not if he thinks she's with child."

He arched his brows and waited.

She stood. "We've got to get her away from here, before the question can be answered."

"Too many Highlanders have been sent away from their homes—"

"Why must everything go back to the clearances with you, Douglas? This isna the English forcing a Highlander from his croft. It's a father protecting his daughter!" She huffed out a breath, dragged in another one, and stomped her way to his side. "Ye dinna *want* to give her to Malcolm, do ye?"

The tic in his jaw was answer enough. It spoke even louder than his "There's no other way."

"Aye but there is. The Nottinghams have just come. I'm sure ye ken."

His eyes, the same grey as Rowena's, went darker under his drawn brows. "What are ye suggesting, Lilias?"

"A replay of history, with a bit of a twist." The smile felt false, but she wore it. "I've seen the young duke around the village in years past. Mistook him a time or two for Malcolm, as it happens. They've the same look about them." But the resemblance ended at the dark hair, the height, the strong features. Every word she'd ever heard spoken about the young lord painted him to be kind, jolly, *good*—and this from Highlanders, who as oft as not despised all English on principle.

A far cry from Malcolm.

"Surely ye're not suggesting—"

"Ye've waited nigh unto thirty years for yer revenge—here's yer chance for it. Revenge upon *her*, but ye'd still be advancing and protecting yer daughter. And getting her far away from Malcolm."

Consideration ticktocked through his eyes. "No." But it was a soft, thoughtful refusal, not a stubborn one. "There's no way to work it—not having kept our distance all these years."

"But Nora didna, and Rowena went with her that summer, ye ken. She has an acquaintance with the young lady. All ye've got to do is send yer wife over now, with Rowena, and with an invitation to dine. Let them all think the new countess has softened you."

"And then when they are here . . ."

She didn't fill in the silence this time. Better to let him make his own schemes, as they were usually sounder than hers. So long as they had the same goal. So long as they resulted in Rowena going far, far from Loch Morar—and from the monster who would destroy her if given the chance.

After some time, he met her gaze again, begrudging respect in his eyes. "I dinna ken what kind of man he is."

"Ye always said ye could judge a man in five minutes." One notable exception aside. "Ye'll have it at dinner, if ye invite them."

"So I will." He straightened, lifted his chin. "I'll not do it unless she convinces me she's a backbone. I'll not send my daughter to England if she's incapable of being a Highlander there."

"Aye, well." Perhaps her smile was equal parts relief and fear that it would yet all fall apart. But she felt it anyway. "Tell her again she must marry Malcolm—ye'll get a rise out of her, now that she's seen him again."

He chuckled—the first amusement she'd heard from him in a fortnight—and turned to his desk again. "How is it that she loves you so dearly and hates me so fiercely, when we're not so verra different?"

Lilias snorted a laugh and lifted her arms. "Soft hands, Dougie. Soft hands."

He shook his head, and she saw it—the boy that had used to play with her brother, pull her braids, and make mischief with her and the rest of the cousins. "When you married Cowan, I feared ye'd lose what was Kinnaird, Lily. I was wrong—ye never did. But . . ." He leaned forward, braced against his desk, that mischief in his eyes. "When the Nottinghams are dining with us, I'll thank ye to remember to call me *milord*."

She made an exaggerated curtsy and let herself out of the room. Only once she was back in the hallway did she press a hand to her stomach and drag in another deep breath. One lion fought—but it left Rowena yet to convince, and Lilias had a feeling the supposedly meek daughter would give her more a fight than the supposedly hateful father on this particular subject.

So be it. She would lie to the girl if she must, she would plan it all out with the Kinnaird and leave Rowena ignorant. Anything, so long as she could save her. Rowena was the closest thing to a daughter Lilias would ever have . . . and she wouldn't see her life ruined.

She wouldn't see Rowena turn into Nora.

Silence descended so deafeningly that Rowena swore she heard the ringing of it in her ears. The hands she had braced upon the table quaked. Her stomach rejected the very smell of the food before her. But she couldn't give an inch on this—she knew it. Even as she wanted to run whimpering from the room and hide under the blankets of her bed, she knew it.

"No." She said again, lest the silence eat up her first refusal and make it null. "I willna marry him. Ye canna make me. I'll run away if I must, to avoid it, but I'll not—I'll not suffer him touch me again."

She expected a roar, a shout, a quick advancement from her father so he could cuff her or box her ears. But he held his seat. Cut off another bite of mutton. Barely even glanced at her. "And where would ye go, Rowena? Gasta Hall? Nay. Ye've nothing aside from what I give you."

"I've a will as strong as yers. I'll make a way." The words sounded true as she spoke them, though she had thought them nothing but a bluff when they formed in her mind. She lifted her chin and darted a glance to Elspeth, who watched her with mouth agape and disbelieving eyes. No help to be found there, though she hadn't expected any. Drawing in a deep breath, she squared her shoulders. "Elspeth's bairn could be a girl, ye ken. Which would mean I'm still yer heir, and ye canna be counting on another babe to follow, can ye? All these years and this is the first—"

"How dare you!" Elspeth stood too, cheeks flushed.

Rowena nearly backed down. She'd never imagined saying

such a thing to her stepmother, all but pointing out that the woman wasn't in the flower of youth any longer. But just now, she couldn't give quarter to manners. "I dinna mean to offend, my lady. But it's the truth, aye? Ye think ye're carrying the next Earl of Lochaber, the next Chief of Clan Kinnaird, but it could just as well be a second daughter. Ye canna write me off yet. And ye canna risk me disappearing—but I'll do it, Father. If ye insist on Malcolm, I'll do it."

For a second, she thought it amusement that gleamed in the Kinnaird's eyes . . . though that made precious little sense. But she hadn't the chance to dwell on it, as Elspeth shrieked and leaned across the table to better scowl at her.

"Ye disrespectful, uncivilized little ingrate! Go ahead and leave—you willna survive a month in the world, and we'll not mourn ye when word comes that ye're—"

"Enough." Father set his fork and knife down. The familiar temper was back in his eyes, heavy as thunder in his brow. But, strangely, it wasn't directed at Rowena. He was glowering at Elspeth. "I invite you to remember that she's my daughter and my heir."

That smug little smile that Rowena detested slid onto her stepmother's lips. "For now, my love. But the bairn's a boy. I ken. I feel it. Ye'll have yer son. Then ye'll have no need of Nora's daughter."

"Half her blood is mine. Kinnaird blood. And as such, she'll have my protection and provision all her days." He turned to Rowena. "It's my duty to see you wed, lass."

For a moment she had actually thought he was taking up for her, taking her side, not just his own. But no. It would come back, again, to Malcolm. She shook her head, but the tears still burned. "I'll not marry him. I'll not. Ye'd have to drag me kicking and screaming to the kirk, and I'd *still* not say vows to that wretch!"

Before he could argue and insist, she spun and darted from the dining hall. The fury gave way to fear, the burning in her eyes swelled and overflowed. Luckily, she didn't need to see her path to know it. Her feet knew every stone of the castle, each dark hall and ancient turn. Within a few minutes she was pushing open the doors to her room, ready to tumble onto her bed and let the sobs wrack her.

"Wena?"

She paused with her hand on the door, ready to slam it closed. A lamp was lit, and Annie had snuggled down into the feather mattress of Rowena's bed, as she so loved to do, a book in hand. Closing the door gently, Rowena tried to summon a smile. The tears would have to either fade or keep. "Escaped your nurse again, did ye, Annie?"

"I told her ye wouldna mind." The little one's cheeky grin faded fast. "Ye're trauchled again. Is Malcolm here?"

With a shake of her head, Rowena sank onto the mattress beside her sister and pulled the girl close. "Father was telling me to marry him, is all."

Annie loosed a gusty sigh and gave her a squeeze. "I dinna ken why he wants you to."

And heaven help her, she never would. "Malcolm will be the next chief, unless your mother has a boy. I canna inherit that, though I can the earldom. Father doesna want the two separated, but he's afraid the Kinnairds will decide to follow other clans and elect their chief if he has no clear heir."

"But—"

"The clan comes first for him, Annie. Always. Before Lochaber, before our own interests."

When Annie scowled like that, it was more than obvious that Douglas was her father. "But ye *are* part of the clan!"

One small, feeble part. "Aye. But my mother was American.

He thinks the years away from the Highlands weakened her family. He thinks . . . He thinks Malcolm is good and strong and will shore up what he deems my flaws."

Annie made a face and snuggled in closer to Rowena's side. "Ye can run away, then. Go to . . . to Africa! I've been reading about Africa. There are great open spaces with high grasses called savannahs, and lions roam there. And elephants. I should like to see an elephant."

Only Annie could make her smile when the very world was falling apart. Rowena trailed her fingers through the girl's dark hair and let her eyes slide closed. "Ye'll come with me, then?"

"Aye." But instead of bright babbling, Annie sighed. "They willna miss me. Not once the new bairn comes. Especially if it's a boy."

"They would miss you. Ye're all things bright and fine, Annys. It's proud I am to call you my sister. I—"

The door swung open even as a rap sounded upon it, and Elspeth blew in with a fevered gleam in her eyes. Rowena and Annie both sat up, ready for the usual berating—but the countess barely spared a glance for her daughter's being where she oughtn't. She headed straight for Rowena's wardrobe. "Ye've nothing. I know ye've nothing, nothing suitable. Ach, what's the man thinking, springing this upon us with but an evening's notice?"

What in the world? Never in the four years Elspeth had lived in Castle Kynn had she pawed through Rowena's clothes—and why would she do so now? Surely—heaven help her—she wasn't trying to find a gown suitable for a wedding? Rowena scooted off her bed. "Suitable for *what*, my lady?"

"For dukes!" The countess flung open the door, pulled out the drawers. "We're to go to Gaoth Lodge on the morrow to call on the ladies—and ye with naught but the day dresses from the January Sale. He ought to be ashamed to outfit his daughter so poorly, no matter that ye've ne'er been to London nor even Edinburgh since school. And now here we are, about to dine with England's most fashionable, with only wool and tweed!"

Dine with . . . call on . . . Rowena sank back down onto her bed, at the foot. "We . . . we're going to Gaoth? The Kinnaird said we may?"

Elspeth sent her a frantic glance. "*May*? He ordered it! And we're to invite the family to dine with us the following eve."

Visions of that summer danced before her eyes. Of Ella, her bright red curls bouncing out behind her, laughing and dancing and singing. Rowena had been just a normal girl back then. Running along with the duke's daughter on every merry chase. Huddling with her under makeshift forts when the rain drove them inside. Heads bowed together over books and papers on which they'd scratched treasure maps and poems and . . .

Magic—that's what it had been.

As Elspeth fretted over her lack of proper white morning dresses, Rowena closed her eyes . . . and let herself hope. If Ella still liked her . . . if she could finagle an invitation to Sussex somehow . . . once there, she could figure out what to do if she were with child.

And if she weren't—well then, perhaps she'd simply stay in England until the countess had delivered *her* child. Then determine if there was any point in ever coming home again.

Four

The rain came down in torrents, forcing the whole company indoors. Brice didn't particularly mind . . . until he saw the strain upon his mother's face. She had been a year out of society, had grown used to quiet drawing rooms and subdued visits. No doubt being set upon by the hunting party in addition to the ladies was more than she had prepared herself for this morning.

His sister, on the other hand, was in her element, laughing as she studied her hand of cards. Miss Abbott was apparently her partner in the whist game, and she looked every bit as happy. She was faring well, from what he had seen, with the crème of Scottish society. He'd witnessed no fumbles, no gaffes, no insecurities whatsoever.

More than one male gaze kept darting toward the whist table. If the gents were eyeing up his sister, he'd have to devise some clever torment to scare them off. Though if someone wanted to raise Miss Abbott to a higher station, he supposed he'd wish them well. Assuming they were deserving of her.

Her brother sidled up next to him at the window. "Our sisters are going to give me an apoplexy if they don't cease drawing the attention of every male guest in a five-mile radius."

Brice laughed and let his shoulders relax. "The question is, would your sister turn down a suit for love of teaching children, or would she send her regards to her new employer and dash off with any handsome gentleman to ask for her hand?"

Geoff shook his head. "On the one hand, she is too picky to accept just anyone. . . . On the other, she has spent countless hours listening to the romantic prattle of *your* sister, so who's to say?"

Another laugh faded when Brice caught sight of movement out the window. A carriage pulled into the drive, which made his brows furrow. Who else could be coming? All the invited guests were already there, and surely no one from the area would just drop in for a call in this weather. Though granted, it was typical enough in the Highlands that it rarely seemed to faze the locals, who referred to their weather as either "raining" or "about to rain."

Geoff had noticed the new arrival too. "I thought you said this would be a restful trip."

"No, no. I said a respite from your schooling. Entirely different."

A footman rushed out when the carriage came to a halt, umbrellas open to fend off the deluge for whomever would descend. Brice could see only a few wisps of white as the passengers got down. Ladies, then. Their cards, once they made it inside, would be taken to his mother, not to him.

So if he wanted his curiosity satisfied . . . He gave his old friend a grin and a nod. "Excuse me, Geoff old boy. I'm going to go and spy over my mother's shoulder."

It required weaving his way through the crowded drawing room, around groups of laughing men and whispering women, sidestepping the card table and avoiding two different couples taking a turn about the room in lieu of outdoor exercise. After exchanging smiles or brief greetings with them all, he made it to his mother in her corner just as the butler entered with his silver salver, two new cards upon it.

Mother's eyes went wide as she took them. Brice's did too. "The Countess of Lochaber?"

"Not the one I met a decade ago, but . . ." Mother took the second card. "And Lady Rowena Kinnaird. Ella will be so pleased. Show them in, please, Mr. Gordon."

With a bow, the butler picked his way back through the room. Mother kept her eyes trained on the door, brows knit.

Brice's probably were too. "Well, that's unexpected. I thought you said he despised the English. Has his new wife softened him, perhaps?"

Mother's lips thinned. "Nothing can soften Douglas Kinnaird. He'll have a reason for allowing this that's to his own profit—you can be sure."

It wasn't the words that made Brice's brows rise now. It was the soft, Lowland burr that invaded his mother's speech as she said it—an accent that so rarely peeked its way through her years in England.

He would have pressed, probed, had they been alone. As it was, he merely turned to await the arrival of their neighbors.

The countess swept in with confidence and a smile, heading straight for his mother. Brice had to admit to some surprise when he saw that she must be forty, at least—usually when a man without a male heir took a second wife, it was one young enough to promise sons. Should he respect the man for choosing based on other criteria? Perhaps affection?

But if the earl had selected his second wife for love, Brice wasn't sure that made him feel any better. As the lady drew closer, he recognized the rapacious gleam in her eye. The one that said she would claw her way to wherever she wanted to be, without much thought to whom she gouged in the process.

A look he knew all too well, having been deemed England's most sought-after bachelor these several years.

The countess curtsied before his mother, pasting on a smile that looked more calculating than sincere. "Duchess, thank you so much for welcoming us. I have been waiting ages to make your acquaintance." Though she carried herself with all the confidence of a born lady, she spoke with a deep Highland burr.

Mother returned the welcome, but the knot in her brow didn't smooth. "It is my pleasure, I assure you, Lady Lochaber. Though forgive me for asking an impolite question—does the earl know you are here? The previous countess came without his permission, and—"

The lady interrupted with a laugh and wave of her hand. "'Twas his suggestion, Duchess. In fact, I was sent with an invitation for you and your family to dine with us at your earliest convenience. We ken, of course, that yer schedule is likely filled to brimming already, but do let us know when ye could join us. Even tomorrow wouldna be too early for us."

Only because he knew her so well could Brice see the shock in his mother's eyes. Her smile showed only grace. "Tomorrow would be lovely. Thank you, my lady." Then her eyes softened, and she moved a step to the side, holding out a hand to the figure hiding behind Lady Lochaber. "Lady Rowena. How absolutely delightful it is to see you again, all grown up."

Brice, too, had to slide a step to see the earl's daughter. And his heir, wasn't she? He always had to remind himself that in Scotland, a female could inherit a title from her father. Rather enlightened of them, really.

The countess made some vague greeting to him, and Brice

responded with the usual pleasantries, taking her hand as expected and keeping his eyes trained on her as was polite. But his ears strained to hear the soft reply of the young lady . . . and failed. Perhaps she spoke too softly, or perhaps her stepmother's prattle was too loud.

Mother touched his arm, though, to draw him over. "You never had the chance to meet my son that summer."

He got his first full glimpse of the girl . . . and knew more than a little surprise. From the neck up, she was what he expected of a young lady. Pretty, in an understated way, with middling brown hair touched here and there with gold. But the frock she wore was of low-quality cloth, the tailoring sloppy and not flattering. For an earl's daughter and heir, she was downright unfashionable—and not the kind that came of a lack of sense. Rather, the kind that came of not having quality to work with. Odd indeed, given the fine linen of her stepmother's dress.

Lady Rowena curtsied, though she didn't so much as glance up at him. "Duke."

Brice took her hand, bowed over it. "My lady, what a pleasure to make your acquaintance." Her hand was small, delicate. And as he lifted it to his lips, he saw bruising peek out from the too-wide cuff of her sleeve.

A familiar pang echoed through him. That pressing upon his spirit, the kind that might as well have whispered *Pay attention* into his ears. He let go her hand but, as he straightened, did his best to capture her gaze.

She did not cooperate. Indeed, she slid halfway behind her stepmother again, doing no more than dart a quick glance up at him.

It was enough to make his brows lift, his smile tickle the corners of his mouth. "A pleasure indeed. I don't believe I've ever met a young lady with such lovely silver eyes."

She directed them downward, her cheeks going pink.

Brice chuckled. "And she will deprive me of seeing them again. As cruel a creature as any young lady, I see."

"Rowena!" His sister appeared, all but elbowing him aside. Foregoing niceties, Ella threw her arms around the girl and gave her a squeeze. "Oh, how good it is to see you! I've missed you terribly all these years, every time we've come." She pulled back, her grin large and brilliant. "Come. I'll rescue you from my shameless flirt of a brother and introduce you to my friends. Oh, we've *years* to catch up on!"

Ella pulled Lady Rowena toward the other young ladies, while Lady Lochaber moved off in the opposite direction to greet a Highland woman who was signaling to her.

Brice stepped back to his mother's side. "Odd."

"Troubling." Mother smoothed out her brow, but it did nothing to banish the clouds from her eyes. "She was as boisterous as Ella a decade ago—and dressed in all the frills and lace that were the height of fashion for girls."

Pay attention, indeed. Something wasn't right here. He could feel it, deep in that place where the Lord stirred within him. With Lady Rowena herself, and with her and Lady Lochaber's sudden appearance at Gaoth Lodge. "What do you think the earl is about? Ought I to be worried?" He was all too familiar with families plotting to match him with their daughters. Perhaps such a plot would explain the young lady's bashfulness.

Mother shook her head. "No, not for the reason you mean. Lochaber would never seek a union."

Refreshing as that may be, he couldn't help but straighten his shoulders. "Because I'm English?"

She sighed. "Because you're my son."

At that, he turned fully to face his matron, blocking her from the rest of the room. "And what has that to do with anything?"

His mother held his gaze for a long, unblinking moment and sighed again. "I was betrothed to him once. I went to London, in fact, to shop for my trousseau . . . and met your father."

No doubt Brice looked as witless as a fish, his mouth gaping open and eyes wide. "How is it we've never heard of this, in all your tales of how you and Father met and fell in love?"

Mother slid to his side, tucked her hand into the crook of his arm, and led him to the far, empty corner of the room. "The betrothal was quiet—my parents hoped to talk me out of it. They were not in favor of me marrying a Highlander in general and were not all that fond of Douglas in particular, though they were willing to indulge me if I was certain. I had no intentions of budging. But when I met Nottingham . . ." Her eyes went distant, dreamy, as they so often did when she thought of his father. "I realized then that I hadn't known what love was before."

"So you broke it off?"

"Again, quietly. And stayed out of the Highlands for nearly twenty years, to avoid him. Douglas was never an easy man. I thought it appealing at the time, but . . ." She glanced over her shoulder, to where Ella and Lady Rowena had sat. Though smiling at his sister, the visitor still managed to look as though she'd rather disappear than stay in the crowded room. "He accused me of choosing your father for his title and nothing else. Of being heartless and mercenary."

The railing of an injured suitor—not so difficult to understand. "It would have looked that way to him."

"I know. But I thought he would have forgiven over time. He married a wealthy American several years later—Rowena's mother. Water under the bridge, I thought, and so eventually we came back to Gaoth with my family. When Nora—the previous countess—brought Rowena to visit, I thought I was right, that all was forgiven. But Lochaber was in Town for the Sessions and didn't know they'd even come. When he found out . . ."

She shook her head, and the tears that were always so quick to gather these days made a sheen over her eyes. "I received only one letter from Nora after that. Apologizing for the fact that we would never meet again. For their safety, she said. I daresay she secreted the missive out, as he never would have let her write such a thing."

Safety? Storm clouds gathered in his soul. How could his mother have even *thought* herself in love with a man who had a cruel spirit? But she had been young, probably not unlike Ella . . . and he could well imagine his romantic-minded sister seeing only the good in someone, blithely ignoring the hints of a darker side.

It was why Brice watched over her so protectively.

"Well. Allow me to say I'm glad you chose the husband you did." He looked to Ella again, and then to Lady Rowena, who had her arms folded protectively over her stomach. Every instinct he had said he ought to figure out why the girl was so reticent, figure out if she had been hurt . . . figure out if there was any way he could help her. Worse, that familiar whisper hovered over his spirit, the same impression pounding, pulsing. *Pay attention. Pay attention.*

He nearly groaned. He had trouble enough at his doorstep right now, given the diamonds even now being set in gold and the ruthless woman out to claim them. The last thing he needed was the distraction of a needy young lady . . . and a generation-old feud coming to call.

The ladies laughed when she spoke. Rowena tried to smile through it, but all she could remember was the teasing of the other girls at school those first weeks in Edinburgh. Mocking her burr, imitating it, somehow making it ridiculous. She'd had to learn fast how to soften its edges, bury it under a layer of polish.

She'd forgotten. How had she forgotten?

"I love your accent. Ignore them." Ella's smile, at least, was genuine. As bright as ever. And praise be to the Lord, as warm. There was no hint in her cinnamon eyes of the cruelty Rowena had expected.

The cruelty every other guest here seemed to hide away behind a mask of welcome.

"I can hardly believe you've come!" Ella gripped her hand and beamed. Her voice, though, was hushed. "All these years . . . we've sent invitations every time we've come. Hoping and praying that something would change and you'd be allowed to call again. Or that we'd run into you in London when you debuted."

They'd invited them? Of course they had. The Nottinghams were the epitome of hospitality. It was the Kinnaird who snubbed whomever he didn't like. Rowena tugged the cuff of her sleeve down, wishing she'd worn gloves to cover the bruising on her wrists. "Father has never taken me to London." Why would he bother, when his goal had always been for her to marry Malcolm and keep the earldom and chiefdom united and strong?

A titter from behind them made Rowena bristle. She didn't turn to see who laughed now, though she could hear the soft padding of slippers, the rustling of dresses as ladies took a turn about the room. "What *is* she wearing?" one of them mock-whispered.

The other giggled. How could a giggle sound so heartless? "I suppose the rumors must be true—Lochaber is too ashamed of her to let her be seen in public. Though one would think his wife could have done *something* with her. Elspeth has always been fashionable, even when she was married to that laird. What was his name?"

Their words disappeared into the other chatter filling the room. Not so from her mind. When she glanced up into Ella's face, she saw lightning in her eyes, flashing in the direction of her guests.

Rowena covered her friend's fingers and gave them a squeeze. "Dinna fash yourself over me, Ella." *No, all wrong.* She must control her tongue, her words. She had done it before—she could do it again. Clearing her throat, she tried to swallow down the Highlands. "They only speak truth. I . . . I shouldn't have come."

"Nonsense." The cheer had leaked from Ella's voice. Determination replaced it. "You are a dear friend—not an acquaintance, as they are. If anyone is welcome here, it is you. And if I have to send them packing, I will. Invitations can be rescinded."

Not politely—not without making enemies. Rowena squeezed her eyes shut. Why must discord follow everywhere she went? "Not on my account, Ella, please. We . . . we havena—haven't—even seen each other in a decade. I daresay that makes *us* mere acquaintances, not dear friends."

"Nonsense," Ella said again. "We were children, openhearted. We shared all our dreams. A summer of such friendship far outlasts the shallow talk that comes with those sorts." She waved a dismissive hand at her fashionable guests, now walking the edge of the room before them. One of them noticed and straightened her shoulders, jutted out her chin.

Rowena's stomach cramped. The ladies would know it was her baffling affection for Rowena that made Ella, the duke's sister, dismiss them. They would know it was her fault, and they would hate her—go back to London or wherever they were from and say nasty things about her. Strangers would laugh, would scorn, without her ever having met them. All of England would speak of the dowdy, ugly daughter of Lord Lochaber.

She should never have come. There was no point. She couldn't leave the Highlands with Ella, even if an invitation were issued. Even if Father allowed it, which he wouldn't. She would find no welcome waiting in the south.

But even gossiping strangers were preferable to Malcolm, weren't they? She shivered and touched a finger to the yellowed bruise hidden under the frayed lace of her cuff.

"You look as though you could use some reinforcements." Another female voice, young and cultured. Rowena looked up just as a young lady about her own age sat on her other side. She was beautiful, too, with dark brown hair and intelligence gleaming in her eyes. "Not that I can offer much, having been the object of their sneers before your arrival, my lady."

This lovely girl?

Ella sighed. "Rowena, this is Miss Stella Abbott—my childhood friend. She and her brother are our steward's children and grew up in the cottage at Midwynd Park."

Not a lady then . . . though she spoke more like one than Rowena ever could, and carried herself with confidence and poise. Rowena managed a smile. "Stella and Ella?"

"The two little bellas," they singsonged in unison, ending on a laugh.

Ella shot a grin across the room, to where the duke and his mother stood in the far corner, looking deep in conversation. "Our brothers tormented us mercilessly as children."

"As *children*?" Miss Abbott shook her head, sending her dark curls bouncing. "That implies they've stopped."

Ella laughed. "The duke and the vicar can only get away with so much teasing in public these days."

"Ha! If any two ever pushed the boundaries of acceptability

in such things, it is they. After a few months with us all together again, it will be a relief to take my post in the new year."

Rowena kept her spine straight only by will, pushing away the urge to hug her arms to her stomach. What had she thought? That she would be the oldest of Ella's friends here this afternoon? Ella already had a childhood friend to keep her company through the end of the year. Rowena would be superfluous.

"Stella is to be a governess." Ella leaned close, her scarlet curls brushing her shoulder and her brown eyes twinkling. "At least until she can nab herself a wealthy husband."

Rowena produced the expected grin.

Miss Abbott shook her head. "I believe siblings are a safer topic. Have you any, Lady Rowena?"

"Aye." A smile slipped out, and her shoulders edged back. "I have now, since my father remarried. Annie—she is eight, and the apple of my eye."

If not for Annie, would she dread the possibility of a babe more? Probably. But having known the girl since she was four, she well remembered the joy of a wee one cuddled to one's side. There were worse things than having someone look up into your face as if you were the whole world.

Someone to love. Someone to love *her*. If only she could have such a thing without having to marry Malcolm.

She tugged on the cuffs again and then looked up when a heavy feeling settled. The duke watched her. He still stood on the far side of the room, his mother no longer by his side. No suspicion seemed to shadow his eyes, no outright question in them like so many of the others were sending her. And yet as his gaze remained latched upon her, she had the distinct feeling that he was peering into her very soul.

Her shoulders rolled forward, and she focused on Ella's expressive hands, gesturing as she spoke to Miss Abbott. She should have told Elspeth to come without her today. Much as she yearned for the chance for a true friend again, it was hardly worth the scrutiny of all these strangers who found her lacking.

All these strangers who seemed to see down to the gaping hole inside.

Five

Lilias peeked into the chamber from behind a massive tapestry that concealed the hidden access. Voices lifted and laughed and filled the cavernous great room. It was strange to hear English intonations rather than the Highland speech that the earl usually surrounded himself with. Strange to peek out and see peers instead of lairds.

The Kinnaird had seen fit to wear his charm tonight. A rare occasion, but when he pulled it out, he could make friends with the very stones of Castle Kynn, so compelling was his smile. He had exchanged only a few words with the duchess—Lilias couldn't hear the conversation from her hiding place, but the lips she read indicated an acknowledgment of many years gone by, many lessons learned, and condolences given.

Lady Charlotte Brice may have believed him when she was a girl. But Lilias had a feeling Charlotte, Duchess of Nottingham, wasn't fooled for a moment.

Now the Kinnaird was with the duchess's son. The duke. Rowena's best hope of deliverance. The young man stood with relaxed shoulders, surely not feeling a trap being set. He smiled, he laughed, he responded to his host with ease.

He was more handsome than Malcolm—Lilias hadn't been able to tell that from the distance at which she had seen him before. About the same age, the same coloring, similar height. He was lither, though, not so bulking and broad. And kinder. *Please, Lord, let him be kinder.*

Her eyes sought Rowena and found her by the window. The girl stood beside the other young man the duke had brought along—a Mr. Abbott, she had heard them say. He smiled at her, gentle and warm, and said something that looked to be serious. Rowena listened with a tilted head, her attention riveted.

Dinner was called, and Lilias straightened her spine, held her breath, and waited for Douglas to catch her gaze.

He did, and gave a minuscule nod.

Her breath whooshed out, indistinguishable above the chatter of the company. He approved. The plan would move forward.

Lilias scurried through the dark passage and came out on the servants' stairs, well away from where the family and their guests would be going in to dinner. She had to hurry. Get to the old croft, make sure there was peat enough for a fire and some flint to strike one. A blanket or two tucked away.

Food and water would look odd, though her hands twitched to add some to her basket as she hurried through the bustling kitchen. But no, it wouldn't matter. They wouldn't be there so long.

Just long enough. That was all.

Had there been any purpose to it, Rowena would have whispered a prayer of thanks. Somehow she'd managed to avoid the too-discerning duke thus far. His friend had ended up by her side instead, and though Elspeth had looked none too pleased, Rowena had known acute relief when she found herself positioned beside Mr. Abbott at dinner.

Rowena breathed in and lifted her fork without the shaking she had feared would possess her. She had been reticent when Mr. Abbott had sidled up to her in the great room and struck up a conversation, but she was glad he had. His presence was easy, calming. His conversation absent flirtation.

She avoided so much as looking at Nottingham, seated across from her. His greeting a half hour before had been another comment about her silver eyes that had made her focus them resolutely on the floor. She didn't want to see the way he took her measure with his every glance, leaving no choice but for him to find her lacking.

At least her evening gown, though disastrously out of mode beside Ella's, required gloves to cover the yellow-green bruises. She turned to Mr. Abbott again. "Ye mentioned a church ye'll be taking over in the new year. Where is it? Near your home?"

"I'm afraid not." But he smiled, eyes gleaming. "Bristol. Very near, as it were, to Ashley Down—the orphanage begun by George Müller. I was beside myself when I learned this. Mr. Müller has long been one of my heroes of the faith. His story is, in part, what inspired me to join the church."

Rowena frowned. "Forgive me, but I'm unfamiliar with him."

"Ah." Eyes lighting still more, he leaned in. "He was a missionary who made it a point to live very meanly, on nothing but prayer and faith, trusting the Lord to provide. Truly inspiring—he would even praise the Lord for an empty plate, saying it was but an opportunity for the Lord to fill it."

Rowena focused on the plate set before her. Rimmed in gold leaf, filled with food she'd scarcely touched. She had never wanted, not when it came to those things. But what about the other empty places in one's life? An empty heart? An empty soul? "I daresay this Mr. Müller had many stories to tell of the Lord's provision." Men beloved by God always did.

Not like her. The Lord never bothered with the likes of her.

His smile was light, unburdened. "We all do, if we open our eyes to it. He is always directing us toward our better good. Sometimes that means trials, but they will lead us to the place where He knows we need to be. And He will always be there beside us, if we but let Him in."

She set her gaze on her plate again. If only it were true. But though her plate was full, her life was empty. Worse—broken, in a shambles. She had nothing left of her heart to offer anyone, even God. What her Father hadn't bruised, what her mother hadn't taken with her to the grave, what society hadn't trampled on, Malcolm had destroyed.

"It's settled, then." Father's voice boomed over the table, drawing all eyes to his face. He smiled, as he had been doing all evening. Why did it strike such fear in her heart? "We should have just enough daylight left after the meal to venture out and see it—and with any luck, the rain will hold off until dusk."

Rowena slid her fork soundlessly onto the table. She had missed something but dared not ask for clarification.

Mr. Abbott could apparently manage the question without any words. Perhaps he and the duke had a language unto themselves, for a mere glance had Nottingham smiling and saying, "There is a druid cairn nearby. Lochaber has offered to show it to us."

"Well, the gentlemen, at least." How strange the warm smile looked on Father's face. "I daresay the ladies would prefer not to tramp through the countryside in their gowns just to see a few standing stones."

Rowena's heart sank. She loved tramping to the circle, evening gown or not.

"Oh, but I'd love to see it!" Ella's eyes were wide and compelling. "Could we not ride there?"

Father managed a look, somehow, that came off as regretful but not condescending. "There isna path enough for a vehicle. Horses can make the trek, but I've never kent a lady to want to ride in evening dress."

Mischief—the exact same shade as it had been a decade ago—sparkled in Ella's eyes. "Sometimes exceptions must be made. Mightn't we go, Mama? It is hardly fair that Brice and Abbott get to while we twiddle our thumbs."

Elspeth sipped at her wine. "Or we could plan an outing for tomorrow, with the whole company."

"I'm afraid we already have plans for tomorrow." The duchess dabbed her lips and sent her daughter a small smile. "Perhaps we could borrow more sensible shoes, at least. It *is* a remarkable place. I would have taken you years ago, my dears, but I could never remember the path."

Father's hand landed on the table, loud enough to draw attention again. Yet, again, without his usual temper. He smiled. "Then if I might be rude and hurry everyone along—we havena *that* much daylight to work with. We'll hurry out and then come back for sherry and dessert and some pipe music in the great room. I've a man, McCloud, who can play the very fairies from their hiding . . ."

A trill of exhilaration coursed through Rowena's veins. She couldn't remember the last time her father had played such a gracious host, couldn't remember ever joining other people her own age on a spontaneous outing. Perhaps it was old hat to Ella, and even to Miss Abbott, but Rowena could scarcely eat for the excitement of it.

Perhaps for just this one evening, she could put aside thoughts of empty places and act like a normal young lady—off on an adventure, small as it may be, with friends.

Everyone tucked into their food with enough speed that the

cook would no doubt be offended when she was told of it, and then they rushed from the table. Elspeth took charge of the women, hurrying them all along to change from their slippers. Minutes later they were all in jackets, boots, and warmer gloves.

And then the crisp autumn air surrounded her, and Rowena squeezed happily into the small, open carriage alongside Elspeth, the duchess, Ella, and Miss Abbott. The men were all mounting horses, her father leading the way toward the cairn. They would only be able to ride so far before they would have to get out and walk, but starting out this way would save a few precious minutes of daylight.

"What is the legend of this one, then?" Ella bounced a bit on her seat, eyes wide and bright upon Rowena. "Men turned to stones? Giants who offended the fairies? Maidens who danced awry?"

"The standing stones are but markers, perhaps ceremonial." Elspeth's tone, factual and precise, clashed against Ella's obvious desire for a romantic tale. "Then at the center is a sunken cairn with portal stones—a burial chamber, no doubt."

Leave it to Elspeth to strip the tale of all its mystery.

Rowena ignored her stepmother and leaned toward her friend. "They say that if ye tread the circle under the light of the full moon, ye'll hear the fairies piping a mournful tune. For it is a prince buried there, one who had always paid them homage, and to whom they had promised the crown. But treachery found him, and he was slain on that verra spot, his blood soaking in and turning the sandstone to its rusty color."

Ella made a show of shivering. "Oh, perfect! When is the full moon?"

The countess sighed. "Not for another week."

Ella sighed too, but it sounded entirely different than Elspeth's had. "Ah, well. It seems we'd have no light from the moon tonight, in any case, so unless the fairies would pipe to the rain . . ."

Rowena hadn't even looked to the sky, but Ella was right. Clouds hung low and heavy, promising rain and hurrying twilight. They may yet run out of daylight, but so long as they could beat the rain back to the castle, they would make do. A bit of shadow would only add to the cairn's allure.

Ten minutes more, and then they all set out on foot up the hill, through the glen. Loch Morar was just below, though on this particular hillside, it could scarcely be made out through the thick evergreens crowding about them. Rowena hung back at the rear of the group, content to listen to the exclamations of Ella and Miss Abbott, the questions of Mr. Abbott and the duke.

Mostly content, anyway. Until she paused to free her sleeve from a twig that had snatched it up and realized that no one even noticed she lagged behind.

No matter. She knew her way, could have found the cairn at midnight on a new moon, so often did she put foot to this rocky path and come here to hide away amidst faded legends and forgotten visions.

The group's shouts of delight told her when they had reached the first of the standing stones. Perhaps there had been more at one point, but now only six remained, sketching out a perfect circle around the sunken chamber. Ella was already scurrying for the portal stones of the burial chamber, the others dispersing throughout the site.

Rowena headed for her favorite part of the clearing, where the limbs of the nearest trees seemed to reach out and embrace the circle. Standing in their shadows, she could put a hand to the cool, red-hued sandstone of the nearest upright slab and pretend she lived in that age long since gone. When Vikings raided, settled, and wove their line into the Anglos, creating that Highland blood Father was so proud of. When chiefs and princes of different lines warred for the right to be master of this place. When no one questioned that something well beyond the human was at work, always.

Perhaps it was God.

Perhaps it was . . . something else.

"Rowena."

She started at the voice, frowning as she turned to search for Lilias in the shadows of the glen. "Lil? What are ye doing out here?"

Lilias was dressed for outdoor exercise, and the pink in her cheeks said she'd been at it for some time. "The Kinnaird asked me to check on Old Maud. Come. Look what I've found."

Rowena followed Lilias through the trees, toward the loch. With what dim light remained, she noted the moisture that had gathered on her maid's silvering hair. "How long have you been about it?"

Lilias waved a hand. "Since a few minutes after you went down to receive your guests. Have you had a good evening, Wena?"

"Aye, I suppose. Though Annie will be jealous that we have come out here without her."

Lilias chuckled. But there was something strained in it, something not so light as usual. Perhaps the ailing crofter's wife had not been on the mend. "Ye can take her out tomorra to make up for it. And tell her all about yer dinner with the duke."

"Oh." A few fingers of fog rose off the loch and slithered over her neck. "I wouldna say I had dinner with *him*. We scarcely exchanged a sentence."

"Ach, Wena. Ye'll have to be devising a better story than that one to entertain the wee lass, ye ken."

Rowena chuckled, ducked under a branch . . . and paused. "Where are we going, Lil?"

Lilias turned back to face her, showing a mischievous grin and the same warm brown eyes she had looked into all her life. "Ye'll see, lass. Trust me."

"Lead on, then." She ducked under another wayward twig and tracked the flight of a golden eagle soaring overhead. "Is Old Maud all right?"

"Hmm? Oh, aye. Though ye ken how she is—always dying, to her own mind. I dinna ken why yer father always takes her seriously."

"As soon as he doesna, it'll be the real thing. And ye ken how Father cares for her—what with her being like a grandmother, his own father's wet nurse when he was a babe." Rowena only saw the old woman a few times a year, lately. At nearly one hundred years old, Old Maud didn't leave her cottage much. Though her ancient husband, every bit as old, still doted on the sheep with his son and grandson.

They walked a few minutes more, chatting about the miracle of their ages, the children that stuck close, those who had gone away. A conversation she had probably had with Lilias at least a score of times over the years. Comfortable and thoughtless and just distracting enough that it took her a long moment to realize it when they emerged from the trees at the embankment that led down into the still waters of the loch. They were a good five miles from the castle now—Rowena could see its mist-shrouded promontory in the distance. Gaoth Lodge would be beyond it. In this direction lay nothing but old abandoned crofts, their sheep long since moved to other pastures. What could Lilias possibly—?

"Trust me," her maid said again, as if reading her thoughts.

"And forgive me. It's for your best, Rowena. Because I love you. Ye ken?"

She had somehow ended up ahead of Lilias, closer to the hillside. So she had to turn around to try to see her lady's maid's face, knowing her own was drawn into a frown.

Before she could register more than the anxiousness in Lilias's eyes, those hands that had nurtured and tended found her shoulders. And pushed.

"Was that a scream?" Brice paused midstep, stopping beside one of the uprights. The *Pay attention* had been echoing in his mind all evening, though just now he wondered if he had been paying attention to the earl when he ought to have been doing so with the man's daughter.

Lochaber lifted his brows but kept moving beyond the circle. "Impressive, sir. I've never met an Englishman who could hear the ghosts howling in the circle."

Brice opened his mouth to argue but then checked himself. It was no ghost he had heard, nor had it come from the circle. But it could have been that eagle in the distance, perhaps. Or some other animal of the glen. If the earl who knew the land far better than he weren't alarmed, he would try not to be.

Still, Brice followed uneasily. He didn't trust his host, didn't trust the easy smiles—not when his daughter had bruises on her wrists. He had thought that perhaps if he was to help, he could learn something from the earl.

It seemed he was wrong this time.

When they returned to Gaoth, Brice would ask Abbott what he thought of Lady Rowena, having actually spoken to her. Brice had tried a few times but had been unable to draw her out. Still, that tugging in his spirit persisted, the one that said there was something he must do concerning the young lady. But how was he to know how he might help her, what she might need, if she would not exchange two words with him, and if her father remained an enigma?

"It's just a wee bit up the hill," Lochaber said over his shoulder. "I canna be sure the two sites are related, of course, but—"

"Lochaber!"

The countess's voice stopped the earl in his tracks and brought a smile to his lips. "Excuse me, sir. Continue on this path and ye'll find it in about two minutes. I'll catch up to you as soon as I see what my wife needs, aye?"

Left with little choice but to agree—and no great regret at a few moments on his own—Brice nodded and kept his feet on the well-worn path while his host turned back to the circle. He was no expert on ancient Celts, to know why there would be another standing stone by itself on the other side of a grove of trees, but such things were nearly as fascinating as young ladies with secrets shuttered behind their eyes.

Though walking two minutes didn't bring him out in the promised clearing. Nor did walking another five, and at that point he became painfully aware of the fading light and heavy clouds. He would have to turn back and reunite with the rest of the group.

A pivot, a step, and then he halted again when he caught the strains of . . . crying?

The wind in the trees? An eagle? Or perhaps one of those infamous ghosts of Loch Morar? Half-expecting to feel the fool for doing so, he called out, "Hello?"

The whimpering sound stopped. Then a faint voice replaced it. "Hello! Is someone up there? Help! Please!"

A woman's voice. Brice headed in the direction from which it had come. "Where are you? Keep talking."

"I've slid down the bank and hurt my ankle."

Bank? He drew up just in time to keep his feet from taking the last step to the edge he now saw in the twilight. Crouching down, he peered over the side and saw a familiar face looking up at him. "Lady Rowena? What are you doing out here alone?" He hadn't even noticed her leave the group. Which made guilt slam him—he had definitely *not* been paying attention, not where he needed to be.

"My maid . . . Lilias . . ." Obvious pain cut her off when she made the mistake of shifting. "My ankle, sir. I fear I've broken it. Can ye go for help?"

If the fat drop of rain to hit his face were any indication, he dared not. She would be soaked through and chilled to the bone before he could return with aid. "I'll help you up myself. Your father should be but a few minutes behind me."

"Oh, ye mustn't—"

"Nonsense." Only sparing a moment's thought to the suit of clothes that was sure to be ruined with the mud—his valet would be mumbling for ages about it, but it couldn't be helped—Brice chose what appeared to be the most gradual way down the hillside.

The loch lapped at the bottom, and he had to bite back a choice word when he saw that the young lady's feet had landed in its frigid waters. No wonder she shook like a leaf. He must get her back in all haste so she could warm up. "Which ankle is it, my lady?"

"My right." Pain kept her voice tight and distorted her face.

Brice knelt beside her. "I'll lift you and set you on your left, shall I? Then together we'll make our way back up."

Though she looked as if she would prefer to refuse—or to cry—she gave a quick nod and reached for him. Brice gripped her under the arms and stood, doing his best to keep the move gentle. Still she whimpered and turned her face away, though he saw the tears that slipped out.

He eased her onto her left leg, careful to support her. "I'm sorry. I don't mean to hurt you."

"'Tisn't you." She glanced up at him only briefly before turning her face to the hill that probably looked more like a mountain to her just now. And tried to stand without aid. "We'd better start. Daylight is fading fast."

And the fat, cold raindrops were striking faster too. "Indeed. Don't be afraid to lean on me, my lady. I won't let you fall again."

It took her a few struggling steps to capitulate on that point, but Brice kept an eye on her countenance, and on the agony that overtook it each time she put weight upon her right foot. Whatever her reasons for not wanting to accept his help, her injury demanded it, and she ended up choking back a sob and all but collapsing against him.

Climbing up the hill would have been a challenge on his own, but the rain made it trickier, and the injured lady added a level of difficulty that had perspiration breaking out on his brow and a prayer hovering constantly on his lips. He had no idea how long it took them to gain the top, but the day's light had all but seeped away by the time they finally reached it.

Where in thunder was Lochaber?

Something went cool within him. "Your father said he would be directly behind me."

Lady Rowena still gasped for breath. "Then he . . . he . . . that way." She nodded toward the trail he could barely make out in the darkness.

Brice pressed his lips against the words—accusations, questions—that wanted to spill out. He wouldn't interrogate the injured girl. Not yet. Not when it could be coincidence, misunderstanding. But as they trekked back along the path and he heard no giggling Ella, no exclamations from Abbott, no murmurs from the Lochabers, that coolness inside turned to cold, hard suspicion.

They stepped into the circle's clearing—empty. And the rain seemed to be picking up its pace. He wasn't a man given to cursing, but in that moment he was sorely tempted. He settled for forcing the lady to take her own weight so he could move to face her. "Where are they?"

Lady Rowena's eyes went wide, fear dripping from them in place of tears. She stumbled back, but then her eyes widened more, her nostrils flared, and she collapsed to the ground with a high keen, hands on the injured ankle.

If she was faking the injury, she had a future on the stage.

Brice passed his fingers through his hair and turned back toward the circle, as if expecting their party to miraculously appear. No, Lochaber would have seen them well out of earshot. And what had he told Brice's mother and sister? That he said he would meet them somewhere? Had they used the falling rain as a handy excuse, created a melee?

He must have had it well planned. Lead Brice off to where Rowena waited. Get the rest of them away. Leave them here, with no horse nor carriage, certainly no car, with darkness already upon them. The rain would only have helped his plan—and in the Highlands one could almost always count on rain.

No doubt he'd be waiting at the castle on the morrow, thunder in his brows and a demand for honor on his lips.

Brice spun back to the girl. "I'll not be bullied. Know that now. Whatever plan this is, I'll have no part of it, even if it means your supposed honor is besmirched. Am I understood?"

Perhaps pain addled her senses, for she looked at him as though he were daft. "Plan? I dinna ken what ye mean, Duke, though clearly ye're fashed."

The Highlands was so thick in her voice he could scarcely understand her. Evidence of strong feeling, he supposed.

He pointed in the general direction of the castle. "Our party has abandoned us. At dusk. When you were suspiciously alone, and I led astray by your father, to where you just *happened* to be. Will you try to tell me it is coincidence? Because I am not such a fool. But I have not carefully avoided such machinations from all of London's slyest mothers just to go blithely along with it here and now. I'll not be bullied into marriage."

"Marriage?" Her bafflement seemed genuine. Which either spoke to her naiveté or outright stupidity.

Brice took a step closer, knowing well it would cause her another moment of fear to have him towering over her. But just then, he cared more for effect than her peace of mind. "I'll ask you again, my lady. What were you doing out there alone?"

He watched the realization dawn through the pain, wasn't surprised when her lips parted, when her eyes slid shut. What took him unawares was the way her shoulders slumped and she curled into herself like a lost kitten. "Lilias."

"Pardon?"

"'Twas Lilias. My father's cousin. She said she'd something to show me, and . . . and then she pushed me. Said it was for my good."

Brice snorted, but he lowered to a crouch. "No doubt both she and your father think it for your good to make you a duchess. But though people often mistake my jesting for weakness, I repeat, my lady—I'll not be bullied. And if this Lilias and your father think I will be, they are in for quite a surprise."

She shrank still more. "Of course. I'll not . . . You should go, sir. I canna walk so far, but if ye appear back at the castle alone, saying ye never saw me, they'll have no choice but to relent and come looking for me. And willna be able to make any demands on you."

And were the weather fair and the darkness not already so heavy, he perhaps would have done just that. But now he heaved a breath and shook his head. "I'll never find the path in the dark. And I can't leave you here in the rain." He wouldn't let an appeal to honor force him into marriage, but his own sense of it certainly wouldn't permit him to leave a young lady helpless, injured, and alone.

Said young lady didn't seem to grasp that. She shook her head and wrapped her arms around her middle. "Ye canna stay with me—ye're right that it must be a scheme. But if we're found well apart from each other . . . Ye can go to the abandoned crofter's cottage. 'Tis the only real shelter within a mile. I'll find a tree to shield me for the night."

Blast that sense of honor—it grated and chafed at the very suggestion. "Leave the lady to the elements while I rest safe and warm? I think not. But I'll see *you* to this cottage, my lady, and then find a place of my own." Or wander about in search of one until he was chilled to the bone and soaked through.

A night of which was far better than a lifetime with a marriage he didn't want. Why in thunder couldn't overeager parents be content to let him choose his own bride?

He held out a hand. "Come. How far is this cottage?"

"Not verra." Her hand shook as she held it out to him. The cold, the wet? Or had he done too good of a job of scaring her?

Blast it, the idea chafed far more than wet wool ever could. Once he got her to her feet again, he fastened on a smile and prayed she could make it out in the dark. "You needn't be fearful, my lady. So long as we are agreed that this scheme will come to naught, I've no argument with you."

A fluttering smile touched her lips and flew away just as quickly.

It wasn't just her hand that shook, he realized as he slid his arm back around her waist, but her whole body. "I assure you," she said, voice quavering too, "I've no desire to marry you, Duke."

A breath of laughter slipped out. "Well now, I'm not as bad as all *that*. I'll have you know that I'm the most eligible bachelor in all England."

They hobbled a few steps, and he glanced down to find her silver eyes wide. "Ye can jest, even now?"

His usual grin found its place on his mouth. "It's a gift."

Her only response was a shake of her head. She indicated a path to the left once they were out of the circle, and true to her word, a cottage's dark outline soon appeared. It looked as though it had seen better days, but the door opened when he pressed upon it, and the inside was dry . . . if it retained a faint smell of sheep.

Brice eased the lady to a seat on a rough wooden chair and headed for the fireplace. So little light remained that he had to feel around the mantel, but his fingers curled around matches, and striking one showed him tinder and peat waiting in the fireplace. "Convenient." Had Lochaber set this up too?

"My father keeps it stocked, in case travelers need it. 'Tis a long and lonely winter up here." Lady Rowena shifted, and a muted groan slipped out.

He got the fire going and then looked over to see she'd raised her injured ankle and slipped off her boot. Most young ladies he knew would never take off their stockings in the presence of a gentleman, but she didn't hesitate. Even in the low light he could see the angry colors on her foot, and the swelling. He winced on her behalf—and then on his own when the rain went from gentle patter upon the roof to a full-fledged torrent.

Lady Rowena looked upward, her brow creased. "You had better wait it out, sir."

A thought that obviously gave her more worry than pleasure. But surely such a downpour couldn't last all that long—though the ground would be soaked now, even under the trees. He warded off the thought by poking around the cottage, soon finding a few rough-looking blankets and an oil lamp he promptly lit and set on the table to brighten the single room.

He draped one of the blankets over the shivering girl, taking the opportunity to get a closer look at her swollen foot. "We should wrap that, my lady. I can cut a strip off one of the blankets, perhaps—there is a pen knife on the shelf yonder I could use."

"There may be a first-aid box somewhere with something better. I've helped fill them."

Turning to do another search, he barely caught her next statement.

"I canna think why he would do this. He hates the English."

"Revenge on my mother, perhaps." There was a small wooden chest in the shadows of the corner, noticeable now with the lamplight, where he'd missed it with only the hearth's fire. Two steps and he was able to lift the top and breathe a relieved sigh when he saw the box labeled FIRST-AID within.

"Yer mother? I dinna understand."

"Apparently they were betrothed once, before my mother met my father. Yours didn't much appreciate being tossed over for an Englishman." He pulled out the box and then pulled out a length of bandage from within it. "There we are."

When he turned, he found Lady Rowena gaping at him. "Betrothed?"

No surprise that Lochaber had been as silent on their history as Mother. "Mm. Though on the other hand, I can't think, if he still harbored animosity toward us, he would want to make us family. So perhaps it is some other motive."

She curled into herself again, turning those large eyes toward the fire. "He'd view it more as being rid of me than making you family."

Her tone stopped him a step away. Such utter despair, such . . . emptiness. As if she were nothing, and expected to be nothing. He eased closer. Surely it was irrational, this sudden desire to soothe that welled up inside. Irrational—and foolish, besides. But there it was, and paired too with that familiar whisper that said it was more than what he wanted to do—it was what he *ought*.

Was this what the Lord had been urging him to, then? Helping her somehow realize her own worth?

A large task for an hour.

He sat on the chair beside hers and handed her the bandage. "You are his daughter, his heir. I can't think he would want to be rid of you."

But the bruises peeked out when she reached toward her ankle, and her nostrils flared. "My stepmother is with child. If it's a boy, then I'm nothing. And even if a girl, then I'm replaceable."

His breath eased out. He could see, from a practical standpoint, why her father would want to secure her a match before the pregnancy was known, if he were only angling for the best possible one. Men aplenty would be happy to marry an heiress, one with a title coming to her, who they wouldn't be interested in if she were a mere daughter with a dowry.

But Rowena was hardly some dowdy old maid. Though her clothes were out of mode, she was young. Pretty. Even more than pretty with the firelight catching the locks that had tumbled free of their chignon and turning them to golden honey. With her eyes gleaming silver.

"Still, I'm surprised your father would resort to this. You're a lovely young lady, and for now his heir. Surely there have been young lords clamoring for your hand for years."

She wound the bandage around her ankle, down over her foot, back up. Her hands still shook, but it didn't hinder her in her task. "The lords are all from English families. Father has never had any use for them."

Until now. Even with revenge as a motive, it made little sense. Brice leaned back in his chair and stared into the dancing flames. "Scottish lairds, then. Surely *they* have been clamoring for your hand."

Even without looking at her, he felt her stiffen, heard the catch in her breath. "One. But he . . ."

Now he turned her way again—and regretted his probing when he saw the look in her eyes. The only words he could think of to describe it were *abject terror*. "Not a good man, I take it?"

She spat something in Gaelic and tied the bandage.

Obviously a touchy subject. And as he didn't yet know whether she was the type to start throwing handy items at the nearest target, he decided it best to nudge the topic slightly. "This cousin that led you off tonight. You're close to her?"

Lady Rowena's face softened, though not entirely. "Lilias. Aye. She's been more a mother to me than my own often was, in those last few years. She came to the castle the same year my parents wed—her own marriage having ended with her husband's death and a world of debt. My mother took her on as lady's maid. Now she's mine."

Cousins as lady's maids? Odd—he'd seen them as housekeepers, of course, but that was the highest position on the staff. But Lochaber probably considered any Kinnaird a cousin and had proven himself more likely to help a clansman than anyone else.

"So . . . she wants you to advance socially? Is that what this is about? Or is it—" he reached forward, caught the hand still fussing with the bandage. Stretching as her arms were, the sleeves had pulled up, revealing the bruises—"something else?"

She jerked her arm away so quickly, so forcefully that she nearly sent herself tumbling off the bench. Perhaps she had anticipated resistance from his fingers, but he'd no intention of holding on to her. Even so, he ought to have known better.

No, this young lady wasn't one who appreciated the touch of a man, however innocent. He held up the offending hand, palm out. "My apologies, my lady, I didn't mean to startle you." But he wasn't about to pretend he hadn't noticed the marks. He nodded toward them, keeping his gaze locked with hers. "You need to get away from here. That's it, isn't it."

Lady Rowena tugged her sleeves down and turned her silver eyes away. "Not like this. Lilias . . . she means well, but I canna fathom why she'd think this the answer."

"Well." His grin might have been forced, but hopefully it would put her at ease. "Obviously she has heard the legends of my unfathomable good looks and unfailing good humor and thought no better man could possibly exist the world over for her darling girl."

The beginnings of a smile touched the corners of her mouth. "Ye're incorrigible, aren't you, Duke?"

He leaned forward a bit, the grin feeling at home now. "The word you're looking for, my dear lady, is *charming*."

"No." But a bit of life had lit her eyes, and her lips curved up a bit more. "I'll stick with incorrigible."

"Oh, cruel creature, you have plunged your daggers straight into my heart." He splayed a dramatic hand over his chest in illustration—and considered it a victory when she loosed a low chuckle.

Perhaps, if the rain kept up, it wouldn't be so tormenting an evening after all.

Six

It was a wonder the waters hadn't carried them straight into the loch last eve. Rowena rubbed her neck, sore from falling asleep leaning against the wall, and noted that the sound of pounding rain had finally ceased. She was as accustomed to rain as the next Highlander, but last night had gone beyond the norm. A leak had revealed itself in the far corner of the cottage, and smoke from the fire had at one point backed down the chimney and choked them.

A miserable night. Yet she couldn't deny that part of her was relieved Nottingham hadn't braved the deluge and left her alone with her throbbing ankle and unanswerable questions. Which only caused her more consternation. Why should she have felt so safe with him? Perhaps he wasn't like her father, dictating to her when she could take a breath. Perhaps he wasn't like Malcolm, forcing himself upon her when the opportunity was given him.

But that didn't mean he was good, didn't mean he was kind to the core. It only meant that he was too much a gentleman to show his true colors to a young lady he had just met.

What had Lilias been thinking, working with the Kinnaird to set this up?

Rowena rubbed the sleep from her eyes, knowledge hovering there beyond the question. Lilias was thinking of the possibility of a bairn, the need for a husband if it were true. She was trying to find an answer that didn't include Malcolm.

But if she thought Rowena would thank her for injuring her and trying to force her to a stranger's bed, then she was in for a rude awakening.

The duke stirred, stretched. And yes, beneath the wariness of him, Rowena felt a stirring too. He was quite possibly the handsomest man she had ever met. If things were different . . .

If things were different, he would never have looked twice at her. He hadn't before this little farce, had he? A few offhanded compliments to her eyes, but otherwise he had regarded her only with suspicion. He was the type for glossy, statuesque ladies fit to grace magazine ads—was probably friends with those she had seen staring back at her in all their painted glory from the circulars.

No. Lilias may have meant well, but she was foolish to try something like this. Even were Nottingham able to be manipulated . . . Rowena was not, could not, be duchess material. And so, it was best to ensure her father couldn't force the matter. "Duke?" Her throat sounded scratchy, no doubt from the smoke-inspired coughing last night. "Daylight is upon us, sir. Ye'd best go."

The duke, bleary eyes open, nodded and pushed himself to his feet. He had fallen asleep against the wall opposite her, as far away as possible in the tiny shack. "Right. Sorry to have intruded so much longer than expected."

"Ye could hardly go out in such rain, not for so long." She watched him stretch the kinks out of his back, run his hands through his hair, and turn resolutely toward the door. "Duke . . . thank you. For being kind in such a trying situation."

He flashed her a grin as if it were nothing—as if her family wasn't trying to ruin his life—and reached for the latch. "And thank *you*, my lady, for not being privy to their plans, or it would have been even more trying."

And he wouldn't have been so kind? Probably not. Rowena shifted, biting back a moan at the screaming pain in her foot when she did. She'd have to look at it, take off the bandage, see if daylight shed anything new upon the injury. She'd wait until she was alone though. Only belatedly had she realized last night that she oughtn't to bare her ankles before Nottingham. Elspeth would be horrified that she had, but she was so accustomed to shedding shoes and stockings to dip her toes into the icy loch . . .

"Are you all right, my lady? Your ankle?"

Rowena opened the eyes that had slid closed with the onslaught of pain and forced a smile. "I'll be just fine, sir."

He focused on her in that way that made her want to squirm—that way that surely saw too much, too well. But if he recognized her bluff, he opted not to call her on it. With a nod, he tugged open the door. "Farewell then. I imagine we'll meet again at the castle."

"Aye." She could hear the dread in her voice. Her father would try to force a wedding. And the duke would, of course, fight him on it. It would prove an ugly scene, she was sure. One she rather hoped she missed.

She'd as soon keep her image of Nottingham as a kind, humorous man a bit longer.

With another nod in farewell, he stepped out. Fog seeped in through the open door, dispersing again with the *whoosh* of its closing. Rowena drew in a long breath, let it out, and allowed her face to contort with the throbbing of her ankle.

It was broken, sure as day. It must be, to hurt so. Her fingers trembling, she reached down to untie the bandage.

Brilliant bruising peeked out, making her stomach flip.

The door swinging open again made it flop. She had the presence of mind to tug her hem back down, but she could wrap her tongue around no wit when Nottingham strode back into the room without so much as by-your-leave. The expression on his face—so stoic but for a trace of . . . amusement?—baffled her.

When her father strode in behind him, a thunderhead in his eyes, some of the bafflement disappeared.

"Is that what you call 'right behind' me, Lochaber?" The duke stopped in the middle of the room and spun back toward the door.

"Rowena!" Father looked almost concerned when he spotted her—she had to give him credit for his skills as an actor. He flew to her side as if he cared. And it almost seemed the breath he sucked in upon spotting her mottled foot was genuine. "What did you do to her, Nottingham?"

She'd never heard that particular tone from him. Had no word to describe it.

Nottingham folded his arms over his chest. "Saved her from a night spent with her feet in the loch, after her cousin pushed her down the hill." He paused, lifted a brow. "I believe the words you're looking for, my lord, are *thank you*."

"Thank you? Ye expect me to *thank you* for spending the night with my daughter? All the neighborhood's out looking for her, and what do ye think they'll say when they find ye've both been holed up here for the night?"

Father looked back to her. Lifted his hand. She winced away, but he didn't strike her. Of course he wouldn't, not in front of the duke. He stroked the hair from her face. Though no affection shone in his eyes when he said, in Gaelic, "Have you no sense, girl? You told him you were pushed? All you had to do was claim to have slipped and let the chips fall!"

Rowena could only shake her head.

The duke lifted the other brow. "Let's dispense with the playacting, shall we? You set this up—a dunce could see that. No doubt so you can try to force us to wed. But allow me to save you some trouble and embarrassment and say, while we're still alone, that it won't work. I'll not be bullied into marriage."

Her father rose, settling into the stance she knew best. The one that kept his spine straight, his shoulders back, and a glare upon his face. Usually, that stance sent men scrambling, women scattering. Usually, when the Kinnaird curled his hand into a fist, everyone knew to run.

Nottingham just stood there, arms still crossed and half a smile still on his too handsome face.

"You've disgraced my daughter, sir! If you think I'll—"

"No. *You* disgraced your daughter. I played the hero." The duke let the amusement fade from his face. "You arranged it well—I'll grant you that. And the rain helped. But it was all for naught, so let's handle this reasonably. You take your daughter back to the castle and tell all those neighbors you've rallied that you found her—*alone*—in the cottage. I'll just turn up far away. No harm done."

"No harm done?" Father motioned to the door, and by doing so drew Rowena's attention to the fact that voices could be heard, though they were muffled by fog and distance. "A search party is scouring the countryside. There's little chance of you slipping away without being seen."

Nottingham's eyes went hard and cold. The smile he put on now looked . . . well, like the smile of a duke. "Covered every angle, have you? Then I'm afraid all your friends and cousins and neighbors will have to be privy to my refusal to be manipulated."

"You would destroy a girl's reputation?"

Rowena lowered her gaze, fastened it upon the strand of wool pulling loose from the knit of her jacket. Stifled the urge to pick at it.

"Don't try to ply me with guilt, Lochaber. I've done nothing wrong, and I won't pay for *your* decisions."

"You think you can run roughshod over my family?" Her father's voice dripped threat.

Nottingham's breath of laughter seemed unaffected by it. "In the past year, I've seen one of my dearest friends kidnapped. I've had a madman point a gun at my head. Witnessed that man's death at the hands of the constable. *Then* lost my father, on top of it all." She glanced up and saw him lean forward, his eyes showing no fear whatsoever. "I'm well beyond petty threats, Lochaber. And I warn you now—don't push me. Don't try me. My good humor has been stretched to its limits."

A chill found the base of her spine and shivered its way up. She thought she knew dangerous men—but it seemed Nottingham was a whole different kind of one.

"Lord Lochaber?" A figure blocked the light from the open doorway—the stable master, and his relief looked genuine when he spotted Rowena. "My lady, ye're well! We feared the worst when that storm wouldna let up. Angus! McDonnell, over here—and with the horses. The lass is injured!"

Nottingham seemed to draw in his next breath with extra care. His focus didn't leave her father's. "Am I understood, Lochaber?"

If he thought so, he greatly underestimated the stubborn Scots blood her father took such pride in. "Your party stayed the night at the castle, sir." The Kinnaird motioned toward the door. "Let us repair there to finish our discussion, aye?"

Any objection the duke may have made disappeared under

the clamor of the arriving grooms and horses, the shouts that went out to the other staff and neighbors combing the glen. Rowena lost sight of Nottingham in the fray, let herself be scooped up by the burly McDonnell and deposited gently upon an old, imperturbable mare.

Her father slid the reins over the horse's head and tethered them to his own mount. When he glanced up at her, she forced the words past her lips. In Gaelic—for though the servants would understand, the duke wouldn't. "Why'd ye do it, Father?"

He froze, then edged closer. "It was that or Malcolm, lass. If ye'd rather the devil ye know, then say the word."

She could say nothing. It took all her strength to hold back the sob that tightened her throat, to keep down the tears that threatened to well. She ought to have just run away after Malcolm stripped her of what little worth she had. Or tossed herself into the loch.

The ride back to the castle passed in a blur of cold, damp air and shooting pain every time her injured foot brushed against the horse. Her discomfort only increased with each person who joined their group, the shouts having gone far and wide, apparently.

One small part warmed within her. She hadn't thought they'd care, any of them, if she went missing. But the joy of their servants and neighbors seemed genuine when they rushed up to her and praised the Lord she was found, safe and whole.

Each time her father was quick to put in that the duke had rescued her, made sure she was safe. Was he trying to appease Nottingham . . . or cement in everyone's mind that they had been together all night? Rowena did her best to smile at whomever spoke and otherwise kept her gaze locked firmly upon the old nag's mane.

More shouting pierced the air when they crossed the causeway over Loch Morar and through the gates of Castle Kynn. She dared look up when their group drew to a halt—and wished she hadn't.

Ella stood on the steps, flanked by her mother and Miss Abbott. The woman Rowena had hoped would become a dear friend—and possibly a means of escape from the Highlands—stared at her with a look of utter betrayal on her face. Asking, no words required, how she could do something so low, how she could set a trap for her beloved brother.

She wouldn't believe that Rowena had nothing to do with it. How could she?

McDonnell lumbered to a stop beside her horse and held up his hands. "Come, lass. There be hot drink waiting, and breakfast besides. Mrs. MacPherson has been cooking up a storm, ye ken. Lilias'll have ye warm and dry and snug in no time."

Lilias. Rowena caught her maid's attention as McDonnell helped her down, asking the same silent question Ella had.

Lilias's eyes had gone wide. No doubt she had seen the mottled foot that wouldn't fit back in her boot. No doubt she regretted having caused her injury. No doubt she wondered if she had done right.

Well, she hadn't. And Rowena would be happy to tell her so when they had a moment alone.

She needed to escape all the eyes, all the questions. All the accusations coming from the Nottinghams and Abbotts. All the whispers going through the Kinnaird clan when they spotted the duke. She looked up into the kind, lined face of McDonnell. "Would ye take me straight to my room, please?"

Understanding warmed his eyes. "Aye, lass."

But her father made it inside ahead of them and barred the path to the stairs, pointing instead toward the drawing room. With a sigh, McDonnell shifted directions.

Rowena wilted onto the chair he chose for her, the same

one she always picked for herself. But she barely registered the comfort of the faded cushions, the fire crackling in the stone hearth, the vibrant colors of the rug she had passed many an hour staring at. She didn't know how much longer she could hold back the tears, but she couldn't well loose them here, now, surrounded by the swarm of families that descended.

Their words were shouts, buzzing and clanging against each other, blurring with the light from the oil lamps lit against the dim day. Elspeth, Father, the Nottinghams. All speaking at once, asking questions, making demands. The duke with his perpetual *"Absolutely not"* and Father with his insistent *"But ye must."* Words like *honor* and *expectation* and *ruined* all battling each other for prominence until the very landscapes on the walls seemed to shiver in their gilt-edged frames.

She squeezed her eyes shut. Pulled tight the blanket McDonnell had draped over her. And prayed she could melt into the chair.

The cacophony kept on until a too-familiar voice shattered it with a furious shout of "Rowena!"

Malcolm. No, no, no. Not here, not now, not with all these people around.

She shrank as much as she could into the chair, pulled the blanket higher. Maybe he wouldn't even spot her in the crowd. Maybe Father would send him away. Maybe . . .

He charged through the room, shoving people aside, and jerked her from the chair.

To keep from falling into his chest, she had no choice but to plant both feet. And then couldn't hold back the cry of pain.

"Glaikit woman!" He shook her hard enough to make her vision swim. "Did ye think I wouldna hear, that I wouldna ken *exactly* what ye were trying to do? Ye're *mine*, Rowena Kinnaird. *Mine*!"

"Unhand her!" Welcome words, but it wasn't her father who

shoved Malcolm away. Nay, 'twas Nottingham who held the brute off with one arm and kept her from falling with the other. His hand curled around her waist, warm and secure . . . But it was not the support she wished for. Why, even before all these people, could the Kinnaird not defend her?

"A *Sassenach*?" Malcolm whirled to face her father, his face mottling red. "Ye wouldna."

Father didn't so much as blink out of turn. "Ye presume too much, Malcolm. Something I wish I had seen in you sooner. Now if ye'll excuse us—I was in discussion with the duke."

"Ye were in discussion with *me* before that Sassenach ever got to the Highlands, and I'll not be dismissed!"

Rowena squeezed her eyes shut and prayed with every meager ounce of faith within her that he wouldn't say it all here and now. That he wouldn't blurt out before the Nottinghams what he'd done to her, what he had taken.

The duke leaned down. "Is he the laird you mentioned?"

A shudder shook her. "I didna ken what kind o' man he was."

Malcolm spun back their way, eyes still ablaze. "Ye needna worry yerself with salvaging her honor, Yer Grace. It'll be o' no concern to anyone when she's my wife."

Nottingham's hand pressed tighter to her side. "I don't believe the lady wishes to wed you, Mister . . . ?"

"Kinnaird."

A glance up at the duke's face revealed, of all things, a return of his amused smile. "Ah, a clansman. How cozy."

Malcolm looked ready to haul off and punch Nottingham in the nose. "The next chief of Clan Kinnaird, and I'll thank you to take your dirty English paws off my future wife."

Nottingham lifted his free hand and made a show of examining it. "Well now. I'm not as tidy as usual, I grant you, but it was for a good cause."

With a growl, Malcolm lunged forward, clamping his hand around her arm and tugging.

She tried to resist, to pull away, to tuck herself to the duke's side. But Malcolm had anticipated her reaction and pulled hard. Then his hand was on her hip and his chest was before her eyes and his musk was overwhelming her and the stones were biting her back again and the pain—the pain clouded her vision, obliterated everything, and she could only beg again, "No, no, *no*!"

The room—*this* room—came rushing back as her father hauled Malcolm a step away, as Nottingham caught her up again, as the women all rushed forward, the duchess shouting something about her ankle.

Her ankle—its throb was so much less now, with that other agony again in her mind.

Malcolm struggled against her father.

The duke glowered with the ferocity of a winter storm. "Don't. Touch. Her. Again."

The brute snarled. "Stay out of it, Sassenach. Ye canna stand between us forever."

The tremors gripped her fast and hard and would have sent her to her knees had Nottingham not held her upright. He stroked his thumb in a circle obviously meant to soothe. And which, oddly, it did. A little.

"Yes," he said, his voice low and tight. "I can. And I will."

Malcolm strained against Father's hands. "What'll ye do? Take her south, hide her away? I'll find her. She's mine, and I'll find her as surely in England as in my own glen."

He would. She had no doubt of that. How had she ever thought it would be enough to leave Loch Morar? Her ghosts would follow her wherever she went.

Nottingham smiled. "And what good will that do you, when she's the Duchess of Nottingham?"

The world stilled. Every breath caught. Rowena couldn't even think of breathing, not when he looked down into her eyes and she saw the soft light in his. The promise. The offer of that thing she craved most—escape. Quietly, he added, "If you'll have me, Rowena."

Her name sounded different, somehow, on his lips without that cushioning *Lady* before it—and punctuated, as it was, with the Gaelic curses that Malcolm spat. The brute roared, fought against Father's arms.

Rowena pressed closer to Nottingham's side and whispered the only word that would come. "Aye."

His mother and sister's shouts were drowned out by Malcolm's as he broke free. In the next moment he'd wrenched her away from Nottingham again, his face as dark as sin.

He'd kill her then and there, she saw it in his eyes as his hands closed around her neck. No one would be able to stop him in time, and she'd never be able to fight him off. She had only one defense, and she barely got the words past her lips before his fingers tightened. "Elspeth's with child."

The implications did exactly as she expected. The fire in his eyes shifted, a different shade of anger snuffing out the murderous rage. His hands dropped from her neck, even if they then dug into her shoulders. "Then ye could well be naught. Is that what ye're saying?"

The words shouldn't hurt, not when she'd counted on him feeling that way. Not when she still bore the marks of a far harsher proof of his lack of love. Why, then, did they pierce like arrows through the remnants of her heart?

"She'll still be my daughter." Father came, finally, to her side. He shoved Malcolm away and supported her himself. "'Tis *you* who may well be naught, Malcolm. Now get out o' my home."

The muscle in Malcolm's jaw ticked, but he took a step away.

Backward, his gaze never leaving Rowena's. His hands still in fists by his side. "Aye. But know this, Rowena." His words were in Gaelic, hard as stone. "If I find you carry my babe, I *will* come for you. No child of mine will be raised by a Sassenach."

Fear curled anew in her stomach. And it didn't vanish when he left.

Seven

Protect her.

That had been the impression that had seized Brice's heart when that blasted Scot charged into the room, and it reverberated still now, as he looked down into the chalky face of the woman who had just agreed to marry him. She shook so violently that he feared she might collapse. And no wonder—her neck now had screaming red marks where the brute's fingers had grabbed and pressed. She was small, delicate. Kinnaird could have—perhaps *would* have—snapped her neck before Brice or her father could have stopped him.

Lochaber had delivered her back to Brice's side to follow and make sure that Kinnaird actually left, and now here they were. Engaged. And for life of him, he couldn't bring himself to regret the impulsive offer. The Lord's command had been crystalline in his heart, His will perfectly clear. Brice was meant to wed this frightened young woman.

If only the Lord were in the habit of handing him reasons along with those undeniable impressions. Because though she was pretty in a quiet way, though she seemed sweet enough, though she obviously needed a protector, though he had been willing to grant the Lord had a purpose for introducing them, she wasn't anything like what Brice imagined his future wife being.

Protect her. It sounded like his own words, his own thoughts. Only clearer, stronger. Truer.

Rowena looked up at him, her silver eyes as big as moons and bright with the fervor of fear. "Ye needna . . ."

But he did. Perhaps Malcolm's motivations were largely tied up in the title he'd thought she was sure to inherit, but it couldn't be only that. Brice had seen passion enough in people. The Scot's might be dark, but it was still passion. The desire to have, to own, to possess—the very same kind that had darkened the eyes of Pratt last summer, when he'd held a shotgun at the ready and demanded a hostage. The same kind that churned within Lady Pratt when she demanded the Fire Eyes.

A curse, without question. The curse of sin, of lust, of covetousness, of hatred.

And Malcolm was too much in its throes to leave Rowena alone just because Lady Lochaber was with child. "You're not safe here, Rowena," he said softly. He'd thought her father the threat—and had seen her wince away from him in the crofter's cottage. But Lochaber paled in comparison to this laird.

"But . . ."

He looked up, met the gaze of his mother and then her stepmother. "Could we have a moment, please?"

The matrons were both quick to nod and usher the rest out. But Ella tossed a look at him over her shoulder that was filled with worry. He gave her a smile. Not a grin, flippant and carefree, but one to let her know he didn't regret anything. Her frown eased a bit.

The Abbotts' didn't. No doubt his friend would have thoughts aplenty on entering so quickly into a holy covenant. And Miss

Abbott plenty about the type of young lady who would trick a man into marriage.

He waited until the door had closed behind the last of them and then led Rowena to her chair. He took the time to pull over a footstool for her to rest her injured ankle upon. Once she was situated, he perched on the ottoman beside her leg and rested his elbows on his knees. "Is that all right?"

Rowena wrapped her arms around her middle and nodded, her expression hollow with the shock of all that had just happened.

His instinct was to reach for her hands, but he suspected that wouldn't have the desired effect, despite how willing she had been to cling to his side in the face of Kinnaird. He settled for clasping his own hands together between his knees. "Right. You have to know he won't give up so easily. You can't stay here."

She shook her head, so slowly it looked . . . mournful. "I'm worthless to him now."

"If Lady Lochaber has a son, which is not guaranteed. And even if it were, that man . . . he has something dark within him. I know you saw it. Who's to say he wouldn't try to kill the babe to keep his standing as heir to the chiefdom, and yours to the earldom?"

A shudder ripped through her, and she met his gaze again. How many times in their short acquaintance had he seen that bright panic in her eyes? Too many. "No. My father would never let him close enough."

"Your father was but a few feet away just now." He pointed at the spot they'd occupied. "But what could he have done had Kinnaird broken your neck? Sometimes one moment is all it takes for tragedy to strike. And no one can be on their guard every second."

Her eyes slid shut.

"We must do all we can to make the risk too great for him to attempt it. Marrying me will help with that. He can't expect to just come and claim you."

Her silver stare opened to him again. "Who's to say he willna come after you too, then? Kill the babe, kill you, and then force me back here?"

Brice nearly snorted—Kinnaird would have to wait in line to get his shot at him. And perhaps it was mere arrogance, but he still thought Lady Pratt the more dangerous adversary. Kinnaird was hot temper and impulse. The lady was cold calculation and patience.

Brice feared ice far more than fire. "The advantage will be ours in England. He won't know the land. He won't have the friends. And the press is always dogging my steps, which will provide another layer of protection."

She went even paler. "The press? But I'm . . . I'm not suited, sir. I'd shame you, be an embarrassment to the Nottingham name."

And the fashionable set would feast on the tatters of her composure for breakfast. But he could handle them too. "It's just trappings, Rowena. Clothes and jewels and the number of footmen one employs. I'll give you those things."

"'Tis more than that, and we both ken it."

"We can handle it. Together." He held out a hand, palm up.

Rather than putting her fingers onto it, she stared at him. "Why do ye want to? Why do ye want to help me? I'm nothing to you."

True . . . until the Lord's words had overtaken his thoughts ten long minutes ago. Until then she had been only a girl he might be asked to help. Until then, the feeling that he was to pay attention and be ready to assist had been vague and open to interpretation. But it was different now. Now he knew the Lord had far more plans for them than an hour's conversation. And though he couldn't yet tell *why* God wanted them together . . . well, the Lord saw what Brice didn't. He always had a purpose. Brice would simply have to discover what it was. "You're something very special to me now, darling. You're the one God made very clear I should have and hold until death parts us."

"God did?" Her voice went weak, her eyes wider. "Why?"

Ah, and there was a piece to that puzzle. Most people in his acquaintance questioned *that* he heard from the Lord, not *why* he heard a particular thing. But she didn't doubt him. Beneath the hurt, beneath the feeling of unworthiness, she obviously had a pure faith. "You'll have to take that one up with Him. I never presume to know His reasons at first, though they usually become clear. He led me to my dearest friends, away from what would have proven disastrous matches. I trust Him to lead me here too."

At last, with a long breath that must have bolstered her a bit, she slid her fingers onto his palm. "Verra well, then. I fear ye'll regret it, but . . . I'll trust Him too. I'll be yer wife."

Who knew such a promise from a veritable stranger could make a grin break out on his face? He clasped her fingers, raised them to his lips, and pressed a lingering kiss to her knuckles. "Let the adventure begin."

No! No, no, no, this cannot be happening. This was worse than the fear a few hours past that something had happened to them. Worse than the realization last night, watching him walking through the mist in the circle, that there would never be another. Worse than the aching questions for year upon lonely year as to whether the old dreams would ever die, whether they would ever dare shift from flirtation to something more.

Worse. So much worse.

The door had been left open a crack, and they were all gathered around it, peeking in. Nottingham and Lady Rowena wouldn't appreciate it. But Nottingham and Lady Rowena weren't the only ones with something at stake right now. Couldn't they see that? Couldn't they see that others' hearts, others' dreams, others' very *beings* would be changed by this . . . this utter poppycock?

He would claim the Lord had told him to propose—he always claimed such when he did something foolish. And because he was him, charmed son of the Duke of Nottingham—and now the charming duke himself—life would play along.

Stella dug her fingers into the doorframe. It was a mistake. They weren't suited. He was too forward for Lady Rowena, she too reticent for him. That truth gleamed clear and treacherous as ice. They wouldn't be happy together. They *couldn't* be.

The duchess let out a slow, quiet breath and shook her head, concern in her dark eyes. "I hope he doesn't regret this," she said to all of them. Or perhaps to none of them.

Ella, her arm through her mother's, nodded her mournful agreement of the question. "I love Rowena, I hate that she's in such a situation, but . . ."

Why couldn't Ella just say it? *But they will destroy each other.*

"He's made his decision though," their mother murmured. "I can see it in the line of his shoulders. There'll be no talking him out of it. We can only pray for them."

No. Stella drew in a long, slow breath. No, that wasn't all they could do. Prayers were all well and good in the echoing beams of a church, or to speak of when one needed to look pious before certain parties—like one's brother. But some things couldn't be left to prayer alone.

Sometimes they must take action. And if no one else would act . . . well then, so be it. Stella would.

It had been a long, silent two days. Lilias chanced a glance at Rowena's face—empty—and carefully pinned the bandage on the girl's foot. So far as the doctor could tell, it wasn't broken, praise be. But the sprain, he had said, was a bad one. She needed to stay off it.

Instead, she'd be hobbling up the aisle of the kirk this morning.

A happy bride she wasn't. Lilias sighed and eased the wrapped foot back to the ground, arranging the layers of white silk and organza again. "Talk to me, lass. Are ye having second thoughts?"

Rowena barely looked her way. She'd not asked her any questions. She'd not made any accusations. Nay, after Malcolm stormed off and the duke proposed two days ago, she'd just asked to be carried to her room and had all but vanished within herself—except for when Annie came in and made her smile.

Just as her mother had done all those years ago. Heaven help her, but Lilias couldn't let Rowena follow in Nora's ill-chosen steps. "Wena, lass. Ye've scarcely said two words."

"What is there to say?" She pushed herself from her chair, not wincing quite as much today when she put a bit of weight on her foot. Hobbling to the full-length mirror, she sighed at the vision of herself.

Though why, Lilias could only guess. "Ye're a sight to behold. That dress . . ." Lilias still wasn't sure where the dowager duchess had gotten it, but it had appeared yesterday amid much flurry. The height of fashion, perfectly fitted to Rowena's petite frame. Not what Lilias had ever imagined her Wena wearing, but it was a taste, surely, of what was to come. Now if only her cheeks weren't so pale. "Ye're all peely-wally, lass."

Rowena pressed a hand to her stomach. "I'm with child, Lil. I must be. My courses are a week late—"

"Worry can cause such things. Ye needna lose hope yet." But it could be true. Otherwise they likely wouldn't be here, preparing for a wedding. She smoothed out a bunching in the back of the gown and then tucked in a curl trying to escape. "And if ye are . . . ye'll have a husband in a few short hours."

Rowena shivered. "He doesna have to do this. Doesna have to help me. How am I to repay him by lying about something so important?"

Lilias forsook the fabric and clasped her girl's shoulders. "Ye canna tell him. Ye pray it isna so, and if it is, ye pass the bairn off as his. Ye ken? Otherwise he'll divorce you and send you straight back here into the jowls of that beast. Unless, perhaps, ye were to tell him of how Malcolm attacked you."

Rowena pivoted on her good foot to face Lilias, incredulity in her eyes. "Ye want me to confess my shame to him?"

Lilias's chin snapped up. "'Tisn't *your* shame, lass. Ye did nothing wrong."

"If it isn't my shame, then why am I the one forced to wed a man I don't know, forced to his bed to cover—" Her heaving breath cut her off, coming too fast, too hard.

Lilias grabbed her before she could make herself light-headed and urged her back to the chair. "Breathe, lass. Deep breaths now, in and out. His Grace is a good, kind man. And handsome, aye? 'Twill be no hardship to let him charm you."

"I canna . . . I *canna*. I canna let him . . ."

Poor lass. Lilias cupped her cheek, careful not to smudge the dusting of powder she'd already applied. "I ken how hard this is for you, Wena. But it willna be like it was with Malcolm. His Grace is no monster. Ye must give him a chance. Ye *must*. Ye understand that, aye?"

Her breathing slowed, though no peace entered her eyes. Lilias leaned over to press a kiss to her forehead. "Lady Ella will be here soon, and then it's to the kirk. Another hour and ye'll be a duchess. Yer mother . . . she'd be so proud to see you today. So proud."

Rowena shook her head, opened her mouth, but the door swung open and Annie gusted in before she could reply. Seeing the way Rowena's eyes lit, her lips turned, Lilias didn't mind the interruption a whit.

The one bright spot, if there *were* a bairn—nothing seemed to light Rowena as did a wee one. And if she could keep from hating a child got on her in such a way, she would flourish as a mother.

Not like Nora.

Little Annie climbed up into Rowena's lap and clamped her arms around her neck. "Take me with you to England, Wena. Dinna leave me here alone."

Rowena closed her eyes and held on tight. "Ye're not alone, Annie. Ye've yer mother and the Kinnaird, and when the babe comes—"

"Then they're as like to ship me off to school as anything, and I dinna *want* to be alone. Take me with you. I'll be no bother, I swear it, and—"

"Ye're never a bother." Rowena kissed the lass's head and rested her cheek atop it. Lilias nearly chided her for inviting wrinkles and red marks but bit her tongue. The bigger lass needed this as much as the little one. "And I wish I could take you. But there's no time, what with us leaving tomorrow for Yorkshire. And I dinna dare ask it of the duke yet. But I will soon, Annie. I give you my word. We'll send for you. Perhaps ye can spend Christmas with us."

There now. A promise of the future, and of a relationship enough with the duke to ask a favor. Lilias breathed a bit easier as she headed to the dressing room to check her trunks one last time. Rowena would do what needed done, and she would learn how to be a duchess.

And Lilias would be there every step of the way to make sure she wasn't alone in the doing.

Brice lifted his hand to knock on his mother's door, though it swung open before his knuckles could connect with the wood. Grinning at the startled look on her face, he leaned into her doorway. "I was hoping I'd catch you before you left."

Mother smiled and reached up to pat his cheek with a gloved hand. "I was about to come check on you and tell you we were headed for the castle. How are you feeling? Nervous?"

"Oddly, no." Or he hadn't been before Macnab had shown up twenty minutes ago. Having the Fire Eyes in hand again though . . . He needed to get them in a safe, fast. He held up the box, keeping his smile light. "I've a gift for you. I commissioned it when we first arrived, and Mr. Macnab just delivered it, having heard we leave town tomorrow."

The old man had nodded his approval of their quick departure too. Apparently Malcolm Kinnaird's dark side wasn't as unknown to all of Lochaber as it had been to those in Castle Kynn.

Mother shook her head, though pleasure lit her eyes. "Oh, Brice, you oughtn't to be giving *me* a gift on *your* wedding day."

"Well, I hardly knew it would be such when I placed the order." He pressed the box into her hands.

She took a step back into her room, waving him in behind her, and untied the satin ribbon holding the box closed. When she opened it, a delighted laugh spilled out. "The missing earbobs! And they're perfect matches too. Mr. Macnab always outdoes himself, doesn't he?"

"He does. It's why I waited until we came here to get it done. I'd a mind to since Father . . ." He had to clear his throat. "I know how you always loved this set. Now you can claim to have found them hidden away somewhere, and no one need know they aren't original."

She laughed. "I have always felt so guilty. To think that they have graced the ears of every Duchess of Nottingham on their—" She cut herself off with a gasp, her eyes lighting up. "What perfect timing Mr. Macnab has! The Nottingham rubies have always been a wedding gift to the new duchess. And now I can give them to Rowena."

"Oh. I hadn't . . . hadn't thought of that, to be sure." Striving to keep his smile in place lest it tip his mother off, he nodded. "I was more concerned with the rings than family traditions—Macnab brought those too." He reached into his pocket and pulled out the coordinating set. How the old jeweler had managed to create something so intricate with so little notice, Brice wasn't sure. But they were works of art, with small diamonds and patterns cut into the gold. Rowena would hopefully be pleased.

And it was still more than a little odd that he had to suddenly think about whether his bride would like something. Odder still that he wasn't well enough acquainted with his bride to know without the wonder.

Mother waved him back out of the room. "The girls and I had better hurry over to the castle to make sure Rowena doesn't need any help from us. We'll see you at the kirk in an hour, love."

"Very good. Tell her . . ." *What?* There was so very much to talk about, and they'd had no time for anything but a how-do-you-do since his proposal. "Tell her I've been praying for her."

He meandered back to his chamber, wishing he had friends here beyond Abbott. Stafford ought to be present, returning the favor of jesting him out of any nerves, as Brice had done for him a little over a year ago. But when he'd returned to Gaoth Lodge the other day set to wire him and Brook, he'd had a telegram from them waiting. Stafford's cousin Cayton had just lost his wife, two days after she gave birth prematurely to a daughter. They were needed in Yorkshire for the funeral today. No doubt they would rant a bit at being left out, but why pull them in another direction?

Abbott was waiting in Brice's sitting room, his face a mask of worry. The moment Brice stepped in, he was greeted with "Are you certain you want to go through with this? You could yet change your mind."

His friend had been full of such wisdom these days. "Of course I could. Which is why I don't intend to."

"You scarcely know her!"

"Oh, bah. How often does a couple really know each other after a Season in London spent flirting and lying? All anyone ever cares about is pounds per annum, anyway." A bit more cynical a view than he usually took, perhaps, but it served his purpose. He strode to the mirror and checked his tie for the fourth time. "At least we are *aware* that we don't know each other. We haven't false pretenses between us."

"Nottingham." Abbott used that solemn tone of voice with him rarely enough that it stilled him as his friend drew to his side. "Please don't be flippant. Marriage is a sacred union, one that ought not to be entered into lightly. I am honored to count you as one of my dearest friends—I only want to be certain you're not making a mistake."

Brice turned so that he could look into Abbott's actual eyes rather than his reflected ones. "I appreciate the concern, Ab. I do. But this is what I'm meant to do."

But it was irritation in Abbott's scrutiny, not acceptance. "Will you claim again that God told you to?"

Apparently it was too much to ask that his wedding day be all smiles and congratulations. Brice drew in a breath that did nothing to soothe the frustration. "You have never doubted me before when I said I felt the Lord pressing something upon me. Why now?"

Abbott spun away. "Of course I've doubted you—anyone in his right mind would doubt you! No one hears from God as you claim to. I've just always bitten my tongue, as it hardly mattered."

Brice sucked in a breath, much as he would have done had his friend punched him in the stomach. That was about what it felt like. "All your talk of your beloved George Müller and his unsurpassed trust in the Lord, and you can say 'no one hears from God' like that?"

His friend flushed. "He was a man of God. Not a duke."

Frustration simmered. No, not just frustration. Hurt. "So I am only permitted to be so close to the Lord if I am a missionary? Is that it? I cannot both follow Him *and* be a good steward of what my family has left me?"

Abbott turned partly away. "You spend most of your day seeing to the things of this earth. Tenants and rents and improvements, sessions and balls and soirees. Then you come and say God spoke to you, when I have dedicated my whole *life* to Him and never—"

"Abbott." Brice's sigh did more than rob him of energy. It left him aching. "You are one of the best men I know—the most faithful. I always thought we strengthened each other in our faith. Do you mean to tell me that I'm a hindrance to you instead? That you resent me or distrust me or . . . ?"

"No! It is just . . ." Abbott sank to a seat in the stiff armchair by the hearth. "You cannot always be right, Worthing. It is impossible."

A lump stuck in his throat. No one called him Worthing anymore, not unless they slipped, forgot his new title. Hearing it from Abbott now took him back to their shared childhood, when it had never mattered that they were unequal in the sight of the world. He had thought it still didn't—more the fool him, apparently, if his oldest friend had been judging his lifestyle all the while. "I never claimed to be always right. I know I make my share of mistakes."

"So then pause for half a moment. Consider that this could be one of them." Abbott splayed his hands, his eyes earnest. "This is the rest of your *life*."

"And I have done nothing *but* consider that these two days! Disbelieve it and resent it if you must, but on this I am without a doubt. I am meant to marry Rowena."

Abbott groaned and rubbed a hand over his face. "Do you not hear yourself? How you sound? Have you paused to actually look at this girl you're marrying and realize that she isn't like any of the young ladies you've flirted with?"

"Of course I realize that—I realized that the moment we were introduced."

"What then? How will you make her happy? How will you get to know her? And how will she respond the first time you let loose some of your typical flattery, aimed at another woman? Have you thought of *that*?"

A valid point, that. Flirting *had* become his way, and he often didn't even notice he'd done it until a gleam flashed in a set of feminine eyes. He had always imagined that his bride-to-be would be so secure in his affections that she would laugh away any slips he made.

But Rowena wouldn't be. Couldn't be. She was so very insecure in general, not to mention in their relationship, which was more potential than reality.

Brice sighed. "You're right, there. And I thank you for the reminder." He raised his right hand and straightened his spine. "I promise you, O Reverend Mr. Abbott, that I will guard my tongue, my heart, and my bride with equal fervor. I will do all in my power to win her heart, give her mine, and make her happy."

Abbott didn't relax. Didn't grin. Certainly didn't laugh. "You're being flippant again."

"But I'm not." Sinking to a chair, Brice caught himself a second from running his fingers through his hair and mussing it. "Perhaps my tone is light, but my meaning isn't. I know this is my life, Ab. And Rowena's. I know we are strangers. I know the path to a steady, unfading love will not be an easy one. And yet . . . and yet I can't help but think that it's *because* we're so different—and that *she* is so different from all the young ladies I've known before—that we will ultimately suit."

Abbott breathed a sigh. "I will be praying for you."

"Thank you. That is all I ask." Since, apparently, outright support was too much to hope for. "And while you're praying, keep our families before the Lord too—that we somehow bridge the decades of bad blood between our parents."

"Well." Abbott leaned forward, forced merriment in his eyes. "If you really want to win the favor of her family, I suggest you put that on."

One glance at the kilt Lochaber had sent over and Brice snorted a laugh. "On second thought . . . I'm really not all that keen on her father's favor, thank you very much."

Eight

She was married. Rowena's hands shook as she fumbled the clasp of the ruby bracelet Charlotte had given her minutes before they headed to the kirk. It was done. Official. She was the Duchess of Nottingham, lady of a manor she'd never seen in a place she'd never been, one of the highest-ranking peeresses in a country she'd never so much as visited, among ladies who would want nothing to do with her.

She was married, and in a matter of minutes her husband, who had been all beaming smiles and soft flirtation throughout the ceremony and the interminable banquet afterward, would come through that door that connected her temporary room at Gaoth Lodge to his. He would come in and expect to kiss her and put his hands on her and . . . and . . .

She couldn't breathe. Her vision blurred. The heavy necklace choked her. She tossed the bracelet into the wooden box and tried to convince her shaking hands to work the clasp of the necklace.

"Easy, lass. Let me help." Lilias strode calmly from the dressing room and brushed Rowena's fingers away. Two quick motions and the necklace sagged, unclasped.

Still it choked her.

Humming, Lilias arranged the gems and gold in the box just so, framing the earbobs. She touched a finger to the gems dripping from those. "'Tis a shame ye couldna wear those too, Wena. We shall have to pierce yer ears so ye may."

The shake of her head wasn't so much at the thought of a needle piercing her earlobe as at the dagger buried hilt-deep in her stomach. She was married. *Married.* To a complete stranger. One who was sure to be disappointed in her. Who would come to resent her for intruding on his life. For standing between him and all the beautiful young ladies he'd no doubt been deciding between.

Or maybe she *wouldn't* stand in his way. Maybe he was like every other powerful man she'd ever heard of. Maybe he even now had a mistress and would dally with whomever he pleased, expecting her to turn a blind eye. How was she to know?

She squeezed her eyes shut. "I'm going to be sick."

Lilias's fingers dug into her shoulders and forced her spine straight. "Ye willna. Deep breaths, Rowena. In and out. In and out. Ye can do this. Ye *must* do this."

She understood the *must.* All of Lilias's arguments made fine sense—if she were with child, which seemed more likely as each day went by, then her bairn would need a father. One who would love, instruct, protect . . . and what man would do that if he suspected the babe wasn't his own? Yes, Lilias had reason on her side.

But reason didn't change that Rowena simply *couldn't.* She couldn't lie to Nottingham about something so vital, when he had sacrificed his future to help her. She couldn't let him touch her just to perpetuate that kind of deception.

Oh, how she wished Annie would come bursting in and toss herself into her lap.

Deep breath, in and out. In and out.

"There now." Lilias soothed a hand over her Rowena's hair, plucking pins out as she went. "See? All will be well, my darling lass. He's a good man. I was talking with his valet when I came with yer things, and Davis said he's been serving His Grace for a decade now. A better Christian he's never met, he says. Kind, generous, upright of character. He'll be a fine husband, Wena. Nothing to be trauchled about."

The words swirled through her head like fog. Vapor. Smoke, cloying and suffocating.

"And tomorrow, he'll take you from this place. From Malcolm. Ye'll never have to face the monster again, and ye'll be far away from yer father too. Safe. Protected."

Unless Nottingham was even worse than Father. As bad as Malcolm, and as adept at hiding it. Two days ago she had been sure he couldn't be, but she had already proven herself a terrible judge of character. She could have been mistaken about him too.

Soon she'd know. Because Lilias would leave and he would come in and she'd be at his mercy.

The last of the pins plinked into the tin box that held them. Lilias hummed a broken snatch of melody as she brushed through Rowena's hair. All too soon the brush came to a rest beside the box of pins, and Lilias patted her shoulders.

"All ready, Yer Grace." She grinned into the mirror as she used that strange title for the first time.

Rowena couldn't smile back. The title wasn't the one she'd always thought would be hers someday. Not Lady Lochaber. She would only be the Duchess of Nottingham now, too high a position for that mere "lady" to be attached to her name. A shiver stole over her. Duchess. Her Grace. A stranger even to herself.

"Aye, it is a mite chilly in here. Come. I'll help you to the sofa and then fetch yer shawl."

Rowena's lips were numb, her tongue useless. She could find no words to object as Lilias helped her to her one good foot and then a-hobbling for the small divan situated by the fireplace. The heat from the fire couldn't touch her. The familiar shawl that soon draped her shoulders felt heavy as shame.

Then Lilias ran the tips of her fingers over Rowena's cheek, kissed her forehead, and smiled. "All brides are nervous on their wedding night. Even I was, though I was head over heels for my Cowan. He'll understand yer fear, but ye . . . ye must let him comfort you, lass. Let him love you."

"Let him love you." But he wouldn't. There would be no love tonight, not the true kind. Only bruising hands and insistent mouths and the stuff of which nightmares were made.

Lilias stepped away, still smiling as if this were a good day. "I'll go and let Davis know ye're ready."

Unable to object, Rowena settled for squeezing shut her eyes and gripping the shawl tight. She could do this. She could. She must.

She couldn't. She *couldn't.* There'd be nothing left of her inside if she did. She couldn't let him take what wisp remained, no more than she could lie to him. She couldn't. Mustn't. Wouldn't.

The shivering intensified until the word no longer suited it, until it deserved to be called shakes, even convulsions. Perhaps she would quake to pieces before he could even come in.

A light rap on the door between their rooms, and it opened. Through the blur before her eyes she could only see the dark head. The pajama-clad legs. The height of him.

Rowena leapt to her foot, gripping the side of the sofa to keep her balance.

Through the blur she made out his smile, small and soft. He didn't come any closer. "I know this is awkward. And we needn't—we're strangers still. I thought we could just talk. Get to know one another."

Talk. She'd thought Malcolm interested in talking, had been fooled by the months of conversation and longing looks. But the words had been deception. A mask over the monster. "Please go away."

His brows pulled down, though the smile remained in place. "Had I known I would end up wedding a Highlander, I would have taken more care to learn Gaelic. What was that?"

She opened her mouth again, but only a sob came out. Heat rushed her face. But embarrassment turned cold and breathless when he advanced.

He moved quickly, like a wildcat coming for its prey. Thinking only of escape, Rowena took a step back.

Her ankle betrayed her, sending her crashing to the floor and flailing at the couch for support that didn't come.

Then he was above her, dark head and broad shoulders, pressing her to the stones by his mere proximity. The blood roared in her ears, her own sobbing filling them. She held up an arm to try to fend him off, but he didn't grab it. Didn't twist it behind her back.

He clasped her fingers with one hand and touched her face softly with the other. "Are you all right?"

His voice was smooth and so very English. A different tone. No threat in it.

But there had never been threat in Malcolm's either, until there was.

He brushed her hair from her cheek. "Let me help you up. May I?"

Her ears strained for Gaelic words, Gaelic curses to bite their way through her heaving breaths and burrow into her mind. Her shoulders tensed, ready for gentle hands to turn hard and strike. To push her down.

They lifted instead, picking her up from the cold, hard floor and cradling her.

She was a child again for one blessed moment, a child in the arms of the Kinnaird before his affection had turned to hate. Safe. Protected. Loved.

A lie. He wasn't her father. He didn't love her. And though he might protect her from one monster, who would protect her from *him*?

"You knocked the cushion from the sofa. I'm going to put you down on the bed, all right? I—"

Bed? She cried out, flailed, pushed from his arms. Soft feathers caught her, but not before she felt her arm connect with something solid, before she heard a grunt of pain from him. She scrabbled to an upright position on the mattress and blinked the tears from her eyes.

He stood there with a hand to his nose, red staining it.

A whimper escaped even as she pushed herself as far from him as she could get, until her back found the wall. She had hurt him, had drawn blood, and he would punish her now. The only question was how.

With every second that ticked by, her stomach churned and knotted. He reached into his pocket, pulled out a handkerchief, dabbed at his nose. Then, inexplicably, crouched down beside the bed, so that he had to look up a bit as well as across the mattress. No anger burned from his eyes . . . but that only meant he was expert at hiding it.

His sigh sounded weary rather than exasperated. But that only meant he was disappointed in her. "I'll not hurt you, Rowena. Never, never will I hurt you." He rested one hand on the edge of the mattress and stretched out his fingers. "Please know that."

Her ankle throbbed, demanding she stretch out her leg and

let it rest. But she daren't. If she did, he could touch her merely by shifting his arm.

He nodded toward the door. "I'm going to leave, all right? I'll send Cowan back in."

Cowan? She pressed against the wall . . . then realized he meant Lilias. Still, she could say nothing, couldn't even nod. Not until he'd stood, backed away, and slipped through the door.

Then the fear holding her taut snapped, and she sagged down to the mattress. The sobs overtook her again. Now what was she to do? She could hardly call him back in, though Lilias would probably insist she try. Would chide her for her foolishness. Would be as displeased as Father always was in everything she did or didn't do.

"Rowena, lass. What happened?" Familiar hands nudged her up, a familiar worried frown looked down on her. Familiar eyes condemned her.

Was there no one left in the world whom she hadn't disappointed? Too heavy to speak, Rowena pulled herself to the pillow and rolled onto her side, facing the wall so her injured ankle remained on top. And so she didn't have to face Lilias.

Her cousin drew in a sharp breath. "Rowena! Ye . . . ye're bleeding."

Bleeding? Had she scraped her leg or something in her fall? She felt no pain beyond the ebbing throb of her ankle.

Lilias laughed and tugged on her shoulder until she rolled to her back and looked at her. Why did she look so happy at an injury? She beamed. "Lass, do ye hear me? Ye're *bleeding*. Ye're not with child! Praise be!"

Lilias embraced her, laughing again in her ear and murmuring more praises.

Rowena went numb. She should feel relief. And did—heaven knew she didn't want Malcolm's child.

But in that moment she knew without doubt that she had wanted *hers*. Someone to love. Life within. A future worth putting her hope in.

She squeezed her eyes shut and told herself to be grateful. To praise the Lord for His mercy.

But she couldn't shake the thought that now she had no one to love her. No one to love. She was yet again only what she was—no more.

Not enough.

Brice waited in the hall for his wife's door to open, turning his hat about in his hands. The others had already eaten, were already loading into the carriages. He'd had breakfast brought up, and some for Rowena as well. Not that he'd so much as spoken to her since last night. Not that she would have replied if he had.

His nose had a minor ache this morning, and his knees a matching one from spending his wedding night in prayer on the cold stone floor. But it had been necessary. Because no matter what Cowan murmured about embarrassing circumstances—which, granted, had brought heat rushing to his face—it wasn't only that which had rendered his bride so panicked last night.

A fear of men in general, thanks to her father? Perhaps in part. But he suspected it wasn't just that either. Not given how similar her reaction to him had been to her reaction to Malcolm Kinnaird the other day.

How, exactly, was one to ask one's bride of less than a day if she had been attacked in the worst possible way by a brutish monster of a man, though?

One didn't. That answer had come through quite clearly during the never-ending night. One didn't push. One didn't press. One didn't insist on answers. One just silently proved that one was different. That one would never hurt, never take, never abuse. One waited.

And one prayed. One prayed that those embarrassing circumstances were truth and not lie, and that one hadn't just agreed to bring a monster's child into one's lineage.

The door creaked open, Rowena and Cowan both coming out into the dim hall. The maid greeted him with a happy smile, the lady with a catch in her breath and a hitch in her step.

Sending a silent prayer winging heavenward, he came forward with what he hoped was an easy smile. He offered his elbow. "Good morning, darling."

She hesitated a moment, but a prod from her maid made a smile stumble its way onto her lips. She tucked her fingers into the crook of his arm. "Morning, sir."

"My wife oughtn't to call me 'sir' or 'Duke.'" He grinned and led her toward the end of the hall. "I would prefer Brice."

She looked up at him with wide, cautious eyes. "Brice?" Had she even known his name? It had obviously been said in the marriage ceremony yesterday, but she had been shaking so, who knew if she even heard it. "'Tisn't an English name, is it?"

The old contention made him grin. "No. It's a Scottish surname—my mother's. And I would be delighted if you would call me by it. I'm afraid that even after a year it feels odd sometimes to hear 'Nottingham' in my own house. That name belonged to my father for so long. . . ."

She nodded, and her shoulders relaxed one crucial degree. "Brice, then. I . . . I'm sorry. For my behavior, and for . . ." She glanced up at his nose.

He chuckled. "No permanent harm done. And I imagine one of these days we'll think it a funny tale—that the bride socked the so-called charmer in the nose on their wedding night."

Her eyes went even wider, and her cheeks went pale. "Oh, but it wasna my fist! And I didna mean—"

"I was only teasing." He patted the fingers resting on his arm as they came to the staircase. She seemed steadier on her injured foot today, but the descent might be difficult. "Can you manage the stairs?"

"Aye." But two attempted steps disproved her. All color fled her skin, and perspiration dotted her forehead, even with Lilias on her other side mumbling about "going all peely-wally again."

Brice halted them all and looked down into Rowena's face, begging her to trust him. "May I carry you down? I know that burly servant of your father's has been doing so, but as I am the only one handy . . ."

Though she swallowed first, she nodded and even murmured, "Thank you."

They were halfway down before he noticed that the family and guests had apparently *not* all loaded into the carriages. There they all stood by the door, at the bottom of the stairs, clapping and whistling like a bunch of hooligans.

Rowena turned her face into his chest and gripped the lapel of his coat. "Dinna tell them. Please. Just let them think what they will."

It was nothing but pride that made relief trickle into his veins at that, he knew. Still. What business was it of anyone else's? "I'll say nothing, rest assured." He gave her a conspiratorial wink and, when they reached the floor, set her carefully down.

She stuck close to his side as they navigated through the jesting, grinning collection of family and friends and servants out to bid them farewell. He relinquished her only long enough for his mother and sister to embrace her and then led her outside and to his shiny red Austin. The sun had made an appearance and gleamed off the chrome.

Rowena's eyes gleamed with curiosity as they drew near. "I've never ridden in an automobile—Father despises the things. Is it yers?"

"Ours." He opened the passenger's door for her and helped her in. "I can teach you to drive it, if you like—after your foot has healed, of course."

Her lips parted in surprise as she looked up at him from the plush leather seat. Her hat was at least five years old, her dress terribly out of mode . . . but with those soft brown curls framing her face and when her eyes were lit with something other than fear, she was rather adorable. He couldn't help but smile.

"You would . . . I could . . . ? You'd trust me to handle it?"

A laugh emerged as he rounded the bonnet, pausing to turn the crank. With the lever in hand a minute later, he took his seat behind the wheel. "I've already taught Ella. The rudiments anyway, though she didn't take to it as much as she'd hoped she would. I think she rather hoped to be as eager about it as our friend Brook, but she says she prefers being in that seat to this one."

"Brook." Rowena's delicate brows had drawn together. "Did I meet her? Was she here last week when we came to call?"

"No." He stowed the crank, flipped on the magneto, and turned the key. "But you will in a few days. We're headed to her home in Yorkshire. Well, her father's home. Whitby Park. She's the Duchess of Stafford now, making her home at Ralin Castle in the Cotswolds. But they're with Whit for the autumn. She and Stafford are among my dearest friends. They're going to be so thrilled to meet you."

The pronouncement did nothing to ease her frown. "I rather think your dearest friends will hate me." She glanced over her shoulder, back to where the rest of them were getting into the carriages. Abbott was even now helping Miss Abbott up, the siblings both watching them with a fair dose of concern.

He might have to have another conversation with those two. Easing forward slowly to keep from startling her, he started them down the drive. "You've nothing to worry about from Brook and Stafford."

Not after he explained things to them, anyway. But as he watched the delight come over his bride's face as they picked up a bit of speed, he had to admit to some worry. Rowena had troubles enough she was sorting through—the last thing she needed was to be drawn into the tumult surrounding the Fire Eyes.

And yet the diamonds were even now among her things. He was driving her, even now, toward what he had planned to be a means of flushing Catherine Pratt into the open.

A few of his prayers last night had been on that subject as well, and on how much—if any—of the matter he should confide to his new wife. But the only sense he got was that he should trust her.

What exactly did that mean, though? Surely God wasn't telling him to invite her into all his secrets, mere days after meeting her, and when she was struggling with so much of her own. He *would* trust her, of course. With all that mattered. With his family, his home, his future. Someday, with his heart.

But the diamonds, for all their being a part of the Nottingham rubies now, weren't really *his*. Not his secret to tell. Not his treasure to entrust. Which the Lord certainly knew. His direction must mean something more, something else.

Neither of them spoke again as they cruised away from the Lodge and turned onto the road that would lead them southward, away from Loch Morar and out of Lochaber. But Rowena watched the scenery roll by, obviously straining for that one last look at Castle Kynn.

Brice angled her a soft smile once the castle had come into view and passed from it again. "We'll be back, darling. Once it's safe for you, we can come whenever you like."

She shook her head and studied her hands. "I've never been anywhere else, but for two years at school in Edinburgh. I'll be a terrible embarrassment to you." She looked up again, her eyes glistening. "What if this was a mistake?"

"It wasn't." And he wouldn't be embarrassed—but he certainly didn't want her to feel like she was an outcast among his usual set. They would have to get a wardrobe commissioned for her while they were in Yorkshire. Brook would know who to hire for the task.

"How can ye be sure, after . . . ?"

"Last night?" Had he not needed both hands just then to manage the car, he would have reached for her hand. "Darling, listen—my intention last night was only to spend some time together, to get to know each other."

When she met his gaze again, hers was cool as the mist. "And if I had welcomed you with open arms? What would your intentions have been then?"

He had the sudden sensation of a crevasse opening up before him. One false step and he'd be down in an abyss from which there'd be no easy return. He opted for the teasing grin again. "Honestly? I have no idea. The situation makes me every bit as nervous as any blushing bride."

She snorted in obvious incredulity. "I hardly think so."

A breath of peace blew over his spirit. "Because you hardly know me. But flirtatious reputation aside . . . my faith has always been the most important thing to me, darling, and God is rather clear on the behavior He expects of His people in that regard. Yes, I've long looked forward to having a wife . . . but I thought I'd know her better than I know my own mind, that we'd both be caught up already in love and desire. You and I . . ."

She still wasn't looking at him, but she held herself so taut that she must be listening very closely.

He smiled. "We have the whole process to go yet, from acquaintance to courtship."

She stared out the windscreen, but he had a feeling she saw nothing of the glen or the road away.

An ache started in his chest and swallowed him whole. She was but a lost child, hurt by those who should have loved her and now whisked away from all things familiar, lashed to the side of a man she knew nothing about.

Brice gripped the wheel and drew in a long breath. "I shall be utterly honest. Someday I'd like children. I'd like a wife who loves me, one whom I love with all my being. And I believe that, someday, we can have that."

Her rigid posture folded until she closed in on herself, just like in the circle the other night when she realized what her father and maid had done. "But what if we dinna?"

"We will. The Lord put us together, and He knows better than we ever could what we need. We've only to trust Him and to discover what He has in store for us. To let ourselves fall in love."

Rather than relax her, the words seemed to draw her into a tighter ball. "Because no one can resist the handsome and charming Duke of Nottingham?"

He told himself the distress in her voice wasn't aimed at him, not really. It was for the whole situation she'd been forced into—the one he knew about, and whatever had inspired it besides.

The words still nettled. "Are you one for wagers?"

"Pardon?"

At least it got her to look at him. Brice flashed his most teasing grin. "I bet you a holiday in the destination of your choice that I fall in love before you do."

Mouth agape, she stared at him for a long moment. Then she shook her head. "And what if you do? What if I dinna reciprocate? Then ye'll want to . . . Yer mind will go to children and that passion ye say ye've kept a rein on, and ye'll either be miserable or . . . or too impatient."

One hand rubbed at her opposite wrist, where the fading bruises were hidden. Or perhaps where new ones had bloomed after the run-in with Kinnaird the other day. Was he the one who had put the first ones on her? And if he had grabbed her wrists so hard . . . if she rubbed at them when talking of a man becoming impatient . . .

Lord, hold her close. Show her she's safe. Heal the wounds on her heart.

He wouldn't have called it peace that enveloped him. But it was calm, anyway, and it allowed him to try a soft, serious smile for her this time. "I will protect you, Rowena. Even from myself. We'll take this slowly, we'll fall in love eventually—*then* we'll worry with the other."

Some steel came into her spine, lifting her from her broken stature and even raising her chin. She had a bit of Lochaber in her, for certain. Did she realize it? "What if we never fall in love?"

It would happen. It *must*, someday, mustn't it? God wouldn't have given him the command to take a wife who would never want anything to do with him.

Or, who knew, maybe He would. Brice shrugged. "I've a young cousin I'll have to groom for the duchy then, I suppose. He's only six at the moment, and a rip-roaring little monster—but we all are at that age, I suppose. If it's what the Lord has in mind, then I'll trust it's because young Ellsworth is meant to be the next duke."

And resign himself to a life of celibacy, to a wife that despised him simply for being a male with a bit of control over her life?

Ducky. He leaned into his door and nudged his hat up a bit so he could rub a finger over his brow. *Just ducky.*

Nine

For the first time in her life, Lilias stepped out onto English soil rather than Scottish. She'd been watching the Yorkshire moors roll past from the window of the carriage she shared with the other ladies' maids and decided they weren't so different, at a glance, from those of the Lowlands, where they'd just spent a week with the dowager duchess's family.

She'd been on her guard the whole time they lingered in Scotland, certain Malcolm would come pounding his way in at any moment. They'd meant only to pass a night with the Brices, to be sure, but the lady's mother had been feeling poorly, and they'd lingered to see her improved.

English soil felt of freedom. Of safety. She'd miss Scotland, aye, something fiercely—for herself. But for Rowena . . .

His Grace's car had needed to stop a while back for petrol, and the carriages had pulled ahead. The duke and Rowena now brought up the rear of the considerable Nottingham convoy, a mile or so back. Lilias took the time to look around her at the grand manor she'd been told was Whitby Park. She spotted a maze to the side of the house, gardens surrounding, horse paddocks stretching out in multiple directions. Lady Ella's maid, Lewis, had said the sea abutted the property to the north.

They went round to the rear of the house—she and the other servants, and the carriage loaded with the family's luggage. The butler and housekeeper would no doubt be at the front to receive the guests, but a lovely young thing met them at the rear door with a smile and a nod.

"I'm Deirdre O'Malley, the duchess's lady's maid, and this is my husband, Hiram Tenney." O'Malley touched a hand to her husband's arm as she spoke, giving him a smile that either spoke of recent nuptials or the kind of love that held fast for a long while. "We offered to show everyone to their places while Mrs. Doyle and Mr. Graham tend the guests."

The rest of the servants Lilias had traveled with seemed to accept this without a bat of an eye as they moved into the kitchen, calling out greetings to those who must be friends. Lilias followed, not surprised when O'Malley held up, obviously waiting for her. She must be the only unfamiliar face, after all, and she put a friendly smile upon it for the young woman.

O'Malley smiled back. "We were told there would be an added guest, but no more. A lady, I presume? Sure and you must be her maid."

"Aye. Lilias Cowan." His Grace hadn't told his friends that he'd married? Lilias pressed her lips together. Rowena had been worse than quiet during the week in Edinburgh, seeming to shrink a little more each time she had to play a part in the family gathering. Try as she might to learn why, Lilias could get no answers from her. Did they ask too many questions? Ignore her? Make her feel out of sorts and tapsalteerie?

She didn't know, but surely it would only make it worse for her to realize His Grace hadn't seen fit to share about his nuptials with those he claimed were his closest friends.

O'Malley must have noted Lilias's expression. She drew her out of the kitchen, toward a set of service stairs. "Is something the matter? We prepared rooms in both the bachelor and lady's wing, so as we'd be prepared, whoever happened to come. It shan't be a problem, I assure you. What is your mistress's name?"

And that was the problem. Lilias hated to reveal a truth to the staff that the master hadn't seen fit to share with the lords, but what was she to do? "She was Lady Rowena Kinnaird until a week ago—but now she's the Duchess of Nottingham."

O'Malley came to a halt in the dim stairway, but enough light reached her to show the shock upon her countenance. "His Grace got *married*? And he didn't tell the Staffords?"

What could Lilias do but shrug? "I heard mention of a funeral they had to attend at the same time."

The maid deflated a bit at that. "Aye, His Grace's cousin's wife. Shame, that—and sure and they would have felt torn between the two. But could Nottingham not have delayed the wedding a bit? They are his dearest friends."

"A delay would have been . . . ill-advised. There were circumstances, ye ken."

Many of the servants she knew would have laughed it off with an *Isn't there always with the lords?* This one narrowed her piercing blue eyes and planted a hand on her hip. "What kind of circumstances? Nottingham only left us for Scotland a fortnight ago—hardly enough time to necessitate the usual 'circumstances' for a rushed wedding."

Lilias sighed. When she'd designed this plan, she hadn't thought much beyond getting Rowena to England. Certainly hadn't considered how all His Grace's friends would react and what they would assume. How much should she share?

Too many of their company had been present that day at the castle for Malcolm's threats to go unknown here for long.

The ladies would whisper of it, or the lords, and the servants were sure to hear.

Still she hesitated another moment before saying, "There was a bit of a threat—a local man. His Grace agreed to wed her quickly to get her away from him."

No understanding softened O'Malley's eyes, nor did her incredulity fade. If anything, it deepened. "And he brought her *here*? *Now*? When His Grace had been planning to—?" She cut herself off abruptly and spun away.

Lilias's back went stiff and straight. Which "His Grace" was the woman speaking of now—Stafford or Nottingham? And what was either of them planning, that a new bride would get in the way enough to cause such a reaction from a maid?

O'Malley hurried up the stairs. "I'll let the head housemaid know we'll need a suite in the family wing for the Nottinghams instead."

Lilias followed, pressing her lips tight. Her heart pounded by the time they reached the landing. And it wasn't from the stairs.

First they'd had to stop for petrol. Then they'd gotten bogged down in a patch of muddy road. And with each holdup, Rowena wavered between relief at delaying the inevitable introductions and guilt over that relief.

Her husband was trying. She knew it, and she wanted to like him for it. But they were so very different. And she so feared giving him hope for a physical relationship if she dared to smile or respond to him. Would this bone-deep yearning for the child she'd been ready to love ever overcome the repulsion brought on by the thought of a man's touch?

Her eyes slid shut, blocking out the sight of purple heather and feathery bracken. She shouldn't mourn the bairn, she knew that. It had been Malcolm's. Or perhaps it had never been at all—how was she to know? Her heart said it had, that she had miscarried. But perhaps the bleeding had been her normal courses, delayed. . . . But shouldn't it have lasted longer than it had? There had been none of the usual pain, either. Did that point to losing the child?

Ought that not to have hurt even worse?

She could have asked Lilias, she supposed, but even the question was too painful. And Lilias didn't understand. Not the mourning, and not her reticence with her husband.

Thus far, Brice hadn't so much as tried to kiss her, other than the obligatory peck at their wedding. But how long would that last? He had confessed—when she asked him how it was that he wasn't already married or engaged, whether he hadn't been courting someone, at least—to having kissed "a few too many" girls. He'd sworn he'd never been seriously involved with anyone other than one courtship that ended with the young lady marrying another, but that didn't make her feel better.

If he expected kisses from those he *wasn't* seriously involved with, how did he expect to maintain his patience with his wife?

"Here we are." Sounding as chipper as always, Brice nodded toward where stone pillars marked a drive, with WHITBY PARK proclaimed upon them in gleaming metal. He turned the wheel, and the Austin obeyed. They'd not gone more than a few feet along the gravel drive before he eased to a halt and snorted a laugh. "Best not to get in their way, methinks."

Rowena lifted her eyes from the upholstery and saw two horses bearing down on them at breakneck speed. There was a white with a man atop it, and a black with a woman. Both riders had golden hair, the lady's spilling out behind her in a whirlwind of curls. Both leaned forward and clutched the reins, both wore a look of pure challenge on their faces.

The lady and the black pulled into the lead so steadily that Rowena had a feeling the man had started the race with her unawares, to have been even with her when Rowena first spotted them.

Beside her, Brice chuckled. "He's always trying to find a way to cheat and beat her—one would think that the laurels Oscuro keeps winning in the races would dissuade him."

She had to presume that the lady, who even now reined in with a laugh and leapt down beside the car, was the infamous Brook she'd been hearing so much about—the Duchess of Stafford. What no one had warned her of was how beautiful she was. Or the fact that she would rush to Brice's side of the car and lean in with utter confidence to kiss his cheeks.

A strange feeling curled in Rowena's stomach. It couldn't be jealousy—she wasn't sure she *wanted* Brice's affection, so why would she care where he had given it before? But still, she had to wonder if this golden figure with the life sparking so sure and strong in her eyes was one of the "few too many."

"We saw the carriages pulling up," the duchess said, straightening again and shoving her mass of curls away from her face. She aimed a smile at Rowena. "I thought we'd head right in to greet you, but no. His Grace the Sore Loser decided he would seize my distraction and try to win a race."

"Can't blame a man for trying." The man—most assuredly the Duke of Stafford, given his wife's nickname—dismounted as well and also came over to clap a hand to Brice's shoulder. He didn't look at all perturbed by his wife's warm greeting. He merely grinned as he hauled her to his side and pressed a loud kiss to her temple.

Brice made a show of looking around. "And where's the little Marquess of Abingdon? Hasn't William got his own horse by now?"

The duchess laughed. "Justin insists he needs to be able to sit up first. Now don't be rude, Brice. Introduce us." She leaned forward, around Brice, stretching out a hand toward Rowena. "You must be one of Ella's friends. I'm Brook. The Duchess of Stafford, if you care to use a title."

Even through the kid riding gloves, Rowena could tell the duchess's fingers were long and slender, elegant. She clasped them for a moment, keenly aware of her own chapped skin under the frayed gloves she wore. "Rowena."

Brice cleared his throat. "The Duchess of Nottingham. If you care to use a title."

For a moment, the blonde scarcely reacted, as if waiting for it to be pronounced a jest. Her lips were still turned up in a smile, her green eyes still sparkling like emeralds. Then she looked to Brice, and all mirth faded.

The lady's husband seemed not so stunned. He laughed and punched Brice in the arm. "Married? You old dog, and you said nothing? I'd such pranks planned for when your day finally came."

Was Brice's smile halfhearted or true? With him turned a bit away from her, Rowena couldn't tell. He chuckled. "Exactly why I acted so quickly. To avoid your shenanigans, Stafford."

The duchess didn't laugh. "This isn't amusing. Why would you marry and not tell us—ring us or wire us to come? By train we could have been there in—"

"Not then, you couldn't have. It was the same time that Lady Cayton died." Brice shifted the car out of gear and looked to Stafford. "How is your cousin?"

"A wreck," the lady answered before her husband could. "But let's not change the subject. Could you not have waited a week?"

Now Brice turned to include Rowena, his gaze soft and his smile small but somehow all the warmer for it. He reached for her hand, held it lightly.

A facade, like they had been putting on before his family? Smiles and acceptance of all the good-natured teasing? She'd been happy enough to play along before his mother and Ella, the Abbotts, the grandparents and aunts and cousins whose names had all swirled together. If they thought all was normal between them, then they wouldn't ask questions she couldn't answer.

But this felt different. More sincere. And she didn't know whether it made her want to cling to his fingers or pull hers free.

"No," he said quietly. "We couldn't. I'll explain it all in a bit."

Her stomach turned. Of course he would tell them . . . but *must* he?

The blonde narrowed her eyes at him, pursed her lips, and tapped a finger on the arm she'd crossed over her chest. She muttered something, but it sounded French, and Rowena's few years of it had long since faded from memory.

Stafford lifted his brows. "Brook."

Admonition? Understanding? By his tone, Rowena couldn't be sure. But whatever it was, the duchess stirred and renewed her smile. "I'm sure Rowena and I will be good friends. You, however." She leveled one of those elegant fingers at Brice's nose. "I'll not forgive so easily. Out. I'll deliver your car to the carriage house for you."

Rowena's turning stomach clenched tight. And threatened to heave when Brice opened the door and slid happily out.

"You mean I get to ride Oscuro?"

"Are you daft?" She gave the horse a slap on the rump, sending him running off up the drive, and leapt into the place beside Rowena, pulling the door shut behind her. "Have a lovely walk, *mon ami*."

"Oh!" Rowena clapped a hand to the door to hold on when the duchess put the Austin back in gear and pulled away far more quickly than Brice ever had. Why did she get the feeling she'd just been kidnapped?

Perhaps because they were barely out of sight of the two laughing dukes when this baffling creature turned cold green eyes on her. "All right, it's just us girls. Out with it."

Both Ella and Brice had described their Brook as bold and fearless, but it wasn't just her beauty they had failed to mention—they also hadn't said how terrifying she could be. "I-I dinna ken what ye mean."

Golden brows lifted. "Please don't play coy. Do you love him?"

They lurched around a curve in the drive, and Rowena's stomach felt as though it kept on going the other direction. She clutched her handbag to her hollow middle. "I-I scarcely know him."

"Then why did you marry him? For the title?"

"No." Rowena squeezed her eyes shut, though that only made her more aware of how the car bumped over the road. "No. I dinna want to be a duchess. I only . . . I had to get away."

The car slowed abruptly, luring her eyes open again. She braved a glance at her companion, but the perfect face hadn't relaxed so much as a stitch. "And why did he marry you?"

"He . . ." She wished Brice were by her side. How was she to answer for him? She had only the words he'd given her. "He said it was God's plan. That the Lord had been clear."

Just like that, the lady was sunshine instead of storm clouds. "All right, then. I daren't argue with Brice on matters of the Lord's will, or I end up being proven the fool. But, Rowena . . ." She eased to a stop in front of the stables, where grooms emerged to catch the bridle of her horse, who'd apparently arrived just ahead of them. "He deserves to be loved. I pray you'll fall quickly for him, and that you find utter happiness together."

With that, the duchess switched off the car and opened the door. Was it possible that she had accepted Rowena so quickly?

No. It couldn't be, not really. She, with her legs daringly encased in trousers and her jacket the height of fashion, with her golden curls and effortless confidence, would have no use for Rowena as a friend.

Yet she paused, turned, smiled. "Coming? I daresay my husband will take pity on yours and walk with him, which means they'll be a while yet. I'll show you inside. You can meet my father. And, if he's awake, my son."

If she ever intended to find a place for herself in this world, she had better make an effort to stand on her own two feet. Nodding, Rowena let herself out of the car.

"You must be tired. Your husband drives at a snail's pace, which doubtless all but bored you to death." Brook rounded the car, linked their arms, and tugged Rowena forward.

She stumbled at the unexpected pressure upon her bad ankle. Standing on her own two feet was still somewhat metaphorical. The injury was improving—it would accept her weight now—but it still protested if she turned it wrong or stood too long. Under her stockings were streaks of black bruises that made her wince each night.

Brook halted again, eyes wide. "Are you all right?"

"Just a sprained ankle. It's on the mend, but—"

"But not when careless acquaintances yank you around. I'm so sorry." She looked genuinely concerned and certainly led her forward with more care on the next step. "Brice would have my head if I contributed to new injury."

The distance between the stables and the house suddenly looked like miles. "He and Ella both speak so warmly of you and your husband. You must have all known each other for a long time."

Brook snorted a laugh. "Not really. Two years or so, soon after I came to England—I was raised in Monaco."

Had Ella perhaps mentioned that? Something about being reunited with her father after being separated for eighteen years. And it explained why she'd lapsed into French there at the end of the drive. Though it raised a host of other questions. Not least of which was how Brice and this woman had come to be so close—and whether she was the one he had courted, who had married another.

Rowena didn't mean to stare. But she could hardly help it as she willed answers to materialize on the woman's flawless face.

Brook grinned. "We are close, and it must confuse you. Brice and I hit it off right away. That's when I first began to realize Justin's feelings for me had gone beyond friendship. He'd always been protective, but Brice made him outright green."

Perhaps it *was* jealousy that unfurled inside her, though tinged with shadows of uncertainty. "You . . . you and Brice were . . . ?"

"Heavens, no." Brook led her toward the steps and the door that opened for them in anticipation. A gentleman stood framed within, somehow looking pleasant without smiling. Brook's father, she would guess, given the strands of grey at his temples. "I entertained a notion for about two seconds, but only because I was trying desperately not to be in love with Justin. And Brice was never daft enough—to use his own words—to think such thoughts of me. Isn't that right, Papa?"

The Earl of Whitby's lips twitched in the corners. "How lucky we are that your Justin can survive you, being the one to cultivate your wild ways to begin with." He turned sparkling dark eyes on Rowena and offered a hand. "Your new family has informed me of the happy tidings. Welcome to Whitby Park, Duchess. Your father is the Earl of Lochaber?"

Her spine tingled. Of course some of the lords would know Father. He didn't make the Sessions every year, but whenever matters that concerned Scotland were to be discussed, he would carve out the time for the trip to London. She managed only a nod, her lips feeling glued together, and slid her fingers onto his palm.

Whitby bowed over her hand, kissing her knuckles lightly. "I remember when he and your mother were recently wed—she and my Lizzie struck up a friendship that spring, being similarly indisposed. You and Brook should be within weeks of each other in age, I should think."

"Oh." An inane response, but her tongue could lay hold of no other words. It should make camaraderie spring up, shouldn't it? But in their twenty years, only one of them had done anything worth doing. Found a home, a father who obviously doted on her, a husband who adored her, a son sleeping in a nursery somewhere upstairs.

A far cry from an aching foot, a stranger at one's side, and a gaping emptiness within.

"Well, there we have it—friends even before we were born." Brook went up on her toes to peer past her father. "Is Abingdon awake yet?"

Lord Whitby tucked Rowena's fingers into the crook of his elbow. "I gave strict instructions for William to be delivered to me the moment his nappy was changed, so I must assume not. But you go ahead and check on him, my dear. I'll see our guest to her room."

The duchess needed no prompting. With another grin, she sped into the foyer and took off at a dash up the stairs.

Whitby led Rowena inside at a more civilized pace, though he watched his daughter's path until she disappeared from sight. "I was so sorry to hear of your mother's passing," he murmured after she'd gone. "I never saw her after that year, but still, when I heard it . . . it was a bit like losing Brook and Lizzie all over again, knowing she was gone too—she who had sat in Lizzie's drawing room in London, exclaiming with her over baby things."

Perhaps tears shouldn't still sting her eyes at a loss so many years old. "I dinna ken what rumors in London may have been—but she did it to herself. She was miserable. Empty." It was none of the earl's business . . . but he was the first in so long to speak to her kindly of her mother. To remember something other than the hollow wisp she'd been in her final years.

"I did hear that." He angled a sympathetic gaze down at her. "I also heard your father pushed her. To be quite honest, neither would have surprised me. Lochaber is . . ."

He understood, somehow. Saw, somehow, her father's nature from what few glimpses he must have had over the years. Rowena nodded. "Aye. He is."

With a pat on her hand, Whitby supported her on the stairs, never asking about her slow pace. Just matching it. "It's good you've come to us. And I don't say that lightly—I far prefer the quiet months with no one but my staff, my daughter, and her husband. But I pray that the moors and the sea and the security of my home can provide for you what it always has for me."

She didn't ask what that was. Didn't need to. Even so . . . this was just a place she was visiting, and she didn't even know for how long. It wasn't a home for her, wasn't her destination. Just a stop along the journey to someplace she'd never been.

Ten

"Are you ever going to say anything, or just stand there with that glower of yours?"

At Brice's question, Stafford exchanged his glower for a sigh and looked off into the distance. They hadn't budged from the end of the drive. Once they started up it, they would have only so many minutes of quiet.

Stafford sighed again and patted his horse's neck. "It is a less than ideal way to embark upon marriage, Nottingham."

"But you understand why I did it. Don't you? You would have done the same in my shoes." After a week of fearful silence from his wife and the constant watchful gaze of Geoff Abbott, he needed to know *someone* out there was behind him.

"If the Lord had made it so clear to me, then absolutely. Yes." Yet Stafford's expression didn't ease. "But if your instincts are right . . . if this Kinnaird fellow attacked her as you suspect . . . You've considered the implications, haven't you? The questions? Do you know when, or if . . . if she might be . . ."

Brice passed a hand through his hair. "Of course I've considered it. I don't think it's . . . That is, they said . . . Not that she's spoken of what happened or not, but . . ." He felt his cheeks heating, and his friend didn't have the grace to hold back a laugh.

Brice let out a sigh. "From what I can gather, timing of certain things preclude it, and I pray it's so. At the moment, however, I'm more concerned for *her*. And for the fact that with every day that goes by, she seems to retreat from me more and more. I never imagined having a wife who all but hated me."

This time Stafford's snort of laughter bespoke normality. "I like this girl already."

He had little choice but to administer a good-natured shove to his friend's shoulder.

With another chuckle, Stafford turned toward Whitby Park. "I suppose this changes everything. You can hardly move forward with your plans for Lady Pratt now."

"Nor can I leave it undone. I need this finished." He, too, looked toward the house. "Now more than ever. This marriage is going to require my full attention, and at the moment—"

"At the moment, we speak of the devil and she appears." Stafford, having glanced back at Brice and hence the road, nodded beyond him.

Brice turned just in time to see the Pratt Benz round the turn. A chauffeur was at the wheel, but there was no mistaking the gleaming golden curls of Catherine, Lady Pratt.

He still found it odd how much like Brook she looked on the surface—when underneath they couldn't have been more different. "Do you think she's spotted us, or can we hide behind the hedgerow?"

Lady Pratt leaned forward to give some directive to her chauffeur and lifted a hand in greeting.

"That answers that. Though I could be back on Alabaster and to the house in half a beat."

Brice took the liberty of gripping Alabaster's bridle—just to guarantee a bit of loyalty.

The Benz came to a halt, its brakes squealing in protest. Lady Pratt ignored her cousin's husband entirely, aiming the full force of her smile upon Brice. "Nottingham, what a pleasant surprise! I didn't think you were due back in Yorkshire for another week." She made a show of looking around. "Did you walk all the way from Scotland?"

He didn't know what to do but play the game. Grin. Shove his free hand into his pocket and be who he had always been. "Your cousin just liberated my car is all, my lady."

One needn't have any great skills in observation to note the flash of ice in her eyes, the way her smile edged toward a sneer. "Charming as always, isn't she?"

"Quite. Never a dull moment with Brook around."

"Yes." She shifted and renewed her smile. "I was so pleased to see that you and your party accepted the invitation to my little gathering, Duke. We'll have a smashing time. I've a ball planned, a fox hunt, a new baritone everyone's been going on about . . ."

She prattled on, but Brice's ears twitched toward Stafford and his soft, "You did *what*?"

He had to give his friend credit—he managed to ask the question without a single shift in his expression, hissing the whole thing from between teeth clenched in a neutral smile.

Brice ignored him for now. "It all sounds lovely, my lady. I'm sure we'll enjoy ourselves immensely—though I do have one favor to ask. I'm afraid whatever arrangements you've made for our rooms will have to be adjusted. I married while in Scotland, and my wife is, of course, traveling with us now."

"Your wife." Something flashed through her eyes, so quick and sharp that Brice had to wonder what *her* plans had been.

Had she adopted her late husband's hopes to marry into the Fire Eyes rather than steal them?

Perhaps it was good his plans for flirting her into a corner had been thwarted. He may have found her far too ready to strike. For now, he opted for a bright smile. "Indeed. A sweet, charming young lady. I'm sure everyone will love her."

A chill swept up his spine at the smile she returned. "Oh, Duke, I'm sure." She shifted her gaze, finally, to Stafford. "I hope your cousin will still come too, sir. I daresay he could use the distraction."

Stafford went stiff as a victim of Medusa. "You'll not convince Cayton to leave his house."

Now her smile went downright wicked. "Oh, I've found it never takes *convincing* with Cayton. Just the right words whispered at the right time."

The fool actually started forward, as if he could do anything but make her day by losing his head. Brice gave Alabaster just enough of a nudge to shift her into her master's path. Stafford, thank heavens, took the hint and came to a halt.

Though his hands were in fists at his side. "Have you no shame? To make such insinuations when his wife is not a fortnight in her grave?"

"I don't know what you mean, Stafford." She repositioned her hat, touched the curls spilling from beneath it. "I only know that Cayton was an immeasurable comfort to me after Pratt's death—they were such good friends, after all—and now I wish to repay him the shoulder to cry on. Is that not merely . . . neighborly?"

"Easy," Brice muttered. Alabaster's ears twitched, though it was the man he'd aimed the command at.

This time Stafford held his tongue.

Lady Pratt tapped the seat of the chauffeur. "Do excuse me

now, gentlemen—I've still much to do before my guests arrive. I'll see you in a week, Nottingham. And give your new wife my congratulations."

A dark cloud passed over Brice's heart, the kind that portended trouble. He let go the bridle and pivoted toward the house, stepping out of the way so Stafford could turn Alabaster around. "I knew she would be ready to pounce. Her mourning is over, society has accepted her again—I even saw her in an advertisement. She has set the stage for herself, now she has only to play her role, she will think, and snatch the diamonds from me."

But if she were allowed to get away with such a crime . . . No. Too many people had died because of those diamonds, or nearly. The feeling of having a gun leveled at his head still jarred him from sleep sometimes.

It had to stop. *She* had to be stopped, before the violence could follow him home to Midwynd Park.

Stafford grunted. "I don't like it. I didn't like it when you came up with this lunatic plan last year, and I don't like it any more now."

Aimed now for the house, Brice led their lopsided trio onward, the horse still between them. "Were it *my* lunatic plan, I may take offense. But as I said then, if you've an issue with it, take it up with the Almighty."

"You're infuriating. You know that, right? It's no wonder your wife hates you."

"Not funny, Stafford." Yet Brice smiled, because it was such a relief to have someone who *wanted* to jest about it with him.

Stafford chuckled. "Oh yes, it is."

Brice angled a look toward his friend—there was still tension beneath the laughter. "Don't dwell on Catherine's insinuations about your cousin. She was only trying to goad you."

Hands closing tight around the reins, Stafford growled. "But honestly, Nottingham, I've no idea what lines he might have crossed. He never loved Adelaide—not as he should have. He wedded her for her money, and everyone knows it."

"But Brook said he is a wreck now, from her death. If he truly didn't care for her . . ."

Stafford sighed and shook his head, angling his face toward the sun that broke through a scuttling cloud. "Guilt, I think. He did seem fond of her there at the end—but the whispers have already started that he got her with child on purpose, knowing she wasn't strong enough to survive it."

People could be so vicious. "I daresay the gossips will also seize on the fact that the babe is a girl, so he still needs an heir. It will make him all the more eligible, and society will expect him to act quickly, to provide a mother for the little one."

Stafford sucked in a long breath and released it slowly. "I know. But if you saw him . . . He is devastated. The way he is doting on his daughter, almost fiercely . . . They were married only a year, but it effected a change in him. I think so, anyway. I hope so."

The stables came into view, and Alabaster pranced as if visions of oats danced before her eyes. But despite the soothing of the salt-laden air, the enchantment of the moors, the pall wouldn't be easily banished. "I don't quite understand how a woman comes to be like Lady Pratt. How she can hate so completely, even before she knows a person."

Stafford handed Alabaster's reins to the groom who emerged, murmuring his thanks. But he kept his focus on Brice. "You'd better be thinking of how to tell that lovely new wife of yours to be on her guard, if you intend to take her with you to Delmore next week."

Brice passed a hand through his hair. Returning to Sussex

was sounding better and better. Perhaps he could just forget he had the diamonds, forget Catherine, forget it all. Concentrate on convincing Rowena to smile at him now and then.

Protect her. The command still pulsed, sure and strong, inside him. But how was he to achieve it?

His only answer was a sudden gust of wind from the direction of the sea that made another chill skitter over him.

The book was there on the carriage bench, just as she had left it. But clutching it close did nothing to make the words stop swirling through Stella's mind like the leaves in the scattering wind.

Lady Pratt. Lady Pratt.

A name, not a person. Not yet. But a name that bore promise. Whoever this Lady Pratt was, she was to be feared. If the two dukes, arguably among the more powerful men in England, uttered her name with such caution, then she was a formidable enemy. *Their* formidable enemy. Someone, it seemed, who would take issue with this sudden marriage.

Someone *else*, rather.

Stella gripped the book tightly. The cover was worn, the gilt of the title faded. *To Have and to Hold.* The page edges had softened from all the times she'd turned them, reading over and again the adventures of the American, Ralph, and his English bride, Jocelyn. The book had gone with her everywhere these last years, ever since the little celebration her father had thrown for her before she left for school. She had read it so many times she all but had it memorized—nearly as many times as she had flipped it open and read the inscription.

To Stella-bell—as you begin your greatest adventure to date, you may perhaps need the respite of a fictional one. Brice

She had known that night, as she traced a finger over the then-fresh ink, that it meant something more than just a random gift to a childhood friend. How could he possibly give her a book with such a title unless it were a promise? A secret. A claim upon her, that *she* was the one he meant to have and to hold.

And now he had wed another.

Stella leaned against the carriage door for a moment and drew in a deep breath. He had barely spoken to her since he had offered his hand to Rowena. There had been no opportunity for her to dissuade him from his promise, no time to assure him that she loved him, had always loved him, and that she was so sorry she had been holding him at arm's length since she returned from school.

She had thought it the best way to win him. A misstep, apparently, but it couldn't be the end of their story. It couldn't. How was she to know that he would have despaired of gaining her love so completely that he would propose to another?

It had been a decision prompted only by compassion, she knew, and the desire to help. The very desire that made him the man Stella so loved. He had rashly pledged his hand, and he would honor it. *Had* honored it. But if he was happy with his choice, why did he watch Stella so closely when she was out for a promenade with Geoff or Ella? Especially when his new wife was nearby. It must be strange for him to watch them interact—the girl he had loved so long and the wife he had hastily taken.

Pushing away from the carriage, Stella tucked the novel into her pocket. She would find a way to make things right. She *must*. She owed it to him, to them. There had to be a way.

It sounded as though someone else may already have one. If so, then Stella would be a fool to ignore them.

And Stella Abbott was no fool.

She stayed behind the carriage, peeking past the corner, until the two dukes meandered their way toward the manor house. Of its own will, her gaze followed the graceful stride of her beloved. She couldn't even remember when he had first captured her heart. It seemed as though it had always been his. That she had grown up specifically for him. Made herself into what he would want her to be. She'd sought an education so she could hold her own in society, but the greater lessons had been the ones she learned with Ella—the angle at which a duchess held her head. The smile one wore in company. The way one spoke, laughed, connived.

Lessons no one had bothered teaching Lady Rowena Kinnaird. And surely Nottingham realized already what a mistake he had made. Surely he saw that his wife would bring him nothing but shame.

He had done his part. He had gotten her away from that raging laird. But a life as her husband? No, he couldn't want that. So how fortunate for him that marriages could be . . . undone.

Lady Pratt.

Sometimes it just required a little help.

Eleven

A fitting with a dressmaker had never left Rowena shaking before. But they'd never been so long before. Nor had she ever been left standing in her undergarments with so many others in the room. In Castle Kynn, fittings were quick, efficient affairs to create her a quick, efficient wardrobe. Nothing fancier than a few serviceable evening dresses meant to see her through several years without needing updates.

At the moment, the two more experienced duchesses—Charlotte and Brook—were debating how long the hem was likely to stay fashionable at such-and-such a length, and whether the waistline was going to change again next season. The dowager duchess kept talking about trends over the years, the younger about the latest mode in Paris.

How Brook could be just as fluent in silks and ruching as she was in engines and horseflesh, Rowena didn't know. But she was ready to escape. She wanted to go . . .

Home. But where was that?

Finally the ordeal was over, and Lilias did up the last button on Rowena's drab grey day dress. The last day, she was assured, she would have to wear it. The seamstress promised her several simple items by the following morning.

One more day to feel like herself. Rowena's right hand went to where the gold band encircled her left ring finger. Perhaps there wasn't a *herself* left to feel like anymore. Perhaps, whomever she had once been, she had given it up when she married the Duke of Nottingham.

Or perhaps Malcolm had stolen it from her.

"You look as if you could use an escape."

Rowena wasn't sure when Ella had slipped into the room, but her warm tone and welcoming smile relaxed something within her. Her old friend had been, at best, aloof these last ten days. Seeing a hint of the old Ella brought out a smile. "I could, yes."

"Well then." Ella held out an arm, over which was draped Rowena's frayed-sleeved jacket and old hat—brown and frazzled next to Ella's pea-green kimono jacket and stylish toque, which she positioned on her head as they turned to the door. "You haven't seen Whitby's maze yet, have you?"

"Only from the windows."

"It's great fun. I ought to know my way by heart by now, but I always take a wrong turn or two—and the earl has the loveliest statuary at the dead ends. They make it worth getting lost." She slid the green silk-satin jacket on as she spoke.

Rowena slid comfortable, worn wool over her own arms.

Ella linked their arms and led her from the room. "From the looks of the sky, we could be in for a storm today, so I thought we had better get our exercise while we may. Though Stella is lost in Whitby's library and wasn't to be budged."

"Ah." So Rowena was second choice. She made sure to keep her smile in place as they descended the stairs at a nearly normal pace.

It faltered when the faint cry of the baby echoed to them.

The way the wailing grew louder, the nurse must be searching for Brook—little Abingdon had the sound of hunger in his cry, and apparently the young duchess didn't subscribe to the practice of a wet nurse, much to the horror of Rowena's mother-in-law.

Rowena could understand though. If she'd had her babe, she would have wanted the pleasure of holding it close. Giving it life. Watching eyelids flutter and rosebud lips purse, little hands curl and uncurl in contentment.

She wanted a babe. Not Malcolm's, but . . . If only she could desire her husband. If only she could master her own reactions, if only she felt as safe by his side when they were alone as she had when they were facing down the monster in her family's drawing room.

Ella chuckled. "Well, had I not rescued you when I did, it seems little Lord Abingdon would have done."

"Mm." Rowena had held the wee one for a few minutes the night before. Not long—she knew her yearning would be on her face, and she hadn't the energy to face all the teasing of procuring herself a child of her own soon. But it had been long enough for her to breathe in the sweet smell of talcum powder and lavender, of young life and easy acceptance.

At the base of the stairs, she looked up and realized that Ella had been studying her. Though no suspicion darkened her eyes today. They shone with their usual light. "Do you miss your sister? I know she is hardly a babe like Abingdon . . ."

Rowena's lips pulled up in a grin. "She would squeal in protest at the comparison. But aye, I do. Fiercely."

"You should send for her when we get to Midwynd." Ella bounced a bit, her eyes lighting still more. "There's nothing like having a child about. She could stay the winter with us. Perhaps even into spring."

Rowena's head buzzed as they gained the out-of-doors. "I had considered asking if she might join us for Christmas."

"Well, of course she can. No, she *must*! I can think of nothing better. We'll tell the plan to Mama and Brice this very evening. I know they'll heartily agree."

Rowena smiled as some of the tension melted away. "Thank you." Everything would look different, brighter with Annie chattering at her side. And perhaps, if she let herself dream, Father and Elspeth would let her stay longer. Forever.

Ella fell to studying her again as they strolled across the lawn between the house and the maze. She made no secret of it, and Rowena said nothing to interrupt her regard. Her friend didn't speak again until they'd entered the mouth of the maze and green shrubbery walls towered over them. "I owe you an apology."

Rowena brushed her palm over the leafy wall. "An apology for what?"

Angling a *you-know-what* glance her way, Ella tugged her to the left. "I've been reserved, and you know well it's not my nature to withhold my affections from those who have claim to them."

Within a few steps, they made their first turn. Rowena was too short to see over the top, so there were just deep green walls all around her and a roiling grey sky overhead. She aimed a small smile at Ella. "But it's been a long time, Ella. We're not children any longer."

"No." Ella's voice was tight and so soft that Rowena could scarcely hear it over the wind that whistled past them. "We're not, and that's the problem. You've married my brother." Turning wide eyes on Rowena, she rushed to add, "Which I don't object to in principle. It's just . . . the method. And though I know my brother made his decisions of his own will, and though

I believe you both when you say you weren't complicit in setting him up . . . I suppose it took my heart a while to catch up with my head on the matter."

"Of course it did." Had it been Annie forced into a marriage with someone utterly unsuited to her, Rowena knew she would have been much slower to forgive and accept than Ella. "I dinna blame you, Ella."

"And that's just the thing." They paused at a fork in the path, and Ella motioned to the left. "The Rowena I knew as a girl certainly would have blamed me. She would have railed at me—she would have demanded I give her a fair chance to prove herself. What happened to that Rowena in the ten years since we first met?"

Rowena blinked and pulled her coat closed tighter. Had she ever really been like that? Quick of tongue and confident? It seemed she'd always lived in fear of her father.

But no, she knew she hadn't. For the first decade of her life, she had been as bold as he had been kind. His shadow had just cast itself over her past, dimming all the good memories. "I dinna ken."

Ella let forth a gusting sigh and led them around another turn. "Perhaps we'll figure out the answer together, then." A wall loomed ahead, the path turning either left or right. This time Ella came to a complete halt, and her brows knit. "Right, I think."

"Ye *think*?"

"Well, I told you I always take a wrong turn or two, but it's no matter. Even if we get lost, it won't take more than twenty minutes to find our way out."

Rowena pressed her lips against a smile. Ella could get lost in her own garden as a child, and it didn't appear that her sense of direction had improved any. "I'm not so sure those clouds will hold off for another twenty minutes."

"A little rain never hurt anyone."

Not in the heat of summer, perhaps, but the air was far from warm today, and Ella's silky jacket wouldn't provide much by way of protection.

Thunder rumbled its agreement.

Ella drew her bottom lip between her teeth. "Definitely to the right. I'm absolutely certain."

Rowena followed, but she somehow wasn't surprised when they arrived at a figure of a frog wearing a crown and looking at them as if to say, *"Hello, fly. You look delicious."*

"Oh, drat." Ella narrowed her eyes at the frog. "Don't look at me that way, Edmund. You never turn into a prince no matter how many times I've kissed you."

A laugh slipped from Rowena's lips, the first in far too long. "Ye've named him?"

"We always seem to meet this way." She stomped forward and planted a kiss upon the frog's granite nose. "Do at least send a princely friend of yours along, won't you?"

Rowena folded her arms around her middle to hold in the warmth. "Perhaps he will."

Her grin bright and unfettered, Ella spun back around and all but skipped back the way they came. "The left. I knew it was the left."

Rowena followed, even as a few stray raindrops plopped onto the flagstone path on which they trod. "And how long will you wait for your prince, Ella?"

"As long as it takes." She flashed a smile, but it was more muted than Rowena expected. "And you have found yours already. I do realize the circumstances are storm-ridden. But I cannot wait to see how the Lord turns it to sunshine for you."

Sunshine to fill the dark, empty places . . . A lovely thought. But probably more fairy tale than reality. "Perhaps."

The wind gusted and ripped through the path, nearly snatching Ella's toque from her head. She held it down with a laughing shriek. Rowena made no objection when Ella increased their pace, but though they'd corrected their first mistake, all too soon they stood before another decision.

Ella looked at the three-pronged fork with flinty determination but a distinct lack of certainty. "I got this one right last time. Or was it the time before?"

They'd be lucky to escape the maze before supper.

Ella held out an arm as if brandishing a sword. "Full ahead, matey."

Rowena followed with a chuckle. "I'm beginning to think it no accident that Miss Abbott chose reading over venturing into a maze with you."

"I don't know why. Life is far more entertaining with a few deviations from the set course." She linked their arms together again. "Who would have thought that you would someday be my sister? But here we are. A detour to a whole new path, but one the Lord planned out all along."

The path led them quickly around a corner, with another in sight. Rowena stopped, tugged Ella around to face her. "Maybe in a few years we'll all understand it. Appreciate each other. But ye needna pretend now. Our friendship was already a decade out of date, and the kernel of it that may have survived was crushed by how this all happened. I understand that."

"Well, I don't." Ella raised her chin, and she would have looked regal had the wind not been blowing the feather of her hat directly into her face. "I was wrong to hold myself reserved. I have apologized, and I will not fall back into that mistake. You have my word."

But could they really recapture the friendship they had once enjoyed? So much had changed in their lives since then.

They turned the corner, and Rowena jumped a foot in the air at the angry Neptune rising from the granite wave, his trident in hand.

Ella didn't bother hiding her laugh. "That must be the very look I wore the first time he threatened to turn me into a mermaid. I barely escaped without a tail—I'm certain of it."

Rowena pressed a hand to where her heart threatened to thunder out of her chest. "What happened to frogs?"

"This is the worst of them—and the grandest."

The rain went from sporadic drips to an earnest patter.

"Ella!" Brice's voice echoed over the hedges, dripping more with frustration than concern. "Have you lost yourself in the maze again?"

His sister clapped a hand over her mouth, though the giggle still slipped past. "Not just myself, I'm afraid. Will you be a doll, Brice?"

Though he seemed some distance away, Rowena still heard his sigh. "Where are you? Wonderland?"

Wonderland?

Ella grinned. "Whitby has the most delightful White Rabbit in one corner, and then the Queen of Hearts and Gryphon in subsequent ones." Louder, she called, "No, dearest, I made it all the way to Neptune this time! With only one wrong turn before now!"

"Bully for you. Couldn't you have had your go at it when it wasn't raining?"

"Well, it *wasn't* raining when we started out, you dolt. And how was I to know it would let loose now, when it's been threatening in vain for all the last day?"

"Oh, Ella-bell."

"Your wife and I are getting wetter by the moment, brother mine!"

A muted mutter sounded. "You dragged Rowena out here? Are you all right, darling? Your foot?"

"Fine." She tugged Ella back the way they'd come. She may not know where to go at the three-pronged fork, but she knew they'd better get back to it.

"I can come in and lead you out, lend you some support if it's aching. Just stay put and—"

"No!" She must have surprised the siblings with her vehemence. It startled even her. But for heaven's sake, if she couldn't even walk on her own two feet out of a shrubbery maze, then she might as well toss herself into the North Sea and be done with it. "Just tell us which way at the triple fork."

He paused long enough that she wondered if he'd heard her. Or if he couldn't remember either. But when he said, "Left," he sounded certain. "Then another left, straight through the following fork, and your third right will bring you out."

Ella ticked it off on her hands, her expression comical. "Left, straight, right, right. Right?"

"Oh, for heaven's sake, Ella, just let Rowena lead." His laughter moved off. He was either heading to the exit or to where he could better call out instructions to them should they need them.

Hopefully the latter. Hopefully she'd be able to slip out sooner than he expected and make her way back to the house alone. Disappear. Leave Ella to laugh with her brother over what was apparently a traditional mishap. The dressmaking group ought to have cleared out of her suite by now. She could go inside, change into dry clothes, perhaps have Lilias run a hot bath. Vanish. If only until tea.

Ella caught her hand and held it tight. "Will you forgive me? For how I've been acting? I must know before we head back in."

How was she to answer the soft, earnest words but with a smile? "Think nothing of it, Ella. Please."

"We can start anew. Not just as friends but as sisters." Her smile was so bright, it was a wonder the rain clouds didn't break up in light of it.

"I'd like that."

"How are we doing, ladies?" Brice's voice came from the opposite side now, closer to them than she would have guessed he could get so quickly.

She shouldn't have resented his nearness. If it weren't for his help, who knew how long they'd have wandered in the rain. Still. She could do nothing, it seemed, on her own. "Perfectly, sir, thank you." She tugged Ella onward.

It took only a few more minutes to navigate the turns, and the rain wasn't falling any harder. She felt only mildly damp under her wool jacket and straw hat—though, to be sure, Ella looked considerably worse for wear, and she went flying past her brother with a laugh as soon as they exited the mouth of the maze.

He had an umbrella, and for a moment he looked ready to chase his sister down and force it upon her. But she was already halfway back to the house, so he must have thought better of it. He held it out to Rowena with a grin. "I ought to have warned you. She has to try, every time we visit."

Rather than step under the shelter and thereby to his side, Rowena merely turned to follow, albeit at a reasonable pace, in Ella's footsteps. "No doubt ye didna think a warning necessary, what with my foot. And the fact that, until today, yer sister has scarcely spoken to me."

He matched his pace to hers and came close enough to hold the umbrella over her head. Whether she wanted him to or not. "I'd noticed that. I was actually looking for her to ask her why she was acting so."

Her legs just stopped, her knees locked, her arms folded over her chest. "Ye think us incapable of sorting things out without your interference?"

Brice stopped too, though a step ahead, and turned to face her. His brows were knit, but only halfway. As though he were afraid to commit to a facial expression. "No. But sometimes we all need a helpful prod or a listening ear."

He looked so caring, so genuine, so handsome. Why did it make frustration boil up inside? "Or a few directions, aye, to make sure the helpless ladies can find their way out o' the terrifying shrubbery."

His brows drew the rest of the way into a frown. "You're angry that I helped you out of the maze? My apologies, Rowena, if I deprived you of the adventure of it. But it is raining, and Ella—"

"I'm not fashed about the maze!" With a shake of her head, she sidestepped him and kept moving.

He leapt into her path again. And his eyes had gone annoyingly soft. "About the marriage, then?"

Blast him. Her breath shuddered when she pulled it in. "Ye've probably ne'er in your life felt powerless. Ye're a duke, son of a duke, raised all yer life knowing what ye were and what ye'd do. Ye're at no man's mercy, free to make yer own decisions. Free to . . . to *rescue* the poor damsel who canna find a way out o' her piteous life without you."

The muscle in his jaw pulsed. He nodded. "I see your point. I asked you freely—you accepted under the most extreme duress. Your only choices seemed to be to marry me or be killed."

"But I canna be what ye'd make me, Brice." She jabbed a finger in the general direction of her rooms. "Frippery and finery—I dinna ken what to do with it, and I dinna ken how to act with such ladies, and I dinna ken . . . I dinna ken *anything* about how to fit into yer world."

He eased her hand back down and held on to her fingers. His were warm. So very warm. Like his smile, framed by the same dimples his sister shared. "Here is all you need to know about being a duchess, darling—do whatever you please. There are very few who can tell you not to. Be whoever you want to be, and be it with confidence. Then watch others imitate you."

She shook her head. "Can ye not see that's the hardest instruction ye could give? I dinna ken who I am."

"I don't know who you are either, Rowena." His fingers tightened around hers. "But I know who you're not. You're not who your father made you. You're not who that Kinnaird fellow made you. You're who *God* made you. And perhaps now you have been given the opportunity to discover who that is. Freely."

The words sank slowly down, into her, lighting warmth in unexpected places. No father scowling at her and thundering about the clan. No Malcolm looming, ready to take and destroy. The beauty of the realization nearly blinded her.

Brice ducked his head a bit, caught her gaze. "And if you really want to spite them, do you know what you should do?" He leaned closer, pitched his voice low. "Thrive. Be happy."

Yes. Prove to her father that she wasn't worthless, didn't deserve his ire. And Malcolm—she would prove to Malcolm that he hadn't destroyed her after all. She didn't bear his mark on her flesh, much as it sometimes felt like it.

She was free of him. Forever. Free to find with another what had been only an illusion with him.

Brice's eyes glinted, dark and spiced, inviting her to believe. In him, in them, in the future.

Maybe she could. Maybe . . . maybe, just now, she *did*. And to prove it to them both, she surged up on her toes, wrapped her arms around his neck, and pressed her lips to his.

The hand she'd let go of settled on her waist, holding her

without pressing her closer. Warm, steady, easy. Much like the mouth that responded just as she needed—a welcoming taking, a gentle giving. The kind of kiss that made her blood sing, made sunshine touch her face. Made her remember that until a month ago, she had looked forward to arms wrapped around her. She had plotted ways to find a moment for a stolen kiss.

There all thoughts of comparison faded. He shifted, somehow, a subtle change in posture or response. She couldn't be sure—didn't much care. His lips caressed hers in a way totally new, a way that made singing blood hum, made her lips part to better taste him.

Oh, aye, he'd kissed a few too many girls before, and at the moment she didn't care if he had done. Because now he was kissing *her*, and it was apt to melt her very bones. She invited him deeper, clung to him, pressed closer. His arm slid obligingly around her waist. Anchoring her, holding her.

Holding her, capturing her. Too close, far too close. He was on all sides of her, hemming her in, keeping her wherever he wanted her. Too big, too strong, too able to toss her to the ground at any moment, and she couldn't fight, couldn't move, couldn't *breathe*. Could only gasp and wriggle backward and know with all certainty that if she didn't get away *right then*, she never would. She'd be sucked into the morass, tossed to the stones, dashed into the loch, and he'd—

"Rowena." His arm had fallen away from her back. He touched her cheek softly and took a step away. "I'm sorry. Too much, too quickly."

She had to shut her eyes against him and fold her arms over her middle to hold it all in. What a blithering fool she was. It had just been a kiss. Just a kiss. But her knees were shaking and her stomach was heaving and her throat still felt as though a hand had grabbed and squeezed and . . .

And he was apologizing, though she was the one who had thrown herself at him. Her own fault, her own stupidity, and now . . . What? At the best, he'd think her a tease. And that would be just as bad as the other option—that he thought her unhinged.

"Not yer fault." Her voice sounded as tremulous as it felt, and thick with her burr, as it always was when her emotions ran above her education. "I just . . . I canna . . . I canna . . ."

"Shh." His fingertips brushed her cheek again. "Will you look at me, darling? Just for a moment?"

It took every ounce of willpower she possessed to pry her eyelids open.

He offered her a tiny quirking of the lips, the kind that bespoke encouragement without a single word. "I don't need to know what happened. I just need *you* to know that I'm not like him. I will never, never hurt you."

He knew—knew or suspected—and as much as it shamed her and made the heat rush to her cheeks, she didn't close her eyes again. But she did grant herself the reprieve of dropping her gaze away from his face, down to the V of his waistcoat, where his shirt and tie peeked out. Relief seeped through the chinks. He knew, or suspected, and he didn't recoil in horror as from a piece of broken glass. He didn't judge. He didn't shove her away.

He just lifted her hand from where it rested on her opposite arm and pressed his lips to her knuckles. Then he wrapped her fingers around the umbrella's handle. "There now. Go inside, warm up. And don't fret."

Oh, she would fret. There was too much to fret about for her not to. But perhaps . . . perhaps his reactions needn't be on her list of worries. He'd been the one to pull away. He'd felt the change in her and respected it. He knew, and he didn't look at her as though she were worthless. Perhaps . . . *perhaps.*

She gripped the umbrella tight and forced a shaky smile onto her lips. "Are ye coming?"

He shook his head and backed away another step, out from the protective canopy and into the steady rain. "You go ahead."

She held the umbrella toward him. "Then take this. I'm already wet, and I can make it to the house in—"

"No, you keep it." He shoved his hands in his pockets in that way of his and fastened his usual grin in place. "I could use the soaking."

He deserved better than her. He deserved a wife who could let herself melt as the heat of his kiss swept through her. One who didn't invite and then run the other way shrieking like a lunatic. He deserved a wife who would send him enticing smiles and then welcome him into her arms.

But he was stuck with her instead. Feeling the sigh from the soles of her feet, she nodded and trudged her way back to the house.

Twelve

"Are they determined to go, then?"

Lilias spun around from where she stood at the edge of the garden, watching Rowena with Lady Ella and the Duchess of Stafford. She pulled out a grin for O'Malley, though it seemed every time the other maid saw her, she was as like to frown as to smile. "Pardon?"

"To Delmore." O'Malley nodded toward the north, where the neighboring estate apparently stood. "For this house party."

"Oh." She looked back to the garden. O'Malley's mistress was laughing, Rowena smiling. Good to see, and to hear her Wena humming of an evening. Coming out of her shell a bit and seeming to enjoy this new company.

Did she need any more proof that she had done right in this plan? As for the duke's plans . . . "His Grace certainly speaks of it as indisputable fact. Is there a reason they shouldn't?" She hadn't forgotten the younger woman's odd comments the day they arrived, but for the life of her she could make no sense of them.

Now O'Malley sighed and tucked a raven wisp of escaped hair back into her chignon. "It isn't mine to tell the whole story, but sure and I can't let you go in blind. Delmore and its mistress—there's darkness there. It's where Her Grace and I were held prisoner last year when the late Lord Pratt kidnapped us. It's . . . I'd like to shake some sense into His Grace, is what, were it mine to do."

Lilias frowned. Lewis and Lapham had told her a bit about the kidnapping, but they had failed to mention it had all happened at the place they were headed to in an hour's time. "And the current mistress?"

"Widow of the criminal. There wasn't evidence enough to arrest her, but we all feel quite certain she was involved." O'Malley's gaze, northward again, went unfocused. "If there's one thing I've learned about the Duke of Nottingham in the last two years, it's that there's no talking him out of something when he thinks it the right thing to do. But sure and you need to know what he's taking you into. You need to pray, if you're the praying type. And if you're not, you'd best become the type mighty quick."

The gust of wind was hardly to blame for the chill that swept up Lilias's spine. "Ye can be sure I will. Is it safe? To go?"

"If His Grace thought otherwise, he wouldn't be taking his family, aye?" Offering a weak smile, O'Malley turned away. "Still. Sometimes we see what the masters don't. Or won't. Keep your eyes open while you're there, Cowan. And your heart inclined toward prayer. We'll be doing the same from here."

Not knowing what other response to make, Lilias nodded and watched the maid stride back into the safety of Whitby Park.

The week had gone too quickly. Rowena rubbed a finger absently over the smooth silk of her new dress and wished they weren't leaving. Or that if they were, it would be to go home, not to yet another houseful of strangers she would have to learn to smile at just in time to leave yet again.

Scarcely away from home all her twenty years, and then to four separate houses in the course of a month—the Brices in Edinburgh, Whitby Park, Delmore, and only then to her new home in Sussex.

"Oh, he's *always* doing that." Ella shook her head, grinning. "I don't know how I put up with him."

Rowena wasn't sure what she had missed, though she had to assume the "he" was Brice.

Brook chuckled. "Trust me, I know. If you recall, the first time we met was in such a circumstance. As if you believed for a moment that he had fallen in love with me in a thirty-second acquaintance."

Aye, definitely Brice. Rowena's chest went tight. She ducked her head to study the handsome little face of Abingdon, who had fallen asleep in her arms a few minutes ago. And to tell herself not to be jealous, given that Brice *hadn't* fallen in love with Brook.

He claimed.

Ella's laugh chimed sterling and bright. "I confess it took me a moment to be sure. Brice being Brice, he could well have up and announced one day that he'd met a young lady and the Lord had struck him with an epiphany that she was to be his bride."

The silence fell quick and heavy. Rowena glanced up, ready to look away again quickly.

But the horror in Ella's eyes at the realization of what she just said was eclipsed by the laughter that soon spilled from her lips again. "And so he did!"

"And aren't we glad of it?" Brook smiled over at Rowena, her eyes certainly clear of any dark emotions. "I'm so pleased we've had these days to get to know each other, Rowena. I only wish we had more of them. Good friends are too hard to come by."

Rowena could nod her agreement to that. "Aye. Though I can't imagine ye have too hard a time of finding them."

Brook breathed a laugh. "Don't you? I'm not exactly what most English expect of their nobility. Am I, Ella."

Ella, of course, grinned. "You're so much better."

"Ha! I like to think so, of course, *mais alors*. Most disagree. I am headstrong and thumb my nose at tradition and am all the time doing what society thinks I ought not."

Her? Rowena gave her finger to the sleeping bairn, who obligingly curled his tiny hand around it. And granted the thumbing of her nose, anyway. But how could society help but love someone so bold? So beautiful?

They couldn't.

"She disbelieves me," Brook said in a mock whisper to Ella, gaze still on Rowena and a smile hovering at the corners of her mouth. "I am being perfectly honest, Rowena. Had your husband not made such a show of being fond of me—he being the darling of London long before I arrived on the scene—I probably would have been laughed out of Town."

"Which you would have happily seized as an excuse to come home. She hates the Season." Ella waved a hand as if dismissing her friend's foolishness.

Rowena was stuck on that *being fond*. A show, she said. But of course she would. She married another, and Brice would surely have laughed off his affections, if he'd had them, wouldn't he have done? Or maybe it really was a show. Which just pointed to how skilled he was at putting one on.

Confusing, all the same.

"Of course I hate the Season. It's a bunch of deceptive nonsense. Isn't that right, Duke?"

Rowena's head snapped up, around. Brice was just stepping into the garden's entrance, his grin as bright as usual.

"I haven't the foggiest notion what you're talking about, Brook, but I don't dare argue." His attention moved from Ella to Rowena. "Are you ladies ready? The bags have been loaded, and it's time to go."

Rowena stood, careful to hold the baby as motionless as she could. "Aye."

"I suppose." Ella pushed herself up too, though a pout had overtaken her dimples. "If we must."

"I wish you wouldn't." Frowning, Brook stood too and approached Rowena with her arms outstretched for her son. She said something in French that Rowena couldn't follow.

Brice sighed. "We've been through this. It's necessary."

"Hmm." Taking the wee one with practiced ease, Brook managed to smile at Rowena in one second and scowl at Brice in the next. "We have different definitions of that word, *n'est pas*?"

"So it would seem."

"And we shall see which of us is right this time—statistically, it has to be my turn soon."

"We shall, indeed, see." Brice offered his elbow to Rowena. But his grin wasn't so bright anymore. "Come, darling. We're in the car again."

Rowena let herself be ushered out of the garden and around to the drive. Wondering more with every step what in the world they weren't telling her.

O'Malley was right—darkness gathered here. Lilias felt it the moment she stepped inside Delmore with the other servants, and it didn't abate at all through the afternoon. She folded away the last of Rowena's new gowns, sidled over to the window, and let loose the shudder that had been threatening to shiver its way down her spine all day.

Her cousin in Ireland would insist they must have built this place over a fairy path. Her grandmother would be more apt to murmur about witches and devils. Lilias didn't pretend to ken what it might be. But something lurked here. Something slithered through the corridors and clawed up the walls. She felt its cold breath. Saw its shadow from the corner of her eye.

Were it up to her, she would never have unpacked—they would have headed straight back to Whitby Park. So close, but a world away.

The door opened, and she spun to see Rowena slipping in, face flushed. "What happened?"

The lass shivered. "Nothing. Just . . ."

"Aye. Ye feel it too." Lilias bustled forward with Rowena's warm wool wrap. The fire had been set an hour ago, but the chill wouldn't leave the room, and the silk Rowena was wearing today may be pretty as the morning mist, but it would be no warmer. "Here, lass. How was tea?"

Rowena sighed, slipped her arms into the wool, and folded herself up into the chair nearest the hearth. "I dinna ken. The men were all elsewhere, and the women . . ." Her brows knit. "I dinna ken why we're here, Lil. Ella and Charlotte—they quite obviously dislike our hostess."

"Well, I should think so." Any woman who chose to live amidst these shadows . . . Lilias shook her head. "I dinna ken why we're here either. Did yer husband tell you how Lady Pratt's husband kidnapped the Duchess of Stafford? Well, it was before she wed the duke, but all the same. The servants at Whitby Park think the lady must have had something to do with it."

Rowena's mouth gaped. "But they . . . they've said nothing to me, none of them. Neither Brice nor his mum nor Ella. And it isn't as though I avoided any of them these last few days, as I had before."

Perhaps Lilias should have kept her own lips sealed on the matter too. But no, O'Malley was right—if their hostess were the type to play in darkness, then they all needed to be on their guard. And one would think that His Grace and his family would recognize as much. She perched on the arm of Rowena's chair and smoothed back the soft brown curls that framed her face. "Ye've been more sociable the last bit at Whitby Park, true enough. But ye still look so sad, lass. What has you so puggled? When ye seem to be getting on better with His Grace?"

Rowena drew her knees up to her chest and pressed her cheek to them. Were Lady Lochaber to see such a posture, she would chide her something fierce. Her mother would have too, once upon a time. But Nora had given up caring too soon. And how was Lilias to enforce what she herself had never learned?

She trailed her fingers through the girl's hair, plucking out pins as she went. The low chignon wouldn't do for tonight's dinner. "I heard you laughing with him last night in the hall. That's something, aye? And I glimpsed you in the garden, holding the duchess's baby. Ye must have made friends."

One of Rowena's shoulders lifted, settled. But it was the look in her eye more than the shrug that made Lilias straighten with a sharp breath. "The babe, is it? Holding hers made ye miss the idea of yer own. But Wena, ye must be practical. Ye must ken 'tis best this way. Ye'll have a child—a legitimate one, the duke's, soon enough. Ye just go to him and—"

"Will ye *stop* it?" Rowena shot up so fast she knocked Lilias from her perch. She was still quick enough on her feet to keep from hitting the floor, despite her years, so she didn't need the hand Rowena held out to steady her. "Will ye stop telling me I must go to him? I canna. Ye ken? I like him, I find him attractive, I *want* to want to, but when I get close to him, I just . . . I canna—"

Her breathing turned to gasps that ate up her words until Lilias could understand nothing but the panic within them. She clutched at Rowena's outstretched arms and pulled her close, ran a hand in circles over her back and prayed the girl wouldn't feel her shaking.

Ye're a glaikit idiot, Lilias Cowan. It was too soon, far too soon. Of course the girl would see nothing but Malcolm before her eyes when a man had his arms about her. "Ye're right. Ye're right, Wena. Forgive me. Ye've no need to rush, no need to pressure yerself. The horror and fear will fade eventually. His Grace will be patient." She hoped. "There now. Breathe, lass. Breathe."

It took an eternity, it seemed, for the gasps and shaking to ease. It left them both exhausted, but Lilias managed to get Rowena tucked into her bed for a rest and took her own in the form of drawing a hot bath for Rowena and turning her attention toward the evening.

The tasks that soothed her, though, didn't seem to have the same effect on Rowena when she forced her through the motions. An hour later, as the lass sat before the mirror at the dressing table, she looked ready to run all the way back to Scotland.

Lilias withdrew the three evening gowns the seamstress had finished in time. "Which one, *a leanbh*?"

The endearment she hadn't used since Rowena really was a "little one" earned her a brief smile. "You decide, Lil."

"Well then. Not much of a decision." She reached for the deep red that would bring out roses in Rowena's cheeks and set off so perfectly the rubies—the only jewels she had at the moment, though the Nottinghams had promised her more as soon as they got to Sussex.

Rowena said nothing as she put it on, though it surely felt

a far cry from any dress she'd donned before, aside from her wedding gown. She sat on the stool as if it were just another tweed skirt, not even looking in the mirror.

A cold draft whistled in through the window, but this time Lilias didn't offer her a heavy wrap. She needed nothing in her way as she fetched the curling tongs from the fire and set about styling each lock, pinning it just so. Only once that was done did she reach for the jewels and fasten them around Rowena's slender neck and wrist.

She stepped back and beheld her creation with a smile. Nora would be proud, if she could see her. So would be the Kinnaird, when next he did. "Stand up. Look at yerself, lass."

Rowena looked as though she would rather slip it all off again and crawl back into bed. But she obeyed and slid over to stand before the full-length mirror in the corner. Eased forward and lifted a hand to touch the silvered glass.

"'Tis you, Wena. Here and now. And as ye were always meant to be."

The girl shook her head. "That isna me."

"It is." Lilias joined her at the glass and rubbed her hands over Rowena's chilled arms. "Ye were raised to be a countess, lass. An heiress, worth every bit as much as any of those women, if you care to tally worth in pounds and land. Ye've nothing to be ashamed of in their presence."

Rowena's gaze dropped, but Lilias had seen the moisture in her eyes. "I dinna care to though. And neither do they. They see only that Father's a miser. Backwards. Backwater. They hear only how I speak, not what I say."

"Aye, and what if they do?" Lilias gripped her shoulders and gave them a squeeze. "Ye're a Highland woman. Daughter of the chief of Clan Kinnaird and the Earl of Lochaber. A heritage worth bragging about if ever there was one."

For a moment, she thought it would pass right through Rowena's ears as most of her other words had lately. But then the lass drew in a deep breath. She straightened her shoulders. And she turned, determined, toward the dressing table again.

Lilias stood back, at a loss as to her intention until she saw her pull the brooch from a box of trinkets. Then she clapped her hands together. "Aye, that's the spirit. Let me help you pin it on."

"I've got it." Rowena moved back to the mirror, hands and eyes both steady as she fastened the tartan flower front and center, where the neckline dipped into a V.

Lilias nodded at their reflection. "Good lass." She would have said more, but a knock interrupted. With a few steps and one hard tug on the door that wanted to stick, she let in the dapper-looking duke—who looked at his duchess as though she'd just stepped from the pages of a fairy tale.

Lilias gave Rowena a smile and slipped silently from the room.

Fragile. That had been the word that had crowded Brice's mind the past few days, whenever he spent time with his wife. She had a delicacy about her that had nothing to do with her slender frame or petite height. Something twined through her hesitant smiles and wary company. Something warning that one false move on any of their parts and she'd run away like a startled hare.

Brice smoothed his tie and wondered where that girl had gone. The one standing before him now radiated . . . beauty. Confidence. The softest kind of pride. His lips tugged into a smile even as his pulse kicked up. "You look stunning, darling."

The girl standing before him, however, didn't smile. She just regarded him with a cool detachment that said he'd made a false move somewhere along the line—but rather than run, she'd turned to ice. Regal as a queen, she waved a hand toward a chair near the fire. "I assume you came early because you have something to tell me. Something you could have mentioned before you brought me here, don't you think?"

Blast. He slid over to the chair and settled on the edge of the cushion, leaning forward to brace his elbows on his knees. "I'm sorry. I . . . you were finally emerging from your shell a bit, and I didn't want to ruin it with talk of unhappy things."

She didn't fold her arms. Didn't scowl. Didn't so much as lift a brow. She just kept regarding him with cold, empty eyes. "A misstep on your part."

Brice sat back, unable to avoid a frown. In high emotions, her accent thickened. Just now, it had all but vanished. "Again, I'm sorry. You're right—I should have spoken with you sooner. What have you heard?"

"Not enough to make any sense of why we're here. Perhaps you should just start at the beginning."

He barely kept himself from passing a hand through his hair. "It's Brook's story more than mine."

She muttered something in Gaelic. He paused, but when she didn't translate, he decided he'd better just let it slide and keep going. "She was in possession of certain jewels, diamonds left to her by her mother. Given to her mother by a cousin, Major Rushworth. But apparently the major's brother and their best friend—the elder Lord Pratt—expected to split the profits when the jewels were sold. When he instead gave them away, they were . . . angry, let's say. Pratt was actually killed over it when the buyer learned he hadn't the diamonds after all. So then Pratt's son, only a child at the time, decided they were by rights *his*. His and the Rushworths'. And when his attempts to marry Brook to get at the jewels failed, he married our hostess instead—thereby increasing their share to two-thirds, with the remaining one for her brother—and he kidnapped Brook. He held her here at Delmore for several days before she escaped."

The story had earned gasps and wide eyes all over England, though the most intriguing detail—that the jewels in question were the rarest diamonds in the world—had been kept from the press.

His wife didn't bat a lash. "Was she privy to it? Lady Pratt?"

Brice held out his hands, palms up. "She says not, and there wasn't evidence enough to arrest her after Pratt was killed. But I cannot believe she was uninvolved. She knew too much, and she married Pratt just days before he kidnapped Brook."

Now she lifted her brows—and for the second time in their short acquaintance, he saw a bit of Lochaber in her. "Well, that certainly isn't proof. It would seem husbands have no difficulty acting without the knowledge of their new wives."

He winced and pushed to his feet. "I grant I deserve that, but they are hardly the same thing. He was plotting out a complicated crime. I am only—"

"What?" Finally, heat came into her eyes and the burr reentered her voice. "What has any of it to do with you? What exactly are ye here to do?"

At the moment, his careful plan looked foolish and impossible. What was he doing, trying to lure a coldhearted viper into attacking him? His every plan hinged on the basic assumption that she would make a mistake, and that he could have the authorities ready to catch her. But what if he was wrong?

And how was he to look his stranger-wife in the eye, knowing the danger she'd run from, and confess to that? On the other hand, how could he lie to her, when she was already furious, thanks to his silence?

He sighed and lowered his hands. "I was there when her

husband was killed. Stafford and I were searching for Brook, and she found us—but Pratt did too. He was about to shoot at me when the constable intervened, shooting *him*. Catherine loved him. In her eyes, his death was my fault."

She slid backward a step and to the side, putting another chair between them. The hands she rested on its back trembled. "I ask again, sir. What exactly are ye here to do?"

They were back to *sir*? Brice blew out a breath and half-turned away from her for her own peace of mind. "Nothing really. It is only . . . if I'm right about her, she'll seek vengeance. And you know what they say about the best defense."

She just blinked at him.

He motioned with a hand. "It's a strong offense. If I can sound her out, figure out if and how she means to act—"

"This isna a game of football on the green! The best defense, when it comes to matters of kidnapping and murder and vengeance, is to be off the field!" She shook her head and retreated farther from him. "Ye must be daft to think otherwise."

Maybe he was. Not just to think that Catherine might tip her hand, but to think Rowena could possibly understand, being tossed into the thick of it like this. He dredged up a smile. "Well, as you say. There's no reason beyond my personal feelings on the matter to think she was involved. I'm as likely to find reason to put it all to rest, which would be a blessing."

"But that's not what ye believe. Ye think she has mischief or worse in mind, and yet here ye are, on her turf. And ye brought yer family with you."

"She's too smart to do anything at her own home, given what happened here before. The authorities have too close an eye on her."

Her eyes went cold again. She turned and strode with stiff elegance to her wardrobe, reached in, and pulled out a wrap.

Her face was as immobile as the statuary in Whitby's maze when she returned to his side and rested her hand on his arm. "We had better go."

"Rowena." He covered her fingers with his. Even through her arm-length gloves, he could feel how cold they were. "I'll not put you in any danger. You have my word."

The eyes she turned on him, silver and compelling, didn't warm. "You think me so selfish that it's only *me* I'm concerned about? I don't want to see you hurt, Brice. Or dead."

"Really." He grinned and led her toward the door. "Well now, that's progress. At this rate, you may well be in love with me before our tenth anniversary."

"Hmm." She led the way into the hall but then, as he paused to close her door, surprised him by stretching up her toes and pressing a kiss to his cheek. Then again, perhaps it was just to put her mouth near his ear so she could whisper, "Only if ye've already fallen for me. I'm planning an ocean voyage when I win that wager."

Teasing him—she was teasing him. He grinned and caught her fingers in his. "So long as you let me come with you."

A cleared throat farther along the hall brought him around. The Abbotts were standing outside Miss Abbott's door, watching them with unabashed interest.

Brice secured Rowena's hand in the crook of his elbow and aimed the grin at his old friends. Abbott's returning smile looked relieved. His sister's was directed toward Rowena. "Look how beautifully it turned out! You look breathtaking, Your Grace."

"Why thank you." Brice drew his wife down the hall. "I do try to clean up well."

Miss Abbott sent her gaze heavenward. "I don't know how you mean to tolerate him for the rest of your life, Duchess."

Rowena merely—thankfully—hummed. Brice covered it with

an exaggerated widening of his eyes. "Oh, you were speaking to my lovely wife? I should have known. She certainly took *my* breath away."

"Your dress is beautiful, Miss Abbott." Rowena leaned across him to study it as they drew nearer. "Such detail in the embroidery!"

At the pride that lit Miss Abbott's eyes, Brice smiled. "She is as talented with a needle as she is with a primer—and has long been putting her skill to use in making herself outshine the ladies in her company. You'll have to keep an eye on her tonight, Abbott, or you'll have gentlemen questioning you about dowries by tomorrow noon."

"No doubt." Abbott offered his sister his arm and a smile. "I'll send them all to Sussex and let Father sort them out."

The siblings moved ahead, and he heard Ella and Mother emerging from their rooms behind them. But he was more concerned with the way Rowena had shifted. Some of that stiff elegance had seeped out, and her eyes were on the ground again.

He leaned close so he could speak to her alone. "What is it, darling? Are you all right?"

Perhaps it was a foolish question, given the conversation in her room. But it wasn't that. These were her old reactions, not those new ones. Fragility instead of confidence.

Which was the real Rowena, and which the one fashioned by pain and hardship?

Or really, at the core, was there a difference? Perhaps they were none of them more than what their darkest moments made them . . . and how they emerged from it when day came again.

Thirteen

Rowena's hand rested on her husband's arm, his opposite fingers resting on hers. Whenever the crowd would jostle around them, he would tighten his grip on her, as if afraid the sea of people eager to ingratiate themselves with the Duke of Nottingham might sweep her away.

She had lost count of how many times she had been introduced by the title that still felt so odd, of the times she had met lord after lord and lady after lady.

And she had wilted a little more with each appraising gaze that swept over her. She tried—she did. She tried to stand tall for Brice. For the Kinnairds. For all she was and all she had been and all she'd become when Brice slid that golden band onto her finger.

But oh, the biting whispers she heard from one set of new acquaintances while Brice introduced the next.

"Lochaber? I heard his daughter was such a disgrace he'd never even bring her to London. What do you suppose is wrong with her?"

"For the life of me, I don't know why some of those Highland lords refuse to educate their children properly. I could scarcely understand a word she said."

"Where do you suppose he found her? Hiding in a sheep pasture?"

No one ever argued with the catty ones, either. They'd titter right along with them and then they'd smile at her husband, say something clever, and ignore her very existence. Brice tried to include her in the conversations—she must be fair and grant him that. But what was she to say to these people?

Her husband's fingers tightened around hers, and he leaned close so he could speak into her ear. "Are you all right, darling? You're so quiet."

She summoned a smile. "Well enough. Although . . . I must tend to a personal need. Will you excuse me for a few minutes?"

He frowned, probably seeing right through the flimsy excuse to her actual need for a moment away. "I'll walk you—"

"I can manage," she said on a chuckle that she nearly felt. Nearly. She may never have been in society, but finding a lavatory was something she had experienced even in the Highlands.

Brice pressed his lips together for a moment. "At least have a maid show you the way—these hallways are a maze."

"I shall." If she went any farther than the hallway this room was connected to, anyway. Hopefully she could find the quiet she sought without losing sight of the doorway. She covered his fingers with hers and stretched up to feather a kiss over his cheek. More to spite the spiteful women than for any other purpose, it was true.

Her husband probably divined her purpose—and no doubt it was why mirth lit his eyes. "Hurry back, darling." He kissed her knuckles, lingering over them, and then released her.

How many times had she put on a show for the clan gathered round the fire at Castle Kynn? So many evenings she had worn a smile she didn't feel, had curled up to listen to McCloud on his pipes when she had wanted nothing but to escape her father's presence. So many times she had played the part of the Kinnaird's daughter when she had felt herself little more than a prisoner.

But she had played the part. She could play it again now, holding her head high as she wove her way through the crowd of hateful gossips, all of whom looked on her with disdain. Normally she would have thought it her gown. Her hair. But she was decked out in the finest of fashions, her coiffure similar to every other lady's. It had to be she herself that they took such issue with.

Her shoulders slumped the moment she cleared the doorway, and she paused with her back pressed to the wall just outside the door. Dragged in a long breath.

"There you are, Duchess."

She jumped at the voice, her eyes flying open from their overlong blink and her gaze latching upon a lavender-bedecked figure.

Lady Pratt—and she smiled with warmth that looked completely genuine. "Forgive me, I didn't mean to startle you. When I saw you slip away I thought I would see if you needed any assistance. And I've been meaning to visit with you. You looked a bit lonesome by your husband's side."

She should be on her guard. Demur and slip away, find Ella or Charlotte. Or cut a swath back to Brice. She should certainly *not* be having a conversation with the woman her husband was convinced was a criminal.

Although, hadn't he said his whole point for the visit was to sound her out? Try to learn what she may be up to?

Perhaps Rowena could discover something. Make herself useful, aid him in his plan. Or at the very least, keep from tipping his hand with rudeness. She summoned a smile and focused on that comfortable place at the lady's shoulder. "I confess 'tis a bit overwhelming. Since we married, I have met only the duke's family, never so many people at once."

"Mm, I understand what you mean." Lady Pratt smoothed a curl and pressed the back of her hand to her forehead for a second. "This all seemed like a marvelous idea when I was sending out the invitations—the perfect ending to my first season back in society. But after so many months of quiet, with no one but the servants and my baby for company, my brother from time to time . . . all the noise and activity can be suffocating, can't it?"

"Aye." She, too, had a baby? No one had mentioned that. And Rowena certainly hadn't heard any crying. "But they are all your friends."

Lady Pratt's shoulders sagged a bit, which brought Rowena's attention up. Her face had sagged a bit, too, and the turning of her lips looked sorrowful. "They are all my something. I don't know that *friends* is the best word. Honestly, Duchess, after all my husband put me through, I don't have much by way of friends. I'm either a sensation, if one believes me innocent of involvement, or a scandal, if one thinks I'm guilty. But never just *me* anymore. Pratt stripped me of that when he kidnapped my cousin."

Rowena searched the tone for deception, for manipulation. She found only the oh-so-familiar exhaustion that came of battling for one's very right to be oneself. "It seems we're all judged by our associations."

"So true." Lady Pratt's smile didn't brighten, though she turned it fully on Rowena. "Yours are, at least now, brilliant. Married to the Duke of Nottingham, who has long been London's favorite. And friends with the Staffords—the most illustrious and sought-after couple in England." She tilted her head, sending curls onto her shoulder . . . and making the shadows beneath her eyes stand out. "Which means, in turn, you have been fed their side of the story. So perhaps I am wasting my time trying to make friends with you. Heaven knows they've never a kind thing to say about me."

Rowena nearly stepped forward to put a reassuring hand on the lavender glove. Nearly rushed to assure her that she wouldn't judge based on gossip. She tucked her hand to her side but allowed herself to say, "To be quite honest, my lady, the Staffords didna mention you to me at all, nor your husband. What little I know came from mine, not them."

Patronization colored the edges of Lady Pratt's smile. "With all due respect, Duchess, if your husband told you any of the story, it was in their words. I daresay you noticed how . . . *close* he is to my cousin Brook."

Rowena's throat tightened. "They are very good friends, aye."

Lady Pratt's smile went close-lipped now, and a little snort of incredulity barely reached Rowena's ears. The lady looked out at her ballroom, green eyes sweeping the floor but not settling anywhere. "Oh yes. They have long been *friends*. We were still close when he first came to call, you know—Brook and I, I mean. I heard all her tales of how Stafford had kissed her before he ran off to Africa to see to business. How Nottingham—Worthing, at the time—made her all a muddle with his smiles and flirtation. I confess, I was jealous. Not because of the attention of the dukes, but because Pratt was on her list of admirers too."

Here she sighed, and her eyes slid closed. "I know now, of course, Pratt was after what she had, not *her*. But at the time . . . I'd loved him all my life. Thought for certain we would marry, be blissfully happy. But the moment she showed up . . ."

She opened her eyes again, shook her head, and her smile went sad, a bit sheepish. "It's no wonder my cousin doesn't like me any longer. I said some cruel things. Let her *think* some terrible things, just to spite her when I saw how Pratt fawned on her. I was jealous, pure and simple. And now that she's the toast of society, I'm paying for my jealousy. Will likely pay for it for the rest of my life."

Rowena looked away from the earnest expression, through the doorway and toward the crowd around Brice. She could barely glimpse him through the throng of people surrounding him, but she caught enough of a glance to see that he was laughing again. He said something to one of the women, and she blushed and fanned herself. Having been by his side for the last hour, she knew that he could elicit such a reaction with the most innocent of words. Innocence, it seemed, didn't stop the ladies from reading meaning into it.

What was it Brook had said? That she had entertained a notion for a few seconds, but that Brice never had. Perhaps she was wrong, and he had dreamed of her, too, before she and Stafford settled things between them.

Or perhaps this was just his way. Making *every* woman entertain wishful thoughts of him. Never feeling anything himself. Perhaps he found his joy in the hunt, in the chase, in the game of flirtation. Perhaps he didn't *want* love, didn't know, even, what it was or how to lay hold of it. Perhaps he merely used the word like any other—to get his way, earn himself adoring admirers, make young ladies flush in pleasure and all but fall at his feet.

Her fingers dug into her side. She had used to dream of love, of a husband. She had thought it Malcolm who would make those dreams come true, aye, but even taking him out of it . . . she had wanted someone who looked at her as though she were the only woman in the world. Someone who understood her every thought. Someone who made her feel . . .

Who made her feel like more than she was.

Brice smiled at something one of the ladies at his elbow said, flashing dimples sure to make a muddle of the woman's stomach. Was Rowena anything more to him than another of the throng? His words were always right, when he spoke them. Promises of what they could have. Encouragement to embrace all he made her.

But what had he made her, other than more of an outcast than ever? And how was she to believe his promises of eventual love, when he hadn't even respect enough for her to tell her of all that drove him?

She turned away, called up a smile. "You say you've a child?"

Lady Pratt's face lit up like a luminary. "Little Byron. Viscount Pratt, but I can't bring myself to call him such, with his father's doings still shadowing the name. He is up on his hands and knees now, rocking. He'll be crawling soon, and the world will never be the same. We'll have to lock up everything of value." She laughed, pressing a hand to her stomach. "Already he reminds me so much of his father. The Pratt I knew when we were children. So curious, so observant, so determined."

Rowena needn't feign her smile now. Whatever Lady Pratt may have done or not done, the love of her child was absolutely genuine. "He sounds delightful."

"I was actually just about to go and say good-night. Would you . . . would you like to meet him?"

She shouldn't. Brice would have a fit. Ella would squeal in horror. Charlotte's eyes would go wide and hard, her lips pressed together.

But why should she dislike someone, distrust someone, solely because *they* did? From what she could see, Lady Pratt was merely a widow who knew well she had made some mistakes, but who was tired of being judged by them. Tired of being only what a man's decisions had made her.

From what she could see, Rowena had more in common with Catherine, Lady Pratt, than she did with Ella or Brook. She smiled. "I would love to meet your son."

Her decision sat easy on her when relief softened Lady Pratt's gaze. This was obviously a woman who knew well the fear of rejection. Something neither Ella nor Brook had ever experienced.

Something Rowena knew far too well.

"We'll hurry—I'll have you back before they miss you, I promise." Grinning, the lady took Rowena by the hand and pulled her along the quiet corridor.

True to her word, Lady Pratt led her onward at the fastest clip their shoes and corsets allowed, prohibiting the need to talk but for a few words of direction here and there. Still, it took them several minutes to navigate to a wing that had a familial, comfortable air about it. No ostentatious fixtures or ornate picture frames. Just generous windows, sweeping landscapes painted with more whimsy than skill, and the happy sound of baby giggles.

Rowena couldn't help but smile at the way her hostess ran the last few feet and pushed open the door. At the way the wee one within squealed with delight at her entrance, straining against his nurse's arms in his eagerness to reach his mother.

"There's my little darling." Lady Pratt took him and held him close, seemingly oblivious to the way he latched on to one of her carefully arranged curls. She smiled at the nurse. "How has he been for you this evening?"

The servant smiled, but there was no covering how harried she looked. "Missing you, milady. And making no secret of it."

"Ah. My precious." Lady Pratt peppered kisses over his baby-plump cheek, down onto his neck. Her efforts were rewarded with a deep belly laugh as he tossed back his dark head in utter joy. Then Lady Pratt turned to Rowena and bounced the wee one to face her too. "Can you say hello to Mama's friend, Byron?"

The boy turned his face into his mother's neck but wiggled his fingers at her. Rowena smiled and waved back. "Hello, wee one. What a handsome lad ye are."

"He gets that from his father too. Don't you, By? He was the most beautiful man." She sidled over to the mantel and picked up a framed photograph.

Rowena accepted it from her and felt her eyes go wide as she looked at what appeared to be their wedding portrait. She'd expected to find that the lady's opinion had been colored by love. Not so. He *was* beautiful, from the black hair to the perfect face and on down through his trim figure. A striking complement indeed to the fair lady tucked into his side, looking so happy.

She couldn't help but note, though, that Lord Pratt didn't look quite so happy as his bride. Putting on a smile, Rowena handed the picture back and focused on the babe. "I daresay the bairn will be every bit as beautiful. He's his coloring, sure enough."

"I pray daily he escapes his disposition. Much as I loved the man, I'm not blind to his faults. He—oh!" Lady Pratt fumbled a bit when Byron lunged for Rowena.

So taken aback was she that she echoed the lady's "Oh!" even as she caught him.

It wasn't she he wanted, though. He grabbed at her necklace, made a happy squeal, and promptly put it in his mouth.

Lady Pratt reached for him again with wide eyes and a panicked screech. "No! Heavens, By, not the Nottingham rubies!"

Rowena couldn't help but laugh—though she also accepted the handkerchief the nurse rushed to offer her. "I daresay they've been drooled on before, if they've been worn by as many duchesses as I've been led to believe."

"Still, if any harm should be done by *my* child . . ." Lady Pratt shook her head and reached for a toy for him to gnaw instead. "That set is legendary. I daresay everyone in the peerage has heard of its long history—and has long seen Charlotte wearing it every chance she got. Honestly, I'm a bit surprised to see she's given it up. I was under the impression the set was her favorite of the Nottingham jewels."

Rowena finished polishing and drying and smiled. "Aye, she said as much—because it was the one given to her on her wedding day, as it was given to her husband's mother on hers, and so on. And so she gave it to me on mine."

"What a perfectly lovely tradition." After pressing a kiss to her son's head and heaving a sigh, the lady passed the lad back to the nurse. "Good night, little darling. I'll see you in the morning."

"Mumumum!"

"I know. I'll miss you too." She blew a kiss to him and said to the nurse, "I'll check on him after the ball has ended."

"I'm sure he'll be fast asleep, milady. Don't worry over us—enjoy your evening."

They slipped back into the hall, and for a moment the mood was somber. Until Lady Pratt glanced at Rowena's necklace again and giggled. "Oh, heavens! I can just imagine centuries of duchesses gasping in horror when he put it in his mouth!"

Rowena chuckled too and touched a hand to the warm gold. "No harm done."

"Well, it's a good thing. I can't imagine any other piece complementing that exquisite gown quite so well."

She didn't know whether to thank the lady for the compliment on her dress or just bask in the warm feeling of approval. Acceptance. She let her fingers fall from the necklace. "Truth be told, I don't even *have* any other pieces yet. My father was never one for such gifts—he always said they'd be mine when I inherited the title." Or never, if he had a son who would someday marry and require them for his wife.

Lady Pratt lifted her brows. "There are no shortage of Nottingham pieces though—my mother always observed that Charlotte had jewels enough for two duchesses."

"Aye, and she said many of them will be mine when we get home. But she brought nothing but jet with her to Scotland, for her mourning attire. And these."

"Of course." Looking appropriately abashed, the lady linked their arms. "I suppose it's gauche of me to even mention such things. My brother is all the time taking issue with what I say."

"Perhaps that's because you so often say what you oughtn't, Kitty."

Rowena might have felt like a ninny at jumping so at the unexpected voice, except that Lady Pratt jumped even higher and splayed a hand over her heart too. "Crispin! Are you *trying* to scare the life from me?"

The man who stepped from the shadows had to be Lady Pratt's brother. He had the same fair coloring, the same general features. Though his expression was muted where the lady's was bright, and he had none of the presence Rowena had grown accustomed to in her companions of late. He seemed more the type to blend in than stand out, even here with just the three of them.

He fell in on his sister's other side. "I guessed this was where you had disappeared to. You had better not dawdle on the way back. Lady Ella was looking for her sister."

Ella. Not Brice? Had he gotten so caught up in the crowd that he forgot she had left? Rowena kept her pace steady and even and tried to ignore that sinking inside.

Lady Pratt sighed. "I was only introducing Byron to the duchess."

Rowena lifted her chin an inch. "Would you call me Rowena?"

The lady's eyes lit up. "I'd be honored. And of course, you must call me Kitty. Or Catherine. Whichever you prefer. I answer to both."

The hint of warmth inside grew. A friend. Perhaps not where her new husband hoped she would make one, but a friend nonetheless. Rowena smiled. Perhaps she could somehow smooth things over between Catherine and Brice. Perhaps, if he saw that she was capable of building bridges where he had not, she would earn his respect. And from there, they could build something real. Something to rival whatever he may or may not have felt for Brook, or for the swarm of other "too many" ladies always around him.

Catherine's brother sighed. "This is all very chummy, but Kitty, *please*. We don't need the duke angry with us."

"Always so reasonable." Catherine rolled her eyes and inclined her head to Rowena as they turned a corner. "This is my brother, in case you hadn't deduced as much. Lord Rushworth. Everyone calls him Rush, though it's one of the most ironic nicknames in England. The man can never be put upon to hurry."

Lord Rushworth didn't so much as smile. "Haste leads to mistakes. As does thoughtlessness, Kitty."

"You see what I've had to suffer all my life?" She made a show of huffing. "And he was so long responsible for me that he can't quite adjust to the fact that I'm an independent woman now. Though, granted, had Byron not been a boy, I would have been back at home again, throwing myself upon his mercy, with only my widow's allotment and no house to call my own."

"Let us praise the Lord he *is* a boy, then. No one wanted you to have to return home." It must be a jest, a tease. The words demanded it, but his tone left Rowena wondering if it was . . . or if it was a barb.

No, it was surely a tease, for Catherine chuckled and leaned into his arm for a moment. "Don't let his insufferable manner put you off, Rowena. He's rather doting, as brothers go. I would have been lost without his support after Pratt died. We got each other through it. Pratt was his dearest friend, you know."

Rowena's brows knit. Everyone seemed to universally agree that Pratt wasn't a good man. Even Catherine. So what did it say of this one, to have been so close to him without the excuse of love, which everyone knew never claimed wisdom or discernment?

Lord Rushworth glanced at Rowena, his expression somehow going even emptier. Had he read her thoughts? A shiver clawed its way up her spine.

Catherine nodded. "It is rather cool in this part of the hall. Magnificent as Delmore is, it's a drafty old place. Half of it's crumbling down around itself, but only so many improvements can be made in a year."

Rushworth snorted. "You've your cousin to thank for those limitations."

The shiver was gone, but unease crouched in its place. Rowena had only heard mention of one cousin, though surely they had more. "Brook?"

"Pay no mind to Rush and his sour grapes. We both know we had no more claim to the jewels than she did, and if our uncle chose to give them to her . . . well. It hardly matters that she doesn't need the money. Or that she'd give the things away." Catherine's smile made a bid for bravery, but emotion flared her nostrils. "My husband went about it all the wrong way—but it was born of desperation. Delmore's income simply can't match her upkeep. And the debts!"

"*Kitty.*" Rushworth let out an exasperated breath and looked to the ceiling. "*Must* you lay it all bare before *her*? Apologies,

Duchess, but really. She won't help you, Kitty. You know she won't. She can't. Not if she means to remain in the good graces of her husband and his people."

Rowena came to a halt, drawing them to a stop along with her. "Are ye talking of the diamonds?"

Catherine turned to her with lifted brows. "You know of them."

She felt almost guilty for needing to shake her head. "My husband merely mentioned that Lord Pratt wanted diamonds Brook had. That's all I know."

Catherine's shoulders sagged. "They aren't just *diamonds*, Rowena. They're *red* diamonds—the rarest gem there is. They were mined in India, and the locals called them the Fire Eyes. The story goes that the gods cut them and gave them to Dakshin Ray, the tiger god. But humans stole them, and they now carry the tiger's curse—that greed, death, and destruction will follow them wherever they go."

Rowena's stomach twisted. The ever-practical English would dismiss such a legend, no doubt. But Rowena had spent all her life among the ghosts of Loch Morar. Had heard all the stories accepted so easily in her home region. Had seen with her own two eyes the ghost boat that always came when a MacPherson died. Had heard the howls of the fabled black dog.

Who was she to say what was real and what was story, when the Lord and His realm was so much bigger than what she could imagine? It had always seemed safest to her to assume her own mind too feeble to grasp it all than to call something poppycock just because she couldn't understand it.

If legend of a curse had followed something for centuries—well then, a wise man or woman steered clear of it. She had to remind herself to breathe. "And Brook has these . . . these Fire Eyes?"

Catherine shook her head and urged Rowena onward. "Not anymore, of course. I don't think she ever really wanted them—she just didn't want us to have them. Again, my own fault for being so nasty when Pratt proposed to her, but . . ."

Rowena pressed a hand to her temple. It was all too much—a story that sounded more like a serial novel in the newspaper than an actual account. Diamonds and proposals and curses and feuds. "But she doesn't have them anymore? Then where are they?"

A snort of a laugh parted Catherine's lips. "I daresay you'd have to ask your husband that question, Rowena."

She came to a halt again and turned to stare at her hostess. "What do ye mean?" The words seemed to shatter as they spilled from her lips, like ice on stone.

"He didn't tell you?" Catherine's eyes shifted, filling with . . . sympathy? "Sorry. I assumed he would have, before he brought you here. Brook gave them to him. Last year."

"Pardon?"

Catherine's hands closed around Rowena's, her eyes apologetic and warm. "I'm sorry—Rush is right, I always speak before I ought. I only meant for this invitation to be a peace offering, an assurance that I'm happy to let things rest, to be done with the whole business. And here I've gone and upset you."

"Why would she do that? Give them to him?" It made no sense, not with anything she knew of . . . of *anyone*. Unless . . . unless the curse had made itself known to her, and she was desperate. She wouldn't want to foist it upon her friend, then, but Brice was always so eager to help someone in need.

She was proof of that, wasn't she? And if he would take a wife to save her from harm, would he not also willingly take on a curse? *Lord, let it not be so*. "I imagine it is only rumor that he has them?"

"I saw her do it. Take them from the necklace where they'd

been hidden and hand them to him. As for why . . ." Catherine hesitated, shrugging. "On that, I can only conjecture. My only real theory was that it was some sort of consolation prize. Stafford won Brook's heart, but she was too fond of Nottingham to send him away empty-handed."

"Nonsense, I say." Still half angled toward the path back to the ballroom, Rushworth smoothed his tie. "My personal theory is that he's as much her lackey as ever and merely doing her bidding concerning them." His gaze flicked to Rowena and softened. "A theory that made more sense before he arrived with so lovely a wife, of course."

She was going to be sick. Thoroughly, eternally sick. What had Lilias forced her into with this marriage? Her husband wasn't just a stranger, he was . . . he was what? In love with another man's wife? Caught up in a web of violence and destruction? Out to ruin a family that was doing nothing more than trying to regain its footing after a disastrous match? Regardless, he had brought a curse into his home. He had willingly accepted items tied to evil. Perhaps *that* was what she had been feeling skitter up her spine since they arrived at Delmore. The clashing of forces beyond her sight.

He had the jewels. The Fire Eyes. He had them . . . and he hadn't seen fit to mention that little detail when he supposedly told her what they were doing here an hour ago.

"Ignore my brother." Catherine slid an arm around Rowena's waist and led her onward. "Whatever Nottingham's reasoning had been at the time, I daresay everything has changed now. *You're* his wife, not Brook. He must love you fiercely to have wed you so quickly, so put all thought of our previous theories from your mind."

"Yes, of course." But he wasn't in love with Rowena. He barely knew her. Certainly didn't trust her.

The question was, did he *want* to trust her? Did he *want* to love her? Because . . . because she knew all too well that being married to one woman didn't guarantee a man's heart was hers. How many secrets had Father kept from Mother?

One, at least. Annie, with her innocent eyes and unwitting resemblance to the man supposedly only her stepfather, was proof of that.

"I'm such a dunce. Forgive me, I beg you. I wanted to be a friend, not ruin everything with such talk before we've any time to get to know each other." Catherine's brows were drawn, lines of distress evident around her mouth.

"Dinna fash yourself, Kitty. Please." Rowena tried a smile again. "I promise—I'm not upset with you."

Her shoulders relaxing, Catherine returned her smile. "Thank you. But let's not talk anymore of such things. Tell me how my cousin is faring—I do still care for her, despite our recent enmity."

Rushworth snorted. "That, I suppose, is why you've been seething that she probably regained her figure more quickly than you did, how she—"

"Well, a girl is entitled to a bit of jealousy, isn't she? It keeps her on her toes." Her grin was so bright, so light-hearted that Rowena couldn't help but laugh. Catherine's step took on a bounce. "How am I *not* to compare myself to her when all of society does it every time one or the other of us steps out? And she forever shocking everyone as she does—trousers and cheek kissing and lapsing into French and Monegasque at the drop of a hat."

But it wasn't bitterness in her tone, nor envy, nor spite. To Rowena's ears it sounded merely like the love of a good scandal, a tale to tell. Catherine, it seemed, was a gossip. Another something Rowena was well acquainted with, being from a tight-knit village. Perhaps not the most admirable trait, but it was hardly criminal.

They spoke of light things for the remaining minutes of travel, but Rowena's mind wasn't really on the activities planned for the rest of the house party or whose dress was the finer among the guests. It had drifted back to things her husband hadn't seen fit to tell her even existed. Of the diamonds . . . and of their curse.

Did he believe it? Understand it? Or was he like all the other English, quick to dismiss it as superstition, despite all the evidence to the contrary?

A tremor started in her hands, and she clasped them together before her hostess could note it. Perhaps he had taken them as a favor to Brook. But did he plan on giving them back, or were they his? Perhaps he meant to sell them—though so far as she had seen, he had no need of funds, nor did the Staffords or Whitby.

But Catherine did. So if her claim to them was valid, why would he not just give the jewels to her?

No. No, if the curse were real, they should not wish it on anyone else.

They turned into the hall where the music spilled from the ballroom, where electric lights were lit and laughter filled all the crevices.

One of the ladies who had sneered at Rowena earlier rushed from the card room. "There you are, Kitty! I'm afraid I need your assistance. My darling husband has been too much in his cups again. Can you fetch servants to return him to his room?"

"Of course." The congenial hostess was back, all vulnerability tucked away behind her smile. "Excuse me, Rowena. Rush."

The two ladies hurried off together. It took Rowena a few seconds to realize that left her alone with Lord Rushworth in the hallway. And that he had turned to her with cold, unyielding eyes and a firm-set mouth.

She folded her arms over her middle, trying to find wits enough to make her excuses and leave. Unable to do anything but stare into those eyes—so very frigid they looked lifeless—and think how familiar they seemed. How like her father's they were.

He edged nearer, but not so close she felt the need to back up. Just close enough that he could murmur, "Don't hurt her. I don't know what you're about, Duchess, but please. She's been through enough. If you dangle friendship before her nose only to use it against her—" Nostrils flaring, he shook his head. "Don't. I beg you."

She shook her head, trying to tell herself he was only concerned for his sister. Not like Father at all. Though her shaking hands were unconvinced. "I wouldn't, my lord. I promise you. I have no ulterior motives."

"I want to believe that, but I don't know if I can." Sighing, he turned to watch Catherine's skirts disappear around a corner. "She's all I have. I cannot help but worry for her. She may jest about how blessed she is to keep all this for my nephew, but the truth is, the debt is overcoming her. And there's only so much I can do to help her now."

"But if you had the diamonds, if you could sell them. . . ." If they could all be rid of the things and their curse, and someone could come out the better for it . . .

His face, for the first time, took on feeling. Soft and gentle, but also dismissive. "An 'if' that doesn't bear thinking about, Duchess. They will never be ours. Your husband would never give them to us, not in a millennium."

But why, when having them seemed to bring nothing but strife and division? Rowena tilted her head. "What if I convinced him? Have you someone who would buy them?"

He hesitated, his face now tormented. "Pratt had someone lined up, but Duchess, don't. I beg you. It's far too dangerous. If your husband discovers you trying to help us . . ."

"He wouldn't hurt me." Much as she doubted Brice's motives in this situation, doubted his heart, she trusted in that much. He had protected her at every turn, had proven he wasn't a violent man.

Rushworth backed away, and that emptiness returned to his eyes, so dark and bottomless it made her shiver. "Not with his fists, perhaps. But there are many ways to hurt someone."

Rustling came from the nearest doorway, though Rowena couldn't see through Lord Rushworth to know who it might be. But then a voice called out, "Lord Rushworth! Have you seen . . . ?" Ella. And when Rushworth turned, she obviously caught sight of Rowena. She sighed, looking relieved. "There you are."

Rushworth stepped to the side with a small, polite bow. "Forgive me for not returning her to you more quickly, Lady Ella. When I heard you asking after her I had a feeling she may have taken a wrong turn somewhere, so I went in search. Such a maze, these hallways."

Just like that, the light of suspicion in Ella's eyes shifted to amusement. "They are, at that. Were you lost, Rowena?"

She didn't want to lie—but what good would it do to confess she had gone off with Catherine of her own will? "I never would have found my way back without someone leading me. Sorry if I worried you, Ella."

"Oh, no matter. You're back now, safe and sound." Still smiling, she dipped a curtsy to Lord Rushworth. "Thank you, my lord, for your efforts on her behalf."

As he bowed again, more deeply this time, and gave Ella a half smile, he came off as charming. Even a bit rakish. "Anything, my lady, to keep the worry from your lovely eyes." With that, he straightened, turned away, and his posture yet again returned to the passive, meek one that she had first noted.

What a confusing man. Which version of him was real? And why did the question leave her skin feeling slicked with fear?

Ella watched him go, bemusement on her face. "He's never even spoken to me before tonight. But that smacked rather decisively of flirtation, didn't it?"

No doubt the belle of every ball she attended, Ella shrugged it off. "Ah, well. We'd best get back to the ballroom. The music has struck up, and my brother would like to dance with his wife."

Would he? Did he *really*, or was it just part of the charm, part of the story he painted for his friends? Rowena trailed Ella back inside, but her heart didn't follow.

What hope did she have of ever being enough for him?

Fourteen

Brice led Rowena down the hall, keenly aware of the tremor in her hand where it rested against his arm—the tremor that had been quite absent earlier in the evening, but which he had noted the moment she reentered the room with Ella and he had claimed her for a dance.

The tremor that perfectly matched the shadow in her eyes. He had wanted to question her then and there, but during a waltz, surrounded by people who made no qualms about eavesdropping, was hardly the time.

His quiet question as to whether she was ready to retire had earned him a quick, grateful nod though. And now a glance over his shoulder proved that no one had followed them, no one else had decided to leave the ball so early. Still, he pitched his voice low. "You said you would find a maid."

No, no, all wrong. That sounded like an accusation, which hadn't been his intent at all.

His wife sighed and kept her gaze focused on the dull, scuffed floorboards beneath their feet. This guest wing was in dire need of improvements. "I didna find one."

"I should have come with you."

At that, she sent him an impatient glare. "I dinna need my husband walking me to the lavatory."

Nor did he figure she would appreciate her husband seeking her out there—hence why he had sent Ella on the search when her absence had stretched too long. "But Rushworth found you."

Her grip on his arm tightened, and a wave of trembling swept over her. If he had laid a hand on her, if he had said anything to upset her . . . "What happened?"

Was the shake of her head a lie? "Nothing."

He let silence envelop them as they turned the corner into the hallway where their rooms were located. "All right, then . . . What did you think of him?"

Her breath shook when she drew it in. "He . . . he reminds me somehow of my father." The gas lamps on the wall caught the feeling in her eyes when she turned them on him. "Is he cruel? To his sister, I mean? She seemed fond of him, but—"

"Lady Pratt was there too?" He regretted the harsh question when her silver eyes went blank, shuttered. "I didn't mean . . . It is only that—"

"Hush." She came to an abrupt halt, clutching his arm to stop him too. Her focus had gone beyond him, toward their rooms. "Is that . . . ?"

He turned to see what had caught her attention, sucking in a gasp when he saw his door quickly shut and the light extinguish from beneath it. Davis? But his valet would have no cause to blow out the lamp—nor to close his door so hastily.

"Stay here." He peeled her fingers from his arm and slid away, hurrying over the distance separating him from his door.

Rowena dogged his steps, muttering something about glaikit men.

They could debate his foolishness and hers later. Right now he indicated she should flatten herself against the wall to remain out of sight. He reached for the door latch, paused with his hand upon it. A deep breath, a *Dear Lord* . . .

Then he sprang. Pushed open the door, let it bang against the wall. He didn't leap through, loath to have someone ready to take a swing at his head and leave Rowena without defense. And quite certain that whoever was within knew he was coming.

Rowena had apparently *not* stayed put. She held out an oil lamp that must have been burning on a table down the hall—and offered no apology in the even stare she settled on him either.

What had happened to the timid young lady he had known these past weeks? He took the lamp and dragged his attention back to his room. Scurrying sounds came from within, a scraping, a muffled, masculine curse.

Rowena's hand touched his arm. "Should I go for help?"

"Not yet." Even if she managed to find her way, it would be too late to help. "Just pray." With that, he held up the lamp and eased through the doorway.

The light shone on all the unfamiliar furniture, but his focus went straight to the dark-clad figure ducking into . . . the wall? "Blast!" He charged forward, catching the hidden door just before it slid shut. "Stop! Get back here!"

As if the intruder had any intention of listening. Brice bullied the door open—a difficult enough task that he had to think the sliding panel hadn't been used in years—and stepped through, holding his lamp high.

The light caught only the heels of black shoes, the shadow of dark trousers disappearing around a corner.

"Brice!"

He had one foot already poised to follow, even as a warning clanged through his spirit. Whomever it was knew these passages, and Brice most assuredly did not. To pursue would no doubt mean being pounced upon. But how could he let the man get away?

"Brice, it's Davis! *Please.*"

Rowena's plea brought him surging back through the hidden doorway. His lamplight now illuminated what he had missed in his rush through the room—his valet sagging unconscious on the floor. Rowena was bent over him, her fingers at his neck.

Relief colored her face when she looked up at him. "Alive, and his pulse is steady."

"Praise God." He slid the lamp onto the table and knelt beside her. "Davis? Davis, can you hear me?"

Davis muttered something that sounded akin to "newfangled butterflies" and rolled onto his side.

Brice rocked back on his heels. "Odd."

"Laudanum, perhaps? My mother used to take it now and then when she had trouble sleeping, and I remember her muttering the strangest things." Rowena pushed herself back to her feet. And froze. "Oh, gracious."

"What?" But he needn't have asked, only to have looked around. Every drawer was opened, emptied. Every one of his belongings turned out. With a sigh, he shoved himself upright too. "Ducky."

Rowena meandered over to the chest of drawers and picked up a roll of pound notes. "Not a random theft, for certain."

Something about the gaze she settled on him, cool and accusatory, made his breath catch. "I need to get Davis onto the bed." And give himself a moment to consider how much he should tell her. And wonder at what Catherine and Rushworth had told her.

He found himself wishing he employed a slighter man as he slid his arms under Davis's and levered him up. His head lolled, more nonsensical murmurs nearly making Brice forget himself and grin. Knowing Davis, he would be aghast at himself for appearing in such a state to Brice.

And for sleeping in his bed, but there was little help for it. Brice dragged him that direction, making no complaint when Rowena took the valet's feet and helped settle him onto the mattress. Davis mumbled something about swimming strangely and rolled onto his side.

Rowena turned toward the lamp. "Ye should check him for injuries. I canna think how someone would have got him to take laudanum, if that's what it is." She lifted the light from the end table and brought it over to the one beside the bed, where another lamp sat, ready to be lit.

In the added glow, Brice noted the blood on Davis's knuckles—not his own, as a dampened handkerchief soon proved—and he also found a knot on the back of his head.

Rowena had folded her arms across her middle. "I can find someone. Lady Pratt or the butler. The constable ought to be fetched."

"No." He pulled a blanket over his unconscious valet and turned to face his wife. "I'll not have the whole house in an uproar over it, nor alarm Mother and Ella if it can be avoided."

She stared at him as if he were daft. "Someone just attacked your man! Rifled through your things—"

"Yes, and praise God he seems all right despite it."

Her nostrils flared, and she squared her shoulders, looking more the Highland countess than terrified lass. "And your things? Are ye not the least bit concerned that he found what he was looking for, whatever it may be?"

"No, I'm not concerned." He might have been, could he not hear Cowan humming on the other side of the door that connected their rooms when he stepped near it, clearly oblivious to all transpiring on *this* side. He stopped before the chest of drawers. Diamond cufflinks, his money, and a rather pricey tie clip all lay scattered across the top. "What they're looking for isn't here."

"The diamonds." Rowena snatched up one of his shirts from where it lay in a heap on the floor and folded it with a few precise, economical, furious motions. "They said ye have them, that Catherine watched Brook give them to you."

He swept the valuables back into the drawer open beneath them. Said nothing.

"Ye'll not even deny it?" She shoved the folded shirt into his chest. "Why? Why would ye take them, Brice?"

She wouldn't understand. Even the Staffords didn't understand. They had only granted him what they deemed his insane request to humor him. "They were having a baby. They didn't need to worry with Catherine and her brother coming after them."

"I daresay it's more her brother than the lady." She snatched a waistcoat from the chair it had landed on. "But regardless. Ye're a fool or worse, Duke, if ye know there is danger attached to them but take them anyway."

"She would have come after me anyway. I was only—"

"Ye brought a curse into yer house!" She kept her volume low, though there was no hiding her furor as she slapped the waistcoat into a drawer. "And for what?"

A chill skittered up his spine. "The only curse is the greed of man. The lust the jewels inspire in them."

She spun from him with a sound of disgust. "Oh, aye, ye English with your logical ways. Ye canna understand it, so ye dismiss it out of hand."

He caught her elbow, though he released her again in the next second when she jerked at his touch. *Blast*. It was going to take a lifetime to figure out how to behave with her. "Rowena, please.

I dismiss nothing. And I wrestled with the Lord for months over this before I accepted the jewels. It was what He asked of me."

"Ye're playing with fire. Can ye not see that?" She sank into the chair by the door, sitting atop another of his shirts.

"It is a risk, but a controlled one." He held out a hand, pleading with her to understand. "But I promise you, I will keep you safe."

"As you did Davis?" She folded her arms across her middle and shook her head. "There are powers beyond human control, Brice. Powers ye best not fool with. Get rid of the diamonds. I beg you. Wherever they are, *please*, get rid of them."

His hand fell to his side. "I can't. They're not mine to dispose of."

"Well, I havena such qualms." Now *she* held out a hand. "Give them to me. *I'll* be rid of them, and pray that the curse goes with them before anyone else can get hurt or worse."

"Rowena."

She surged back to her feet, thrusting that outstretched hand his way. "I canna live under a curse. I canna. Dinna ask it of me. Get rid of them, or let me."

"If the curse were only some disembodied power out to get us, perhaps I would. But it's not. It's *people*, Rowena, *these* people, and they would never believe us if we said we'd tossed them into the sea. If I let them stand to watch, they would insist I had thrown imitations." He took her fingers slowly in his. "There's no point in getting rid of them. We must end it, once and for all."

Her eyes, large and dry, shouted sorrow as she slipped her fingers free. "Then give them to Lord Rushworth. Let *him* have the curse o'er his head. We can help Catherine break free of him, we can—"

"She is no innocent!" He shoved his now-free hand through

his hair and half-turned back toward the bed. "She does not want to be free of her brother. She wants the Fire Eyes—nothing less."

"Do ye know her so well?"

"Do *you*? After, what, a five-minute conversation?"

She lifted her chin. "I know men like her brother. I know how they treat the women in their lives. That tells me enough."

From what *he* had seen, the sister was every bit as conniving and cruel as the brother could possibly be. But there would be no convincing Rowena of it, not tonight, anyway. He drew in a long breath, made himself go still. "I'll not hand the diamonds over to them. I can't. Justice must be served here, once and for all."

"Justice." She shook her head, backed away, fumbled for the door latch. "Ye'll not find it. Ye'll find only the curse, and ye'll drag us all down with you."

"There is no—"

"I dinna expect ye to listen to me. Why would you?" She tugged the door open. "Ye barely know me. So be it." She stormed into the hallway. "*You* talk to him. Perhaps he'll listen to another cool, logical Sassenach."

Brice flew to the door, ready to be horrified to see whoever lurked in the hallway. Mother? Ella? The last people he wanted drawn into this. But it was only Miss Abbott who stood there with wide eyes and obvious confusion, her hand resting on the latch to Ella's door across the hall.

Her gaze focused on the room behind him and must have caught sight of the melee still within. "What happened to your room?"

Rowena's door slammed, making him wince. "Just someone trying to ruffle me. It's nothing."

Miss Abbott's brows arched. "Your wife seems to disagree."

"She does." But she didn't understand. She hadn't been fighting this battle as long as he had. Brice pasted a weak smile onto his lips and stepped back into his room. "We will work through it. Good night, Miss Abbott."

He closed the door against her soft "Good night, Your Grace." Then turned to face the mess that had been left for him.

Fifteen

Catherine, Lady Pratt. The lady behind the name hadn't disappointed. Lovely. Charming. Seemingly sweet.

But Stella Abbott didn't miss the cold calculation in the lady's eyes. The steely, unrelenting something in Lady Pratt's stare said clearly she would do anything—*anything*—to have her way.

Exactly the sort of something needed in a good ally.

Stella cast one more glance over her shoulder to be sure no one followed her and turned down the quiet corridor. Lady Pratt had excused herself half an hour before, and Stella had noted where she went, though she didn't follow immediately. Best to go unnoticed.

The house party had spread itself over the entire estate. Some of the guests were out on a foxhunt, others putting together a play they would enact the final night. Others probably taking advantage of the plethora of open rooms at Delmore to betray their spouses and pretend it didn't matter, since their spouses were likely betraying them too.

Sickening, all of them.

But it meant Catherine, Lady Pratt was alone—or mostly. She sat in the solar at a small writing desk, her brother resting in an armchair near at hand, a book open in his lap. The brother, if Nottingham's word on the matter could be trusted, was as dangerous as the lady. Another good ally, in that case.

Stella tapped on the open door, making sure her face reflected what it should. A sweet smile, a bit of the bashful guest who knew well she was inferior to her hosts.

But not for long.

Lady Pratt looked up, lifted her brows, and put on that careful society smile that perpetuated the lie that she was an innocent. "Good morning. . . . Miss Abbott, isn't it? Have you lost your way, or can I help you with something?"

Stella closed the door behind her with a satisfying, muted *click*. Her smile faltered though. If Nottingham discovered she had sought out his enemies, purposefully to cause him trouble . . . But it was for his good, their good. She must remember that, must keep her focus on the goal. "It is *I* who can help *you*, I think."

The lady put down her pen and turned on her chair, a bit of her feigned innocence eclipsed by calculation. "Oh, *really*." Condescension dripped from her tone. "And how, pray tell, can you do that, my dear?"

Chin held high, Stella took a few more steps into the room—she would have to let Catherine think herself superior, but Stella knew better than to show any intimidation. Not in the company of a predator. "Perhaps I should say we can help each other. If you meant to unnerve Nottingham last night with that search of his room, you've missed the mark. He was expecting something like that, I think."

The lady's gaze flicked to her brother, though other than that she made no response. "I've no idea what you mean. Cris, dear, have you heard of anything that transpired in the duke's room last night?"

Stella looked to Lord Rushworth, but he didn't so much as glance up from his book in response to his sister's question. "I've heard nothing to that effect, no. And one would think the duke would make some noise about such a thing."

Now Stella smiled, though it felt small and rather mean. "That just shows how little you know him. I will give you enough credit to assume you realize he's only here to draw you out. Please return the favor and don't assume me stupid. I assure you, I am not."

Now the lady leaned one arm onto the back of her dainty little chair, her regard heavy and intense. "And yet you expect me to admit to guilt for something I didn't do?"

Stella's smile froze, but she refused to let it fade. She wouldn't cower . . . but she reminded herself to let the lady think herself in control. "What could I possibly do to you, even if you *did* admit something to me? You could destroy me—don't think I'm unaware of that. One word from you, and I could lose the position I've worked so hard to attain."

"Now you're stroking my vanity." But Lady Pratt smiled and relaxed a little. "I admit you have me curious. How exactly do you think we can help each other?"

Looking back years from now, would this be the obvious point of no return? When it all went from thought to action? Maybe. But it would not—*could* not—carry any regret. Even if, as Stella met Lady Pratt's eyes, a single knot of unease pulled tight deep inside.

But it must be done. It *must*. "I don't know what it is you want from the duke. The search suggests an object, but I would have otherwise thought it merely revenge."

The lady toyed with the necklace dangling from her throat. Gold and gems that would provide meals for most of England's families for months, yet she played with it as though it were nothing more than glass beads and pyrite. "There is, of course, the hypothetical possibility that someone searching his room would have *both* motives—an object *and* revenge."

"But that isn't how you meant to achieve either, is it? I heard the two dukes talking at Whitby Park. Your original plan, before he came back from Scotland married, was to make yourself a duchess."

An overstep, perhaps. Lady Pratt went cold again, hard as she said, "Now your theories begin to clash—first you say I want revenge on him, then that I wanted to *marry* him?"

Stella's new smile felt more like a smirk. "I think there's no better position from which to exact revenge than from a man's side—and from his bed."

Lady Pratt sat up straight again, her mouth agape but amusement in her eyes. "Here I thought you pious, Miss Abbott."

"A common misconception." Everyone had always thought her like her brother. Or like Ella, seeing only the good. As if one had a hope of advancing, of acquiring one's dreams, if one did nothing but pray or giggle all day long.

The lady pushed to her feet. "I like you, Miss Abbott. I didn't expect to. Usually Nottingham only surrounds himself with spineless idiots who think the world is all sunshine. Like his insipid sister."

Stella snapped her spine straight—it was one thing for *her* to grow tired of the disposition of her oldest friend from time to time, but it was quite another for this woman to insult her.

Lord Rushworth objected before she could, though. "Leave Lady Ella out of this, Kitty."

Interesting.

Lady Pratt sent her gaze heavenward and shook her head. "Predictable."

"Just focus on our guest." Sounding irritable, Rushworth waved a hand.

"Fine." Leaning now against her desk, the lady folded her arms. "You think you know my motives, but do, pray tell, expound on your own."

A beat of silence. Two. Then Stella whispered the words that had been burning inside for a fortnight. "I want that marriage over. They don't belong together."

Another rush of nothingness, then Lady Pratt's lips curled upward. "Oh, how quaint. You think you have a chance with him, that the Duke of Nottingham would really sully his hands with the likes of *you*."

Though she dug her nails into the palms of her hands, Stella took care to make sure the lady didn't see it. "One might make the same observation about *your* intentions. Did you really think you had any hope of manipulating him into marriage? Knowing how he despises you?"

The lady's nostrils flared. "My amusement is fading quickly. Do get to the point, my dear, before I ring for a servant to escort you out."

Another miscalculation? No. The lady needed to know she wasn't dealing with a spineless idiot who thought the world nothing but sunshine. "Given his conversation with the Duke of Stafford, I must assume this is all related to the business that led your husband to kidnap the duchess. If the papers had even a kernel of truth in their reporting, it's tied to diamonds, right?"

The lady examined her fingernails. The lord turned a page in his book.

Neither denied it. Stella nodded. "I've no idea if he has them. But if he has, he isn't stupid enough to travel with them—and certainly not to bring them here with him. They'd be at Midwynd."

"Obviously." Lady Pratt's tone dripped venom. "And if I *were* interested in finding something in the duke's possession that he had, perhaps, stolen from me . . . and if I *did* want to scare him into revealing their location . . . well then, one might assume I would be prepared to attack on multiple fronts, wouldn't one?"

What did that mean? That she had something else planned already, certainly, but . . . "You need someone who will be there to watch him when he reveals the truth of their location."

How mean her smile looked, small and victorious. "I already have someone. Someone far closer to him than *you*."

Don't step back. Don't back down. "The new duchess?" A guess, based on her disappearance last night, which coincided with their hostess's. But a right one, given the sparkle in the lady's eyes. Stella breathed a laugh. "Don't be a fool. Perhaps right now she feels too much the outcast from his world to trust him implicitly, but how long do you think that will last? A few more weeks of his incessant charm, and she'll turn to mush in his arms and believe anything he tells her."

They couldn't let that happen. Couldn't. Nottingham was too compassionate a man to let his wife fall in love alone—he would convince himself he loved her too, even though it was impossible, even though his heart was Stella's. He would cling to the words until they became true in action if not in fact. Then the mission would be lost.

But right now there was a chasm between Nottingham and his new wife. One that search through his room last night had pushed wider, since it apparently led to an argument. Now was the time to act. *Now*.

"Hmm." Lady Pratt raised a finger, waggled it. "I still fail to see where this will help *you*. Unless you intend to make me promise you money to make you more alluring to your beloved duke."

The thought made nausea churn. "I can't be *bought*, my lady. I have no care for money. What I want is your word. If I help you get whatever it is you're looking for, you help me end their marriage. Once and for all."

Lady Pratt stalked forward so quickly it required every ounce of willpower not to back up into the door. "You're daft. Either to think you can trick me into something so incriminating or to think I'd actually do it. There's only one way to permanently end their marriage, and I'll not mortgage my future with murder charges. I'm not the fool my husband was."

All right, so the lady wasn't quite as blinded by greed as Stella had hoped. No matter. "It needn't come to that anyway. There are grounds for annulment. They could easily argue that they were forced to marriage under false pretenses."

The lady's brows jumped upward. "I assumed some sort of trap was involved, but Nottingham would never admit before a court that he was forced to anything."

"There *was* a trap, but that wasn't what forced their hand. It was a threat to their persons."

Oh yes, that was most assuredly interest in the lady's eyes. "A threat by whom? Her father?"

"No." But this conniving woman didn't need to know the name *Malcolm Kinnaird* yet. He was a powder keg, one that ought not to be employed unless all other options were exhausted. "All you need to know right now is that it's one you can utilize if necessary."

"What would you—hypothetically—recommend? Since you say whatever transpired last night was insufficient."

Such care the lady took with her words. But that, too, was no matter. They all knew. That was enough. "There is one thing they both hate. One thing that will make the duchess close herself off to him from pure fear, and which will bring back to him the nightmares your husband and his shotgun inspired. One thing, my lady, that will work to both our benefits."

"Violence?" Lord Rushworth shut his book and sat up straight. Somehow, his smile looked completely benign, his eyes without a shadow as he said, "I daresay that can be arranged."

For the first time, the teeth of fear bit Stella—hard.

Brice glanced at his watch, unable to ignore the scratching of impatience. As far as he knew, no one at Delmore realized he was gone—and he would just as soon keep it that way and get back before the ladies finished their tea. Before Rowena could look at him with those big silver eyes and silently ask, *Why did you leave me?*

"Average height, average weight, dressed in dark colors. Your man didn't get a look at his face either?" The constable sat at one of the tables in Whitby Park's library, jotting down Brice's account onto a pad of paper. Stafford, Brook, and her father were there as well—his whole point in coming here rather than finding the constable in Eden Dale. The fewer times he had to recount it all, the better.

He shook his head. "He said he came up behind him while he was in the hallway outside my room—he had no recollection of entering it again at all."

The constable tapped a finger on the table. "They must have knocked him out and then administered a hefty dose of laudanum to keep him asleep so long."

Brook gave an exaggerated shudder and held little William closer. "I maintain that whoever invented that stuff ought to be hanged."

The constable spared a smile for her but no more attention. "And you're absolutely certain nothing was taken?"

"Not so much as a pin. We actually left most of our belongings here and only took what we needed for the house party to Delmore."

Stafford grinned. "He's not *entirely* witless."

Whitby's lips twitched up too. "Witless enough to invite you to this conversation though, Stafford. It would have been over by now had he not."

Stafford splayed a hand over his heart. "I am merely lightening the mood—a favor Nottingham was always so kind as to do for me when it was I engaged in an interview with our esteemed constable."

The esteemed constable cleared his throat and tapped his paper. "But this telegram you just received from your home in Sussex—will your local constable be favorable to communicating with me, do you think? To determine if there is anything in common about the two crimes?"

At that, Brice paced to the window, as if it would show him Midwynd instead of the maze. "I'm certain he will. But I believe my steward when he says that nothing was stolen or destroyed. I don't know what other commonality there could be, and with the footman missing, there's no one to question."

Just another mess in Brice's bedroom there. Which oughtn't to have surprised him when he read the telegram from the elder Mr. Abbott an hour ago. And honestly, it wasn't the assault to his belongings that disturbed him—it was the idea that one of his employees had likely been bought. When he thought he'd always made it perfectly clear that if they or their families were in want, they need only to come to him.

Perhaps he had been too long away from home. He turned back to his companions.

Pursing his lips, the constable shook his head. "You obviously think Lady Pratt and her brother responsible for both. And I'm not disinclined to believe you, Your Grace. But there's no proof. As many people as you say are at Delmore right now—"

"But who else would have a reason to ransack his room?" Brook stood, too, and bounced the baby in that way women always did.

The constable spread his hands. "I realize that. But one person *having* a motive does not necessarily indicate guilt, Your Grace, as you well know. Perhaps if we could put out to the staff that anyone who saw anything would be compensated for sharing it . . ."

Perhaps. But just as likely, someone had already been paid by Catherine to feed them lies.

A knock sounded on the door they'd closed behind the constable. Whitby stood, brows drawn. "Excuse me. It must be important, or Mr. Graham would never disturb us."

Mr. Graham didn't get out more than a "Pardon me, my lord, but—" before a figure pushed past him. Brice only vaguely recognized Stafford's cousin, Cayton. Last he'd seen him had been at the Staffords' wedding, and this gaunt, sunken-eyed figure bore little resemblance to the man he'd stood beside while his friends took their vows.

Cayton headed for Brook, paused, and then redirected his course toward his cousin. "Take her for a minute, will you?"

Apparently the bundle in his arms was his daughter. She made not so much as a peep as Cayton transferred her gently to Stafford's arms and then proceeded to collapse on the couch.

Stafford settled the babe comfortably against his shoulder but scowled at his cousin. "If you need a nap—and arms to relieve you of Addie—you do realize you've hired a nurse to provide that, right? You needn't drive an hour here just to achieve it."

"I thought I'd come for tea, give Tabby a respite, take your advice to get out. But I scarcely slept last night, and by the time we got here . . ." Cayton flung an arm over his eyes. "Wake me in the morning."

Whitby eased forward. "If you'd like a room—"

"No, my lord, I don't want a room—and I beg your pardon for bursting in on you." This the man delivered from under his sleeve. "What I want is a day when I don't feel as if the world is caving in on me."

Brook handed little Abingdon to her father and took Cayton's daughter—Addie, apparently—from Stafford. Then with a discreet motion to Whitby, they left the room with the little ones, the constable hot on their heels.

Brice angled toward the door, prepared to follow them out without being noticed. A mourning husband no doubt didn't want a near-stranger privy to his grief. Though frankly, most mourning spouses he'd seen hadn't made such a show in the presence of any near-strangers. But who was he to judge?

He moved silently.

"You needn't leave, Nottingham."

Blast. Feeling doubly awkward now, he pivoted a few steps from the door and saw that Cayton had sat up again and was merely leaning forward, elbows on his knees, and rubbing his face. Brice cleared his throat. "I don't want to intrude, my lord. I thought perhaps you could use some time alone with your cousin."

Cayton didn't so much as glance at Stafford. "My cousin, try as he might, cannot understand. You may. I'm told you just married—was it for love?"

To keep himself from bristling, Brice slid his hands into his pockets. "Not exactly." But it wasn't for money—not like Cayton. Though heaven forbid he say something so callous now, when the man was obviously eaten up. Was it just with grief, or was guilt at play, as Stafford had suggested?

Cayton looked up, their gazes locking for perhaps the first time in their very limited acquaintance. Brice's feet propelled him back to his chair. Not just because of the raw pain in the man's eyes that demanded a listening ear but because of the gentle nudge in his spirit that told him this was as much why he'd felt he should come to Whitby Park as to tell the Staffords about last night. He sat.

Eyes bloodshot, heavy circles under them, Cayton swallowed. "You've only been married a few weeks?"

Brice nodded. And began to pray, silently and intently, for this man and his motherless daughter. "A bit over a fortnight. And I only knew her a few days before that."

Cayton nodded and leaned back against the cushion, letting his eyes slide closed. "Obviously our stories aren't all that similar. Everyone knows I married Adelaide for her money. But we'd known each other most of her life. And she . . . she loved me. She'd always loved me . . . and I had cared for her—though I barely remembered she was alive a few years ago. Once I met Lady Melissa . . ." He shook his head, his larynx bobbing when he swallowed.

Brice had never paused to think how Adelaide must have felt. Married to the man she'd long dreamed of, knowing he was in love with another. Perhaps some people would glory in the victory, all feeling aside. Based on the one time he'd met the late Lady Cayton, he did not believe she was that type of person. "That part of the story I know. I was there, in fact, when Lady Melissa discovered your engagement."

Cayton's lips pulled up in a sickly imitation of a smile. "Yes, I recall how she flaunted being on your arm in Hyde Park that day, flirting as if her life depended on it. As if I weren't well aware that it was Brook you were courting, not Melissa."

A strange unease squirmed to life. "I wasn't courting Brook."

He had been happy to let London think so, at the time—but Stafford's own cousin? Shouldn't he, of all people, have realized that Brice had never pursued his cousin's wife like that?

"Right. Of course." Cayton shot a look to Stafford.

Stafford, the insufferable oaf, only grinned.

Brice leaned forward. "I'm not saying that just because Stafford is here, as he well knows. I'm not nearly daft enough to want to chase that woman around all my life—much as I adore her. It was merely convenient to let society think me pursuing her."

Cayton stared at him. "You surely realize that's not what anyone thought then, and it's not what they think now either."

Leaning back again, Brice drew in a sharp breath. "What do you mean, what they think now? It's obvious to anyone that the Staffords are in love, and why would Stafford and I be friends if . . . ?"

The slanted look Cayton sent him stopped him. The man breathed a laugh. "You can't be that naïve, sir. Everyone thinks you and Brook . . . and that my dear cousin is too besotted a fool to notice. No offense intended, cousin."

"Could have fooled me." Stafford's amusement with the situation had given way to a glower.

Brice blew out a long breath. "Define 'everyone,' if you please, my lord."

Here Cayton paused, obviously trying to sort through memory no doubt clouded with lack of sleep and recent grief. "I think I've heard the musing from multiple sectors—and I assure you, Stafford, that I always try to inject reason and assure them that you're no fool, and that you'd sooner shoot Nottingham than let him near your wife if that were a danger—but I believe most of it originated with Kitty."

Of course it did.

Stafford transferred his scowl to Brice. "And you do realize, I hope, that you just took your new wife into that viper's den, where her ears will be filled with such nonsense."

"She's with Mother and Ella. No one would dare say such things around them." Would they? He kept his focus on Cayton. "Though I can guess at how it would make a wife feel to hear rumors about her husband being in love with another woman."

Cayton's face twisted with pain. "She never asked me about it. Certainly never called me out." He looked down at his hands. "She just . . . tried. Tried to be what I wanted. Tried to make me love her. But you can't just make yourself love someone." His gaze flew up again, begging for agreement. "Can you?"

"I don't know." Brice was certainly no expert on love. He'd never experienced it, not the kind Cayton spoke of. But he could see where Stafford wouldn't be the one to ask—he and Brook had fallen in love the good old-fashioned way, with generous amounts of fighting and running from the truth of their affections. No convincing of themselves required.

Brice, though . . . He felt affection for Rowena, certainly. And the more he looked at her, the more beautiful he realized she was. The more he wanted to take her into his arms—if she would allow it. The more he *wanted* to love her. But was wanting to love enough to make it so?

He sighed and said again, "I don't know. But I have to think that even if we can't force a feeling to bloom, we can choose it. Love is not just a *thing*, after all, it is an action too. We can act in love. We can be faithful to love. We can carry it out until our hearts catch up."

It was true—it *must* be true—but Cayton didn't look convinced. He just stared into middle space and shook his head. "I tried. Perhaps not at the start, but at the end I did. When I realized she was with child, and when she grew so weak with it . . .

"I know what the gossips are saying—that it was all part of my devilish plan to rid myself of her. But it wasn't. It wasn't." He pushed himself to his feet, though he swayed a bit upon them and looked as though he might keel over at any moment. "She'd told me that she was healthy enough, that the doctors assured her of it. They hadn't, but I didn't fathom that sweet Adelaide could lie. I didn't. She . . . All she wanted was a child."

This must be a conversation Stafford had already had with Cayton. He didn't look surprised or distressed. Just moved to clap a hand to his cousin's shoulder. "And she got to hold her. She got to see how beautiful she is, how perfect, despite being early. Her last day on earth was one of the purest joy, Cay. Cling to that. She loved you, she loved your daughter, and she knew *you* would love your daughter. You needn't kill yourself proving it. Let the nurse do what you've hired her to do and for heaven's sake, man, *sleep*."

Cayton shook him off, staggered to the window, and leaned against the frame. "I told her I loved her—Adelaide—there at the end. I said it because I *did* love her, in a way, and because she wasn't recovering from the blood loss and I didn't want her to die thinking herself unloved. But she didn't believe me. She looked me in the eye, smiled that beatific smile of hers, and said she knew I didn't, but it didn't matter. That I'd been a good husband, and she knew I'd be a good father."

Brice flinched, glad Cayton was turned away so he couldn't see it. But it wasn't the late Lady Cayton to whom his mind went—he could barely even recall what she looked like. No, it was Rowena's face that surfaced in his mind's eyes, with her luminous silver eyes that harbored such hurt in their depths.

Who did she have, right now, to love her? Lilias Cowan, who no doubt had acted out of love, but who had nonetheless had a hand in forcing her away from all she knew? Her father, who would raise his hand to her? The stepmother who, whenever Brice had seen her, had only sneers for her stepdaughter?

Her stepsister, who she wouldn't see again until they could convince the Lochabers to send her to them for a visit. His family, who were trying to bring her into the fold, but who were still more strangers than friends.

Then him. He had the advantage over Cayton—he wasn't in love with anyone else, wasn't trying to move past it. His heart was his own, and the Lord's. And God had instructed him to marry Rowena, to protect her. Love would come.

But what if it took longer than he anticipated? Or longer to convince her? What if this Fire Eyes business came to a head in a more dangerous way than he was aiming for, and Rowena was caught in the middle? What if she were hurt or killed? How would he live with himself?

No better than Cayton was.

"You can let this eat you alive, Cayton," Stafford was saying, pulling Brice back to the present and away from that nebulous future, "or you can let it make you stronger. You can turn it over to the Lord, turn *yourself* over to the Lord, or keep flailing about like a drowning man when you know well that's where salvation lies."

Again, Brice got the impression that this part of the conversation had been said before. Stafford looked determined as he said it. Cayton weary. The earl sighed and rubbed at his face. "But I don't know how to be like you. It's never made any sense to me."

"Then let's pray it does. Let's pray right now that your heart is opened and your mind made clear on who God is and what He wants from you and for you."

Cayton lowered his hand and stared at his cousin as though he were a hydra. "You want to pray for me—*here*? Now?"

Stafford just grinned. "Actually, I meant to make Nottingham do it. He has an uncanny way of knowing just what to pray."

Brice had a feeling he wouldn't be making it back to Delmore in time for tea.

Sixteen

A scream shattered the peace of the afternoon, but it wasn't the sudden sound that made Rowena's heart gallop—it was its sudden ceasing. A scream, with so many guests in attendance, could mean only that someone was startled or saw a mouse or slipped on a stair. But that quick silence . . . Rowena knew that silence. It was the kind that came with a hand over one's mouth, with the stones cutting off one's air. It was the sudden silence of pain.

She wasn't the only lady who stood, all thought of cards forgotten. But she was the only one whose hands shook, probably the only one whose stomach heaved. The others looked curious, nothing more, as they rustled from the rooms in their afternoon silks and linens, chattering about who may have fallen and if any ladies weren't in attendance.

A warm hand touched her arm, and she looked over into Ella's questioning face. Rowena tried to summon a smile, but it wouldn't come. How could it, when she kept hearing her own strangled screams echoing back at her?

Her mother-in-law had come up on her other side and now

took her elbow. "I'm sure it's nothing, dear. Someone probably stubbed a toe or took a tumble."

Rowena couldn't work any words past her tight throat. She nodded, though even that felt wobbly and strange. They filed out of the drawing room amidst all the others, but once in the main hall no one seemed to know where to go.

Then came a second scream from one of the ladies near the stairs, and this one kept going until it became a ringing in Rowena's ears. The group shifted, and she saw the shoes. Black, serviceable. Then the stockings, revealed by a skirt bunched up far too high. Bloodied. Then the figure prone on the ground.

Gasping for a breath that wouldn't come, Rowena had to spin away. Still, the image had burned itself onto her eyes. The ripped gown, the skin already bruising, mottled, the head lolling against the floor. Was she dead? Unconscious?

Was that how *she* had looked after Malcolm attacked her? Limp and lifeless? It's how she had felt. How she still felt far too often.

A cacophony descended, swirling about her with buzzing voices and frantic screams, with a flurry of skirts and pounding feet, and then the arrival of masculine legs. Scores of them, it seemed, all encased in black or grey trousers, all looking the same. Rowena gripped the step she sat on, not sure when she'd come over here and sank down upon it. Vaguely aware of Ella's red hair at her side.

One of the ladies sashayed back toward the drawing room with a dismissive wave of her hand that snatched Rowena's focus. "It's only a maid." Disdain oozed from her voice. "I don't see why everyone is so upset."

Only a maid. Rowena squeezed her eyes shut. Obviously that woman had never employed family down on their luck. Had never sought out a maid when she needed a mother, had never preferred the company of staff to family. Obviously that woman had never felt hands pushing, hitting, bruising—if she had, she would know that station didn't protect one from horrors.

Nothing did.

Deep voices soon drowned out the women's, though Rowena couldn't make sense of what any of them said. Not until, some time later, one broke through the melee with an authoritative, "Now, see here! Everyone back, now."

She glanced up in time to see a man in a coat striding in from the open door, heard the word *constable* on Catherine's lips.

He wore a frown under his hat and surveyed the lot of them as if they were criminals all. "Did anyone see what happened? Who discovered her?"

More buzzing voices, too many speaking at once. Rowena watched the constable when she could, though it required peeking through the banister of the stairs when he passed by. He had a competent air about him, and she could just see enough of his face to watch realization dawn when he beheld the maid.

Rowena turned to Ella. "Is she alive? Did they say?"

Ella pressed her lips together.

The constable stooped down and went about something Rowena couldn't see and didn't much care to watch anyway. He'd brought others with him, men in uniforms that made the whole afternoon seem unreal.

The ladies began to drift back to the drawing room, faces pale and voices hushed. When the men started making noise about returning outside, however, the constable stood up. His face was stone. "I'm afraid all the men in the house—guests and staff alike—must remain in here until I've had a chance to speak with each one."

One of the lords whose name Rowena couldn't recall huffed.

"And why is that, sir? You cannot think that any of us would have stooped to injure some maid. And if you'll question us, you ought to question the women too. Perhaps one of them—"

"The girl appears to have been violated, my lord." The constable lifted his chin and glared at the man, who blanched. "I daresay the women had nothing to do with that, though certainly I will be questioning whether any of them heard or saw anything to help us. And yes, I think it quite likely that one of *you* would deign to treat a pretty maid so. The only question is which of you—and whether you meant to kill her or only to have your way with her."

Rowena squeezed her eyes shut and stood, though it made her head spin. She had to get away from this. Back to her room, though that wouldn't be far enough. Outside. Down the drive. Along the road until her feet were blistered and her stomach empty and unable to threaten to heave, until she was so tired she forgot who she was. *What* she was.

Only a maid. Or as Malcolm would have said, *only a woman*.

Air—she needed fresh air, a damp breeze, a chill. A hill to climb until her legs burned. Yet with the first step, her foot slipped on the marble stair and she had to grasp for the banister.

Strong hands caught her before she could so much as open her eyes. Though when she did, she wasn't surprised to see Brice there, his face etched with concern. "What's going on?" His voice was hushed, barely discernable above the din.

Rowena pulled in a breath, but she couldn't remember how to form it into words. She just stared into his dark eyes and wished he'd pull her to his chest until it all went away. More, she wished she wouldn't want so desperately to be released if he did.

He glanced to his sister. "What is it?"

Ella touched a hand to his arm and stepped down—without a stumble—to the floor. "A maid was attacked. In the worst way, it seems, and . . . and killed. I'm going to find Mama now that you're here."

He nodded, but his gaze had flown back to Rowena. Tangled with hers, her pain reflected in his eyes. If she had doubted before if he knew, there was no question now, when he looked at her in that way that said he understood exactly how this affected her. Brows pinched together, he leaned forward to feather a kiss over her forehead. "We're going home. To Midwynd." He touched her cheek, though his hand didn't linger. "Now. Go and tell Cowan to pack your things. As quickly as everyone can be mustered, we're leaving. Even sooner if we must—you and I can take the car if they're too long."

Pure gratitude swelled, and she nodded almost frantically. Leaving wouldn't change the horror, wouldn't keep the nightmares from finding her. But it would help. It *had* to help. She had to leave—*now*.

Spinning around, she scurried up a few stairs while Brice called out to his sister and mother. And then paused when that same sniveling lord who had questioned the constable charged up to him.

"You'll do no such thing!" The man pointed, his face scarlet and his chins jiggling with his outrage. "The constable just said we were none of us to leave until this is settled, and that goes for dukes as well as us lowly barons. Isn't that right, constable?"

Brice looked over to the constable, who lifted his brows and sighed. The man looked more weary with it all than anything. "When did you get back, Your Grace?"

Back? Rowena's fingers curled around the railing.

"Back?" The lowly baron harrumphed, which made his girth jiggle. "Our company not good enough for you, Duke? Did you leave us this afternoon?"

Brice didn't so much as glance as the baron. "I just walked in the door, constable. If you need to verify my whereabouts—"

"I know well where you were, and with whom, Your Grace. You and your wife may leave, though I would like to see if anyone else in your party saw or heard anything." He waved a hand and turned back to one of his men. "Assemble everyone, if you please, Barnes. The women in the drawing room, since that's where they were all headed, and the men . . ."

Rowena would no doubt leave dents in the banister from where her fingers gripped it. He'd left. After the incident last night, after their first true argument, he *left*. And why? To go to Whitby Park—she would stake her life on it. She hadn't intended to believe the gossip about him and Brook, but . . . but their first argument, and that was who he went to. Was it for the purpose everyone here would whisper about, or because of the diamonds?

Did it matter, if he would not tell her which or why or even that he'd done it? Did it matter, if the fact stood that he dismissed *her* thoughts about the jewels and then sought out Brook's opinion? Did it matter, if the curse hovered ever over them?

And had just struck again. Her stomach felt likely to heave, so thickly did the darkness choke her. He could call it whatever he liked, he could blame it on man and man's lust and greed, but it was more than that. Perhaps that was the tool it used, but it was more. She could feel it.

Before he could look her way again, she raced up the rest of the stairs and prayed she could find her way to her room. Prayed that Lilias would be within. Prayed that she could flee this place within the hour and that, somehow, the curse wouldn't follow.

And yet still a twinge of guilt struck. No one else could leave so quickly, so easily. Some not at all. Poor Catherine, having to endure such violence in her home, when all she'd wanted was to forget the past and begin her future. Would this reflect somehow on her, though she could have had nothing to do with it? Would it be another scandal she would be part of by association?

Would she, too, be haunted by the violence that was already too much a part of her life?

Rowena hurried down the corridor, turned right at the corner. She had hoped they could be friends. As she'd lain awake last night she'd kept seeing Lord Rushworth's cold, emotionless eyes. Kept feeling the shiver that had overtaken her in his presence. Perhaps he wasn't *exactly* like her father, but she knew the eyes of a cruel man when she felt them pierce her. And cruel men were always cruelest to their families, it seemed. Perhaps he had spoken words that sounded concerned for her, but the Kinnaird could do the same. He always knew what to say to outsiders to make them think whatever he wanted them to. But that never stopped him from raising a hand to her in private.

What if Rushworth was the same? What if keeping Delmore was Catherine's only means of staying free of him? What if all the lady needed was a friend who understood, who could help her escape him?

Yet here Rowena was, running away. Unable to convince her husband to be rid of the diamonds—the only things that could give Catherine independence from her brother, freedom from the debts her husband had incurred, which effectively strapped Catherine to the only financial support she would have for her and her son when Pratt funds ran too low. Unable to offer any consolation, any encouragement.

Unable to offer the same rescue that she had herself so recently been given.

Please, Lord. Perhaps . . . perhaps if she could help another in a similar situation, it would fill one of those empty places inside. If only God would grant her the strength to do so. The means.

But she could do nothing from here. She couldn't. The violence was too suffocating, the darkness too complete. She would leave now, but she wouldn't give up on her new friend. She would find a way to help her. To convince Brice to relinquish the Fire Eyes.

Perhaps, if they could use the jewels for such a noble purpose, then it would break the curse. Perhaps, if they bathed them with enough prayers and righteous tears, God would separate the jewels from the evil that had so long clung to them.

All was quiet in the guest chambers, even in her room when she entered it. No Lilias bustling about, preparing her gown for this evening. She was probably taking her tea with the other servants—though the constable's men would be interrupting them even now, most likely, and unless she had something to offer them by way of information, she would soon return. She would know Rowena would have fled up here, and she would follow.

Rowena wasn't about to sit around and wait for her. She grabbed the small valise from her trunk and opened it upon the bed. A nightgown, a change of clothes, her toilet. What else would she really need before the others could catch up? The book by her bedside, her jewelry. That would do. She slapped the lid closed and headed for the chifforobe where Lilias had hung her coat and hat—new, like everything else she had here with her. Unfamiliar.

Breath hitching, she sank onto the edge of the bed without putting the garments on. Everything had become unfamiliar—everything but the darkness in Rushworth's eyes. It had followed her. Maybe it would always follow her. Maybe she ought to be more concerned with the curse that seemed to be on *her*—to be always the victim of a man—than with the one on the jewels.

She squeezed her eyes shut. She could outrun that curse. She could, thanks to Brice. There would be no cruel father or beau awaiting her in the south. Just more newness. Sussex. Brighton. A place she'd only seen photographs of once or twice, when a friend at school had holidayed at the coast there. An estate called Midwynd that was as shrouded in mystery to her as the isles in Loch Morar of a foggy morning.

A rapping sounded at her door. Rowena couldn't bring herself to budge. "Come in."

Catherine stuck her head in, apology bright in troubled eyes. "You're leaving? I can't blame you, of course. I would too, were I you."

Rowena motioned the lady in and forced herself to her feet. "I'm sorry, Kitty. It's no reflection on you, I assure you. It's just . . . I dinna . . . I dinna do well with violence."

"I understand." Of course she did—and wasn't her tone indeed knowing, soft? Catherine swept over and clasped Rowena's hands in her own. "I promise you, I do. You needn't explain. I would leave too, if I could."

Her feeble smile made Rowena's heart squeeze. "I feel as though I'm abandoning you."

"Nonsense." Catherine gave a reassuring squeeze of her hands. "I'll be well. The constable is an able man. He'll have everything solved soon, and life will return to normal."

"Yes, but . . ." But how long would the lady's brother hover here? And how was Rowena to help her, when they'd barely known each other a few hours? She must gain her trust somehow. There would be no freeing the woman from anything until she admitted it. Rowena drew in a breath and gave her a small smile. "You should come to Brighton. It's pleasant in the winter, I hear. We could take tea together. Get to know each other better."

Catherine's eyes lit only for it to fade away in the next moment. "You're so sweet, Rowena. But your husband would be furious if I showed up in his domain." And her brother, no doubt, loath to let her out of his manipulative sight. It had taken Mother years to convince Father to let Rowena go to school—and he had snatched her home again the moment Mother was gone.

"My husband accepted this invitation, didn't he? What could he possibly say about you taking a holiday in a resort town?" And surely, once he got over his suspicions of this woman, he would see the same aching spirit that he had identified so quickly in Rowena. Surely he wouldn't begrudge her their help. Not when he had given his whole life to help *her*.

Catherine smiled and tightened her grip again. "Perhaps I shall. If so, I'll let you know. And Rowena . . ." Her smile went soft, and she let go Rowena's hands, perhaps so she could twine her own fingers together. "Rush told me what you said. About helping. I appreciate that—more than you could know—but please, don't put yourself in any danger for my sake. I'd never forgive myself if something happened to you."

"Nothing will happen to me." Rowena folded her arms across her middle. Nothing would happen just because she opposed her husband, at least. If something were to happen, it would be because he refused to get the cursed gems out from under their roof. She must convince him of that necessity. To sell them and use the money to achieve good. That would counteract the bad. Break the curse. It *must*.

Catherine sighed and looked toward the door. "Forgive me if I have little faith in any of our safety when there is a constable in my house and one of my maids dead."

The shudder wouldn't be suppressed, and with it came the

images. The blood, the stocking-clad legs, the dress hiked up too far, the shoes peeking from under the stairs.

Rowena frowned. "It was an odd place for her to be, don't you think? I mean, in such a position. If someone were to . . . to attack her . . . why there, so near everyone?"

Catherine shook her head. "One of the constable's men said it looked as though she had been in the closet beneath the stairs. It is connected to others in the bowels of the house, so who knows where the man actually found her. Their conjecture was that she had got away and was trying to go and find help when he . . . stopped her."

Sinking back onto the bed, Rowena forced air into her lungs. "That was no mere happenstance, then. Whoever did it must have followed her. Been *hunting* her."

With a snort, Catherine waved that off. "More likely is that she arranged to meet someone and then it didn't go as she planned. Hannah was always looking for a way out of her lot in life, and it could be she thought to blackmail one of the lords—or convince him to set her up as a mistress. Which I will, of course, tell the constable when he speaks to me."

So desperately she wanted the idea to bring a morsel of comfort—maybe, just maybe, the girl hadn't been violated, had gone to someone's arms willingly—but it wouldn't take hold. Rowena had been alone with Malcolm of her own will too, had wanted to give him a kiss before he left the next day. That didn't mean she had been offering any more than that. It didn't mean she deserved the treatment she received.

"I had better get back down there. I only wanted to speak with you before you left."

"I'm glad you did." Rowena pushed herself up again, though she felt so very heavy. "Would you . . . would it be all right if I were to write to you?"

The light reentered Catherine's eyes. "Of course it would. And I'll write back—though using a different name, or who knows if it would make it to you. My mother's maiden name, perhaps. Julia Rigsby."

Should she offer to do the same, for Catherine's safety? No—Rushworth would probably be glad to see his sister corresponding with her, given that Brice had the diamonds. Let it appease him. She smiled, nodded, and clamped all other emotions down until the door clicked shut behind Catherine . . . and then she fell back onto the soft mattress and let it envelop her. Closed her eyes.

A mistake. Images came. The mattress turned to stone, hard and cold, and the coat that had half-fallen on her became as heavy as Malcolm. Her collar choked her. The fragrant potpourri on her bedside table turned dank and musty, suffocating.

Fighting him off had been impossible—fighting off the memories proved even harder, for the impressions wouldn't leave her. They were always there, waiting to pounce. Would they be so always? Or would they eventually fade? The nightmares cease?

At length she managed to get her breathing under control and sat up. Her face felt clammy, but she had just moved toward the basin when another knock sounded. Lilias, she hoped. "Come in."

Brice entered, though only a step. His face was guarded, yet his concern for her nevertheless clear. "The constable is talking to our party first, but it will still be an hour or more before they will all be back to their rooms to pack. We could wait if you preferred, or we could leave now—"

"Now." Abandoning the thought of freshening up, she darted up and grabbed her coat and hat again.

The memories wouldn't leave her—but the more distance between her and all the reminders, the better. Then, when her mind was clear enough, she could focus on how to free Catherine—and for that matter, the Nottinghams—from the Fire Eyes' curse.

Seventeen

One Month Later
Midwynd Park

The screams awoke him. They weren't loud—they never were. But Brice's ears had become attuned to the sound of Rowena's face turned into her pillow, Rowena's anguish pouring out in the dead of night.

He rose, slipping his arms into the robe he'd taken to keeping draped on the chair just beside his bed. The fires were banked, the room cool. He'd grown accustomed to that too. Silently, he slid over to the door adjoining their suites—the one she kept locked, never seeming to realize he had a key. But oh, how grateful he'd been that he had, when those screams had first woken him their second night here.

The key slid surely into the lock, turned with a promising *click*. The door had squeaked that first night, but not since. Not since he'd ordered it discreetly oiled and planed. The last thing he needed was her waking to realize he was in her room, sending her into even more of a panic.

But he was the only one near enough to help. He could have

asked Cowan to take a room up here, he supposed, but . . . but it didn't seem right somehow. It *should be* a husband who gave his wife comfort in those moments she needed it most.

He knew her room better by night than he did by day, knew which board to avoid and when to sidestep the table. Knew exactly how she'd look with the moonlight trickling through the window and glazing her with silver. Small, fragile . . . lonely. She slept on her side, a pillow clutched to her middle, her face buried in it.

And she cried.

The words varied from night to night. Sometimes she muttered of mazes and closets and Hannah. Sometimes of stones and fog and Malcolm. Sometimes in Gaelic that he couldn't understand. Always with the same panic. The same fear. The same sorrow.

He eased to a seat on the edge of the bed opposite her face, though he was fairly certain she wouldn't wake up. She never did. He wasn't even sure she remembered these nearly nightly dreams. In the morning, she always seemed cheerful, her eyes without shadow as she bombarded him over and again with pleas to be rid of the diamonds.

In what had become routine, he touched a hand to her shoulder. "Shh. You're all right. They're gone." His voice barely made a whisper in the room, as light as the fingers he trailed down over her back. The same soothing motion his mother and nurse had once used to calm him after a nightmare when he was a boy. Fingers up, fingers down, a circle around. The softest touch, the softest words. There but not there.

He prayed as he continued his ministrations, as her pillow-muffled sobs quieted into gasps, then into whimpers, and finally into silence.

A stirring inside told him he must go. *Now.*

The prompting always came sooner than he wished it would. Every night it was harder to force his knees to straighten, to force himself to leave when everything within him shouted that his place was here, by her side. Holding her until the nightmares stopped coming. Everything within him told him that if they could get to know each other as just themselves, all thoughts of curses and victims and diamonds aside, then their marriage would improve. Everything, that is, but the voice of the Lord.

He stood, careful to hold in the sigh. As he had twenty times before, he slipped back through the door, slid the key back in the lock. Listened to it turn.

As he had twenty times before, he settled on his knees on the rug beside his bed and let his head fall to the mattress. "How long, Lord? How long until we sort through this? Until she lets me comfort her when she is awake? How long until she lets me be at least a friend? Until she trusts my decisions? Everything I try, every time I think I'm making progress . . ." It seemed there was a wall between them, and though she stretched from one side and he from the other, neither could cross it. Between them always loomed this curse.

He was beginning to think it real. For neither he nor his wife had any greed or lust for the jewels, and yet they were coming between them. Just as the curse said they would.

He prayed the wall would come tumbling down. But the Lord offered no assurances. No peace. No direction on what he should say to his wife in the light of day. Just that same, eternal instruction he had been hearing in answer to all his prayers lately. *Listen.*

Listen. He *was* listening, had been all through his six weeks of marriage. Listening for the Lord to reveal how to act and when. Listening for that next instruction. But it seemed he'd have to wait for it. Wait for her to understand. Wait for a time not yet upon them.

He crawled back into his bed and stared up at the darkened ceiling. He didn't like it. Not when one thing he was waiting on—Lady Pratt to make her move—could well interfere with the other. Not when he didn't know who among his staff he could trust. But he would wait, listening.

Even if it killed him.

Where in the world could he have put them? Rowena peeked behind yet another painting of yet another long-gone Duke of Nottingham. No safe. She hadn't expected one, really. There was only the one built into the wall, Brice had said, and he had made no secret of it to her—rather he had told her not to ever bother using it, because everyone in the house knew it was there.

But there had to be a strongbox or something *somewhere*. He wouldn't have put the red diamonds just anywhere, would he? He'd keep them close—she was sure of it—and secure.

Not that she intended to toss them into the sea without his knowledge, tempting as it was, nor turn them over to be sold without his permission. But maybe, if she could hold them in her hand before him, he would finally listen to her. Maybe they could have a conversation as . . . Well, not as equals. They would never be equals. He was so . . . *much*. Handsome and kind and funny, always so quick to make her laugh, to take care of her and everyone else in his charge.

But the longer they drifted beside each other, putting on a happy face in public but so very distant when alone, the more she wondered if maybe her husband didn't *want* to trust her. Didn't want to value her. Didn't want to love her.

She still wasn't enough.

If she found the diamonds, though, perhaps it would at least rouse him to anger enough that he would cease with smiling at her when he didn't really mean it.

She let out a long breath and stared down the hallway. She must be daft, to *want* her husband to grow angry, when all she'd ever wanted was to avoid her father's wrath. But anger she knew how to deal with—this smiling silence she did not.

In the distance, she could hear the murmur of the housekeeper giving a tour, the hushed exclamations of her audience as they took in the grandeur that was Nottingham. Rowena should get away before they turned the corner and glimpsed her. Only once had she made the mistake of getting caught by one of the tour groups, and oh, the *staring*. She'd felt like a stuffed pheasant on display.

The ancient dukes weren't watching over the diamonds anyway. Bidding them all farewell with a curtsy, she hurried around the corner.

And nearly screamed when she collided with Mr. Abbott.

He steadied her with a chuckle and promptly released her. "I must say, Your Grace, you're the only one I've seen who curtsies to the paintings as one would to the dukes themselves."

She grinned and motioned him to follow—no need to explain why. Mrs. Granger had turned the far corner, and her tour-guide voice echoed along the gallery. Only once they were safely a hall away did she speak. "One never knows when a ghost might be sticking around, and I'd just as soon not offend any o' Brice's ancestors."

Abbott arched a brow that said a sermon was forthcoming.

She'd already heard this particular one—thrice. Any time she dared mention something he deemed "superstitious nonsense." She tried to check her tongue against such things, but it was so ingrained in her to speak of spirits and ghosts and brownies.

Of blessings and curses. She hurried to cover it with another grin. "I'm only jesting, Mr. Abbott."

"Of course." His green eyes didn't look convinced. But he smiled and held out an envelope to her. "I was seeking you out to give you this. The post just arrived while Father and I were coming in, and I knew you'd be eager for this one."

"Annie!" She drank in the careful, childish script and scurried with barely a glance to the nearest sitting room. The red one, apparently, that was seldom used. But she found a seat in an ornate, dreadfully uncomfortable chair and ripped open the envelope.

A few more weeks! I can scarcely believe the Kinnaird and Mama said I could come, but I'm so glad, Wena. I cannot wait to see for myself all the things you've told me about. The white cliffs of the Seven Sisters—you'll take me there, won't you? And to the aquarium in Brighton. And the Royal Pavilion!

Smiling at the enthusiasm that came through so clearly, Rowena read through the remainder of the letter. The rest of Annie's want-to-dos, as well as her list of ought-I-to-brings. And there, nestled into the bottom paragraph, the news that made Rowena's back go stiff.

The Kinnaird says to tell you he hopes you are doing well and becoming comfortable in your new home. Mama always mutters that it's sure to outshine you, but he snaps at her when she says such things, going forever on about how a Kinnaird could never be outdone by some Sassenach's house. Sometimes I'm so glad I'm not a Kinnaird. Speaking of—Malcolm continues to come by at least once a week. He makes Mama nervous. She is convinced he means to harm the wee one if it's a boy and has made your father swear to her that Malcolm will be barred from the house if so.

I canna wait to leave and come see you. Do you think perhaps you could just never send me home?

With a sniff, Rowena touched that last line. She'd had the same thought, had even mused it aloud the other evening, and Brice had smiled at her and said Annie was welcome as long as her parents permitted her to stay.

When it came to her sister or any passing fancy, he was quick to indulge. But when she tried to speak to him of serious things, of the most important things—Catherine, the Fire Eyes, even whether they had ever tracked down that footman who had ransacked his room at Midwynd while they were at Delmore—he shut her out.

He did it with concern in his eyes, it was true. But a solid marriage was not built on coddling, was it? Granted, she had little experience when it came to such things. Still, it seemed to her that if they were ever to become more than strangers, then it wasn't enough to shower her with gifts, reach for her hand in public, and then refuse to talk to her of what was obviously eating him up inside.

And if he wouldn't . . . then how could she help but pull away her hand again? He said such lovely things, the word *darling* rolled so easily from his tongue. But what did he offer her that he didn't offer to everyone else too? What of his thoughts, his hopes, his fears, his heart?

She received only his charm. And much as she felt that pull that wanted to let it melt her, she couldn't.

"Good news from home, I hope?"

"Oh." She hadn't even realized Mr. Abbott had followed her in. Giving him another smile, she folded the letter and tucked it into her pocket. "The excitement one would expect of an eight-year-old preparing for her first trip."

His smile was always so warm, sincere. Free, thankfully, of any expectations. "I can well imagine. And she will be in true ecstasy when she sees the room you've remade for her."

An indulgence, that. One into which she'd poured her heart. Draping fabrics and whimsical toys, a new canopy for the bed—Brice had even agreed to have an artist come and paint a mural on the wall. The man had a few touches left, but it was utterly charming. Annie would think she'd stepped into a fairy world.

Mr. Abbott no doubt went away muttering about fanciful nonsense after he'd seen it last week.

She stood, her hand still over the pocket. "If you'll excuse me, Mr. Abbott, I have some correspondence to see to."

"Of course." He clasped his hands behind his back and followed her into the hall. Mrs. Granger never included this part of the house on the tour, so they were safe from the prying eyes of the curious. "Might I say, Your Grace, how good it is to see you feeling so at home here? I confess I feared you would feel a stranger for some time yet."

Perhaps her smile faltered, but she kept her face directed ahead so he wouldn't be able to tell. "Everyone has been verra welcoming." Mrs. Granger had even, in a fit of rapture, caught her up in an embrace.

Yes, it was easy to feel at home at Midwynd, which was all generous windows and sunlight, brilliant whites and bold colors. It was easy to take over some of the tasks Brice's mother said she was happy to relinquish. Easy, in some ways, to be the duchess.

Except when it came to the duke.

They reached the back stairwell that would take Rowena up to her private suite. She paused here and turned to give Mr. Abbott a warm smile. "Thank you again for bringing the letter to me straightaway."

"My pleasure, I assure you. Nothing makes your eyes light up like word from your sister." At that, he turned partially away. "Your Grace, I . . . You have made a home here, but I must ask. Why do you cling so to the ways of the Highlands? You are in a world now where you can flip a switch to turn on a light, but still you carry an oil lamp with you after dark. You are among friends, yet you choose to wander about alone . . . and are always speaking of these antiquated superstitions."

For a long moment she just stared at him, unable to grasp why absolutely *everyone* in England was so sure that they were right, that her opinions were useless. Her fingers curled into the soft fabric of her expensive day dress. "In the month I've been here, your precious electric has gone out three times, aye?"

Mr. Abbott sighed. "Briefly, but—"

"And the servants' hallways aren't wired yet, aye? But I go regularly to check on any ailing staff members, or to ask Cook for something, or to talk with Lilias."

His shoulders rolled back, the light in his eyes shifted. Resigning himself to a lecture, that was all. Not really *listening*. "Certainly, Your Grace. That of course makes sense. I only meant—"

"Ye only meant that you, like everyone else, want me to be something other than what I am. But I'm not, Mr. Abbot. And I ne'er will be, and ye might as well try to convince yourself and your family and your good friend the duke o' that truth."

Hands held up in surrender, he produced a tight smile. "No one wants you to be but who you are, Your Grace. I am only concerned. You speak so often of things like ghosts and fairies and—"

"And ye're so enlightened that ye know for a fact ye're right and I'm wrong, and it pains you?" She shook her head and smoothed out her skirt again. "Ye've read your Bible, Mr. Abbott, I ken ye have. So tell me. What do ye make of the fact that Saul went to a medium and called Samuel up from the dead?"

His brows knit into a frown.

"Or perhaps ye'd prefer a New Testament example, since ye're all about the modern and enlightened. So what of when the graves opened and the dead were seen walking about after our Lord's death?"

Impatience wracked his shoulders. "Your Grace, you are deliberately—"

"Or the way the disciples prayed over a handkerchief and sent it to the sick, and they were healed—proving power can be put on an object, aye?" And so curses could be too. Why were they willing to believe in the one but not the other?

Mr. Abbott sighed again. "We do not live in that world anymore."

She shook her head. "Has it ne'er occurred to you that ye dinna see these things because ye dinna believe? And worse, ye look down on those who do?"

He took a step back, contemplation flashing through his eyes.

Good. Perhaps she could make *one* man hear her anyway. She eased back a step too. "I believe in the unseen, aye. Call it superstitious, if ye wish. But I fail to see how ye can trust God to fill yer empty places when ye're not willing to grant He can still do miracles today."

While she had the final word, before he could wrap his tongue around all the pretty, high-sounding phrases he'd learned in seminary, she turned and fled. Up the stairs, down the hall, ignoring the scratchy feeling inside that said something must change soon.

What, though? How?

She arrived at the door to her small private sitting room and reached for the handle. But she paused when impressions flitted before her eyes as they too often did. Dark, fanged beasts pursuing her. Endless mazes below stairwells. Lifeless Hannah. Cruel Malcolm.

Drawing in a deep breath, she focused on the sensation that always chased these dark ones away. A soothing voice. A gentle touch.

Dreams, all. Nothing but memories of dreams, and so she would thank God that He sent fair ones to scare away the foul. Even if Mr. Abbott would likely dismiss *all* her dreams as a bunch of nonsense.

She pushed into the room. As with most in Midwynd, this one was well lit by the generous windows, and she entered to breathe in the autumn sunshine and the scent of faded roses and fresh paper. She sat at her desk and pulled out a sheet of the latter.

A few minutes later she'd dashed off a letter to Annie, promising trips to all the sites in Brighton and Hove and the nearby countryside. When the wee one arrived, Rowena would tell her all the stories Brice's family had been filling her with—of how the estate name had been taken from what they'd once called the River Ouse, of when the prince regent had stayed there a century before, while the Russian-styled Royal Pavilion was still being built.

For now, she tucked that letter into its envelope and then pulled out another piece of clean white paper. *Dear Julia . . .*

It still felt odd, after four letters, to write to Catherine under a false name. And she still sat for far too long, wondering how to forge through a letter enough of a friendship to inspire the woman to trust her. To admit that Lord Rushworth was cruel, to reach out for help.

She prayed, for the thousandth time, for the opportunity to help.

It had been ten days since she'd received a letter in response, but hopefully that meant that, as she had sworn she would try to do in her last letter, Catherine was closing up Delmore and preparing to winter in Brighton. All her guests had finally been dismissed by the constable after a prolonged week, when the prime suspect—the valet of the sniveling baron, oddly enough—disappeared from the house one night, thereby proving in the minds of the constabulary that he was guilty.

Rowena hoped they were right, and that they would soon catch the fellow. But mostly she was just glad the investigation was over, for Catherine's sake.

With any luck, she was on her way, or already in the area. In which case the letter Rowena wrote wouldn't reach her for a good while, so she didn't bother trying to put anything but niceties in it. What else could she even report?

The diamonds must be in his room—though he hadn't seemed terribly alarmed at the news that someone had searched his chamber here. He'd told her about it in the car on their way from Yorkshire, and the thought of one of his servants betraying him had upset him, but he'd not been alarmed.

Which meant he had the Fire Eyes so well hidden he was confident no thief would ever find them.

A wife might, though, were she really one. If she had ever so much as stepped foot in the chamber that had been his since he outgrew the nursery, then perhaps she would know its secrets and hidden crevices. But then, if she were wife enough to see such things, if she knew him well enough to know his hiding places, she would also be wife enough for him to have listened to and valued her thoughts on the matter.

"Julia again, is it?" Lilias's voice, sharp and terse, made

Rowena jump upon her seat and spin. She found the woman standing just behind and to the side, hands on her hips and a frown on her face. "I've kent you since ye were a newborn bairn, Rowena, and ye've never been friends with a Julia. So kindly tell me why ye're writing to one of a sudden."

She turned back to her innocuous letter, wondering what it might be like to have a servant who was only a maid. "Ye dinna ken every friend I ever made, Lilias Cowan. Now I'm in England, I thought to renew an old acquaintance from school."

She had, in fact, received letters in the last few weeks from nearly *all* her old classmates. As soon as announcements and articles began popping up in newspapers and periodicals about how the most eligible bachelor in all the empire was no longer eligible, "friends" had popped out of the woodwork.

She needn't look to see Lilias's incredulity—it came through clear as crystal in her grunt. "One of the lasses ye said were so cruel to you, who never wrote back when ye first left Edinburgh? And why should ye be bothering with such a one now?"

"It's been a long time. Bygones and all that." She'd sent them all very brief, cool acknowledgments of their felicitations. And had decidedly *not* extended invitations to any of them to drop in on her at Midwynd if ever they were in the neighborhood.

This time Lilias's silence spoke as eloquently as her grunt had. Only after a long moment did she sigh. "I worry for you, lass. Ye've this shining new life, and rather than grasp it with both hands, ye're scurrying around behind yer husband's back."

"I'm doing nothing wrong." Only trying to protect them all. Even if her stubborn husband wouldn't budge, wouldn't listen. Wouldn't let go the diamonds that he seemed to think he was protecting for Brook.

It always came back, it seemed, to Brook.

Another sigh that sounded akin to the winds gusting over

Loch Morar. "Ye said to fetch you at four so ye could bathe before the soiree this evening."

The sun dimmed. Though at least tonight's event was only a musical soiree. No dancing, no supper, limited time for her to be snubbed by the elite of Sussex who, despite all Brice had promised on their way home, had been no quicker to accept her than Catherine's friends had been in Yorkshire.

Lilias's hand landed on Rowena's shoulder and gave it a light squeeze. "What is it, lass?"

"Nothing. I'm ready for that bath." She stood, leaving the letter to "Julia" unfinished, and followed Lilias from the room.

Please, Lord. Please let Catherine come soon. She needed a friend in the worst way.

Eighteen

The housekeeper's parlor was warm from the fire crackling in the hearth, the conversation filled with laughter. The upper staff were lingering over their sweet—and why not, with the masters all out for another evening in Brighton? They had no urgent tasks awaiting them, no guests to see to. Lilias enjoyed the moments of peace and smiled along with the others over Mrs. Granger's tale of the six-year-old lad who had gone into a tantrum during the tour that afternoon.

Davis laughed at the housekeeper's description, going so far as to toss back his head.

"It wasn't funny," Mrs. Granger said, though she smiled. The woman smiled a full three hundred percent more than had the housekeeper at Castle Kynn. But then, she wasn't in service to Douglas Kinnaird. It surely made all the difference in the world. "I knew Her Grace was in the gallery, and I cannot tell you how I feared his mum wouldn't get him calm by then and he'd end up ripping right down the hallway and stomping on her toes, so unhappy was he to be there."

More laughter twined around the table, and Mr. Child sent his sparkling gaze toward Lilias. "She's a curious one, isn't she?

I swear every time I turn about, Her Grace is studying some new stone or mantel as if it contains the keys to paradise."

Lilias returned the smile. In part at thought of Rowena . . . and in part because the butler put her in mind, in some way she couldn't quite name, of her Cowan. "She was as a girl, aye. But having never been away from home much, she soon learned all the secrets there were to learn in the castle. Must be a bit of an adventure for her, having someplace new to discover." Away from the iron fist of the Kinnaird—and the threatening shadow of Malcolm.

"Such a sweet young woman." This came from the dowager duchess's lady's maid, Lapham. She toyed with one of the berries that she had proclaimed herself too full to eat, swirling it about in the cream. "It's no wonder His Grace decided so quickly to wed her. Something about that hesitant demeanor of hers that just makes a body want to pull her close and pat her head."

Mr. Child snorted a laugh. "Yes, Lappy, I'm certain His Grace wants to *pat her head*. Exactly the response of a young man when faced with a lovely young lady."

Lapham slapped at the butler with her napkin—something no one ever would have dared do to McDonnell in Castle Kynn.

Mrs. Granger chuckled. "I've certainly been praising the Lord this month that His Grace fell for someone like Her Grace and not one of the many debutantes who have visited over the years and measured the whole place as if fitting it for new drapes."

Mr. Child looked to the ceiling. "This from the woman who sobbed for a week straight when she heard that the Baroness of Berkeley was betrothed to the Duke of Stafford."

Lifting her chin, Mrs. Granger obviously fought back a grin. "Well, I didn't know at the time that Her Grace was waiting for him in the Highlands, did I? Only that the most charming young lady who had ever stayed at Midwynd had got away. That one would have kept us on our toes."

"That one would have given me a heart attack." Mr. Child splayed a hand over his chest in illustration. "And His Grace was wise enough to know it and take pity on me. Far better that he chose Her Grace."

Perhaps it was that perpetual amusement in the butler's eyes that reminded Lilias of her late husband. The way he could be so serious when facing the under staff or the masters or the public, but was so quick to turn a jest behind closed doors.

"It was her eyes that got him." Davis raised his glass in salute. "If I hear him reference 'those silver eyes' one more time . . ."

Lilias smiled into the laughter. She'd always thought Rowena's eyes beautiful—but at the castle, where Douglas shared the feature, no big to-do had ever been made over them.

"Ach, no. 'Twas the accent," Mr. Child said in a fair imitation of it, his gaze drifting for only a split second to Lilias. "There's nothing like a Highland burr, aye?"

Would it not have been so obvious, she would have pressed a hand to test her cheeks and see if they were as hot as they felt.

Mrs. Granger grinned at her. "I daresay—"

"Mr. Child! Come quick!" One of the footmen—there was a matching pair of them, twins, and Lilias hadn't yet learned how to tell them apart—burst into the parlor. Was it excitement or horror on his face? "Humphrey has returned—Old Abbott caught him sneaking round the back, trying to get in."

Because the others all leapt to their feet, Lilias did too, though she hadn't a clue who Humphrey might be. She turned to Lapham, who was the closest to her. "Who is—?"

"The footman who ransacked the duke's room while we were away and then took off." Lapham tossed her napkin to the table and scurried out with the rest of them.

Lilias followed, though more slowly. From the thunderclouds in everyone's faces, they took it as personally as the duke had that one of their own had betrayed Nottingham.

And they said only Scots had such allegiance to their clan.

The group spilled into the kitchen, where the aging steward held a protesting young man in a chair by the scruff of his neck.

Mr. Child headed straight for his office. "I'll ring the constable."

"I've rope to hold him until he gets here." The other twin footman—or the same one?—bent to tie the lad's legs to those of the chair, amidst some colorful cursing from the captive.

Old Abbott looked about to box the boy's ears. "Watch your tongue, you fiend, there are females present."

As if a thieving traitor had such sensibilities—and he proved it by spitting on the floor, in the direction of Mrs. Granger. "Let me go, ye ol' badger. I'll not talk—not to you, not to no constable, not to no one."

"You will if you know what's good for you." Mrs. Granger huffed—and made a show of stepping directly on the spittle on the floor. "To think that we fed you, clothed you, accepted you as one of our own. Didn't His Grace even send extra home to your family last Christmas, when he heard your mum hadn't enough for a goose?"

The lad's eyes burned—but not with the life most of them here boasted. No, it was a dark fire in them. One Lilias had seen often enough to recognize. He sneered. "Oh, yes, a fine Christmas goose they bought too. Surely that kept them from wanting all the rest of the year. All thanks to the duke's eternal generosity."

This time Old Abbott *did* deliver a cuff to the lad's ear. "You'll speak with more respect of your betters, boy. And it isn't his title that makes him so—it's his common decency. Something *you* are surely lacking. To stoop to thievery—"

"I didn't steal *nothing*. And well you know it." Yet it wasn't disappointment now in his gaze, or shame. Certainly not shame. 'Twas . . . victory.

"And did you come back to try to remedy that?" With her hands on her hips, the tall housekeeper struck an imposing figure indeed. "Or are you daft enough that you meant to beg your job back?"

He didn't shift, didn't lift his chin, didn't try to square his shoulders—which were now rolled back, his wrists being bound behind the chair. Yet somehow defiance settled upon him like a cloak. "Humphrey Umstot doesn't *beg*."

Old Abbott folded his arms over his chest. "Then why are you here? To find whatever it was you were looking for before?"

Humphrey didn't answer. Didn't twitch. Just curled his lips up in a mean little smile that curdled the cream in Lilias's stomach.

Trouble had come to call. And she hadn't a clue how to protect Rowena from it this time.

Brice had no idea how he'd managed to lose his wife this time. He'd been determined to keep her hand firmly on his arm all evening, but for when they were in their seats. And he certainly hadn't needed the whisper from his mother or sister to tell him to do so—though they'd taken it upon themselves to give said whisper anyway. As if he couldn't see for himself that the usual Brighton and Hove visitors and residents hadn't received Rowena all that warmly.

Jealousy, Mother had said with a nod.

Pure viciousness, Ella had pronounced.

Some combination thereof, he had decided. And he would have been happy to have stayed home of an evening instead of taking part in the usual post-Season engagements that had peppered their autumns and winters in the past.

But Rowena had vehemently objected, had insisted that their routine wouldn't be disturbed for her sake. That Ella ought to get to enjoy this first year she could take part in such events.

If Rowena would stand as straight and speak so boldly with silk on her shoulders and jewels around her throat as she had that morning in her day dress and old, worn shoes, then no young lady in Sussex would ever dare speak ill of her.

Dash it all, where *was* she? He'd only stepped out for a minute, to find the lavatory. And Ella had given him a nod to assure him she would take over the watch. So why was he seeing Ella's brilliant red head without the soft brown curls that should have been by her side? It was one thing for Ella to lose herself every time she took a turn but quite another for her to lose his wife when Ella herself hadn't so much as budged from the aisle between the two blocks of chairs set up for the recital.

"The best soprano I've heard since Collette Sabatini was touring England twenty years ago," an older gentleman said as Brice brushed past.

"At the Royal Pavilion," a lady was saying to a different group, swishing her fan in front of her face. "Tomorrow."

A flash of light on fair blond hair caught his eye. Made him freeze. It couldn't be—could it? He only knew two blondes of that shade, and Brook wouldn't just show up at a random soiree in Brighton without notice. But surely, *surely* Lady Pratt wasn't so audacious.

Of course she was—he knew she was. But if she were in town, he would have heard. He paid people to keep him abreast of such things.

A lady in a peacock green dress shifted out of the way, proving that yes, indeed, it was Catherine, Lady Pratt, on the arm of her brother. Dash it all—and they were talking to Rowena. He sidestepped the people in the aisle, nearly tripped over a chair, but he managed to keep his smile in place. His face clear. His posture casual as he approached. Though it took every ounce of willpower he possessed to keep his gait easy and relaxed as he joined their cheery little group and claimed his wife's hand.

"There you are, darling. Lady Pratt, Lord Rushworth, good evening—I didn't realize you were in the area." He smiled, but they weren't either of them stupid enough to believe he meant it. And Rowena obviously realized it too, given the way she stiffened.

Rushworth nodded a muted greeting. "Evening, Duke."

Lady Pratt gave one of her sickeningly sweet smiles. "We just arrived in Brighton yesterday, desperate to get away from all the nonsense over that maid—I'm sure you understand. I, of course, wrote you to let you know that the primary suspect had fled, and . . . well, when I wrote your direction upon the envelope, I thought Brighton would be just the thing to clear it all from my mind."

She was good—he'd give her that. The perfect intonation to convey both regret over the maid and weariness with it all. Her back remained straight, her fingers didn't grip her brother's arm too hard. The only indication of her true purpose that he could note was the way her attention drifted, for just a moment, to the diamond-and-ruby collar necklace Rowena wore.

None of the gems were large enough to be the Fire Eyes. She had never seen them, but surely her parents had told her of their size when they instilled in her the idea that they were hers by rights. He pulled Rowena a few inches closer to his side. "Have we received a letter from Lady Pratt, darling? I don't recall seeing one—though I have been praying that the tragedy at Delmore would be quickly resolved."

Rowena sighed. "Aye. I told you about it last week. Or tried to."

Dread sank in his stomach. Last week . . . she had indeed brought up Lady Pratt—and he had cut her off with a rather frustrated claim that he was tired of hearing about her.

Blast. It was no wonder his wife held herself always aloof. Why had he not listened? The dread turned hard and twisted. *Listen*. So often he had gotten the impression he must, but he had assumed it a command to listen for the Lord's whisper.

What if, instead, the Lord's gentle command had been bidding him to pay attention to what his wife had been trying so hard to tell him? If he had failed to hear her on the simple matter of the resolution of matters at Delmore, what *else* had he missed? It wasn't the first time he had misinterpreted the Lord, it was true . . . but it may have been the direst.

He had always prided himself on being attentive. How could he be so with everyone else and fail so miserably with his wife? He was a royal dunce.

Lady Pratt laughed and waved a hand. "Oh, isn't that always the way with husbands? Our words just drift right over them sometimes." Her gaze drifted yet again to the necklace.

Brice drew his wife back a step, even as he smiled. Catherine wouldn't try something so obvious as snatching the thing right from her neck, but he didn't know how quickly she might be developing subtler plans. Though the diamonds and rubies were also family jewels, his mother had never really worn them, always preferring the Nottingham rubies when a gown called for red. Which meant that no one really *knew* they were family gems, so Catherine may well think he'd had the piece commissioned to hide the jewels.

On the one hand, it made him glad he'd instead hidden them among the iconic ruby set—and that thanks to his wife's unpierced ears, they never left her room. On the other hand, it made him wish he'd only draped emeralds and sapphires and topaz around Rowena's neck these past weeks. He should have known Catherine would show up at some point and see his gifts.

He looked down at Rowena. Shadows drew hollows under her eyes, and her face was otherwise pale. The company? Perhaps, but he didn't think so. "Are you feeling all right, darling?"

For once, the only thing in her eyes when she looked up at him was gratefulness. "Not really. I'd thought it just a light headache, but I'm afraid I'm feeling quite peaked now."

"And here I've been chattering at you!" Catherine surged forward, abandoning her brother's arm in favor of taking Rowena's other one. "Forgive me, Duchess. We can catch up another time. In fact, why don't you join me for tea tomorrow? I'll send the direction for the house I've let. If you're feeling better, of course."

She actually left her a graceful way out of the invitation, which gave Brice pause. Though Rowena offered a polite smile and, after a hesitant glance at Lord Rushworth, said, "Thank you, Kitty. I do hope I feel well enough."

His stomach went tight. She wouldn't listen to him if he tried to warn her against going—and why should she, when he hadn't listened to her? But he had to convince her not to go. Even if she thought Catherine needed help, thought she could offer it, he could surely appeal to her distrust of Rushworth.

He must. He *must* keep her out of their clutches.

"Go home and rest." Catherine patted Rowena's arm and then stepped back beside her brother again. "So good to see you this evening, Duke."

He forced his teeth to unclench. Forced niceties to his tongue. "And you, my lady. I hope you enjoy your stay in Brighton."

Her lashes fluttered down, but not before he saw the malicious gleam in her eyes. "Oh, don't worry, sir. I'm sure my visit will provide everything I seek."

From anyone else, he would have assumed she meant rest and reprieve. From Catherine . . .

He steered Rowena away. "Would you like to go home?"

"Could we?" She pressed a hand to her stomach. "I hate to pull you away from the concert."

"There will be other sopranos, or this one another time. Your health is far more important." Seeing Ella still stood where he'd left her, he headed that way. Mother was there too. Perfect. He interrupted the ongoing conversation as unobtrusively as possible, speaking only to his mother. "Rowena is unwell, so we are going home. Would you like me to send the carriage back for you, or—"

"Oh, poor dear." Mother turned her full attention on Rowena, and her brows knit. "We'll all go. No point in making Jones drive back out in this rain. Is it a headache?"

Rowena nodded. "In part."

"I'll call for the carriage and our wraps." He lifted Rowena's hand to place a kiss upon her knuckles before he stepped away. Since she would only let him do such things in public, he would take full advantage. The moment watchful eyes were no longer upon them, she would turn away with that perpetual sorrow draping her shoulders.

Until the nightmares seized her again, anyway.

Fifteen minutes later they had all climbed into the carriage under the umbrella Jones held for them, and after another half hour they pulled into the drive at Midwynd. Though glad for Jones's sake that his family had come home with them, he rather regretted the chatter they provided. He had to speak with Rowena about Lady Pratt and Lord Rushworth. And now, unable to have accomplished it on the drive, he would have to see her to her room for the conversation.

Perhaps he ought to wait for morning and pray she was feeling better? No. If she chose not to join them for breakfast, she could well avoid him until teatime. So after they'd dashed into the house and turned over their wet overcoats and capes and hats, he took her hand again. "I'll see you up."

She didn't bother arguing with him, given that he saw her to her door after nearly every outing.

Mr. Child appeared, clearing his throat as he approached. "Pardon me, Your Grace. But Humphrey returned while you were out. Old Abbott caught him sneaking in. The constable has him in custody in town, though my understanding is that thus far the boy has said nothing beyond cursing us all."

Rowena shuddered under his hand and turned her wan face up to his. "You'll need to see to this. I'll—"

"No." Was that disappointment in her eyes? He added a soft smile. "Morning will be soon enough to go back out. Constable Morris will have it all in hand. Thank you, Mr. Child. Did he cause any disturbance this time?"

"No, Your Grace. Not beyond stirring up the staff, who were all outraged at his audacity. We can't think what he was about, trying to get back in."

An excellent question. Another search for the jewels? Was his purpose only to upset them? Was it mere coincidence that he showed up just as Lady Pratt and her brother came to town?

Brice pasted on a smile. "Let us pray the answers are forthcoming—tomorrow. For now, I'm afraid my wife is feeling under the weather, so if you'll excuse us, I'll see her to her room. Good night, Mother. Ella."

Behind them, the others continued to discuss the Humphrey situation, but Brice ignored them all. He'd spend some time praying about it—again—tonight. Let all the questions swarm then. For now, Rowena. *Lord, give me the words to talk to her. Give me the ears to listen.*

She tugged her hand free of his under the guise of lifting her skirt for the stairs. "Ye needna see me up, Brice. Go and tend to this. I know ye must."

"There's little I could do just now anyway. And you're more important."

"Am I?"

He snapped his gaze to her, expecting her to have shrugged off her peakedness in favor of pique. But no, she still looked ill, tired . . . and emotionally weary on top of it all.

Well, no wonder. How could he have been so blind to how he was treating her? He'd thought . . . He'd thought her wrong. Himself right. And so, all his prayers had been geared toward convincing *her* to listen to reason. "Of course you are." Yet he knew she didn't believe him. "I am very sorry if I haven't made that clear."

She didn't even look at him. "Oh, ye've made your feelings *verra* clear. Ye've let me ken exactly where I rank in your affections."

"Rowena." He halted her on the landing, leaping before her to block her way. Wishing her eyes betrayed anger, uncertainty, disdain—anything but the disappointment that made them dull as smoke. "I've made a mull of this, but it wasn't by intent. I want . . ." He wanted to hold her. To draw her to his chest and let their hearts beat in rhythm. To be given the chance to know her well enough to understand the sparks flitting through the smoke of her eyes.

To make her nightmares go away—for good.

With a shake of her head slight enough to prove the headache was still present, she stepped around him. "Why pretend anymore, Brice? I'm not what ye want. I'll never be what ye want. I'm not . . . enough. Ye've no respect for me."

"That isn't true! I realize I haven't listened as I should, but it's only because—"

"Because ye know best?" She picked up her pace, though her face went even paler. "Oh, aye. Yer judgment is perfect. Except, apparently, when ye judged that ye had best marry me."

"Rowena." He felt the puppy nipping at her heels as he followed her toward the family wing, mentally going over every memory from the past six weeks. All the times he had reacted from that basic assumption—he was right, she was wrong. All the times he had followed it up with a charming smile, thinking . . . what? That charm and flirtation would be enough for a marriage? That she would overlook where he ignored her thoughts if he showered her with attention in other ways?

He was a blithering fool.

"Darling, please. I've acted an idiot, and I'm sorry. I thought . . . I thought I was giving you time to see my side. I didn't realize I was dismissing yours so fully." They reached her door, though she didn't even glance at him. "I won't do the same now. I swear to you. But we *must* discuss the danger you would be in if you went to Catherine's tomorrow with Lord Rushworth there."

He expected her to shut the door in his face. Instead, she left it wide behind her. He took that as an invitation, though he was careful to advance no more than two steps inside when he saw Cowan wasn't within. The last thing he wanted was to put her in a panic.

She finally came to a halt with her back to him, her hand pressed to her dressing table. "So ye grant he's the problem, then? Not her?"

"I . . ." He paused to draw in a careful breath. "I readily grant he is a problem. He is dangerous. I am not, however, as convinced as you that Catherine would be any better were she free of him."

"Why will ye not let me help her?" Tears burned her eyes, and panic burned her voice. The sweep of her arms was tremulous.

"Ye canna ken what it's like to be always under the control of a man like that. Ye canna. But ye helped me, ye got me free of Loch Morar, of Malcolm, of Father. Is that what you want to hear from me, Brice? Ye saved me. Rescued me. My noble prince, as Ella would say. But it means nothing—*nothing*—if I canna stand on my own. If I canna help another."

Given a century, he wasn't sure he'd understand this woman. But in that moment, he knew for a fact that if he spent a century trying, it would be years well spent. The vulnerability made him want to shelter her forever . . . and the steel made him want to kiss her until it melted, and melted him along with it.

Somehow he doubted that would go over well just now. He took the time to draw in a long breath and let it soothe the questions. Let it back out slowly, measuring the moments. "I appreciate that you want to help. I admire it. I would love to see you give aid to others who have suffered as you have. It is just that I am not certain Catherine is one of those women."

She shook her head, looking so very different from the first time he'd seen her. No hiding behind anyone now, no ill-fitting clothes, no arms folded protectively over her stomach. No bruises, thank the Lord above, marring her perfect ivory skin. Now she stood in the finest silk, her spine straight.

Her eyes flashed, lightning dissipating the smoke. "I grant that ye saw *my* truth quick as a flash. But ye're not infallible, Brice. Ye're blinded, in this case, by yer dislike for her husband. But Lady Pratt is just a doting mother and a widow." She tugged the gloves from her hands with enough force that he half expected the seams to rip. "One too long whispered about and judged. Too long reviled. One who could verra well be a fine woman if taken apart from the men in her life."

Cowan slipped into the chamber from the dressing room entrance, but Brice kept his focus on Rowena. "I realize you see yourself in her. But, darling, this is what she does. She appeals to one's vulnerabilities in her deceptions."

Rowena slapped her gloves onto the table. "Why can ye not admit that perhaps ye're wrong? Why can ye not see that she's a victim, an outcast—"

"An *outcast*?" He reached for the magazine his mother had handed Rowena earlier that day, flipped it open to an advertisement. "Does this *look* like an outcast to you? Would anyone pay her to pose and say that 'Fuller's Biscuits are the *only* biscuits I serve with tea' if she were reviled? She has made herself into a celebrity, Rowena, and she revels in every bit of it!"

She stared at the colorful rendition of her supposed friend, and a crack appeared in her wall.

He strode a few steps nearer, now that Cowan was in the room to help her feel safe. "Please, darling. Please don't be taken in. This is her skill—convincing whomever she's with that she is like them, that she commiserates, that she's the perfect friend. But she'll betray you, just as she did Brook when—"

"I am not *Brook*!" The questions, the crack he'd seen forming, snapped away, replaced by the anger he'd wished for five minutes earlier.

Stupid request, that.

She slashed a hand through the air. "One would think you would be the first to realize that, given how little you esteem me and how highly you esteem *her*! Tell me, darling, how much of the gossip is true? Exactly how close are you? Is it merely that you were in love with her once, or was your little trip to Whitby Park from Delmore that day not so innocent?"

Cowan gasped and dropped whatever it was she'd had in her hands. "Rowena Kinnaird, mind yer tongue!"

Now was not the time to correct the name, nor the fact that a lady's maid oughtn't to be using it. He didn't even glance

Cowan's way. Instead, he covered the rest of the distance between him and Rowena, stopping just near enough to reach over and tip up her chin. Just near enough that she'd be able to see the fire in *his* eyes too.

"Look at me, Rowena." He waited for her to obey, though she did so with a clenched jaw and rebellion in her eyes. And that was his fault too, wasn't it. His wife shouldn't have to wonder whether he was in love with another. His wife should be secure in his affections. But she wasn't—and how could she be? He may have spoken of finding love at some point in time, but then he had let this diamond business remain always between them.

No longer. It was time to realign his focus. To fall in love with his wife, and to convince her she could trust him with her heart too. "I have *never*, either before her marriage or after, been romantically involved with Brook. Look me in the eye and believe me. She is a dear friend, as is Stafford. Nothing more."

She averted her face, knocking away his hand. "It doesna matter."

Pressure built up in his chest. "Of course it matters. *You* are my wife, Rowena. You, no one else, and that is just as it's meant to be."

She tugged off the ruby-and-diamond ring that matched the necklace and threw it to the tabletop. It bounced, slid, shot off the table and onto the floor, where Cowan scurried after it. "What does that even mean to you, Brice? That I must obey you, even when ye insist on something that everything within me screams is false? Does it mean I must fall in love with you just because ye compliment my eyes and hold my hand in public? Ye dinna trust me, ye dinna believe me, yet ye seem to think that ye've only to deliver a few lines of flattery like ye do with every other woman in Britain and have me falling at yer feet with the rest of yer adoring throng."

She slashed a hand through the air, her cheeks going pink over the pale. "Well, ye'll not find me there."

His determination sizzled into frustration. "I don't want you at my dashed feet, I just want you to give me half a chance to be something to you other than a stranger."

Rowena fisted her hands and looked ready to stomp. "Maybe I dinna *want* ye to be anything but a stranger! I dinna *want* to get sucked down into yer infernal charm, unable to see anything but what ye want me to see. I'll make my own decisions, my own friends, be my own person—"

"Good! If you recall, I told you weeks ago that I *wanted* you to be your own person. So why in blazes you now think otherwise, I cannot discern!"

Her color rose still more. "Because ye willna accept me for who I am! I can only be the Duchess of Nottingham now, not permitted to wear wool or speak with a burr or believe what I have spent my whole life believing. I canna turn around without your oldest friend lecturing me on superstition or you calling me daft for believing in curses."

His usual gut reaction beckoned—spin away, refuse to engage in what he deemed a ridiculous argument. Hold tight the explanation, the understanding he was content with. But a quiet *Stay* resonated within him, and this time he didn't think he was misunderstanding. He shoved his hands in his pockets to anchor himself. "I love to hear you speak. I care very little what you wear, so long as you have what you need and are happy in it."

She snorted. "Your society disagrees."

"Yes, they do. And you can either conform to their expectations or defy them. Whatever your choice, I will stand beside you. But I think it the other that really bothers you, and that *is* my fault. My failing. Your opinions and beliefs are worth no less than mine."

"Dinna—" She loosed a laugh that sounded half sob. "Dinna agree with me—when we both know ye dinna really—just to sound . . . *perfect*."

Stay. He clenched his hands within his pockets. "I know well I'm not perfect."

"But ye *are*, and I hate you for it! For yer perfect life and yer perfect faith and yer perfect plans. I hate you for yer perfect friends and yer perfect confidence and—and I *hate* you, and I wish I'd never met . . ."

The color drained from her cheeks, her shoulders hunched forward, and she pressed a hand to her mouth. A second later she was dashing toward the lavatory attached to her dressing room. The sounds of retching soon filtered through the door.

Brice sighed as the need to stay built, pressed upon him. He pinched the bridge of his nose and motioned Cowan to follow her mistress as she so obviously wanted to do. "Go ahead, see to her. Help her change. I'll be back in ten minutes."

"Yer Grace." Cowan, frown etched in her forehead, slid the ring onto the table. "She didna mean what she said. She doesna hate you. She just . . . She has so many years of hurt stored inside."

Though it took effort, he forced the strain from his countenance, forced a partial smile. "I know that—I assure you. And I'm not returning to argue with her more. I'm returning to prove to her she's wrong. That I'm ready to listen."

He was going to stay.

Nineteen

Never, in a lifetime of humiliations, had Rowena ever felt as miserable as she did with her head hanging over the toilet and the bitter taste of her words to Brice overshadowing the sickness. Tears trickled down her cheeks as her stomach heaved again, and the cool, familiar hands that smoothed the curls away from her face did little to bring comfort.

"There now, lass. It'll be over soon."

No, it wouldn't. The vomiting, perhaps, but not the bigger problem. She squeezed her eyes shut and sagged against Lilias, spent. "I'm a fool."

"Aye." Lilias was never one for indulgence. "But he'll forgive you for it. And ye need to let him. Rowena . . ." Letting out a long breath, Lilias held her tight and rested her cheek against Rowena's head. "Dinna be like yer mother, lass. Dinna let yerself be so eaten up by regrets that ye do something glaikit."

Mother . . . foolish? Rowena could barely even call her mother's face to mind anymore, but for when she pulled out the old, faded photographs. Nora had been beautiful, once upon a time. The enchanting American heiress out for an adventure, visiting the land her grandparents had fled in the clearances.

By the time Rowena left for school, Mother had been as faded as those pictures.

Was that her future, too, if she stuck to this course? "I'd never kill myself, Lil. Ye needna worry."

"'Tisn't the leap from the cliff I fear you taking—it's the years of waste leading up to it. The decision yer mother made to blame her husband for her own choices."

Rowena sat up, though it made her stomach roll again, and turned to see Lilias's face. "How can ye speak so? My father suffocated her. Took the life from her long before she took her own. He beat her—"

"I ken what he did, and I'll make no excuses for him. But yer mother was no saint, Wena. That summer when he first lost his head with you both—it wasna just the visit to the duchess that set him off so. 'Twas who *else* was at Gaoth that year."

Else? Try as she might to send her mind back, Rowena could remember no one but Ella, Charlotte, and an eternal parade of guests that were all faceless to her. "Who?"

Lilias pressed her lips together and shook her head, but then she sighed. "An old beau, from the States. He came to Scotland with the Carnegies, and when the Nottinghams and Brices paid their obligatory visit to Skibo, he came back to Lochaber with them. Because he kent yer mother was Lady Lochaber and wanted to see her again."

But Mother wouldn't have . . . She wasn't so foolish that . . . Surely not, under Rowena's very nose, with Lilias—her husband's own cousin—attending her . . .

She lunged forward to retch again. All those times Mother had sent her to Gaoth, all those days Rowena had happily skipped along at Ella's side—what had Nora been doing? Rowena spat out the last of the acrid bile. "Why? Why would she do that? Father doted on her then. On both of us."

Lilias passed her a washcloth and stood to run water into a glass. "She was never happy in the Highlands, lass. Not after the first year or two—after the romance of it wore off. She wanted her home. Her family. Threatened time and again to go back to them. That's when yer father started cutting off communication. She pushed him for years, and then when he came home that summer and found the Nottinghams there . . . When he realized her old flame had been in his castle . . . Well, ye know the result of that."

"Aye." She could still remember the utter shock the first time his fist struck her, when she heard Mother sobbing in pain from the other room.

Taking the glass from Lilias, Rowena held it for a long moment as the older woman turned her to pluck pins from her hair. She stared into the clear water. "But . . . why did he take it out on me?" The words emerged as the barest whisper.

Lilias dropped a hand to her shoulder and squeezed. "He was blind with rage, Wena. And then . . . then he wanted to make you stronger. Wanted to ensure ye were like *him*, not yer mother. And that's how his father taught him."

"But I'm not like him."

Lilias sighed and plucked out the last of the hairpins, her fingers then moving to the buttons down Rowena's back. "Well and good. But dinna be like her either, lass. Dinna blame yer husband for everything wrong in yer life. His Grace is a good man. Better than yer father ever was. And he'd never betray you as ye accused him of doing. As yer parents did each other."

Cold air snuck beneath the silk. She shivered—and couldn't seem to stop once she started. She set her water down and nearly tripped as she stepped out of her gown. Her fingers fumbled the hooks on her corset.

"Poor lass. Ye look ready to fall over. Here, put on yer nice, warm flannel."

She did—though it did little to warm her. Praying her stomach remained steady, she headed for her toothbrush and powder.

Lilias paused in the doorway with the silk in her arms. "Rowena . . . yer husband's coming back in a few minutes. When he does, remember . . . ye're not yer parents."

Coming back? Her stomach roiled, though thankfully it didn't heave again. She brushed the bitterness from her mouth and hurried as much as she could back to her chamber. Turned off the electric lamp and crawled into bed with only the fire in the grate for light. Perhaps if she pretended to be asleep, he'd go away. She couldn't face him now, with those words still echoing in her ears.

"I hate you. I wish I'd never met you."

Her chest hurt as much as her stomach. It wasn't true, had never been—certainly not in the moment when he stood there and apologized for all she had resented these weeks. Why had *that* pushed her to say such terrible things? Why could she deal better with his disregard than with humble attention? Nothing made sense anymore. Not her marriage, not her life . . . not what she thought was a budding friendship. It was all a muddle. Reasons and motives and goals all mixed up and as confused as Ella in the maze.

It had seemed clear for that one moment, that day at Whitby Park. When Brice had told her to spite them all by being happy. By thriving. By discovering who she really was. But Malcolm would gloat if he could see the distance between her and Brice. And Father—Father would probably agree with her. Father would say she shouldn't trust a Sassenach not to disappoint her.

But since when did she think her father's thoughts?

The door clicked open, shut again. Lilias? No, the step was too heavy. She squeezed her eyes shut and tried to regulate her breathing. She didn't want to give Malcolm reason to gloat . . .

but she needed time. She couldn't face Brice yet. Not yet. Just a few more hours—a night between her cruel words and seeing their effect in his eyes. That was all. In the morning she would face him, and the consequences. In the morning, she'd be ready to talk through it all with him. Settle things.

The mattress shifted, and her spine went tight, despite her attempts to remain relaxed. He would know she was awake. She needed to stay calm. He wasn't going to insist on any marital favors tonight. He never had before, and he certainly wouldn't with her having just lost her dinner a few minutes before. He wouldn't. She could—*must*—stay calm. She would simply ignore him, and he would eventually be content that she was well enough and go away. He would . . .

A touch on her shoulder, so soft she barely felt it. And her tension eased. A brush down her back, back up, around, and peace edged out the mounting panic. The darkness that she hadn't realized was pressing closer slid away. Breathing became easier.

Tears pressed against her closed eyelids.

"Shh. You're all right." Why did the whisper, as soft as the touch, settle into her mind like the refrain of an old hymn? "Rest, my darling. Just go to sleep. I'm right here."

A mere minute ago, his words would have sounded like a threat. Just now . . . the promise of it brought those tears squeezing past her defenses. "Why are ye being kind to me?" Her voice came out quiet, too, and husky with her tears.

He settled more, behind her, his fingers keeping up that blessed caress on her back, brushing aside the curls in a way that made her scalp tingle. "You're my wife. I just want to comfort you. To be here for you."

Now she *had* to face him, to see him, despite the fact that turning over dislodged his touch—and put her in a position she'd never been in before. Lying face-to-face with a man, their noses only inches away. As she turned she could see the golden flecks in the center of his eyes, the dark fan of lashes that no man had the right to boast. What she couldn't see was any deception in their depths. Any dark intentions.

But there was pain there. Caused by *her*. And how did she dare claim she wasn't like her father?

With a quick breath to bolster her, she lifted her hand and rested it against his strong jaw. "Brice . . . I dinna hate you."

He moved his head just a bit and kissed her fingers. "Rowena . . . I don't hate you either."

It shouldn't make her smile . . . but it did. "I'm sorry I said all those hurtful things. I just—"

"I know. Dinna fash yerself." He said it with a burr, and with a wink. Then he made a show of turning onto his back and making himself comfortable on top of her blankets. "I can't blame you for being annoyed with me, given my utter perfection—perfection *is* annoying, isn't it? Though in your list, you left off a few vital items. Like my perfect handsomeness. And my perfect dancing. And my perfect horsemanship. My perfect teeth."

She should have been alarmed at him making himself so comfortable. Instead, she laughed and grabbed a pillow with which to bash him in the face. He caught her wrist, used it to pull her down onto his chest . . . and stilled that quick burst of panic with those magical fingers against her back again.

She felt rather like Father's hunting dog—an utter monster until one found that place he loved behind his ears, and then he turned to a pile of mush. Brice, it seemed, had found a way to do the same to her. And she obligingly melted into his side and closed her eyes to better enjoy the touch. "What're ye doing?"

His hum vibrated in his chest, under her ear. His scent, fresh and crisp, filled her nose—nothing like the musk Malcolm always wore. He positioned her arm for her, over his chest . . . and yet it felt more like a request than a command.

"I'm settling in," he said softly, "for a night with my wife. In which I solemnly swear that I will not be swayed by any amorous intents—my goal being solely to provide comfort to her and, if all goes well, convince her that I'm not an utter cad."

She rested her cheek against his chest too and tried to convince her stomach to stop churning so. It was distracting her from the music of his caress. "Ye oughtn't. Ye could catch whatever I have."

His fingers stilled, rested for a moment, turning their position, just like that, into an embrace. Then he lifted his head to press a kiss to hers. "I might. But do you know what?"

She opened her eyes and shifted her head enough to look at him. He was smiling a soft, beautiful smile.

"It'll be worth it."

It was her heart, not her stomach this time, that lurched.

Brice awoke, not to muffled screams in the middle of the night, but to the soft light of dawn and an arm gone numb. An arm gone numb, to his delight, from the head resting upon it. He wiggled his fingers but otherwise decided to suffer the discomfort.

Definitely worth it.

He traced a finger over the arm draped across his stomach and smiled. He may end up sick—Rowena had run to the lavatory three times before finally falling asleep just like this—but it was a price worth paying. She hadn't just tolerated his presence; she had snuggled against him and taken comfort. She had reveled in the innocent touch upon her back. She had somehow, without really saying anything at all, opened up.

Thank you, Lord. Thank you. Now if you would please help me not to wreck it all. . . .

Rowena's breath hitched, and her eyelids fluttered open. Smiling, Brice kept up the soft tracing of his finger, praying it would ease her into realizing he was still with her. When she smiled back at him, his heart swelled until it nearly hurt. "Good morning, darling."

She actually, miraculously, snuggled closer. "Morning."

"How are you feeling?"

"Mm." Her eyes closed again. "Dinna ken yet. Though at the moment I'm inclined to say I'm quite lovely."

His fingers found her long locks and twined through them. The hot iron's curl had loosened overnight, leaving naught but a hint of wave. "No question about that."

She rewarded him with a sleepy grin. "Even charming first thing in the morning. Maybe I *would* hate you, if I didna prefer, just now, to be charmed."

"Shall I press my luck, then?" He turned onto his side so he could face her . . . and find a new position for his tingling arm. "Beautiful as you always are, I've never seen you more so than now." With her defenses down. Her face soft, absent of fear or caution. If he *really* wanted to press his luck, he would lean over that tiny, enormous inch and touch his lips to hers.

Her hand, which had settled on his back when he turned, slid over his shoulder to land on his cheek. The eyes she opened shone with vulnerability. "Did you really never love her? Or anyone else?"

"Never. My heart is waiting for you to claim it, Rowena."

"I thought I . . . or *didna* think I'd . . ." She sighed and tucked her head under his chin. "I like having you here. Beside me. I didna think I would, but . . . I canna recall the last time I slept so peacefully."

Was that an invitation to stay there again tonight? Perhaps . . . But he'd let her issue it explicitly rather than declare it again himself. "No nightmares last night."

She drew back, brows arched in question. "How do ye ken about the nightmares?"

The urge to tell her was too strong, too directly opposed to his good sense to be anything but the Lord. He wrapped the loose curl around his finger. "You cry. Scream into your pillow. I can hear you nearly every night."

Her eyes went wide. "I *scream*? Loud enough to wake you?"

"I'm a light sleeper." *Tell her.* That voice that sounded like his own thoughts, only stronger. He pressed his lips together, aiming a silent *Are you certain, Lord?* heavenward and then giving himself a mental shake. Of course the Lord was sure. Brice was the one plagued by uncertainty. He pried his lips apart though. "It began our second night home. I thought . . . I thought you were being hurt, so I rushed in. You were well, of course. Just the bad dream. So I . . ."

Her brows lowered, her eyes relaxed, the corner of her lips tugged up. "You did what you did last night. Soothed me. That's why it seemed so familiar, so . . . comfortable."

"I couldn't just let you cry, alone. But I swear to you, darling, I never would have taken advantage, I never—"

"I know, Brice. Ye're a good man." Her hand slid down to toy with the front of his shirt. Hopefully she couldn't detect the way his heart pounded beneath it. "How often? Do I have such nightmares, I mean?"

"Two nights out of three."

"And do you always . . . ?"

He nodded. "I can't bear to let you suffer it alone."

"All these weeks I've been focused on what ye weren't doing—and yet ye've been doing whate'er ye can to help me."

She shook her head and splayed her hand over his heart. "I'm an oaf."

He leaned over but angled his face up to kiss her forehead rather than her lips. "You've reason to be upset with me. I dismissed your concerns because I didn't want to entertain them. But I was wrong to do that, darling. I just pray you'll forgive me, that you'll give me a chance to listen now, and to win your heart."

"I'll do better too. I promise. I just . . . even wanting to be with you, I dinna ken when I'll be ready to . . ."

"I know." He wouldn't lie and say it would be easy to have her in his arms as he did last night and not want more—but he would never, never make her aware of any struggles. He swore that silently to her. She had pain enough to overcome on the subject, and she didn't need his impatience added to it. "I promised you at the start that I wouldn't push you, that I'd wait as long as it takes for you to be ready. That hasn't changed."

"Thank you. But I . . . I'll try. I'll stop avoiding you. And I . . . I'd like it if . . ." Her nostrils flared. "If you would . . ." Face washing pale, she levered herself up, darted to her feet, and ran to the lavatory with a hand to her mouth.

Poor thing. Brice levered himself up too and swung his legs over the side. He would wait for her to reemerge, see if he could wheedle the end of that sentence from her. But then he had best get to his own room and ready for the day.

He had a visit to the constable to arrange.

Rowena emerged five minutes later, pale and shaking, and made him seriously reconsider that plan for the day. She sank down beside him on the bed and leaned into him, making no objection when he slid his arm around her.

She moaned into his shoulder. "I guess ye've no worries about me trying to have tea with Catherine today."

A topic they had avoided last night after the initial quarrel. Brice ran his hand up and down her arm. "This isn't exactly my preferred way of winning an argument."

"'Tisn't yer doing. And I had best think on what ye've said about her. It's just . . ." She sat up straight only to let her shoulders slump and lift a hand to rub at her face. "I could swear I saw something in her. Something hurting."

"Perhaps you did." How was he to know, really, what had gone on in her life? How was he to know, for that matter, whether people like her and her brother were born or . . . or made? He may well have blinders concerning them. Blinders his wife didn't share. "If you are right, we need to figure out what it changes. What our actions should be. Though perhaps that conversation ought to await the return of your health?"

"Aye." She attempted a smile, quickly fading, and scooted farther onto the mattress, under the blankets. "You had better see to that business with the constable."

He must. But . . . "I could stay with you."

Despite the circles around her silver eyes, soft light lit them. "I appreciate that. But ye have duties. See to them, then come and check on me. And . . . and if ye'd stay here again tonight . . ."

He really did hate that such a crucial victory came at the cost of her health—but he would take it, however he could get it. "I was hoping you'd ask." He leaned over and pressed a kiss to her cheek. "And you know, just to throw this out there . . . you needn't be sick to enjoy my delightful company."

Her answer was a grin that almost eclipsed the obvious discomfort she felt, and a playful push against his shoulder. "Get on with you. But hurry back."

He left the room with a grin that no doubt made him look the fool. But what did he care? His wife was beginning to like him.

Half an hour later, he was dressed and groomed and praying he'd find the breakfast room empty. He didn't much care to answer any questions about why he looked so happy when his wife was ill and there was a traitorous footman in the clink in town.

No such luck—though Mother and Ella were nowhere in sight, Abbott was pouring himself a cup of coffee . . . which was odd. The Abbotts rarely dined with the family at Midwynd, unless there was business to be discussed. They usually kept to their cottage at the corner of the property for all their meals.

His old friend greeted him with a nod. "Forgive me for making myself at home—Father asked me to await you and let you know he's ready to go into town whenever you are."

Though his tongue demanded a leisurely cup of tea to start his day, Brice settled for grabbing a muffin. "You needn't apologize for taking a cup of coffee. He is at your house?"

Abbott sighed and waved him to a seat. "Have your tea first—he is having his. We weren't expecting you to rise for another twenty minutes or so."

That would have been his usual time to come down, yes. But he didn't usually have an employee held in jail. Still, he hated to interrupt his steward's morning ritual, so he poured himself a cup of tea. And determined to drink it quickly. "Will you be going with us, Abbott?"

"I see no reason to. I thought I would put some more prayer and study into the topic of my first sermon from my new pulpit. I cannot make up my mind for the life of me." Abbott settled into the chair across from Brice's. "They mentioned in the kitchen that Her Grace is ill. Nothing serious, I hope."

Brice would have done better to skip the tea, after all—it tasted like water to him. Maybe he was already coming down with something too. "Let's pray not. She was ill several times last night and already this morning, but she slept well, at least."

His friend seemed to think nothing of the implications that Brice had been there to witness it. But then, why would he? No one beyond Davis and Cowan could know that he was a complete stranger to his wife in those respects.

"Everyone is in an outrage over Humphrey—or *most* everyone. A few of the under staff have been mute on the subject, and Father and Mr. Child have agreed to keep a close eye on them all." Abbott regarded him with an unrelenting stare that made his bite of muffin turn to dust. "On the one hand, it seems foolish to assume anyone else is involved. But on the other hand, something more than what we know is obviously at work. It appears Humphrey was searching for something particular, to return as he did. Have you any idea what?"

Brice washed the tasteless muffin bite down with a sip of the tea.

Abbott leaned forward. "Nottingham. You have been acting oddly for months. Perhaps it is merely your new responsibilities weighing on you—I was happy to assume so. And then you stumbled into marriage. But there is something more, and I'd have to be a dunce not to see it. Tell me, please. Tell *us*, so that we can help. Father and Mr. Child need to be aware of it if more servants are likely to be bought and convinced to partake in such activities."

Brice sighed and shoved his plate and cup aside. Old Abbott had a head start on him—surely he was about done with his breakfast. "They do, yes. You're right."

His friend regarded him with lifted brows when Brice stood. "But not I? You'll not tell me what's going on?"

It wasn't the brows that gave him pause. It was the hurt in the eyes beneath them. "Ab, it isn't that I don't trust you—on the contrary. But I don't want to pull you into this mess."

"I would pray with you. For you. Support you."

Brice passed his fingers through his hair. "You've a new life you're planning, one you've worked hard to achieve. You don't need to be distracted with my troubles."

Abbott looked far from mollified. Indeed, his movements were jerky with anger as he stood, abandoning his steaming cup as well, and strode to the door. But once there, he paused, turned. And speared Brice through with righteous indignation. "I thought that was what friends did—carried each other's burdens. But perhaps I always thought more highly of our friendship than you did. Perhaps you don't need my feeble prayers added to yours."

"Geoff—"

"Do you think I haven't faith enough to handle the hardships of life? That I do not believe God bigger than anything we might face—the seen and the unseen?"

Where was this coming from? "I have never doubted your faith."

"Just the worth of my support? Perhaps we are not truly friends, then. Perhaps I was merely taken in by your affability. Perhaps *you* don't even know where your charm ends and genuine regard begins."

He would have retorted—but it was the second time in less than twelve hours that someone had made that accusation. Either Abbott had been listening at Rowena's door last night—highly unlikely—or there was some truth to the allegation that he relied too heavily upon his personality. He sighed and pinched the bridge of his nose, squeezing his eyes shut for just a moment.

But when he opened them again, Abbott was gone.

He took a moment to pray, though he wasn't sure what he was praying for, exactly. For his own blinders to be removed. For his pride to be torn down before it could destroy him—though his wife and friend had done a bonny good job at that already.

For his relationships to be strengthened through these travails, not weakened.

And for Abbott's faith—whatever that little peek into his insecurities had been about. Not unlike their conversation before Brice's wedding, was it? Was he questioning his calling to the pulpit? Now, after working so hard for so long?

Brice shoved himself up and strode out of the breakfast room, the house, and across the acre to the steward's cottage. His knock was answered by Old Abbott's ancient mother, who greeted him with a wrinkled smile and waved him in. Her son still sat at the table, newspaper before him, Miss Abbott by his side.

She greeted him with a smile too. "Morning, Your Grace. How fares your wife this morning?"

It still felt odd when his childhood friends called him that. But he managed a tight smile. "Still unwell, I'm afraid."

"I'm so sorry to hear it. Ella and I were hoping to convince her to join us this morning for our archery practice."

Old Abbott grunted. "So long as you keep it to archery. Yesterday I caught my son teaching them both to handle a pistol—for which I owe you my apologies, Your Grace. I told Geoff he oughtn't to have let Lady Ella handle a gun without your permission, but he said he didn't think you'd mind. I don't know where he would come by such a notion."

It was a notion he had never considered. But now that he did . . . given the current circumstances, it might not be a bad idea for the ladies to know how to defend themselves. Heaven knew it had saved Brook's life when she was attacked in her stables almost two years ago. He didn't advocate the use of violence, but if one found oneself with a weapon pointed at one's head, one ought to know how it worked. "It's a wonder she hasn't asked me to learn before, honestly. I don't mind at all, if Geoff would like to continue the lessons. He has always been a thoughtful, thorough, careful marksman. I trust no one more to give such instruction."

"See, Papa?" Miss Abbott gave her father a cheeky grin. "I told you it was not a problem. Which is good, because I'm shaping up to be an excellent shot—as good as Geoff, he said."

Brice chuckled. "Then remind me not to get on your bad side."

Old Abbott sighed. "Very well, I'll make no further complaint. Only promise to be careful, Stella." He stood, folding his paper and setting it aside. "Shall we then, Your Grace?"

"Indeed." He smiled his farewell to Miss Abbott. "Try to stay out of trouble, Stella-bell."

She dimpled. "I would, but what fun would that be?"

Old Abbott shook his head and then reached for a hat to cover it with. "She's going to be the death of me," he said as they stepped out into the brisk September air. "I swear one of these days I'm going to step through my door to a telegram saying she's run off to Gretna Green to elope with some chap I've never even met."

"Only if he's rich enough to justify it!" Miss Abbott shouted after them.

The second shake of the man's head didn't surprise Brice . . . but the lack of amusement in his eyes did. "Were her mother here, God rest her soul, she would never permit Stella to act as she does. But the harder I try to keep her in hand, the worse it gets."

Brice frowned and led the way to the stables. He considered suggesting the car, but the roads were a muddy mess from last night's rain, and his Austin would likely not make it down the lane. "I daresay you have nothing to worry about, sir. For all her jesting, she is a good girl with a solid head on her shoulders."

"I pray you're right, Your Grace—but fear you're wrong. I don't know where she came by these grandiose ideas of marrying so far above her station, but I've a terrible feeling it'll lead her to heartache."

It was on the tip of Brice's tongue to observe that the world was changing, that social lines were beginning to blur—what with nobility posing for postcards and advertisements and more and more often marrying out of the genteel class. But the lines in the man's face were those of a father concerned for his daughter's heart more than her social status. A flippant answer would do nothing for such worries.

While they waited for the carriage to be brought around and then rode into town, they spoke of the more menial matters of the estate—the ones Old Abbott could recite in his sleep and which Brice was finally beginning to get a handle on. But as the countryside gave way to shops and houses, silence fell.

He hadn't seen the former footman since they left Midwynd in the spring. And the man had only been employed with them for six months before that. But that wasn't what made him seem almost unfamiliar when they arrived at the jail and the constable led them to a cell. It was the way he looked up at Brice with hatred in his eyes. Definitely not something he had noted in the fellow's gaze before.

He nodded to Constable Morris. "Could I have just a moment to speak with him?"

"You can, Your Grace. But he likely won't say much—he hasn't to the rest of us."

Brice smiled and made a show of leaning against the bars, casual and comfortable. If he weren't mistaken, the particular flavor of revulsion in Humphrey's eyes would take umbrage at that. Perhaps it would goad him into opening his lips.

Indeed, the moment the others had shuffled off, the young

man sneered. "His Grace himself deigned to come, did he? Ought I to feel important?"

Brice chuckled. "Let's cut to the chase, Mr. Umstot, shall we? We both know who hired you to do what you did—though no doubt you'll go mum again rather than give their names. But you've chosen the wrong side. Whatever they've paid or promised, I could have given more."

He must play to his greed. More, try to figure out what Catherine's plan had been—had she paid Humphrey simply to upset him . . . or had he actually been looking for the Fire Eyes?

Humphrey leaned back against the wall, arms folded across his chest. "Think so?"

"Mm. But do you know, especially, why you've made a grave error?" Brice tipped his head down. "Because never, in a lifetime, would you or anyone else find it."

Humphrey sat forward, hands braced now on his knees. "Oh, don't be so sure, Your Grace. They've already found them."

Them. Brice had deliberately said *it*. So he must have known what it was he was looking for, to realize it wasn't just one thing.

Never mind the claim itself. To that, Brice just grinned. "Funny. I happen to know otherwise."

What had he ever done to this man, that he snarled at him with such revulsion? "Didn't say they'd been handed over yet, did I? But they will be. They've another on the inside, ready to meet."

He wasn't about to show any concern over that, though his mind immediately began to run through the list of every servant in the house—and, blast it, why were there so many? No doubt the whole point of telling him this was to send him home in a panic to dig out the Fire Eyes from their hiding place . . . where some other traitor would indeed be waiting to seize them.

Fat chance.

He straightened, slung his hands in his pockets, and smiled again. "Good luck to them all, then, and to you. We've only trespassing to accuse you of, so I imagine you'll be out of here soon enough." He turned, as if he hadn't a care in the world. He wouldn't threaten. He wouldn't brandish his power.

Humphrey already knew exactly who he was, of what he was capable. He had deemed the Fire Eyes worth the risk.

So be it. Let them all imagine his reactions. Let them guess at his next move. He'd surprise them all.

He'd do absolutely nothing. Nothing but wait for them to move and be ready to pounce . . . as soon as he figured out who else in his house was waiting to betray him.

Everything all right, Lily?"

Lilias looked up, shocked to hear the familiar version of her first name from anyone but Rowena—but upon spotting Mr. Child a few steps away in the moonlit slumbering garden, she smiled. First that he would approach her, and all the more that he would call her by a given name. She sat on a bench that was cold as the night air, her fingers folded in her lap. "Just worrying o'er the duchess is all."

"Still sick?" He took a few slow steps toward her. When she motioned him to the seat at her side, he moved far more quickly and settled beside her with a lovely muted smile.

"Aye. It's been five days. The poor lass ought to be better by now." But every morning Lilias entered to the sounds of Rowena retching. Every day saw the duchess so exhausted and spent that she could do little but lie about. Every evening His Grace had to practically kick Lilias from Rowena's chamber, assuring her he'd take care of her.

He did—she knew that. Rowena, despite her misery, smiled whenever she spoke of him now. Her eyes lit up when he came into her room. That, at least, was good to see. This was not the way she would have chosen for it to happen, but seeing them fall in love brought a balm to Lilias's heart.

It couldn't quite eclipse the worry, though. Rowena had never been sickly. What was causing it now? If it didn't relent, if she wasted away, if it was some disease she caught in England, where Lilias had forced her to come, she'd never forgive herself.

"Probably nothing to worry about." Mr. Child leaned back against the cold iron bench and grinned—actually grinned. "I daresay you would know better than I if it's good news rather than bad, but the timing's right, isn't it? It was always right about now that my late wife, God rest her soul, would start feeling so poorly."

Lilias just stared at him for a long moment. She already knew of the late Mrs. Child, of the four children who were grown and off making their own way in the world. She knew exactly what he meant by *good news*.

And it made her own stomach clench up so badly *she* nearly retched. "I hadn't considered that." Because Rowena had bled. And had never lain as a wife with His Grace. She *couldn't* be with child. . . . Except the bleeding had been so short. Painless, Rowena had said. Light. And it should have come again in the time they'd been here. Should have, but it hadn't.

Heaven help them.

Warm fingers closed around her frigid ones. "Forgive me if I've overstepped by saying such a thing. I only meant to offer a happier alternative to the duchess having a serious illness."

"Think nothing of it, Mr. Child." Lilias's smile wasn't as forced as she'd expected it to be. Not given how perfectly right it felt to have her fingers tucked in his. How long had it been since a man had held her hand? Just held it, to give comfort and perhaps a touch of pleasure? Over two decades—that was how long. Since Cowan had clutched it in his last moments. Since she'd been a lass herself, no older than Rowena. But oh, with so many life lessons stored inside already, and four years of a happy, if hard, marriage behind her. "It would indeed be a far happier reason. But I canna be sure, ye ken."

He studied her for a long moment in the moonlight, making Lilias infinitely aware of how frazzled her hair no doubt was, how plain the wool jacket she'd put on. How faded the serviceable grey dress beneath it.

How very different from when she sat in the moonlight with Cowan as a lass, so sure of her own beauty and charms. When there were no lines on her face, no sagging in her figure, no grey in her hair. When she hadn't felt the fool for entertaining notions of romance.

She turned her face up to see the smattering of stars studding the night sky.

Mr. Child didn't release her hand. "You've said you've served her family since before she was born. You must care deeply for her, as I do for His Grace and Lady Ella."

Lilias smiled up at the winking diamonds above. "Even more, I'd wager. She's a daughter to me, the only one I've ever had. I daresay I mothered her as much as Lady Lochaber ever did." She'd cried for her when the Kinnaird lashed out against her. More, certainly, than she did for Nora. And more than Nora ever did for Rowena, so busy was she crying for herself.

"Her Grace is a lucky young lady, indeed, to have you. And I daresay she has no fear of you taking a position elsewhere."

Was that a question? A probing? An asking if she would be here as long as the new duchess? Lilias smiled up into the night. "Nay, she's no fear of that. She may perhaps occasionally wish me elsewhere, as every young woman does her mother, but we have got each other through some difficult times."

"Well." He squeezed her hand. "Let us hope that ahead of you lies far more good times than difficult ones. And new life to love rather than sickness, eh?"

"Aye." But even as she agreed, she had to fight back the sting of tears. Their every action since the wedding night had been based on the assumption that there was no babe. No need to lie to His Grace. No need to rush Rowena into the marriage bed.

But if she *were* with child . . . there would be no lying now, even if they wanted to—which she knew Rowena hadn't to begin with. There would be no choice but to throw themselves on the duke's mercy. Nothing to do but pray he chose to protect Rowena rather than toss her out.

He liked her, Lilias could see that. Might be coming to love her. He was kind, and he was gentle. He was *good*. But he was still a duke. He had a long family legacy to uphold.

"Look at you, shivering. You must be chilled to the bone, Lily." Mr. Child stood and tugged her up with him. "Come inside, have a cup of chocolate before you retire."

There was nothing to be done about the other just now anyway. Rowena was safely tucked in her husband's arms. His Grace was soothing her, taking care of her. Tomorrow she would speak to Rowena, first thing. Examine the possibilities with her. Tomorrow they would consider the consequences. Tonight . . . tonight, let them enjoy what ease they could.

Tonight Lilias would let herself revel, if only for a few minutes, in the security of a warm hand around hers, in the fact that he didn't let go as they walked back to the house. Tonight she would let herself dream that she'd be at Midwynd for years to come, have a chance to discover whether maybe a second chance at love waited with this good man at her side.

Tomorrow she could well find herself out on her rear, a weeping mistress by her side instead.

Brice awoke on his fifth morning in Rowena's room with words echoing in his heart.

Love her.

The command was clearer than any he had heard before, resonating. Replaying itself. Turning into a veritable refrain within him. *Love her. Love her. Love her.*

Her hair was fanned out over his chest, a few strands tickling his nose. He smoothed it down, lingered a bit over the long silken locks. And wondered why the Lord thought to wake him with such an insistent command when he'd fallen asleep eight hours before wondering if that was the word for how he felt about the fragile, strong woman in his arms.

Love her.

Usually the Lord's promptings brought peace. Just now, it brought irritation. He didn't have to be *told* to love her. He was leaning that way all on his own. Which the Lord obviously knew. So *why*?

Rowena shifted, turning onto her back. Yes, his stomach went tight when he looked at her, saw the curves that he'd so quickly grown accustomed to feeling pressed against him all night. Not that desire was love. But when paired with shared laughter, with whispered dreams of *someday* like they'd taken to falling asleep to, with a baring of the heart . . .

Love her.

It was going to be a long day if the Lord kept this up. Brice sat up, careful not to disturb Rowena, and slid out of bed.

"Brice?"

He must not have been careful enough. Her voice still sounded sleep heavy, though—perhaps she could catch a few more minutes. He leaned over and pressed his lips to her cheek . . . and then to her lips, because he couldn't help himself. "Go back to sleep, darling."

Instead, she looped an arm around his neck and kissed him again, softly. "Dinna leave yet. I dinna want the day to start. Perhaps if it doesna, I willna be sick again."

Well . . . he had nothing all that pressing awaiting him this morning. Nothing that wouldn't wait twenty minutes, anyway. Just more names to go over with Old Abbott and Mr. Child, servants' histories to examine. Hints to find as to who might be in the pay of Catherine Pratt.

Though he still needed to get up, if only for a few minutes. "I'll be right back, I promise." A quick trip to the lavatory—and perhaps a minute with his toothbrush and powder, if more kissing was promised. "Two minutes."

She grinned sleepily up at him and let her arm fall. "I'll be counting."

Chuckling, he raced for the lavatory. The *Love her* refrain hammered him all through his ablutions though, which nearly wiped the grin from his face.

By his estimation, he was at a minute forty when he moved to the doorway again, humming as he stepped from her lavatory into her dressing room.

The voices from the bedchamber brought him to a halt at that second doorway, though. Cowan, the outer door clicking shut behind her even as she said, "Oh, good, His Grace isna here. I must talk to you, lass."

Rowena levered herself up in bed, brows knit. "He'll be right back. What is it, Lil?"

The maid perched on the edge of the bed, her back to Brice, and gripped Rowena's hand. "It's this sickness. Were it the flu, it would have passed by now. But if it's . . . that is . . . The bleeding, Wena. Perhaps it was too short. Perhaps it didna mean what we thought. This sickness—it's just how yer mother was, when she carried you. I fear ye may yet be with child."

The floor fell out from beneath his feet. The walls closed in, pressing his chest until he could scarcely breathe. But the dagger—the dagger was Rowena's gaze, which flew straight to him and pierced his heart.

Cowan twisted, spotted him. Her cheeks washed as pale as Rowena's. "Yer Grace—I . . . she . . . It isna what it seems."

He held up a hand to stop the tumble of words and took one more step, just enough to emerge from the dressing room and into the bedchamber. But he couldn't bring himself to step any closer. Not just then.

Love her.

His nostrils flared. But the facts still managed to crystallize in his mind. "You were attacked."

Not her fault. He knew that. Wouldn't judge her. Not for the violation, not for the result.

But for the lies, the tricks . . . the quick plot for a marriage to cover up those consequences—his chest burned at those. And how many prayers had he offered up, that if he were right about his suspicions, this consequence wouldn't be an issue?

Love her.

Rowena's hands shook as she gripped the blanket—looked to the floor, as she hadn't done around him in days. "Aye. As ye figured out long ago."

"When?" He hated to ask, didn't really want to know. But he had to. Whatever he did, whatever decisions he made, he had to know. "When did he . . . ?"

Cowan covered her mistress's hands with hers and raised her chin. "Just a fortnight before you arrived, Yer Grace. Near enough that no one would know the difference, no one would think it not yer bairn."

Not his bairn. No, not his babe. Some monster's, who would attack a girl who'd dared to trust him. Who would hurt her, abuse her, misuse her. All no doubt to force her to marry him. Oh, but Lilias Cowan and Douglas Kinnaird had outsmarted the monster, hadn't they? "That was your plan all along. Force her to marry me so you could pass off the child as mine."

God, why? When I prayed, when I did as you urged me, when I married her to protect her? Why?

Cowan went even paler. Rowena's shoulders slumped, and tears slipped down her cheeks. Accusations, those.

Love her.

His wife shook her head. "I didna ken if I was with child or not, Brice. I didna, I swear to you. And I didna have any intentions of lying. If I *had* kent, I would have told you. I couldna keep that from you."

No, not when she was too terrified of a man's touch to allow the full cover-up Cowan no doubt had intended.

"Then our wedding night . . ." Her breath was heavy and tremulous, like it had been each morning when the sickness—oh, that wily sickness—struck. She pressed a hand to her stomach. "I thought it my monthlies. I did."

Love her.

His insides felt hollow. Burned out.

Cowan rubbed a hand over Rowena's back. "We're at yer mercy, Yer Grace. I beg you—"

"No." Tears streaming unchecked—either at the topic or from the sickness she seemed determined to hold in check—Rowena scooted away from Cowan, to the edge of the bed. "No, ye canna ask him to raise this child, Lil. Ye canna. I will raise the babe. I'll love it. I'll not judge it for its father . . . But it's too much to ask of Brice. He deserves better than this, better than me."

Love her.

Pressure mounted behind his nose. His choices were few and stark. He could divorce her, and make it clear in a court of law that the babe she carried could not possibly be his. That meant exposing what she had suffered to the world. Exposing that their marriage had been, thus far, a farce. Preserving the Nottingham line.

He could put her away quietly, a separation but not a legal one. Not have to face her, but still support her and the babe. Still be bound as the legal father to the child, which meant if it was a boy, that boy would still be his heir. The next duke.

He could keep Rowena as his wife but insist she go away somewhere to give birth to the child, and then find a home for it, praying no one ever found out. Force her to abandon her baby.

Or he could let the deception do its work. Let the world think the babe his. Be the child's father. Be Rowena's husband.

Love them.

Not since his own father lay lifeless on the steps had he so wanted to weep.

"And Joseph was minded to put her away quietly . . . but an angel appeared to him in a dream—"

He shook away the old story. He was not Joseph. How could the Lord expect him to be? Why, why would He ask him to do this, when all he'd ever wanted was a wife to love him, his own children darting about his feet? To preserve the centuries-old legacy of Nottingham and keep the duchy in the Myerston family for another three hundred years? If he'd known seven weeks ago what was truly at stake . . .

Would he have disobeyed the Lord? The Lord, who knew the moment that life was conceived?

Brice's eyes slid shut. She was his wife. Was this meant to be his child?

Love them echoed on within him.

He swallowed, and it felt like a rock stuck in his throat.

Pay attention. He saw her as she had been that first day at Gaoth, little more than a shadow. *Protect her.* The terror, the devastation when Kinnaird had wrapped his hands around her throat. *Trust her.* The hope that had dared to bloom in her eyes as he took her away from Lock Morar. *Listen*. The disappointment he'd caused every time he ignored her concerns. *Stay with her.* The way she'd begun smiling at him these last few days. *Love her.* Those endless eyes, regarding him a moment ago with a resignation that said she expected the worst. That she still thought it was all she deserved.

Brice forced himself to draw in a deep breath and let it seep back out. He wanted to slam into his own room and let the injustice of it all fill him. He wanted to scream that he'd done his best to protect her, but this was too much. He wanted to tell that voice inside to shut up, to leave him alone, to let him be angry and hurt for once.

Maybe it would be excusable. Maybe it would be understandable.

So why did the echo of her words break his heart even more than the realization of what they'd done?

He opened his eyes again and looked at her. At the defeated slope of her shoulders, at the hopeless bend of her neck. The pale cheeks, the fingers twisting around themselves. Just like the first day he'd met her.

No—she wouldn't turn into that girl again. Not on his account. If he did that to her, he'd be no better than Malcolm Kinnaird. No better than Lochaber. And he *had* to be better—because that wasn't who he was, and because he had sworn not a week ago that he'd prove that very thing to her.

He abandoned his spot and moved to the bed, forced his knees to bend, his hand to reach out. He settled on the side of her away from Cowan and rested his hand on her knee. Rowena looked up into his eyes, hers shining silver behind the magnifying tears.

Cowan muttered something in Gaelic. Then in English, "I beg you, Yer Grace, make no hasty decisions. Consider what ye'll do."

He didn't spare a glance to the woman but rather kept his focus on his wife. "I don't need to consider it." He did, of course. It would take hours of prayer and consideration to figure out how to live out the promise he was about to make. But that was between him and God—no one else. "I would never punish you for another's sins, Rowena. I'm your husband. I will love you. Protect you. Remain at your side. And I will be the best father any child could ever want."

Her arms came around his neck, and she sobbed into his shoulder. "I'm sorry. I'm so sorry. I didna ken. That it was possible, aye, but . . ."

He splayed a hand across her back and held her tight for a moment. But he wasn't quite as strong as his words. He drew away with a shaky smile and pressed a kiss to her forehead. "God knew. He knew, and He put us together. He told me to marry you." And he intended to have a long conversation with the Lord about that when he was alone.

He needed to be alone.

Rowena sniffed and pressed a hand to her stomach. "It willna be easy for you. I ken that. But I . . . I thank you for being willing to try."

Brice summoned a smile. "I certainly have some digesting to do. But we will be all right, darling. We'll be a family. We'll be happy together."

She nodded, nostrils flaring. Then, apparently unable to control it any longer, she made a mad dash for the lavatory.

Brice sighed, rubbed at his face as he stood, and turned toward the door that connected their suites.

"Yer Grace."

He paused but didn't turn more than a quarter of the way around. Just enough to see Cowan twisting the bedsheet between her hands.

"Ye're smart enough to ken it was me who planned it all. I'll not lie and say otherwise. Rowena ne'er would have done such a thing. Ye're a good man to forgive her, accept her . . . but I understand if ye willna offer the same to me. If ye . . . if ye want me to leave."

And take from his wife the one person who had loved her all her life? He wasn't such an ogre. Even if he had no desire to talk to the woman at that moment. "You would do anything for her—I realize that. And I even appreciate it. But Cowan . . ." He met her gaze, felt his spine stiffen. "Don't ever lie to me again."

"Aye, Yer Grace. Ye have my word."

It would have to do. With a quick step, he passed through the door to his room and closed it softly behind him. Davis wasn't within yet, and he didn't ring the bell to call for him. He just slid into the nearest chair, braced his elbows on his knees, and buried his head in his hands.

He had been so sure that he wouldn't have to worry about this, even having discerned what he did. So sure the Lord wouldn't punish him with another man's child. And yet here he was. Barely making any progress as a husband, but now he would be a father.

Centuries of expectation settled on his shoulders. Centuries of the same bloodline, passed down from duke to duke. Why, why must he now accept that Malcolm Kinnaird's son could well be the next Duke of Nottingham? Was it wrong of him to pray the babe was a girl instead, as it had apparently been wrong to pray it didn't exist? *Why, God? Why is this your plan for us?*

A warm breeze passed over his heart. A warm thought filled up the hollow inside. *Because I can trust you with them. Because you need them. Because the life you will live together is better than the lives you could live apart.*

He steepled his hands and let his chin rest against them, staring blindly at the unlit hearth across his room.

It wasn't how he'd wanted his life to go. Wasn't what he'd dreamed would happen, even when he obeyed the urging to marry Rowena. He'd thought they'd just get to know each other. Fall in love. Start a family of their own.

Love her.

His lips curved up. He'd always thought love to be something that just happened. Or, as he'd said to Cayton that day at Whitby Park, an action they could take until their hearts caught up with their hands. But maybe it was more than that. Maybe it was a choice. Maybe it was as much about determination and dedication as discovery. Maybe it wasn't a feeling, wasn't an emotion—if it were, it would be changeable, fleeting, like anger or happiness or sorrow. But it shouldn't be. Couldn't be. Love had to be firmer than that. Which meant that love, like faith, couldn't be based on feelings.

It had to be based on what *didn't* change. On what he *knew*. And he knew that Rowena was the wife God intended for him.

He leaned back in the chair and rested his head against it. Looked at the mural some duke of ages gone by had commissioned for his ceiling.

He would love her. He would love the child. He would trust that the Lord knew best.

He *would* . . . even if he couldn't feel it right then.

Twenty-One

Rowena folded her coat-clad arms over her stomach and let the brisk wind off the Channel whip away some of the nausea. It made a difference, somehow, knowing *why* she was ill. Made her realize there was no point in huddling in her room, afraid of spreading some dreadful disease.

The sunshine was already doing her good, as was the bracing air. She stooped to pick up one of the smooth, polished pebbles of the beach and held it tight until her fingers gave it warmth. Then she stroked her thumb over the even surface.

It looked so lovely and easy, this stone. Yet she knew it had become so only through years of tumbling about in the water, all its rough edges being sanded away. Were she Ella, she would find hope in that—the certainty that something good waited on the other side of the trials.

She slid the stone into her pocket and turned her face up to receive the sunshine. He hadn't come last night. Rowena had dismissed Lilias, had crawled into bed, had lain there waiting for the door to open between her room and his. But Brice hadn't come.

She understood—she did. He was being tossed about now,

too, as surely as these stones in the tide. The news he had received yesterday . . . He had reacted nobly, but the commitment certainly would be easier to say than to live. To feel. She must give him time.

But she had missed his arms around her—and had been so terrified of falling asleep and falling back into the claws of the nightmare, of screaming and thereby obligating him to come when he didn't want to, that she had scarcely slept more than a few minutes at a time.

"Your Grace?"

Starting, she spun around, digging up a smile when she saw Mr. Abbott jumping down the short embankment between Midwynd lawn and this last section of beach before the land rose too steeply away from the Channel to grant easy access. Up on the bench overlooking the beach, Lilias still sat, and Mr. Child with her. They hadn't much liked the idea of her coming all the way here on her own, but she still thought it rather an overreaction that the butler had taken an hour away from his duties just to chaperone her.

Mr. Abbott came to a halt a few feet away and stooped down much as she had done to pick up one of the smooth brown stones.

"Good morning, Mr. Abbott. Taking some exercise?"

"Not exactly. I will be giving the girls their marksmanship lesson in a few moments and thought to seek you out first and invite you to join us."

"Kind of you." She looked past him, along the coastline to where Brighton was just visible in the distance. From here she could barely make out the distinctive onion dome of the Royal Pavilion, harkening to a land she had seen only in books. The pier stretched out into the water though, unmistakable. So very different a view from what could be seen from the shores of Loch

Morar. "But you needna teach me, sir. I learned long ago how to handle a weapon, along with all the other Highland lasses."

"I didn't know that you'd feel up to it in any case. But we were all so glad to hear that you had got up and come outside today." He shifted his weight from one foot to the other, his gaze flicking out to the water before settling on her again. "I have been praying."

Why should that make him so nervous? "Thank you. I am much improved."

"Not just for you. For . . ." He turned to face the Channel and flung the stone, skipping it twice over the waters before it sank. Sighing, he turned to her again. "For my own faith as well. I have been thinking on what you said—that I do not believe in the unseen."

"Oh." She slipped her hand into her pocket and gripped the stone resting within. Perhaps she ought not to have said such a thing to him. But who would have thought he would do anything other than dismiss her words?

Mr. Abbott called up a tight smile but directed it to the gulls that landed noisily a few feet away. "You were right. As much as I admire those who believe so completely, I . . . I think some part of me thought it could be achieved only by someone else. Or only if I met a specific set of criteria. That maybe if I studied enough, learned the proper words, it would come. That *He* would come and reveal himself to me. I thought it could only happen in a few specific, orderly ways. And I completely dismissed that there may be an enemy working against Him, even though Jesus spoke of it at every turn."

A blast of cool air made her shiver. "Ye canna have one without the other."

"Exactly." His gaze locked onto hers again, and again he looked as he had that night at Castle Kynn when he spoke of empty places. "I wanted to ignore the darkness that underscores the light. I wanted to control how the light might show itself. That was wrong of me. But, Your Grace . . . I *do* have faith. I have faith in the miraculous. In the unseen." Fervency lit his words now, and his eyes to match.

She nodded and wished the wind would cease. "Good."

"I don't pretend to understand what kernel of truth might lie in our legends and myths. In our curses and blessings. But I promise you I will never again dismiss such tales as pure superstition." He held up a finger, brows raised. "So long as you don't expect me to throw salt over my shoulder. Or refuse to go to sea on a Tuesday."

"Friday." She bit back a grin. "But, aye, I grant that those things *are* superstition."

A smile softened his countenance as the breeze toyed with the hair beneath the brim of his hat. "Then we have reached a truce. And I thank you, truly, Your Grace, for making me dig deeper. For making me put my hand more firmly in the Lord's."

Rowena wrapped her arms tight about her middle. How was it her words had achieved such a thing in this man, yet she still felt so uncertain?

Mr. Abbott motioned toward Midwynd. "May I help you back up the bank, Your Grace? You look chilled."

Lilias would no doubt be insisting she return in a few moments anyway—except that she looked deeply engrossed in whatever conversation she was having with Mr. Child. Still, Rowena nodded. "Aye, thank you." She walked on her own over the smooth, damp stones but accepted his hand up when they reached the two-foot cliff. She had yet to see the real cliffs in the area—white chalk ones much like Dover's famed precipices. They would visit them when Annie arrived, though.

"You know . . ." Once on even ground again, Mr. Abbott

released her hand. "I have been studying the lore of the British Isles this past week, trying to find a way to prove to you it was nothing but nonsense."

Only because he had begun where he did was she able to smile. "I daresay that made for an interesting week's reading."

"That it did." His eyes went thoughtful. "They all seem to hinge on the basic belief that there are spirits that prowl around tormenting us, and that we must guard against them. Scare them away."

"Aye."

He gave her a smile and angled toward the path that would lead to the side lawn. "But only a third of the angels fell—what of the others? They are conspicuously absent from the legends."

She had meant to walk with him a ways, but her feet came to a halt. "Aye."

"There's much I don't understand about it all, and much I probably never will. But this I know, Your Grace." He pointed heavenward. "All authority rests with Him. Aye?"

He tried to say it as a Scot and failed miserably. But it made her smile. His words made her nod. And their meaning rooted her to the place long after he had strode away.

He didn't have to throw her own words back at her—that one couldn't believe in either darkness or light without granting the other. But was that not what she had done as surely as him, just in reverse? Feared the darkness, the curse, the evil . . . without granting that there was One strong enough to overcome it.

That, in fact, such darkness was still like all other darkness—an absence of light. Of Him. But the Lord hadn't abandoned His children to the darkness. Much as she might have thought so for those cold, empty years, and especially those weeks between Malcolm's attack and Brice's arrival.

But He had been there still. Working even then for her good.

Preparing a place. One full to overflowing with family and promise and security and . . . and love, if she were brave enough to claim it.

Was she? Striding past Lilias and Mr. Child, she pressed a hand to her stomach. Over the past twenty-four hours, that truth Lilias had spoken had become sure in her heart. She was with child, and she would love her bairn. She would—despite its father.

Then there was Brice. He wasn't like other men. He had promised impossible acceptance, he had promised love. Promise—wasn't that as strong as a spoken blessing, opposite a curse? He had spoken words that proved he was far more than just a charming face.

But he couldn't do it all on his own. She had to rise to the occasion too. She had to love him.

Her fingers clung to the stone in her pocket. He wouldn't be like Malcolm. And more, he wouldn't be like Father.

She wouldn't let the fear and pain ruin it. She *wouldn't*. Hurrying over the distance between her and the house, she barely noted Lilias and Mr. Child calling to her to hold up. She would find Brice. Now. This very minute. She would throw her arms around him and hold tight. She would swear to him that no curse—be it the tiger's or from her own fear—would defeat them. They would cling, together, to the Lord. And surely, surely if they clung to Him, He would knit them tight as a family too. They could choose to love.

A gunshot made her jump. She splayed a hand over her heart but relaxed when she heard the laughter coming from the side lawn. Just Ella and the Abbotts. Within a few more steps they were visible, the siblings laughing and Ella with a pistol in her hand.

Miss Abbott looked about to fall over with mirth. "You hit

that poor tree! Did you see the bark fly? It's a full five feet from the target, Ella!"

Apparently Ella's aim was as bad as her sense of direction.

The redhead huffed and handed the pistol to Mr. Abbott. "We can't all be as natural as the two of you. Blame it on my peace-loving family—it must be in our very blood. I've never even seen Brice go on a hunt."

Mr. Abbott checked something on the weapon and set it down on a table that they must have brought out. "He at least knows how to hit a target—though you'd be hard-pressed to make him aim at anything living, be it a grouse or a villain."

"Oh, I know. I daresay even if he'd had a gun in hand last year, he'd have let Pratt shoot him before he'd have defended himself." Ella turned, as if to see her brother through the white stone walls of the house. Instead, she spotted Rowena and squealed with joy.

A moment later, arms were about her, a mass of red curls tickling her nose. "You're out! You're up! Are you well? You must be, to have ventured from your room. I was beginning to think you'd run away and no one told me—except that Brice was nearly as absent, but always had your greetings when he returned."

Rowena smiled at her sister-in-law and gripped her arms—largely to keep them from squeezing the life out of her again. "I am . . . not so terrible. Still a bit uneasy in the stomach, but I daresay it's not catching at this point."

"I should think not, or Brice would have been felled by now." Ella gave a happy little sigh, looking contented as a cat napping in the sun. "We were just having target practice—we'd grown bored with archery, and I can never convince Stella to play me at tennis, so it's our newest sport. Perhaps we'll join the gentlemen next time on their hunting adventures. Wouldn't that spoil it for the lot of them?"

With a laugh, she spun back to the Abbotts, though she kept hold of Rowena's arm. "Would you like to learn? Brice said we may."

Rowena shook her head. "I learned years ago, but it ne'er much interested me. I was just going to—"

"Walk? I'll walk with you, then. Stella, you've frightened me off! I'm taking a promenade with Rowena!"

The Abbotts smiled and waved them on.

Apparently her seeking of Brice would have to wait a bit. A delay she didn't entirely mind, given how long it had been since she had taken a stroll with her friend. They said nothing until they'd rounded another corner and the lawn gave way to a copse of trees that would lead the way to the River Ouse, if one followed them far enough. Weeks ago Ella had shown her their favorite spot under the boughs, where a bench had been situated to give an advantageous view of both the house and the countryside. Near it was the miniature house that the former duke had commissioned for Brice and Ella to play in as children. Unused now, but it always made Rowena smile to see it. To see how their father had thought of them.

She turned back to Ella and wished the tree limbs didn't block the sun. "Sorry I didn't let you visit. I was so afraid of bringing the entire house down with the same thing."

Ella laughed. "It wouldn't be the first time any of us had got sick. But no matter—we all rather began to think Brice was making the whole thing up just to keep you to himself for a few days. Which made us realize you'd not had a proper honeymoon. You ought to plan a trip, you know. Somewhere grand and romantic. France or Italy or the Alps."

"Perhaps." She smiled at the mention of the trip Brice had wagered her . . . then let it drift away. That was contingent upon him falling in love with her before she did him. And given the blow she'd dealt him yesterday, she wasn't so sure that was possible. He had promised to love her, yes—but it would take time. She knew that better than anyone. "Though Annie will be here soon, and hopefully we'll get to keep her with us for a good while."

"And no doubt we'll all adore her just as much as you, so it's no great thing to leave her in our charge for a fortnight. Although . . . Mother had another theory about your illness." Ella grinned and flounced onto the cold wooden bench as if it were plush with upholstery. "One that might make travel a bit difficult in a few months."

"Oh." Perhaps she didn't need the sun after all—she now felt quite warm. What was she to say? What would Brice *want* her to say?

Ella's head fell back with laughter. "Mother cautioned me not to say a word to you—she said you two ought to realize it for yourselves, and decide for yourselves when to share, if it's in fact true. But I couldn't help myself—the look on your face! It hardly matters whether it's true just now or not—that look . . ."

Rowena sat beside her friend and pulled out a smile. Perhaps a bit self-deprecating, but a smile nonetheless. And then she said, with the utmost determination, "What a curious bird that is—I've never seen the like. Do you know what it's called?"

Rowena waited for an hour. She had changed into her nightclothes, had lost her dinner—which she'd taken with the family—and moaned out the misery of it. She'd dismissed Lilias for the night, assuring her she was well and that her husband would be in momentarily. But again, Brice didn't come. She'd heard his steps in the hall, the low rumble of voices from his suite . . . which, granted, she could *only* hear because she'd pressed her ear to the door.

But her husband didn't come. And didn't come. And didn't come.

She had tried to find him earlier in the day, but he had apparently gone somewhere with Old Abbott. And now . . .

She understood why he remained away. But that didn't stop the tears from burning as she sank onto the chair facing their adjoining door.

She had hoped he would save her the need to reach out, she admitted it. She had hoped and prayed all afternoon that he would simply slip in, as if last night's lonely hours had never happened.

But he didn't come, and it was far too easy to think that perhaps she ought to just give him time. Time to digest it, to pray his way through it. Time to reconcile a lifetime of hopes and assumptions with a hard truth. Time, just like she had been demanding since they married.

But she'd been wrong—she hadn't needed time, she'd needed *him*. "Lord . . ." Her voice faded to nothing in the room, a dim echo under the crackling of the fire and the steady *tap-tap* of the newly come rain upon the windows. She hadn't prayed much in recent years. Perhaps she had tried these last weeks, but it had been halfhearted.

Now she stared at that closed door and opened the one upon her heart. "Lord, I know I've been a negligent daughter to you. I've never . . . never really thought myself worthy to approach you. Mr. Abbott would say we're *all* unworthy but that you love us anyway. Brice would say I've the kind of heart you love best—a broken one."

She shuddered, and her lips quivered. Perhaps her heart had long been broken. But *his* oughtn't to be. He'd always sought the Lord first, above all. He spoke of his faith as easily as Father did his clan. It was such a part of who he was, of all he did, and he should have been rewarded for that. Not punished with the likes of her.

"No. No, I must stop thinking that way, aye?" It rang of the heartbreak . . . but He could take away the sorrow and replace it with joy. Heal the broken places and make them stronger than before. "I am your child, not just my father's. Loved by you if not by him. Shaped into your image, not his. I can love Brice as he needs to be loved. I can be what he needs. I can, if you'll just show me how, Lord."

The fire crackled. The rain tapped. And that door stayed shut.

She gripped the cushion beneath her as her throat went tight. The door had a handle on this side as surely as it did the other, didn't it? What was stopping her from going through it just as Brice had done? When she'd needed him—even when she hadn't realized she had done—he had come. Had comforted, had silently proven he was all he should be, all she could need.

Well, he needed *her* now, though he might not think so. He needed her to hold tight to the closeness they'd forged over the past days. To fight for him, for the right to be by his side. He needed her to prove that it wasn't just the babe she wanted—it was him, too, and a promise wasn't enough. They needed the *now* as well as the *someday*.

She stood on shaky legs, before the determination could fade. She took a deep breath, before the nausea could overtake her. She strode forward, before she could scurry back to her own bed, her own blankets.

The slab of wood stood sentry between them. She raised a hand but just pressed her palm to the smooth surface rather than knock. There would be no question who was at this door—if she asked leave to enter, he could just refuse to answer. And the thought of rejection . . .

But she had rejected him at every turn. He had the right to

do the same. Even if she had every intention of ignoring him if he did, as he had done when she first felt the sickness.

With a bolstering breath, she rapped her knuckles against the wood.

A beat of silence, just long enough to make her wonder if he was nestled under his covers with his back to the door and his eyes squeezed shut, praying she'd go away. But then the door whooshed open and she was looking at his cotton-clad chest rather than the wood.

"Are you all right?" Concern laced his words even before her gaze traveled up to see it shining in the warm chocolate depths of his eyes. He cared. He might not have come to grips with it all yet, but he cared.

It emboldened her enough to duck under the arm he'd stretched out to hold the door open and step, for the first time, into his room.

"No. I missed you." It was all deep woods in here, and jewel tones. Sapphires and emeralds, a splash of ruby. Elegant and in the best taste—perfectly suited to him. She turned her back to it all to face him though and summoned a smile. "And I got to thinking that it was glaikit to ignore it. I could go to sleep, but I'd only fall back into that nightmare—and then I'd be crying and ye'd come in anyway, aye? So we might as well save you a rude awakening."

The corners of his lips tugged up. "Considerate of you."

"Wasn't it just?" She tried to summon some of Ella's perpetual bounce as she made a show of striding to the bed that was turned down for him, settling herself comfortably into what must be his spot. "Ye know, I do believe I like your room even better than mine. Such rich colors."

He shut the door with a soft click and sidled her way. "You could redecorate yours—I said as much when we arrived."

Flashing a cheeky grin didn't feel quite natural . . . but it felt right. "Or we could just spend our nights in here instead."

Amusement twinkled in his eyes—praise be to heaven. "Are you wooing me, Duchess?"

"Just trying to win that bet." She held out a hand and prayed he'd take it.

He did, and sat down beside her on the bed with a sigh. "I'm sorry. I know I should have come last night, I just—"

"Shh." Both her hands around his, she lifted his hand and pressed a kiss to the broad palm. "Ye needna explain it to me. I understand. And I want to give you space, as ye've given me. But . . . but we've made such progress this week. I dinna want to lose it."

"I don't either. I don't." He tugged his hand free but then wrapped his arm around her and pulled her close, onto his lap. Rested his head against hers. She couldn't remember when last she'd felt so safe. "I just didn't want to come to you with such thoughts as I have ricocheting through my head. Worthless, all of them, and I know it. But I can't silence them all."

At least he was trying. And trying to protect her from them. It was more than she'd done for him, really. Much as she'd thought herself trying, she hadn't gone about it the right way, had she? She had been just as guilty as he of not entertaining the possibility that she had been wrong. Of believing a curse was stronger than anything they could build together. "I've been so terrible to you. So quick to believe the worst, about you and us."

Laughter rumbled in his chest. "Well, I *am* so perfect it's beyond reckoning."

"And verra annoying." She looped an arm around his neck and tugged his head down so she could press her lips to his. And, oh, how perfect it felt. "Brice . . . I still dinna ken which of us is right about Catherine. But I want to say here and now that, if it's a choice between helping her and peace with you . . . I choose you."

He went so stiff on the mention of her name that he needn't even speak to convey his thoughts on that. But he held her close. And he sighed. "I don't know either. Everything in me shouts that she is dangerous, every bit as much as her husband was, and as we both agree her brother likely is. But it occurs to me that I don't know *why* she is the way she is. Yet I have been assuming her beyond redemption. That is surely wrong of me, regardless of which of us reads her aright. I ought to be praying for her. And . . . and I ought to be willing to grant that perhaps the Lord revealed something to *you*, so that you could help her. So that we could end this in a way I never anticipated."

She tipped her head back so she could look into his face. "What are ye saying?"

Another sigh, and his eyes slid shut. "If you feel you should go and visit her . . . if you are convinced that you must . . . then do. With my blessing."

Relief swamped her, even as she wondered if she should turn down the offer on principle. But she couldn't. She would always wonder, if she did, whether she could have helped. Whether she had turned her back on someone in need.

She pressed her hand to Brice's cheek, savoring the feel of his stubble against her palm. *Her husband*. How had it come to be so? And how had she passed so many weeks at his side without giving in to the urge to lean over and feather a kiss onto his lips? "I *do* feel I must. But I swear to you, I'll go in with my eyes open. After much prayer. And I'll not go again, not unless the Lord makes it clear I should and providing you agree about that."

His arms tightened around her. "I want at least two able-bodied men with you in the carriage or car. And someone to go in with you."

At that, she shook her head. "The men, aye—but if anyone goes in with me, it's certain she willna speak honestly."

His jaw clenched. For a long moment, he made no other move. Then he swallowed. "All right. But position yourself before a window, and we'll make sure one of the men can see you. If you are in distress at any time, you must make a signal."

"I will. I promise."

He stroked a hand through her hair . . . and down onto her back as she so loved. "I can't lose you now, darling. I can't. Tread carefully when you go, and know that I will be here praying from the moment you leave until the moment you return."

"Ye willna lose me. Our life is only beginning." She rested her head against his shoulder and looked to the rich tapestry above his bed. The soft pillow bidding her snuggle in. Her pulse kicked up a bit. It was different, somehow, planning to spend the night in *his* room. Different, but she wouldn't relent from her course. She could trust him. She could rest with him.

She could love him.

"You must be exhausted. I heard you tossing and turning all last night. My fault, no doubt, and I am beyond sorry." He shifted them, turned, and lowered them both together until the pillows welcomed her head. "Everyone was so glad to see you today."

Her lips smiled even as her eyes closed. "A bit suspicious though, I think, when I was so choosy about what I ate."

"Mm." His nose traced the curve of her jaw and made little tingles whisper over her. "I daresay it won't take them long to come to their own conclusions about it. We had better tell them ourselves." His voice held no dread at the prospect. "Tomorrow at morning prayers? We can't exactly hide for long that you're still sick."

Tomorrow? She sucked in a breath. Better to tell them than

to keep dodging the question. And better to smile in joy than hide away in her room. Still . . . "Are ye certain ye're ready?"

His hand moved to her stomach and rested gently upon it. Even that light pressure made her feel ill, but she'd never in a millennium say so. He sighed a bit. "I'm certain. This is my child—I will not keep the joy of that to myself."

Rowena blinked back the burning brine. He was trying. So obviously trying, but so obviously not feeling that joy yet. "Ye needna pretend. Not with me."

"I'm not pretending. I'm just . . . torn. Selfishly. But so sorry for what you suffered."

She breathed a bit easier when he moved his hand and turned her head to look at him. "It was a nightmare—as ye well ken. But I'll confess here and now that I'd more than resigned myself to the thought of a bairn. I'd come to want it—despite how this babe came to be, and that I wish it were yours instead. But it's different for you."

"No. If anything, it should be easier. I didn't go through what you did. But still I received the blessing of a beautiful wife and a child of our own." He kissed the tip of her nose.

Her heart melted a little more. "It could well be a girl. If it's a girl—"

"It doesn't matter. Know that now, darling." He smiled, and amusement returned to his gaze, as light as the finger he trailed over her arm. "I admit that I had the same thought, railing against the idea of another man's son being the next duke, compromising the bloodline. But let's be honest. Do you really think that in three hundred years of history, that's never happened in the duchy before? I always rather thought the fourth Duke of Nottingham bore more of a resemblance to the portraits of the then-Earl of Ashford than his own father . . ."

It shouldn't have made her laugh, but a giggle escaped. "I

could hardly believe the third Duke is in your ancestry. Frighteningly ugly, wasn't he?"

"And yet those features never show up again in the gallery—for which I may just owe my inconstant great-etc. grandmother eternal thanks, if she betrayed the old dog. I hear he was a foul-tempered, boorish man too."

He would never advocate inconstancy—she knew that. But wasn't it just like him to find the humor in a thing? Turning onto her side, she wrapped her arm around him. "I thought God had abandoned me, deemed me unworthy. But He led me to you . . . so I must be loved by Him indeed, to have been given such a blessing. I'll be a good wife to you, Brice. We'll have our own children after this one—

"This one is our own. I mean that. Girl or boy, this is my child." His hand was in her hair, cradling her head. His eyes were as deep as Loch Morar but far warmer.

She'd thought it a curse when Lilias pushed her down that embankment. Thought it a cruelty when Father demanded they wed. But when his lips took hers, she knew it was the best thing that had ever happened to her.

Blessings already—Fire Eyes or no Fire Eyes.

A baby? *A baby*? The words spun around Stella's head, dancing with incredulity. A baby. His and hers. Nottingham's and Rowena's. They clasped hands as they said the words, gazing at each other rather than the collection of family and staff. The words that said all was over. All Stella's chances gone.

A baby.

Charlotte squealed. Ella laughed in glee. They both flew from their seats to embrace the happy couple, words like *blessing* and *thrilled* ricocheting about the room.

But this was no blessing. This was nothing to be thrilled over.

"Oh." Mrs. Granger grabbed Stella's hand, blinked back tears that she smiled through. "Oh, I couldn't be happier. Look at them—what fine parents they'll make. Won't they?"

How was one to smile into a face one had known all one's life and convince her one was happy? But Mrs. Granger was scarcely paying attention, certainly not waiting for an answer. She was creeping forward with the other upper staff, waiting their turn to offer their sincere congratulations. Mrs. Granger, Mr. Child.

Even Father, beaming the smile of the ignorant. Of one who

had no idea what this news did to his daughter. Who, if he *did* know, would scowl and lecture and ask her for the millionth time why she couldn't be content with what he'd given her, like Geoff.

A baby. It would surely look odd for her to sink to the cushions of a chair when everyone else was on their feet, but her knees were shaking. She leaned on the wall to cover it. *A baby*. They were together so little until Her Grace took ill . . . had only a time or two seemed to even tolerate each other, there in Yorkshire. And oh, how green and oily her heart felt when she stopped to consider how it all came to be. Their arms about each other. Lips upon each other.

No. No, it wasn't right. They weren't in love—wasn't it obvious? They had no business creating a child. But they must have conceived right away, to be so sure already of . . .

Wait. Stella straightened again. *Wait, wait, wait*. What was it that brute of a Scot had said when he barged his way into the castle? The words certainly weren't spoken in the accent McLucky had used at school in their impromptu Gaelic lessons, but they had been clear enough. Could he have said . . . ?

Yes! *A baby*—Kinnaird had spoken of a baby. And not Brice's, to be sure.

Her lips curling up, it was an easy matter to slip from the room, from the house. Around to the little cottage their family had always called home. Fetch a coat, fetch a hat. Borrow a horse. A quick trip to Brighton and Lady Pratt, and this little bump would disappear. Not that loosing the Highland brute on them was a *good* plan, but what choice did she have?

Precautions could be taken to make sure Nottingham wasn't harmed. But Kinnaird must come. He would, at the least, drive a wedge between them. He would shout the truth—or the possible truth, anyway—to the world, and the lie would be shattered. Their marriage would shatter with it, for even Nottingham wasn't so good that he would forgive his wife for trying to pass another man's babe off as his. That would be that.

And at the most . . . at the most, Kinnaird might end the marriage more quickly than a divorce or annulment would. And then who would be there to comfort the bereaved widower?

The wind blew brisk and steady off the Channel, a harbinger of autumn. Then winter, and then her new post would begin, and she would leave here.

But she couldn't, mustn't. Once she was gone, her chances would go with her. She must act now. Before this smoldering fire inside grew to fever pitch. Before he forgot their love in the excitement of a child and a wife who looked at him as Rowena had been doing that morning. Before all their history, all their years together, all those dreams turned to dust.

Kinnaird. He would solve it all. Though Stella didn't dare try to get in touch with him herself—if Nottingham found out, that would be the end of her newfound hopes—but Lady Pratt could take care of that. Then it would all be finished.

Twenty minutes later Brighton came into view, bright and golden in the morning light. Gulls cried overhead, horses clopped, the occasional automobile puttered. Stella steered her horse around a parked milk wagon and entered into the town she'd always called her own. She'd come here countless times during her life, but her favorite trips had always been by Ella's side, where she could pretend that her purse were as heavy with silver as her friend's. That they were sisters, duke's daughters both, with the world at their feet.

Sometimes she had pretended that the passersby wouldn't know, to glance at them, which was the real Lady Ella—as if all of Sussex hadn't been exclaiming since Ella's birth—sometimes in admiration and sometimes in disgust—about her brilliant red hair.

It was no wonder she always tried to claim it was auburn. Though she never minded being the center of attention, Ella had always preferred to earn the spotlight, not to be forced into it. As children she would sometimes hide behind Stella. Push her forward. As if she, too, wanted her to be the duke's daughter.

Stella checked the direction on the letter she'd stashed in her handbag, the street sign at the corner, and turned her borrowed mount down the avenue. She would never be a duke's daughter. But she could be a duke's wife. A duchess. Higher than Ella, higher than Geoff, higher than the insufferable gentlewomen she'd had to kowtow to at school. Then it would be *she* Brighton bowed to as she passed. *She* people sought out for favors, for friendship. *She* Brice took into his arms and gazed so fondly at.

After securing her horse outside, she mounted the steps before the front door and rang the bell. It took a long moment before a servant answered it, no doubt not expecting any callers for another hour.

He greeted her with a sneer that would have gotten him sacked had he been *her* butler. "Servants around back."

Servant! Stella lifted her chin and realized only then she had been dressed to help Grandmum prepare their little garden plot for autumn. Why had she not thought to change before she came here? "Only one of us is a servant, and I assure you it isn't me."

The butler made to shut the door in her face—she stopped it with both hand and foot. "Your mistress gave me instruction to come." She thrust forward the letter she'd received two weeks ago. The one Stella had nearly ripped up, in which Lady Pratt had arrogantly demanded news of her progress.

Snatching the missive from her hand, the butler studied the handwriting for a moment and then grunted and let her in. "I'll thank you to exit from the rear. We can't have the ladies who will be calling seeing riffraff going through the front door."

Curses upon dull cotton dresses! She should have donned her linen morning suit, the one whose embroidery she had slaved over for two solid weeks. Then he would know with whom he dealt. Then he would fawn over her as he would those insipid ladies who would be laughing their way up the stairs in an hour. She snatched the letter back. "Just show me to your mistress."

He directed her toward the drawing room, from which came the sound of a squealing brat. Stella paused just inside the threshold, trying to curtail her disdain. As if she needed any crawling, gurgling reminders of why she was here.

And hadn't the lady funds enough for a nursemaid? Why did she soil her frock by rolling about on the floor with her baby?

Catherine, Lady Pratt looked up—and sneered. "What are you wearing?"

Blighted cotton. "Never mind that. You wanted news?" She waved the letter. "I'll give you news. But you have to swear to me you'll take immediate action."

She outlined it all quickly as she could, the fire inside banking a bit more with each new spark of interest in Lady Pratt's eyes.

When the lady smiled that mean little smile, Stella knew she had done right in coming.

"Don't worry." Lady Pratt set her son upon her lap and motioned Stella toward the door. "I'll take care of everything. I know *just* how to use this."

For the first time in days, Stella breathed easy. Soon Rowena would be gone. And Stella would be stepping into her rightful place.

Rowena followed the servant into a drawing room in the rented house, wishing she hadn't handed over her handbag and wrap—she could have done with something to clutch. She had been so sure that she was meant to come here, to try one more time to help Catherine. She had been so calm as she bade Brice farewell with a soft, lingering kiss and climbed into the carriage.

But seeing one of the burly guards surveying the rented town home, receiving his instructions on where to sit and how to signal if there was trouble . . . her stomach knotted, and she knew that it wasn't to be blamed on the bairn.

Inside the drawing room Catherine was laughing and tickling her wee one, who gave a great belly laugh in return. He crawled up into her lap with all the familiarity of a child who knew his mother better than his nurse and settled happily there.

Could she be a monster *and* a good mother? Rowena was none too sure.

The servant cleared her throat, disapproval in her eyes. "The Duchess of Nottingham, my lady. Shall I take the boy up to his nurse for you?"

Joy lit Catherine's eyes as she looked up, soothing a bit of the concern in Rowena's heart. The lady waved the servant away. "No, no, the duchess doesn't mind my little Byron. Do you, dearest?"

"Not at all." Rowena smiled and hoped the sincerity of that statement came through, rather than the conflict within her. Settling onto a chair near her hostess's spot on the floor, she couldn't help but gaze at the wee lad and wonder what her own babe would look like. Would he or she have the dark hair of Malcolm? No, of Brice. They looked enough alike that anything inherited from the monster they could attribute to her husband instead, and happily. Brice's hair. Brice's height. Her grey eyes?

Catherine transferred herself and little Byron to the chair beside Rowena's. She grinned. "I see you're not wearing the rubies to be slobbered on today. Wise of you."

Laughing before she could check herself, Rowena touched a hand to her throat and the simple pendant she'd chosen for the day. Well, the one Brice had chosen, had fastened around her neck for her. He'd even pressed his lips to where neck and shoulder joined, sending a flurry of happy tingles down her spine. "Not for fear of drool, I assure you."

Catherine smiled. "I'm so glad you could come by today, Rowena. I was beginning to worry for you. Have you been sick this whole time?"

"I have, yes. I . . ." It would be so easy to fall into small talk. But would small talk lead her to true revelations? She had so little experience in honest friendships. *Please, Lord, guide me. If I can help her, help me to know how.*

The babe squealed and stood on his mother's knee, clapping chubby hands to her cheeks. Catherine laughed. "Well, By is happy you are feeling better. Aren't you, my little darling?" She anchored him with one arm but focused her smile on Rowena again. "I was afraid your husband would have been upset with you after that soiree. He was none too pleased to find us in Brighton, I know."

"You needna have worried." Rowena clasped her hands together and forced a smile—told her tongue to deliver only English syllables, to leave her Scots at home. "I didn't realize your brother would be joining you here."

"I do detest traveling alone. Though, of course, when Rush is going ever on about the expense of letting a house, I almost wish I had."

Though she was listening for it, Rowena couldn't tell if there was anything hidden in the tone of voice. Catherine spoke evenly, off-handedly, a laugh seeming to hover on her lips.

How often had Rowena laughed off dread and disappointment? But she had never been so skilled at it. "Your brother . . ."

She swallowed, moistened her lips, and forced a smile. "He reminds me in some ways of my father."

"Your father's a miser, you mean?" Catherine tilted her head back with a laugh.

No mirth, even feigned, would come. Rowena nodded. "Aye, that he is. And controlling and stern and always hovering to make sure I didn't do anything that would reflect poorly on the clan."

Catherine laughed again. "Rush *can* seem stern, I imagine. But you needn't be concerned over his scolding of me, dearest—and you are concerned, aren't you? Sweet of you. But he is all bark."

"No, he isn't." That she could state evenly, without a trace of shaking. That she knew to the very core of her soul. "I know the look of a man who is all bark, Kitty. And I know the look of one who takes his greatest pleasure in hurting others."

"You . . ." Now Catherine's good humor faded, hardened. But it wasn't gratitude that filled her eyes, nor sympathy. It was . . . fury. "You little twit. You think my brother is cruel to *me*? That he—what? Controls me? Hurts me? You think me so weak that I would *let* him?"

A sting, but she ignored it. "'Tisn't a matter of weakness—"

"That is exactly what it is! I would think you would recognize it, given that you haven't a backbone to speak of."

Rowena snapped straight. But *she* had lashed out before, hadn't she? Attacking the one who wanted to help rather than the one who was the problem. "Kitty, I—"

"If you want to save someone from violence, you're about a decade too late." She put little Byron onto the floor and sat back up with blazing eyes. "And it's *he* you would have had to offer your pathetic aid to. You want to bond?" She swept an arm out. "My brother isn't like your father—my *father* was like your father. My brother is the only reason I never felt his fist. *He* always took it for me. For our mother. He is the only one in this world who has *ever* fought for me, and if you dare to insult him—"

"I'm sorry." And yet Lilias's words clanged about in her head. *"He wanted to make you stronger . . . and that's how his father taught him."* "I don't mean to insult him, or you. I just recognized—"

"You're too stupid to recognize the nose on your own face." Catherine surged to her feet. "I am not a victim, *Duchess.* I don't need your help in managing my brother, or whatever you came today thinking to offer. There's only one thing I need from you." She leaned in, towering over Rowena's chair much like Father would have done. "The diamonds."

Much like Father . . . but not. His tone, but not his voice. His posture, but not his build. Catherine was but a few inches taller than Rowena, a few pounds heavier.

And if she clapped her hands, her guards would come bursting in.

Nothing to fear. Which was, perhaps, why it was more sorrow than terror than filled her. "You don't want the diamonds, Kitty. Not if you really think their worth will fix what's wrong with your life. Not when their curse feeds on that very thing."

Catherine straightened and let out a disgusted breath. "I should have known a Highlander would latch ahold of the ridiculous curse nonsense. They are just jewels, Rowena. Lovely, rare jewels that will soon grace the throat of a Russian princess and in so doing set me for life."

"Ye're wrong." Rowena stood too, slowly but without qualm. "If ye want them for only selfish purposes, ye'll taste nothing but the curse."

"You want to talk about curses?" Catherine's lips curved

up into a smile small and mean. "Let's talk about Malcolm Kinnaird."

"What?" Now she froze, all blood seeming to rush from her head so quickly it left her dizzy. Frost blew across her heart.

Catherine laughed, but there was nothing light in it, nothing pleasant. "Let me make this so clear there is no mistaking it, even for a dolt like you." She leaned forward, somehow still looking like the doting mother with her babe hanging on her leg—but for the utter disdain in her green eyes. "Find the gems, or I send a little note to one Malcolm Kinnaird saying you're carrying his babe and trying to pass it off as Nottingham's."

Her stomach lurched, the bile rose, panic clawed at her neck. But through it cut another dagger altogether. How could she know that? How? The only people who knew she was with child at all were the staff at Midwynd, the family, and surely, *surely* none of them would have rushed over here and told her.

Would they have?

Catherine smirked, even chuckled low and deadly in her throat. "Wondering how I know you're with child? Oh, I have my sources, my dear Rowena. Remember that. I know your every move."

Please, Lord God. Give me strength. My own is never sufficient, but yours . . . please. Please.

"I know your comings. Your goings. I know that the duke just announced the *good* news this morning, never guessing how you've duped him. Do you think he would be any less upset about that than about the Fire Eyes?"

Rowena sucked in a breath. Catherine didn't know quite as much as she thought, whoever her source. "You've got it all wrong. I am with child, yes, but the babe is my husband's." He had claimed the wee one—and more, wanted no one to know otherwise. Certainly didn't want Catherine spreading such terrible things around the society he so enjoyed. Having everyone, for generations, speaking of how he'd been cuckolded.

But Catherine just smirked. "Perhaps, perhaps not. But what, do you think, will this Malcolm believe?"

A shudder overtook her, too fierce to be controlled.

Catherine obviously noted it, given her mean little laugh. "Oh, this *is* good. The self-righteous duke who always made a point of being so much better than the rest of us ends up with a wife who's already given herself to another."

Given? Rowena dug her fingers into the cushion. "Ye dinna ken of what ye speak."

"I know enough, you dithering fool. You've made your bed, lied to the duke—now you'll pay the price. Do exactly as I say, or the enraged clansman my darling friend has told me about will be knocking on your door—and I daresay he will act first and ask questions later. The only question is, who will he kill first, do you think? You, who betrayed him, or the man you ran off with?"

Heaven help us. Rowena's throat ached with the memory of his hands around it. The long-faded bruises pulsed on her wrists. The murderous rage in his eyes filled her vision. And in her ears echoed that low Gaelic threat. *"If I find you carry my babe, I will come for you. No child of mine will be raised by a Sassenach."*

How did he mean to make good on that threat? Kill Brice and steal her away? Kill her and the babe rather than let her child be raised English? Kill them all?

She was going to be sick. Squeezing her eyes shut, she forced her breath to stay even. Forced composure into the limbs that wanted to fold and curl up. Forced her hands not to clap together and draw her men into the house—she could handle this herself. She *must*. "Why would you do this? I have been nothing but a friend to you. Wanted nothing but to help you."

Catherine picked her son up again, settled him on her hip. And when she smiled, Rowena saw what Brice must have been seeing all along. The woman who had posed for magazine advertisements, who was all confidence and sultry smiles. The woman who was just like her brother. "Do you think I need help from the likes of you? I take care of myself. Your only use, *dearest*, is in getting me those diamonds. Now go home like a good little coward and fetch them."

"I'll never."

"Oh yes you will, Duchess." She sat down, all casual unconcern, her son in her lap. "You'll be back here in three days, with the Fire Eyes in hand. Or Malcolm Kinnaird will be knocking on your door."

Shaking too much to answer, Rowena strode from the room. She wouldn't have even paused for her things had a servant not been standing there with them.

Her guards waited outside, looking about to storm the house when they glimpsed her face. So she schooled it, forced a smile, and shook her head. "Dinna. All is well."

A blatant lie, but a necessary one. All was so very far from well. But she held it in until she'd climbed into the carriage. And only after the men had closed her firmly within did she let the shaking come, let the tears clog her throat.

It wasn't fair. She had just finally come to appreciate all she'd been given, to see that the Lord had been there all the lonely years she'd thought herself abandoned by anyone who might have loved her. She had only just begun to realize that Brice was the man her heart needed. She had only just found the strength to reach out to another she thought was in need.

Why had she chosen so foolish a recipient?

She dashed at the tears, but more replaced the ones she wiped away as the landscape rocked past her out the window. She had been right in one thing, at least. There was pain there, there was violence. She *had* recognized that in Rushworth, and the echo of it in Catherine too.

But Brice, too, had been right. Catherine had let it turn her into as much a monster as her brother had. And now what was Rowena to do? Even if she wanted to, she couldn't just hand over the diamonds. She had no idea where they were, and though she now had access to Brice's room . . .

No. That was no answer at all. That was the curse—that was destruction. That was feeding the beast instead of slaying it. She wouldn't take part in such deception. She wouldn't let the curse win.

She would tell Brice what Catherine had threatened. They could find an alternative solution together.

Together. The promise of it wove a strange peace around her, and she blinked away the tears. If anything could counteract the curse, perhaps it was that.

Brice stepped out into the morning sunshine and focused on the drive. Today would be another day spent poring over all the information they had about employees' histories—which would manage only to make him feel like a spy. At no point thus far had he stumbled across anything that made an *Aha!* sound within him.

But there would be no focusing upon such tasks until his wife had safely returned.

He wasn't usually one to prowl about the front of the house where any tourist could spot him, but it afforded the best vantage. He would stay right there until he saw that carriage roll up. He would pray. Worry for his wife. And yes, worry, too, about who in his house was set against him. If Humphrey had spoken true, then one of them had been bought. But he felt no closer to discovering who it was than he'd been a week ago.

A knot loosened in his shoulders when their familiar carriage came into view, the horses moving at an unhurried trot. Nothing had gone terribly wrong, then, or they would be rushing. She was safe, safely home. He strode forward as the vehicle drew near, but his relief vanished when he caught sight of Rowena's face at the window. He arrived in time to help her down and knew he was frowning. "You've been crying."

Her attempt at a smile did little to mollify him. "You were right. I was too, but . . ." She tucked her hand into the crook of his arm and tipped her face up to look into his. "Could we walk?"

"Of course." He intended to learn exactly how Catherine had proven them both right—and preferred no one else be there to overhear the conversation. "The Abbotts were helping their grandmother in the vegetable garden, so perhaps toward the wood."

Rowena nodded her assent and waited until they were protected by the ancient trunks and optimistic saplings before she drew in a breath and turned toward him again. "I was right that there has been mistreatment in her life—but it was her father, and her brother took the brunt of it. It has knit them together, I think. And, as you feared, made them both monsters."

Brice let his breath ease out and gripped her fingers. "But you were right to want to help."

Rowena moved her fingers so they fit between his, held them. "And you right to warn me away from her. To think that I believed if they could use the diamonds to restore Delmore, free her of him, it could break the curse. To think that I promised to help them." She shook her head.

Brice drew in a quick breath and came to a halt. "Of course.

You are the one they were banking on, the one Humphrey mentioned." A relieved laugh slipped out. "I should have realized long ago! They don't have another spy in the house at all."

And his wife would most assuredly not be helping them any longer.

Though she certainly scowled at him now. "You didna mention that Humphrey implied such, or I could have told you that a week ago."

"I-I didn't mean to keep it from you, darling. I—"

"It doesna matter." Indeed, her frown smoothed out and a bit of a smile found a place on her lips. "We were focused on happier things last week, when I wasna losing my dinner. But *mo muirnín*—" she turned to him and rested her hands on his chest—"she intends to use me yet. She's given me an ultimatum. If I dinna hand over the jewels in three days' time, she'll . . . she'll tell Malcolm I'm carrying his bairn."

Had he thought it fear tickling him before? No. That was but a pinch compared with the pressure now threatening to squash him. His arms slid around her waist. "How? How does she know?"

Rowena shook her head, tears trickling down her cheeks. "Someone must still be feeding her information."

So there *was* still another traitor in his house. One who must have been there when they made the announcement. One who must have sent word to Catherine in all haste, to have beat Rowena there. *No, wait* . . . Not just someone there this morning. Someone who'd been there in Scotland too. Or who had overheard them talking yesterday.

But that would mean someone so very close to them. *Davis? Cowan?* No, he couldn't accept that. He *couldn't*.

And it didn't really matter, did it? The damage was done. For now, they must focus on lessening the potential effect. "We'll alert the constable. Hire more guards if we must. Leave the country if it comes down to it, go somewhere Malcom Kinnaird can't follow. But he will *not* touch you again, Rowena. You have my word."

She buried her face in his chest and slid her arms around him. For a second, he feared she'd turn those luminous eyes of hers up at him and say it wouldn't be enough, that for the sake of her child—*their* child—they must give Catherine and Rushworth what they wanted. He feared that he'd be unable to say no, that all noble thoughts of justice and freedom from the curse would crumble under the fear for her and the babe.

And she did turn her gleaming silver eyes on him. She reached up and touched his face with her small, gloved fingers. Her lips even pulled into a tremulous smile. "When the shock has worn off," she said softly, "as it settles more in your mind, ye'll wonder. Ye'll wonder if I fear the curse more than I believe in us. Ye'll wonder if in a panic I'll take them to her. But I willna. I promise. She'll not have them, not when it will just keep the curse going strong. I dinna even want to ken where they are anymore. Dinna tell me—dinna ever tell me."

"Rowena." He held her close, shut his eyes against the world. "I trust you. Implicitly."

"And I you. But still—I dinna need to know."

He relished the feel of her in his arms, the floral scent that drifted from her hair. How grateful he was that she didn't pull away anymore. So grateful she looked up at him without the fear, the caution, the distrust. They'd come so far, so quickly once they got over those seemingly insurmountable bumps. He ran a hand up her back. "You're more important than the diamonds, you and the baby. If it comes down to it—"

"No." Her finger touched his lips, stilling the words. "There is another way. I dinna ken what it is yet, but I'm sure of it. If a curse is darkness, then there's only one way to break it—with the light of the Lord. He'll provide a way."

He smiled to realize she'd grown there too . . . even if *he* didn't feel the Lord's peace at the moment. "We'll pray."

"Yes. And He'll answer." Her hand slid around to the back of his head, bidding his heart to thunder. "I'm so sorry I doubted. Doubted you, doubted us, doubted God. But He's proven me wrong on every count. And especially about you. Ye've accepted me and my bairn. I owe you everything."

He shook his head—slightly, so as not to dislodge her hand—and tried to unglue his tongue from the roof of his mouth. "One cannot keep accounts in marriage, darling. You owe me nothing."

But oh, the way she smiled. Small and warm and private, the kind of smile that promised things he dared not put to name. "Don't I? I would think that, at the least, I owe you my heart."

She pressed on his head, and he obligingly lowered it, though he paused an inch from her lips. "Don't you know, darling? Hearts can't just be given. They must be exchanged. I can take yours only if you take mine too."

"Is that how it works?" She strained up until her lips touched his, making him forget the cool air and the warm sun both. Making him forget there was a world outside her arms. No birdsong, no whispering wind, no snapping twigs. "How fortuitous."

"Isn't it?" He held her flush against him and claimed her lips with his.

No! He knew? He knew the babe wasn't his, and he accepted it anyway? Stella nearly collapsed. Her stealth, so prized a few minutes earlier, gave way to clumsy feet that stepped on twigs and fists that pummeled trees on their way back out into the garden.

They spoke of hearts, of unity, of working together. *No, no, no!* It was to drive them apart! Kinnaird was to be a wedge between them. He was . . . he was . . .

He isn't here. And Lady Pratt hadn't promised to fetch him, had she? *No.* She had said she would use it. But apparently she deemed it enough to use the knowledge as a threat. All that stupid woman wanted were those stupid diamonds, and she didn't see far enough ahead to realize that they would be most easily acquired through the destruction of this ridiculous marriage.

The world went grey. Cloudy. Beset with fog. No one else would solve the problem. No one else would provide the answer. Stella clutched at the soft wool cloak she had put on to fend off the wind. She could depend on no one else. No one else could ever make her what she was destined to be, no one else could give her the desires of her heart.

It was up to her and her alone. If she wanted the love, the husband, the title . . . if she wanted all her dreams to come true . . . if she wanted *anything* in this world . . . then she'd just have to take it.

Lilias listened, unabashed, to the laughter seeping out from beneath the drawing room's door along with the strip of lamplight. It warmed her more than any fire to hear it, and to hear it sound so bright. So light. So free. She pressed her fingertips to the closed door and smiled through it.

Maybe her methods hadn't been right—though she hadn't a clue how she could have managed it differently—but the outcome was. Her Rowena had found happiness. A husband who would love her and the bairn—whom she could love in return.

Soft footsteps padded up behind her, silent but for the muted squeak of the soles upon the floor. "Are we eavesdropping, Lily?"

Her smile only grew as she let her fingers fall and turned toward Mr. Child. "Aye, and happily so." But she stepped away from the door and motioned him to follow. "They're content. I just have to listen now and then to assure myself of it."

"Well, if you've had enough of it . . ." He pulled his arms from behind his back, revealing her coat and his. "The moon is out and the night mild. I thought perhaps I could talk you into a stroll, since the duchess isn't likely to retire for another hour."

Unless the sickness struck earlier than it had in nights

past. . . . But even if so, the duke would gladly see to his wife for a few minutes until she could be fetched. She accepted the coat and, once Mr. Child had helped her into it, pulled out the knit gloves she'd stowed in the pockets.

He led the way out the back, held the door open for her. And when she'd paused to await him, he didn't offer his arm. Instead, he took her hand in his and gave it a little squeeze that made her heart dance like a schoolgirl's. "It's a lovely night indeed, Mr. Child," she said in an attempt to school her reactions.

Useless, given the way he smiled at her. "You could call me Franklin, you know. If you're of a mind, and given that I've taken the liberty of calling you Lily without even asking your leave."

She hadn't felt so giddy since Cowan had pulled her away from the feast all those years ago, down to the shores of the loch, and kissed her under the starlight. "I'd like that. And I dinna mind that liberty at all. There are too few people left in the world to call me Lily."

"It suits you. You're fair as a lily, especially in the moonlight."

Heat stung her cheeks—and made her laugh. "Listen to you, complimenting me as though I'm still a lass. And me blushing like one."

Mr. Child—Franklin—rubbed his thumb over her knuckles, making her wish she hadn't put on her gloves. "I can't imagine you were any lovelier twenty years ago."

"I'd heard the duke was a silver-tongued charmer, ye ken—but no one warned me his butler was too." Smiling, she bumped her shoulder into his.

Franklin grinned. "And from where do you think he learned it?"

They rounded the corner of the house, to where the light from the drawing room windows spilled out onto the lawn. With the moonlight flooding down from above and the golden rectangles angling out from the house, it painted the shrubbery and trees in sharp relief. But why was a shrub moving when there was no wind?

"What in thunder?" Franklin must have noted the same, for he let go her hand and put a hand on her arm, bidding her stay still. "You there! Show yourself!"

Lilias nearly rolled her eyes—he would have done better to remain still with her, and they could have crept up together, unnoticed. But no, at his shout there was further rustling in the shrubs, and a darting shadow. Franklin took off that way, but a frustrated "Blast!" soon sounded. "Lost him."

"Did ye see him at all?"

"No." He huffed back up to her, a hand at his side. "I saw only a clear reminder that I'm not a young man anymore and oughtn't to be chasing intruders about just to impress you. Brilliant, aren't I?"

She took his arm, rubbed a hand over it. But she stayed focused on where the figure had been. "Whoever it was, was watching the family. Is that Humphrey fella still locked up?"

Franklin shook his head. "He'd done nothing really, other than trespassing—for which he was fined. But we've someone keeping an eye on him, and he's in Cornwall."

The moon still beamed and the wind stayed calm . . . but Lilias felt colder. "Who, then? Who would be spying on them?"

Pressing his lips together, Franklin shook his head again and led her toward the rear door at a quick pace. "I certainly don't know, my dear. But we'd better tell His Grace posthaste."

Foolish as it was, she almost wished they could keep it to themselves. With such news, the laughter would die. The light would fade. And Rowena's smile would turn to a worried frown again.

They were walking. Around and around the house, through the gardens, into the wood and back again. Rowena shifted her hand on Brice's arm but kept her gaze locked ahead of them. Not that she really saw the lawn sprawling before her or the blue sky covering them above. Only the list in her mind with most of the suggestions already crossed out.

The problem was that they weren't just trying to stop one villain—they were now forced to deal with two, who would be coming at them from different directions.

Well, hopefully not. If they could bring Catherine to justice quickly and efficiently, she might not have time to contact Malcolm. He might never know. Never enter the picture again. Never intrude upon the life she was building at Midwynd.

If only her breathing, quick and shallow now, would remember that.

"Do you need to rest?" Brice drew her to a halt, his brow creased more deeply than it had been a minute before, when merely talking about murderous men and thieving women.

"No." She forced that old panic down and drew up a smile. "I think better these days when I'm moving."

Brice lifted her hand and kissed her fingers, then replaced it on his arm. "I keep coming back to the same idea. But I don't like it."

She studied his handsome profile, but it gave her no hints. "And why is that?"

"Because it may require you going back to Catherine, to draw her here."

The idea of facing the blonde again didn't exactly please her—but it wasn't nearly as terrifying as the thought of facing down Malcolm. "I can do it. Whatever ye need me to do. Tell me yer thought."

"We give her the jewels."

Rowena's legs froze, her feet rooted themselves to the ground. "We *what*? Have ye gone daft?"

Apparently not, given his grin. Or perhaps that was evidence that he *had*. "Well, not *the* jewels. Just . . . jewels. That could be mistaken for them."

"Are there such things?" She still couldn't quite wrap her mind around red diamonds. But oughtn't any gem that someone would kill over be unmistakable? Oughtn't anything worth so much, cursed so much, be identifiable at a glance?

"Rubies." He said it calmly, evenly. Knowingly. "They have been mistaken for rubies for much of their existence, apparently. I can get some that are a close match in size and color and clarity."

Her feet still weren't inclined to budge. "You can get them. In three days?"

"In one." He sighed and tilted his head back to watch a cloud scuttle by. "I have already done this legwork. They won't be the *closest* match, but she's never seen the real things. She won't know that."

"Even so, aren't rubies of such size and clarity rather dear? Too dear to just toss willy-nilly into the hands of a criminal?"

A fortnight ago, she would have considered the quirk of his brow condescending. Today it looked merely amused. "Well, I don't intend to let her *keep* them, darling. The whole idea is to have the constable there to arrest her whenever she takes them."

Of course. Though if something went wrong . . . Well, they wouldn't be as dear as the actual Fire Eyes. "So we put rubies in a hiding place. I go to Catherine and tell her I've found them but can't bring them directly to her for some reason, that she must fetch them herself—and for some other reason, *she* must be the one to do it, not some hired lackey. But of course, we're lying in wait. When she steals, she's arrested."

"Exactly. Simple, safe, and effective."

Hopefully. Though she wasn't sure it was enough to break the curse. Rowena tugged him onward again, toward the paddock where the horses were being put through their paces. She wasn't much of a rider, but she did enjoy watching the creatures leap and trot and turn. "We have only to determine those reasons. Why would I not be able to bring them? And how do I convince her she must, herself, be the one to get them?"

Brice rocked his head back and forth in thought. "Well, with our happy news, you can claim to be constantly watched. That I or Mother or Ella are always at your side, and that they're stashed in a place you can't easily get to—which has also yet to be determined."

"True. Though wouldn't a letter be more believable then?"

Brice's countenance went contemplative. "That would be my preference. It is just that I fear that she won't take a letter seriously enough. Perhaps a trusted courier?"

Which would involve finding one. "One of the Abbotts?"

He tilted his head. "Perhaps. I daresay Geoff would appreciate the chance to help."

"As for the other—how to convince her to come herself . . . Will greed suffice? Reminding her that if she entrusts the task to anyone else, they could make off with them?"

"I should think so. And there we have it. She's arrested, and we have a few years at least before we have to worry with it again—time enough to get a story in circulation about selling them far, far away from here, so that if and when she wins her freedom or someone else looks for them, they follow a trail to the other end of the earth. It's all finished before Annie arrives." Brice traced his fingers over hers.

Oh, to be able to think of other things. Of Annie, of the coming wee one . . . of the fire his kisses had begun to ignite inside her.

As if reading her mind, Brice drew her to a halt under the boughs of a wide tree and aimed a warm smile into her face. "You've blossomed so, these last two months. When first I met you, you would sooner have cowered in a corner than face down a woman who would insult and threaten and steal."

Or a man who could ignite passion within her. She returned the smile. "I'm sure I've much healing yet to do. But I—"

A crack shattered the air, and bark flew from the tree. Then came shouts, shoving, a whirl she couldn't begin to process. Brice's voice, yelling something about *down*. Another, calling their names. Hands pushing, shoving her to the ground.

"Nottingham!" Footsteps, swift and heavy. She could see the feet, recognized the polished but inexpensive shoes. They matched the voice.

"Abbott! No, don't—"

Another crack . . . a thud. She craned her head around, then wished she hadn't when she saw the blood gushing from Mr. Abbott's head.

An animalistic keen rent the air, and she didn't know if it came from her own throat or someone else's.

"*No*. No!" Brice took only enough time to shove Rowena behind the tree before diving for the bloody, still form of his oldest friend. "Geoff! Geoff, speak to me!"

But Abbott made no reply. He didn't twitch. The only movement was the spurting blood, drenching his friend's face in crimson.

"Brice, get *down*!"

He heard Rowena's frantic cry, of course, but the words meant nothing. He reached Abbott, touched a hand to his face, his neck. Was that his pulse or Brice's, thundering so hard he could feel it in the tips of his fingers?

"Brice!"

But the air was still. Of those earth-shattering shots anyway, though now footsteps pounded from every direction. Brice rested a hand on Abbott's chest, trying not to look at the terrible wound on his head. Trying to focus on whether there was the faintest rising and falling, a beating of the heart.

Voices joined the footfalls, shouting a dozen questions at once. As if he had any answers. As if he could do anything but fall back, impotent, when Old Abbott stumbled to his knees by his son's still form. When Mr. Child put a hand on his shoulder and asked, "What happened, Your Grace?"

He could only shake his head. "I don't know. We were walking, talking, and I heard—I could scarcely believe it—a gunshot. But not coming from where they had all been practicing. Bark flew from the tree. Then Geoff was shouting and running our way, trying to help, I suppose, and . . ."

"Brice." Rowena crawled up to him, wrapped her arms around him, buried her face in his shoulder.

His arms came about her without the need for thought. Thankfully, because he couldn't think, could only stare at his friend with that terrible dark circle on the side of his head. Then something shifted, clicked, and he shook himself. "Run to the telephone, Mr. Child. Call the constable straightaway, and the doctor. Hurry!"

The butler rose and took off with a speed that defied his age. Others had joined them—grooms and stable hands, gardeners, servants from the house. Mother, Ella, and Miss Abbott, all of whom looked about to fall over. Especially Miss Abbott, who advanced on shaking legs and all but collapsed at her father's side, over her brother.

Brice pressed a kiss to Rowena's head and staggered to his feet, his wife still latched to his side. His gaze fell on Davis, just emerging from the rear door beside Cowan. "Davis—would you get the women inside? They shouldn't—"

"No. I'm not leaving you." Rowena's arms went tight around him. "Not with someone trying to kill you."

"You think it was on *purpose*?" Ella, eyes wide, gripped their mother's arm. "Why? *Who?*"

Brice drew in a quick breath. "There were two shots—one too many to have been an accident, I should think. But it's hard to say who the target was. The first bullet struck between us, on the tree."

Rowena shook her head. "But I was already on the ground when the second one was fired. They must have been aiming at you, to have hit Mr. Abbott."

She had a point. And in part it brought relief, to realize she wasn't the target. Not that he particularly liked being in a gunman's crosshair. But better him than Rowena and the baby.

For the first time, he prayed the child was a boy. That if something happened to him, Nottingham would live on through that tiny life inside his wife.

Was that why God had brought them together, and her already with child? Was that why He had insisted Brice understand, love her, accept the baby as his own? Was he destined to die for the sake of justice—or to protect his wife?

He stood up straighter, held her tighter. He prayed not. But if so . . . then so be it. So long as they lived on.

Ella shook her head. "But . . . but *who*? Who would do this? Humphrey?"

"No, not Humphrey. He isn't in the area."

But assuming himself the target didn't exactly narrow it down. He was the one Catherine was after . . . though he was also the only one who knew where the diamonds were, so why would she risk silencing him before he could confide the secret?

And he was also the one Kinnaird would be more likely to take a shot at, if he'd so quickly traveled from the Highlands.

Neither of which he particularly wanted to tell the entire household.

Old Abbott rocked back on his heels, drawing all attention to him and to the terrible reality, rather than speculation. "He is alive, at least. Barely, I think, but alive. Praise God for that."

"We need to pray for him." Brice lowered to his knees again, Rowena alongside him, and gripped Geoff's hand. Still warm, promising life. Yet how would he have the strength to cling to it?

Brice closed his eyes, opened his lips, and prayed for a miracle.

How had it all gone wrong? Her brother lay in the hospital, unconscious, death looming. Unable to lift a finger. Unable to breathe a word. Unable to open his eyes and accuse. Clinging to life by the slenderest thread, but clinging.

Cling. Keep clinging.

He could live, that was what Ella had kept repeating all afternoon. Like Phineas Gage in America, who had taken a railroad spike through the skull and lived to tell about it. Like countless men in war. On and on Ella had gone, even dragging out some random book to show her the standard procedure for treating a bullet wound to the head—a procedure the medics wouldn't bother with if survival weren't possible.

But Stella cared little for whether the silver coin even now bound to the wound on Geoff's skull would keep infection at bay. The how didn't matter. All that mattered was that he lived. He had survived the operation to remove the bullet, so perhaps there was hope. There *must* be hope.

"Oh, Geoffrey," Father mumbled, his voice barely piercing the shadows that clung to the room. "*Why?* Why you, son? Not that I would have wished such a thing on His Grace, but why did you have to be there?"

Why indeed? Stella pressed her fingers to her eyes to try to make the images go away. It had all gone so wrong. Never, as the plan formulated, had it occurred to her that someone else might arrive to intervene. An oversight. A grave one.

No, not grave. Don't think about dying. Pull through, Geoff. Pull through.

Father looked up, and their gazes tangled. He sighed. "You ought to head home, Stella. I'll stay here with your brother. The duke said there would be a carriage waiting for us."

The duke. Eyes sliding shut, she shook her head. It had all gone so terribly wrong. That first miss . . . but he had acted so quickly. He'd pushed Rowena down, out of her sights, and the look on his face—not fear, not for himself. His every movement had been to protect *her*.

The rage had shifted, then. Turned, twisted.

She shouldn't have pulled the trigger again. She'd known it the second she'd done it, had nearly let loose a scream of dismay. Killing *him* was never what she'd wanted. Rowena must be removed, yes, but she never should have let herself grow angry with Nottingham. Even if he had spoken words of love to the sniveling twit. Even if he had forgiven her betrayal. Even if he had barely so much as glanced at Stella in the last week, nor said how-do-you-do.

But she hadn't meant for it to affect Geoff. Her father. Her family.

Geoff. *Cling to hope. Cling to life. Fight. Fight!*

Her eyes slid shut. Geoff had never been one to fight. Not *in* life—but *for* it, surely he would. He must. Just like all those other lucky men Ella had been so quick to find examples of.

Because if he didn't . . . She muffled a sob with her fist. He shouldn't have been there. It wasn't her fault he'd come running up as he'd done. She hadn't meant to hit him. Hadn't even seen him there, not through the rage that had greyed out her vision. But it hadn't been aimed at him, not at Geoff.

"Stella. My dear, please. It's growing late. Go home. Update the Nottinghams and your grandmother."

Stella grimaced. Grandmum would spend the evening fretting and lecturing, berating Stella for not being at her brother's side, for being in the manor with Ella instead of among her own. And she wouldn't be able to retort, would she, and say she *hadn't* been with Ella?

Because it was even more her fault than Grandmum could know. Than anyone could know. Because if they did, if they ever found out . . . if they somehow found the pistol she'd stashed in the shrubbery and not yet had time to fetch . . . She buried her face in her hands. She could be arrested. Go to prison, all hope of a life with Nottingham gone. All hope of *any* life gone. And if Geoff died—but he mustn't. He *mustn't*. "Please, Father. Just let me stay here."

"Stella." He sighed, sounding so very old. "Geoffrey wouldn't want you to neglect yourself, or for your grandmother to be kept waiting for news. Eat. Rest. One of us should, and Geoff would want—"

"Will you *stop* it?" She lurched to her feet, spun away but then back to face him, her back to the door. Her brother had a private room solely because Nottingham had insisted on it. Otherwise they'd be in the ward with all the other patients. "Stop talking about what Geoff would want, as if he were the perfect, selfless child. He wasn't, you know. He *was— Isn't*, I mean. He isn't."

Father rested his elbow on the arm of the chair and his head in his hand, as if merely talking to her wearied him. "I never said nor thought your brother was perfect. But will you really argue with me right now about whether or not he's always wanted the best for you? For all those he cares about?"

Of course not. Sainted Geoff, always putting everyone else first. How was anyone to compare to him? To live up to the standard he set? But he wasn't so perfect. He *wasn't*. "He resented the duke, did you know that? Resented him for his faith, when he'd never studied as Geoff had. Is *that* what a perfect child would do? Hate someone for being *good*?"

Father didn't jerk to attention, didn't gasp, didn't so much as blink. He just sighed again. "Please, Stella. He had his emotions firmly in hand, he spent hours on his knees to keep his focus where it belonged. He did not begrudge what the duke had. He only wanted to have such faith *too*. And he confided in me just this morning—"

His voice broke, but he sniffled and smoothed out his features again. "Just this morning he said he could see how His Grace needed such faith to get through these times. How relieved he was to realize it has aided him and Her Grace as they've fallen in love."

"No!" She didn't mean to scream it, but a whisper wouldn't have been ardent enough. Nothing would be ardent enough, but it helped to grab the nearest thing at hand—a clipboard—and fling it to the floor. "No. He doesn't love her. He *can't* love her, they aren't meant for each other. It was all a mistake, all a terrible mistake. They shouldn't have wed. It was a mistake. A mistake! I didn't mean to . . . I didn't . . . I love him. That's all that matters. Love. All is fair, as they say, in love."

Father's brows had knit, drawing lines in his face that had already deepened in the past few hours. They made him look as ancient as Grandmum, as doddering. As if he even remembered what it meant to be in love—if he'd ever known. No doubt he'd married Mother simply because she was an appropriate choice. Propriety—it was all he ever cared about.

"Stella." Father shook his head. "Lower your voice, I beg you. Sit down. And please don't say such things. You don't love him—"

"I *do*! Who are you to tell me my heart?"

His visage went fierce. "Your father—that's who. Though heaven knows you always resented being born to the steward instead of the lord. And that's all this talk is about—you wanting the life of a lady."

"It is *not* what it's about! I wouldn't care if he was a stable hand or a miller or a . . . a pickpocket. I love *him*, and he ought to be married to *me*, not that spineless Highland goat!"

Father washed pale, and his eyes went large. "She doesn't mean it, Your Grace. She is . . . It's just a tasteless jest."

Something inside went from sparking and hot to cold as a stone. Slowly, Stella turned. And there, staring at her as if she were a stranger speaking Swahili, stood Nottingham. His hand was still on the knob she hadn't heard him turn, and he had frozen in the doorway.

At least the she-goat wasn't with him. Stella lifted her chin and refused to let any embarrassment creep in. What had she to be ashamed of? She was every bit the lady Rowena was. Perhaps she hadn't been born to a nobleman, but her family was as fine as those moody Kinnairds—better, really. And *she* at least knew how to conduct herself in society. How to stand without cowering. How to greet lords and ladies without stuttering or lapsing into an incomprehensible accent.

She met his stare, though she nearly took a step back at the look in his eyes. *Horror* was the only word to describe it. Horror, at *her*! His old friend. The girl he had teased all their lives. Had flirted with long before *Rowena* ever entered the picture. Had said time and again would steal some nobleman's heart—and who could he have meant but himself? Why would he have given her that book, that inscription?

Forcing a swallow, she drew in a breath. "I'll not apologize for my heart, sir." There, see? Even now, she could speak without trembling, without quaking. She could hold herself erect. Not like *her*. "I'm only sorry I didn't confess my feelings long ago, before you were forced into this awful marriage."

He slid inside, pulling the door shut behind him. "I wasn't forced into anything."

Sending her gaze to the ceiling, Stella waved that off and pivoted. "You were—by her circumstances, if not her father. But that which is between us is stronger than—"

"Miss Abbott, there is nothing between us." He looked at her as if she were a wild animal that might attack at any moment. As if he weren't the one attacking, spitting out *Miss Abbott* like stones meant to build a wall between them. As if she weren't his Stella-bell, hadn't always been. "Aside from friendship. You have always been like a sister to me, but—"

"A *sister*?" She advanced on him, fisted her hands in his lapels. The closest she had been to him in a decade—but it wasn't how she'd always imagined. He wasn't gazing down at her with longing. He wasn't pulling her closer. His hands gripped her wrists, but not to hold her there—to push her away. Something hot and desperate dug its claws into her chest. "Darling, *please*. Give me a chance. I'll prove we're meant to be together. You deserve better than her, some rag tossed aside by a Scottish laird. You deserve—"

"Stop." He forced her back a step, forced his jacket from her grasp—and looked at her as he'd never done before. With a thundering anger. "It was you. It was you who told Lady Pratt about Kinnaird."

She tugged against his grip, but he held her fast. "For all the good it did—she's useless. I don't know why you fear her."

"Have you any idea what you've done?" Now he released her and stepped back as if she were a leper, that horror in his eyes again. "What you've brought upon us? Don't you realize that *that* is most likely why your brother lies near death?"

"You think Lady Pratt did this?" And she should let him—she should. It would serve the woman right if they somehow pinned it on her. But those claws kept digging, her insides getting hotter. Bubbling, until the absurdity of it all came out in a wretched laugh that pierced the room a second before she clapped a hand over her mouth.

"Stella." Father appeared at her side, his face frozen in a mask of dismay. "Stella, what have you done?"

Why must he look at her like that, why must they *both* look at her like that? As if she were the one who had betrayed *them*. As if all this were *her* fault. She shook her head, and then shook it harder when it did nothing to make those bubbles stop overflowing. "Nothing." Her voice didn't sound right. Too high, too insistent. "I did nothing."

But they stared at her, both of them. They stared, and their faces both screamed that she was a disappointment. That she was worthless. That she was *riffraff*. "It wasn't my fault." Couldn't they see that? "I was only trying to undo a wrong. You shouldn't have married her, Nottingham. Surely you know that. It was a mistake, and as soon as you're free of her, you'll thank me for it."

The muscle in Nottingham's jaw ticked. "I don't want to be free of her, Miss Abbott. I love her."

She winced at the blow. "No. No, you can't. All those times you told me how beautiful I am, all the jesting about me marrying a nobleman—"

"Oh, Stella." Father pressed a shaking hand to his forehead.

"You knew they were just that—jests. You knew he was complimenting you as he does Lady Ella."

Nottingham's nostrils flared. "You thought . . . Miss Abbott, I am sorry if I misled you. I promise you, it never once occurred to me that you would take my words as anything but those of a brother."

Misled her? *Brother?* She jerked her head to where Geoff lay in a stark white hospital bed. A silver coin over the hole in his skull, as if that could save his life. That life on the cusp of extinguishing. And Nottingham meant to tell her it was all for naught? That he didn't even love her?

"No." Now her voice was only a whisper nearly lost in the new shaking of her head. "All I've done to try to win you. All my hours of planning, and you expect an apology to make it better?" It all came boiling up, over.

She flew at him again, not really seeing anything but the fog. The same fog that had blinded her when she'd had him in her sights. Now she had only her fists and her nails, though she couldn't seem to get any purchase with them. Her feet were stuck in a morass, vines gripping her waist. "No!" Struggle as she might, she could barely reach him. The hateful, traitorous man. "I wish I'd killed you! I should have aimed at you from the start rather than that worm of a wife you love so well! It should be *you* on that bed, not Geoff!"

The vines suddenly dropped, and she fell forward, her knees striking the cold tile floor.

"Stella." Father. It had been his arms holding her back. Now he recoiled from her when she looked at him. "What . . . what are you saying?"

What? What had she said? No . . . no, she couldn't have . . . A sob ripped its way past her lips. "It was an accident. I didn't mean to . . ."

"You just said you tried to kill the duchess." Father's voice shook. "Stella . . . why? Why would you throw your life away like this?"

What did he mean? "I haven't. I was only . . . I didn't mean to hit Geoff, Father. You must know that."

He shook his head. "Is that supposed to console me? You tried to kill a duchess. A duke. You'll be imprisoned—"

"No!" She looked to Nottingham, but he wouldn't meet her gaze. His was locked on Geoff. "You can't turn me in. You can't. I didn't mean to hit him. I didn't mean . . . It's all a big mistake. You can't. You can't."

Father's face adopted the same somber lines he had worn at Mother's funeral. "I'm sorry, Stella. But you've left us no choice."

Brice squeezed his eyes shut, but it didn't go away. Didn't change. He pressed his palms to his temples, but the pressure didn't ease. One of his best friends—his oldest friend—still lay near death . . . and it was still his fault.

Rowena's hand rubbed circles on his back, just as he had done for her when she was the one reeling. Little comfort came. "I shouldn't have . . . I don't know. I never considered she would . . . What have I done, Wena? I'd thought it all in good fun. Innocent, harmless."

"It was." Her burr came through, melodious and comforting. "'Tisn't yer fault how she took it, *mo muirnín*. I've heard the things ye've said to her. Ye did nothing wrong."

Then how had it all turned into *this*? And how could Rowena now say there was nothing wrong with the way he'd always flirted and teased, when it had caused her such confusion? He shook his head and opened his eyes, though the sight of Ella, eyes red, curled up in a miserable ball in the corner of his sofa, did nothing to ease him. "Ella-bell?"

She shifted, looked to him. "I didn't have the least suspicion, Brice. Shouldn't I have? We spent all our days together these past months, and yet . . . she never breathed a word. Not a word, not about anything but the position awaiting her and the gentlemen she hoped to meet in Hertfordshire."

He had no answer. They had all, it seemed, failed to see the disturbed depths of Stella Abbott. Though perhaps her father had at least had an inkling. He had expressed concern over her desires, hadn't he?

And he had been the one to call the constable on his own child. To hold her still until Morris arrived, all the while watching over his other child in the hospital bed.

Lord, that poor father. Give him your succor. Save his son. I beg you. And Stella . . . I don't know what to pray for Stella. She was dangerous, clearly. Somehow able to admit to an action without accepting any responsibility for it. Something, somewhere, had gone awry inside her. *Heal her too, Father.* He didn't know how else to phrase it.

Rowena, perched on the arm of his chair, feathered her fingers through his hair. Funny how she'd been the calm one when he came home and broke the latest terrible news to everyone—including that *she* had been the one Stella had meant to kill at the start. While everyone else fell apart, himself included, she'd been the one to comfort and assure. He leaned in, rested his head against her side. "Perhaps we'll wake up and find this whole day a bad dream."

Rowena trailed her fingers down his neck. "No. But what we'll find is that the Lord is still lord. He isn't cruel or absent, He's directing us. Even in this. He's leading us to the place He needs us to be."

Ella sniffed. "That sounds like something Geoff would say."

"And so it is. Something he said to me that first night at Castle Kynn. I wasna so sure I believed him at the time. But I've seen the truth of it since. And truth doesna change at the next crisis."

He wanted to pull her into his lap and hold her tight. He wanted to smile at how she'd grown. He wanted to cry at how her new strength had to be tested now, like this.

"He'll recover. He will, I know it. Terrible as it seems, a head wound can be better than one to the chest or stomach." Ella unfolded her legs and pushed herself to her feet. At once determined and so very sad. "I'll leave you two to find what rest you can. Sorry to have intruded so long."

"Ye're no intrusion, Ella."

But the knock at the door felt like one—because anyone knocking would be a news bearer. And he couldn't fathom that any news to come would be good. Still, he had no choice but to bid, "Come in."

Mrs. Granger stepped half in, her gaze settled on Rowena. "Pardon me, Your Graces, my lady. But there's a visitor."

Who, that the staff wouldn't have turned them promptly away on a night like this? Brice drew in a deep breath, praying it was the Staffords, somehow knowing they'd need the support of friends. "Who is it?"

Her focus stayed latched on Rowena. "It's your father, Your Grace."

Twenty-Five

Rowena padded down the stairs, wondering where her peace had gone. Up in their rooms, with the horror of the day upon them, she had felt the Lord's hand, felt His presence, though logic said she shouldn't. She'd been able to push aside the sickness that wanted to churn—and the tears that wanted to come at realizing Stella Abbott had wanted her dead. She'd been able to hold tight to the hope that Mr. Abbott, who had so recently claimed to believe in the miraculous, would pull through.

Yet hearing that her father was at Midwynd shattered it all.

"It's all right." Brice gripped her fingers in his and kept pace beside her. "I'm here with you. He can't harm you. He has no control over you."

"Aye. But why is he *here*?" Not more bad news . . . *Please, God*. But what if something had happened to Annie? Why had he come a week before he and Elspeth were scheduled to bring her, but alone? She held fast to Brice's hand and wished the stairs would go on forever.

But they ended too soon, and then the hallways refused to stretch into eternity. In but a few moments she stood before the parlor door, wondering why she'd rather face Stella Abbott with a gun in her hands than the man who had raised her.

Brice lifted her hand to his lips and pressed a lingering kiss to her knuckles. "When you're ready."

She would never be ready to face her father again, apparently. It would have been easier with Annie as a buffer between them, her happy chatter covering the fact that Rowena had nothing to say to the Kinnaird, and he likely had nothing to say to her.

Except here he is. Indulging in a deep breath, she straightened her spine, squared her shoulders, and set her chin at what she hoped was a confident angle. "I'm ready."

Brice, however, held her in place. She turned her face to him, ready to ask what the matter was, but his lips settled on hers before she could speak. A soft kiss, and yet one that strengthened. Not just her, she saw when he pulled away with a bit of light back in his eyes, but him too.

"Rowena." His voice was as soft as the kiss, barely a whisper in the hallway. His fingertips traced her cheek. "I love you."

Her breath balled up. He'd said before that he *would* love her—he'd spoken of giving her his heart. But he'd never stated it so simply, so truly. He loved her. A sentiment that man waiting in the parlor had never once expressed. One her mother had said often enough, but which she had disproven with her choices—for didn't love put the other person above one's own desires? Malcolm . . . Malcolm had claimed it, but it had been a lie.

Had she ever really been loved before now by anyone other than Lilias? For who she was—strengths and weaknesses, both? For all she could be and all she had overcome?

She cupped his cheek, too, and looked deep into his chocolate eyes. "*Tha gaol agam ort.*"

His lips twitched up. "Which means?"

"I love you."

"That's what I hoped it meant." He wrapped his arms around her, seemingly content to ignore their guest who was no doubt pacing the parlor impatiently. "I should really learn a bit of Gaelic."

She looped her arms around his neck. "I'll teach you. Let's start with *An toir thu dhomh pòg?*"

He did his best to imitate her and then lifted his brows. "What did I just say?"

Smiling felt odd today. But she must take whatever joy she could find, whenever she could find it. "You said, 'Will you give me a kiss?' And the answer, Duke, is yes. I will."

He was chuckling as their lips met again. "A very important phrase indeed. I shall have to perfect it." For now, though, he held her close and kissed her deeply, sending tingles along her nerves.

Rowena held tight and let the realization come that she wanted more than his kisses. That if he had been killed today, she would have regretted not being his wife in the physical sense. She would have been sorry she hadn't invited more than kisses that made her senses swim. Perhaps the fear still lurked somewhere inside . . . but he never lit the panic anymore. He banished it.

When they stepped apart, she could sense the calm again. She could grip his hand, manage a tight smile, and nod. She could face her father.

Brice opened the door, and she stepped through without a tremble.

Douglas Kinnaird wasn't pacing. He was standing at the window, staring out into the darkness, and when they entered, when he turned, it wasn't with a scowl for keeping him waiting. It was with a sigh that sounded . . . relieved. "Rowena. Nottingham." He greeted them with a bare nod. "Forgive me for dispensing with pleasantries—but ye've trouble coming. Malcolm is on his way."

The calm fled again, and Rowena stumbled in its absence. "Now?" Catherine had said . . . but then, why should she believe anything that woman said? Or perhaps Miss Abbott had contacted him. It didn't much matter *who*, really. Just *that*.

"Blast." Brice rubbed a hand over his face. "When?"

Father looked at him rather than her. "McPherson reported that the telegram came in yesterday for him. He delivered it, but he gave me a copy too. I left straightaway—and had McCloud get Malcolm drinking at the pub. It willna have bought much time, but perhaps a day. The wire . . . it said . . ." Father glanced at her, then back to Brice.

She stood as close to her husband's side as she could manage. "He knows everything, Father. Including that I'm with child—Malcolm's."

Spitting out a Gaelic curse, Father turned away, then back. "Lilias—before you left, she'd said it wasna an issue."

Not a conversation she particularly wanted to have with her father. "We were mistaken." She wove her fingers more tightly through Brice's. "Father, why'd ye come?"

Now he looked at her as he so often had in the past—as if she were daft, or stupid. "Ye think I'd just let him come and hurt you again?"

He'd let him the first time, hadn't he? And then threatened to make her marry him, to be hurt by him for the rest of her life. "Ye could have wired. It would have been faster . . . and easier."

Father lifted his chin. The lamplight caught the silver in his hair, but it also sharpened the shadows in his face, the angles of his broad shoulders. Made him look fierce, like the chief he was. "Ye think I'd leave yer safety to a pack of lily-livered *Englishmen*?"

Brice snorted. "No need to walk on eggshells around me, Lochaber, really. Tell me what you really think."

"Pardon me, Duke." Not that his tone actually asked forgiveness. "Ye've a lovely home, and I can see ye're taking fine care of my daughter. But ye havena the foggiest clue how to meet an enraged clansman."

"I suppose I should break out the broadswords and battle axes?"

Father didn't look amused by the humor that made Rowena want to smile. But he bit back the retort she'd expected. Though his hand fisted, his nostrils flared, he shook his head. "'Tis my fault he's still a problem. He's my responsibility, and I failed to get him in hand when I should have done, years ago. Now it's my family paying the price. I ask yer leave, Duke, to let me help."

Silence pulsed, but then Brice nodded. "My way, my terms. We'll take care of this peaceably, as much as possible." His fingers tightened around Rowena's. "There has been violence enough already."

Was it any wonder she loved this man?

Father didn't look to think it a smart stance to take. But he nodded. "As ye wish. But Malcolm willna think that way. He'll have bloodlust in his veins, and ye're likely to be his target, Duke."

Brice didn't even seem to hear him. His eyes had narrowed. "Do you know who sent the telegram?"

"Nay, there was no name. The best McPherson could figure out was that it came from Brighton. Have ye enemies who would want him to know?"

Rowena rested her hand on Brice's arm. "Too many. Was it Catherine, do you think?"

Shaking his head, Brice focused on the nothingness across from him. "It wouldn't make sense. Her best hope is scaring you into doing what she wants, but if he's already here, then you'd have no incentive to give in to her. Your focus would instead be on getting away from *him*."

"Stella, then."

"It seems the safest assumption. That it was she, and that Lady Pratt doesn't know Malcolm is headed our way. Still, we had better act quickly. Once he arrives, her threat loses its potency, and she'll come up with something worse."

A shiver overtook her. "He could be here by tomorrow."

"Then we move first thing in the morning. I'll ring the constable straightaway and—"

"Pardon me." Father glared at them both. "What the devil are you two talking about? Who is Lady Pratt?"

Brice had already turned toward the door, urgency making him all but vibrate. Their fingers were still linked, but his grip had loosened. He met her gaze. "Are you . . . ?"

"I'm fine." And she was, mostly. She squeezed his fingers and let them go. "Go and ring the constable. I'll fill in Father on what is going on."

His eyes asked *Are you certain?*

She smiled to assure him she was.

He strode from the room, and she wrapped her arms around her middle, chilled now that he wasn't beside her. For a long moment, she stared at the empty doorway, not really wanting to turn back and face the Kinnaird.

But she heard him shift, and then he was at her side, though a long stride away. "What did he do when he found out?"

Drawing in a long breath, she prayed for an extra measure of peace. "He did what only the best of men would do—promised to love me and the bairn, to protect us. He kissed me and swore to be the finest father a child ever had." She kept her body facing the door but turned her head to look at him.

She'd gotten her petite stature from her mother. The shape of her face, the color of her hair. What did she have of him but for his eyes? And his propensity to assume the worst, apparently, to judge too soon and too harshly.

What a legacy to have inherited. "I'm surprised you bothered coming, Father." She heard the rigidness in her tone, and it came out in the clipped accents of the English. "That you would worry at all with what he did. You have another heir on the way. You'll not need me anymore."

Cursing, he turned to face her, granite for a face. "How is it ye lived yer life in my castle, yet ye ken so little about me?"

She turned to him too, and felt a surge when she did so. How many times had she dared to face him down before? Once? Twice? "What is it I'm supposed to understand? I ken only what ye took such care to teach me—dinna disagree. Dinna disobey. Dinna speak out o' turn or look out o' turn or ever ask for anything. And dinna, above all, ever expect affection." So much for English inflection. She spread her arms wide. "Those are the lessons I learned at yer knee, Father. Pray tell, what did I miss?"

He muttered another low curse and shook his head. "Lil said I'd handled you wrong. That ye needed soft hands."

"Instead of cudgels, you mean?"

"I did what I kent to do!" he shouted. Then he heaved out a breath, slashed a hand through the air. "Hate me for it if ye must. But it was with a cuff that my father taught me how to be a Kinnaird, with a cuff that his father taught him. And ye're a Kinnaird, Rowena. My firstborn, my daughter, my heir. Mine to protect, to try to shape into someone worth the air ye breathe—unlike yer cowering traitor of a mother."

Her eyes slid closed, but she bit her tongue. For the first time, she listened for the hurt in his words. The hint of a man who had tried to make his wife happy, who had spent a decade doing everything right, only to lose her when he dared leave her alone. "Lilias just told me what she did. That summer."

"Then ye ken." His voice didn't soften. If anything, it sounded rougher than it had before. "Ye ken that it wasna my fault."

Her fingers curled into her palm, and she opened her eyes again. "Not that she strayed. But ye decided how to react, Father. Ye decided to punish *me* for it, not just her. And that . . . no—that I dinna understand." She pressed a hand to her abdomen, where that precious little life grew safely inside. "I dinna understand why ye hated me for her offense."

His larynx bobbed. "I never hated you, lass."

But he wouldn't say he loved her. Perhaps his lips didn't even know how to form the words. And it shouldn't require words, should it? Brice had proven his heart through his actions long before he whispered it to her in the hallway a few minutes ago.

Father though . . . "Perhaps you didna. But that's what yer actions said every time ye hit me. Every time ye insulted me. Ye say ye wanted to make me worth the air I breathed—but ye taught me the opposite. That I *wasna*. That I wasna worth the air, or the land I stood on, or the castle that was more important than I was. Your actions told me that my well-being was worth less than the sheep in the pastures, less than the least of the clan, less than anything. That's what I've spent the last decade feeling like—*less*. Then ye wonder at how I dinna stand tall with the pride of a Kinnaird."

His posture went even more rigid. "Ye're standing tall enough now."

Perhaps his lips didn't know how to form an apology, either. He wouldn't say he was sorry. He wouldn't ever admit he had chosen the wrong way to teach her what lessons he thought she needed to learn. He wouldn't ask her forgiveness.

The question was . . . could she forgive him anyway?

She turned away, back toward the door.

"I dinna ken why ye had to run off to England to learn it, but there it is—ye're standing as a Scotswoman should. Defiant and strong, not giving in when trouble comes. Ye do the Kinnairds proud, lass."

And yet still he couldn't bring himself to say she did *him* proud. Still wouldn't even admit that she had to run off to England because he'd given her no other choice.

The silence stretched until it crackled, but Rowena hadn't any words with which to break it. None that wouldn't be more venom—and she pressed her lips against that. She wouldn't be like him. Not anymore, not even with him. She'd laid out her complaints, she'd made her accusations, and what had it gotten her? An assurance that she wasn't hated. That she was worth something to the clan.

He'd never be the father she wanted. That was hers to learn to accept. He would never laugh with her, never put an arm around her, never be one for long talks by the fire of a cold winter's eve. He wouldn't cheer her on in her victories or soothe her tears in her failures.

But he would leave his world to come to hers when danger threatened. He would admit, at least, to handling Malcolm wrong.

Was that enough?

"What's this other business the duke is tending? About that Lady Brat?"

The mistake made her lips curl up. "Pratt. She wants diamonds that Brice has and will stop at nothing to get them. She threatened to unleash Malcolm on us if I didn't discover their whereabouts and get them to her."

A glance at her father showed his brows were arched, his arms folded across his chest. "Are the gems hers?"

"No."

"Valuable, I take it?"

"All but priceless."

"And she thinks to threaten my daughter into becoming a thief on her behalf? Greedy English b—"

At *her* raised brows, he cut himself off, cleared his throat—and finished with "Brat."

"Pratt."

"I'll call it as I see it."

She smiled, actually smiled. In the presence of her father, over something he'd said. On a day like this, it felt akin to a miracle. "Aye, well. I daresay we willna argue that one with you."

He nodded, tugged his waistcoat, and drew in a breath. "I'll help however ye need me. With this Lady Brat, and with Malcolm when he arrives. With whatever ye require."

She would have preferred a few simple words. But whether or not it was enough, this was what he offered. All she would get from him. She nodded, then tilted her head and drew upon that well of calm inside. "Promise me one thing, Father."

"What?"

"Annie. No matter what comes between you and Elspeth, or what Annie might do, ye'll never raise a hand to her like ye did to me, or to the coming babe either. If they displease you, then send them to me. I'll take them."

He stared at her for a long moment in that baffled way, shaking his head. "Ye know who ye put me in mind of?"

As if he hadn't shouted it at her a hundred times. "My mother."

"Nay. Lilias. Blasted nuisance, she is . . . but a fine Kinnaird." He nodded and turned to the door too. "Ye have my word."

Perhaps that *would* be enough.

Twenty-Six

"And *that's* meant to be a secure hiding place?"

Brice hammered the board back into place and told himself not to grit his teeth. Mother had taken him aside and cautioned him to be kind, to be receptive, to grant Lochaber a way to help. According to her, this was a great step on his part, one that should be encouraged.

And he would only be visiting for a few days. All right, a week—he'd announced his intentions to stay through when his wife brought Annie in six days' time. One little week, and then Brice wouldn't have to see the man for months.

See? There was reason to smile as he straightened from the floor of the old playhouse nestled in the trees. It had seen better days, having not had a child's laughter to brighten it for many years. But then, that was rather the point. "I think it a perfect hiding place. No one would expect priceless gems to be hidden out here—hence, no one would look for them without a tip."

Lochaber grunted. "I do hope ye havena put the real things in a place so insecure."

Why, again, had the man followed him? All he'd done to help was stand about criticizing while Brice pried up a board in the corner, slid in the rubies his jeweler had obligingly delivered at first light, and nailed the wood back into place. "Well, you haven't stubbed your toe on them yet, have you?"

Lochaber didn't so much as chuckle. "If they're as valuable as my daughter said, they ought to be under lock, key, and guard."

And announce to the world where they were? "Your opinion is duly noted." He ducked out of the miniature house and headed back for the real one—it was within view, which was part of the reason for his choice of makeshift hiding place. The constable's men would be watching from the windows, and when they saw Lady Pratt—and hopefully her brother too—approaching, they would give the signal to the men who would be hiding in the woods. Said men would make their move once the thieves had the jewels in hand.

Quick, simple, effective. Once caught in the act of stealing, they would have little hope of escaping the charges. And Brice intended to have the story of his selling them to a wealthy sheik ready for the telling whenever they got out.

Lochaber's attention had drifted to the path Catherine was to follow, assuming she listened to the advice Rowena would impart on where to sneak onto his property. "And what if they dinna play along? What then?"

He couldn't think about that. "They've been seeking the Fire Eyes for a lifetime. They won't stop when they're so close. Greed will take over."

The curse would bite.

Lochaber shook his head. "But it all hinges on them getting the note, reading it, acting right off. What if Lady Brat is out calling? We havena time to wait. Malcolm could be here on the afternoon train."

"Have you always such a cheery outlook?"

Halting, Lochaber emitted a noise that sounded suspiciously

like a growl. "'Tisn't wrong o' me to think things through and point out the flaws in your plan, lad. How else will ye fix them?"

"All right." The man probably had a point. . . . Though a nicer way of putting it wouldn't be ill received. "What do you suggest, my lord?"

"Dinna leave it to a courier—that's what." Lochaber lifted his chin. "I'll deliver the message myself, and if she isna at home, then I'll track her down. Say Rowena entrusted me with it where she wouldna anyone else. And I'll employ my particular charm to ensure she does as we want."

"Charm?" It came out too scoffing, but Brice couldn't help himself. "You mean, you'll antagonize her?"

For the first time since that trap of a dinner, Lochaber smiled at him. "Exactly. Ye've yer way, Duke—and I've mine."

Well, if anyone could succeed at chafing Catherine into acting, it was likely the Earl of Lochaber. "A fine change to the plan—and I thank you for volunteering."

"I told you I'd help. I'm helping."

Brice moved onward again. They really hadn't any time to waste, and he'd scarcely seen Rowena since they rose two hours ago. She'd been perfecting the letter she'd send to Catherine, he'd been dealing with the jeweler, the constable, hiding the rubies.

Mother and Ella had gone, at his request, to spend the day at hospital with Old Abbott and young. He suspected they would pay Miss Abbott a visit at the jail as well, given the look they'd exchanged. And they'd promised to send an update on Abbott's condition.

No bad news had come thus far. He must have made it through the night. *Please, Lord, let that mean he'll pull through altogether. Please. As all the others whose names Ella keeps reciting, let him pull through. Heal him, fully. Grant him the miracle he needs.*

As they neared the door, Lochaber said, "I'll fetch the letter from Rowena and head out directly. It's early yet to pay a call, but I think that'll work to our advantage, aye?"

"I should say so."

"Duke."

Brice paused with his hand on the latch and looked over his shoulder.

Lochaber stood without a smile now—but also without a frown. No judgment in his eyes, if no warmth. He held Brice's gaze for a long moment. Then he nodded.

Approval? Appreciation? Merely acknowledgment of the danger they were inviting today? Though he couldn't be entirely sure, he suspected it was a combination of it all. And so he nodded in return.

They found Rowena sealing the letter into an envelope, stamping her personal *N* design into the pooling wax. Upon their entrance, she held it up. "Here we are."

Her hand was steady . . . but the writing on the envelope wasn't. It looked hurried and harried, just as it should. "Perfect. Your father will be delivering it."

Her eyes went wide, but she nodded. "I suppose it would make sense to her. If she asks, he can say he merely came down a few days before Annie and Elspeth. Just dinna mention Malcolm, Father. She must think she is in control there."

"Aye. I'm not a dunce." He took the letter, slid it into his pocket, and spun on his heel. "I trust your drivers know how to get me to this woman's house?"

He didn't wait for a response, and Brice didn't try to halt him. Instead he held out a hand and, once Rowena put her fingers in his, pulled her to her feet so he could wrap his arms about her. "How are you feeling?"

"The toast seems to have settled, for which I'm thankful.

Though to be perfectly honest, I'd rather skip this day altogether and wake up to tomorrow—wherein Mr. Abbott shall have proven Ella right and awakened, Catherine shall have been arrested, and Malcolm shall have been discovered to have passed out in the pub in Lochaber, thought the telegram a dream, and given up all thought of coming here."

"Mm." He rested his head against hers. "That would be lovely."

She nestled against him and trailed a finger down his tie. "Brice . . . when all this is over, I . . . I dinna want to wait any longer. To be yours in every sense, I mean. Had I not been so miserably ill last night when we went upstairs, I would have . . ." She blushed to a halt.

Who knew he would have found a reason to grin today? "Giving me incentive for getting through this day?"

"In one healthy piece." She smiled up at him. With the kind of smile that tied a man in knots. "I love you. I canna promise that there willna be any panic, but I think I'm ready. I ken ye'll never hurt me. And when ye kiss me . . ."

He did so now, just a featherlight touch of his lips on hers. "When I kiss you?"

"I ne'er want you to stop. I canna think of anyone, anything but how ye make me feel."

Were it a different day, he would have accepted the unspoken invitation to test that now, to kiss her until they both melted. But the pressure he'd felt since the minute he woke up this morning pressed harder upon him, and he drew away a few inches. "My darling, I want . . ."

She inched away too, but her smile was all soft light. "I know."

"But we must . . ."

"Aye. 'Tisn't the time. Constable Morris will be here any minute. And until he arrives . . ." She caught his hand, tugged him toward the settle. "You lead the prayer, *mo muirnín*. Ye're better at finding the right words."

No words felt sufficient, not today. Not with so many lives teetering on the balance. But he did his best to put voice to the cries of his spirit. For the Abbotts. For the constabulary. For Mother and Ella. For him and Rowena. That Lochaber would be able to influence Catherine as required.

That they would be protected from Malcolm.

But there were praises too. That her father had come to warn them. That Geoff had survived the night. That no one else had been harmed yesterday.

When he breathed his amen and opened his eyes, he found they were no longer alone in the drawing room. Much of the upper staff had slipped in, bowed their heads, and joined the prayer. Davis and Cowan, Lapham and Lewis, Mrs. Granger and Mr. Child . . . who had a hand on the small of Cowan's back. Brice slanted a glance at Rowena, but she didn't seem to have noticed.

A conversation for another day.

The butler reclaimed his hand and tucked it behind his back, clearing his throat. "The men have arrived, Your Grace. Shall I show those who will be positioned inside where to go?"

"Please. And I'll take the others outside. Rowena—"

"As I promised. I'll stay inside, out of the way."

Brice sent her a scowl. "I did *not* say out of the way."

His wife grinned. "Out of the way, out of harm's way . . . the result is the same."

"Hmm." He touched a finger to her chin and then stood. "Just be safe—that's all I ask."

Cowan bustled forward. "We'll go to the upstairs sitting room. Not as good a vantage as the men will have, but we'll be able to glimpse a bit."

Mrs. Granger nodded. "I'll bring up a tray of tea things. I've already put out to the inns and hotels that we'll not be conducting tours today, as requested, Your Grace."

"Thank you, Mrs. Granger." Brice kissed Rowena's hand and then turned her over to the older women, who would no doubt coddle and try to distract her until it was all finished. Would have driven him crazy—and probably would her too—but caring for her would keep *them* busy and out of harm's way.

And keeping the household from any more injuries was everyone's top priority today.

He met the group of trusted men in the entryway and led them out the back, to the various places he and the gardener had chosen this morning. Every possible path of escape would be covered by at least one man, the more likely ways by three or more. In the garden, they would be concealed by hedges and sheds, behind gates and statuary. In the woods, the spryer of them would opt for height in the trees and the majority would crouch behind brush that would conceal them from whichever way Catherine might come.

All would be listening for the bird call of their fellows in the house, watching for her arrival.

By the time Brice got them all situated, he could hear the crunch of gravel from the front. Lochaber came around the side of the house just as Brice was heading back through the garden to the rear door.

He didn't quite know how to read his father-in-law's face. He certainly didn't look pleased, but he didn't look any more displeased than usual, either. Brice headed his way. "How did it go?"

Lochaber spared a curt nod. "I daresay she willna be far behind. Piece of work, that one. Are ye well acquainted?"

"Only well enough to know I have no desire to know her better."

That earned him a brief smile. "I've met a few like her before—not my favorite people, but I ken well enough how to speak to them."

"Well, I appreciate you doing so. I think all is in place—"

"Sir!" Mrs. Granger's voice broke in, sounding frustrated. "I beg your pardon, but when I said no tours, I didn't mean you could take yourself on one!"

Brice barely stifled a moan. Apparently they hadn't gotten the word out to everyone in ample time. If they'd had the leisure of choosing their own day for this all to transpire, it wouldn't have been on one when tours were normally given. "Excuse me. I had better intervene—we have had tourists sneak away before, but their curiosity usually flees rather quickly when they realize they've been caught by the master of the house."

Lochaber muttered something about the lack of wisdom of giving tours in general, but Brice ignored him and turned toward the corner of the house where Mrs. Granger's voice had come from. The poor woman must have been chasing the fellow all the way around, for her next shout sounded short on breath and growing ever more in outrage.

Another day, it would have been amusing. Today . . . He paused when a dark-clad figure rounded the corner.

Tall, broad. Dark hair falling over his forehead, dark eyes. And lips that curved up into a dark, cruel smile when he spotted Brice.

"Blast." How did he get here so quickly? And why was he raising his arm as if . . . ?

"Get down!" Apparently not trusting Brice to act, Lochaber charged into him, knocking him to the ground behind a granite maiden.

Even as they fell, a crack split the air, and a *chink* came from the statue. Screams, shouts, thundering steps. Brice pulled himself from the white gravel digging into him, careful to remain behind the wide granite base. Lochaber followed suit behind him.

"Put down your weapon! Hands in the air!"

The answering Gaelic shout didn't sound inclined to obey. Footsteps, but not away. No, closer. Brice's gaze darted to the door—too far, with no cover between. The nearest tree was a good thirty feet behind. Could they edge around the statue, avoid him?

Lochaber cursed, peered out, cursed again.

When Brice looked up, he was staring down the barrel of a pistol. Malcolm Kinnaird wasn't smiling now, but he also wasn't firing. He grabbed hold of Brice's collar and wrenched him to his feet, shouting at the encroaching officers, "One step closer and the duke gets a bullet in the head!"

Ducky. Just ducky.

Lochaber stood too, looking ready to pummel the man. "Easy, Malcolm. Think before ye act. Ye kill him, and ye willna get away. Ye'll be locked in a Sassenach prison the rest o' yer days."

The cold cylinder pressed to Brice's temple wasn't moved by the earl's logic. But he felt no panic, not like yesterday. Just a calm that held him absolutely still.

"Call off yer hounds, Sassenach," Kinnaird hissed into his ear. "Give me Rowena and my bairn, and we'll leave you in peace. No one harmed. No one hurt."

Brice glanced about the garden. All the men were out of hiding, all had their weapons at the ready. The odds were in his favor—except he already had a pistol at his head. But if he could just put some space between them . . . "They'll not make a move without my command." Not entirely true, given that they weren't *his* men, but they certainly wouldn't charge in at the moment. "Put away your weapon and we'll talk. Inside, like civilized human beings."

"Oh, I dinna think so. I'm not glaikit enough to go into yer house. Send yer guards away and his lordship in for his daughter."

The men kept creeping closer, though Brice hoped the hand he raised discreetly at his side would halt them. He didn't particularly relish the thought of Kinnaird getting nervous at the approach of a dozen . . . Wait. A dozen? He scanned the faces again and realized the men from the woods had joined the fray.

"I'm not jesting!" Kinnaird yelled loudly enough for them all to hear. "Now, Lochaber. Go and fetch Rowena. If ye refuse, it'll be a bullet in the duke's head and one in yers as well. I may die or rot for it, but at least I'll know he willna be—"

"Malcolm, *stop*! Let him go. I'm here!"

Now the panic came, full and hot, and Brice jerked his head toward the house. "No. Rowena, get back inside! Now!"

She stood in the doorway, her face still pale from that morning's sickness, her eyes wide with fear. Why, then, would she put herself in the path of the monster who had haunted her nightmares? Why would she . . . ? But he knew. The same reason he would sooner take a bullet than let her suffer at his hands again.

Love did strange things to one's logic. And to one's fears.

"There's a good lass." Kinnaird pressed the gun harder against Brice's temple and dug his fingers into his neck. "Here's how it'll work, Sassenach. She comes with me, and ye dinna try anything clever. If ye do, I shoot her instead. Do ye ken?"

All too clearly. One way or another, one of them would die if they fought. Yet they *must* fight, with their wits if not with weapons. "You would kill her? When you've gone to such trouble to get her back?"

The gun was warming against his flesh . . . which made it all the worse. "Better dead than—"

"With a Sassenach. Right. Very enlightened of you, I can't think *why* the Scots and English were ever at odds."

Kinnaird shifted his grip on the gun, pushed Brice back around to face the officers rather than Rowena. "Stay back. Ye'll have yer precious duke soon enough. Rowena!" He gave a sharp Gaelic command.

Rowena edged forward, taking slow, cautious steps. He could barely glimpse her in his periphery, couldn't see her face. Couldn't exchange any silent message.

He didn't have to. Lochaber still stood before him, unencumbered and able to see them both. He glanced from Rowena to Brice, showed three fingers against his leg and then looked to the ground.

"Faster!" Kinnaird barked.

Lochaber flashed one finger.

"Well, if ye want me to move faster, perhaps ye should try not scaring the verra life out o' me with that gun. Put it down, Malcolm, and let him go! I'm *coming*."

Lochaber flashed a second finger.

"I'll put the gun down when I'm good and ready."

Lochaber flashed a third finger. Brice lunged to the side and down. Lochaber charged with a shout that would have done William Wallace proud.

A shot. Feminine screams. Masculine shouts. A veritable earthquake of thundering footfalls, another blasted shot that bit the ground not an inch from his nose, spraying dust into his eyes. He blinked it away and got to his knees, casting about for . . .

There, there was Rowena, crawling toward him. Unharmed, praise the Lord. He had to get to her, get her to safety, then find some way to help Lochaber, who was trying to wrestle the gun from Kinnaird's hands.

"Brice." Her voice was but a croak, but it was speaking his name, so what did he care? He scrabbled to his feet and stumbled for her, pulled her up into his arms.

A guttural scream ended the shuffling sounds behind them. He spun.

The constable's men had converged upon them, and one stood on the wrist that had formerly held the weapon. A second claimed the gun, and four more held the beast down. Morris wiped his brow and repositioned his hat. "You're under arrest for the attempted murder of the Duke of Nottingham. And if you don't stop struggling, Clive here's going to have my permission to pound you into submission."

A hulking man slammed a hand against his fist and grinned.

Brice buried his face in Rowena's hair and held her so tight even air couldn't fit between them. "What were you doing down here? We agreed—"

"I saw him, heard him. I couldna let him kill you. I couldna."

"I know. But you nearly felled me of a heart attack." He leaned back just enough to tip up her face. "We're safe."

"Aye." But her brows drew together. "Are *all* the men here?"

He spun back around, did another quick count—but his math in the heat of the moment hadn't been amiss. They'd left the woods unguarded.

His stomach turned to a stone. "Constable Morris."

Morris looked up, around, and seemed to come to the same conclusion he just had. Muttering a curse, he took off at a run for the trees.

Brice and Rowena hurried after him. But he didn't need to see the twigs disturbed that they had carefully placed. Or the door standing ajar on the old playhouse. He knew, even before he ducked in and saw the board torn up.

Morris swept his hat from his head and slapped his leg with

it. "We missed her. She came at just the right time. What a blasted lousy coincidence."

Leaning into the doorway, he sucked in a breath. "Somehow I doubt that."

"Well, she's not going to get away with it." Morris slammed his hat back on his head and brushed past Brice and Rowena. "She can't be more than a few minutes ahead of us. We're going to catch her at her flat, with the gems still on her person, that's what." He paused a few steps away, glaring. "You might as well come. Identify your possessions then and there so she can't claim they're hers. I daresay it'll be safe enough with a whole retinue of us arriving en masse."

Brice nodded. It would allow him to stop in at the hospital too.

Rowena tucked her hand in his. "I'm going too. I'm not letting you out of my sight."

"You needn't worry for me, darling." But he gripped her hand. And was glad she did. "I don't intend to find myself the target of a gun again—ever."

"Good. But even so."

"Even so. Together." They must get this finished—and move on with actually living.

Chaos greeted them. Rowena followed behind Constable Morris and Brice, but they looked every bit as confused as she as they pushed open the door that hadn't been latched and stepped into the bowels of pandemonium. Everything inside the house Catherine and her brother had let was in a riot, servants shouting and scrambling and crying, no one paying any mind to the fact that a slew of uniformed officers had just entered.

"What in thunder?" But no one answered the constable's mutter.

Rowena shook her head. It didn't look as though the household were trying to beat a hasty retreat—no one had anything in their hands, no boxes or trunks to be seen. And that surely wouldn't incite so many tears.

Then a vaguely familiar maid came running down the stairs, sobbing. "It wasn't my fault, my lady, I swear it! I *swear* it! I was right there in the next room the whole time, just knitting. I didn't do anything!"

"You stupid wench!" Catherine tore down the stairs after the maid, in a state Rowena had never seen her in before. Her hair was half down. Her face streaked with tears and white as the chalk cliffs. And she shook so violently Rowena could see it from the door. "You killed him! You *killed* him!"

Bile burned Rowena's throat. The nurse—it was the nurse who stumbled in her haste, who fell down the last three steps and then beat her fists against the floor. *No. Dear Lord, not little Byron. Please, not her baby. Don't have taken her baby.* She gripped Brice's arm, bidding him go no farther.

Constable Morris, however, lurched forward to catch Catherine when she made to throw herself atop the nurse. She beat against him, trying to get to the girl. "She killed him! Arrest her, make her pay—she killed my baby!"

"I didn't! I swear it!" The nurse crawled behind the constable's legs, barely comprehensible through her heaving cries. "I love the boy. I would never harm him. He just stopped breathing. He always naps so sound, never making a peep, but I checked on him. I did, like I always do, after an hour, and . . . and he just wasn't breathing! It was the crib death, my lady, not me. Not me!"

Catherine's scream made Rowena wince away, move behind

Brice. Not that he could shield her from it, from the pure, undiluted sound of a heart fragmenting, shattering, piercing one's being down to the soul.

How well she knew that scream. She'd loosed it herself when Malcolm had attacked her—but to lose one's child? It was all she could do to keep from being sick at the thought.

The scream ended on a shuddering sob, and Catherine's fists let off pounding at the constable, clinging to him instead. "She killed him. He's gone. My precious angel, my beautiful boy—it's all her fault. I was only away from the nursery for an hour, visiting with my friends in the parlor, and . . . and she *killed* him."

Only then did Rowena note the three ladies crowded in the parlor door, all pale faced and tear streaked. Ladies who certainly didn't look newly arrived, given the half-eaten biscuit one still clutched in her hand.

Catherine hadn't been at Midwynd.

"Easy, my lady. Easy." Constable Morris guided Catherine away from the nurse. "Rest assured there will be an inquiry, but if it was crib death . . . these things happen, terrible as they are. We lost one that way, too, when she was but three months old."

Catherine's knees buckled, and the constable lowered her to the lowest step. He looked to her guests. "You were with her? For the last hour?"

The ladies all nodded. From within the parlor Lord Rushworth pushed past them and went to his sister, gathering her close. She wept into his shoulder.

The constable sighed and edged closer to the ladies, away from the mourners. "And Lord Rushworth—he was with you too?"

The eldest of them, as if shocked, still looked to where he'd brushed by. "I didn't realize he was there at all."

"Oh, Lucinda—he was there the whole time, he greeted us when we came in."

"No, not the whole time," the third put in. "He stepped out for a moment, remember? For ten minutes, perhaps."

Not enough time to have gone to Midwynd and back.

Fearing she was about to be ill, Rowena stepped back outside, tugging Brice along with her. "They didn't take them. They may have had someone else do it, but it wasna them. And now . . . this . . ."

Brice shook his head and looked back to the door, his face wreathed in pity. "I wouldn't have wished this on them. I wouldn't wish this on anyone."

The curse? Happenstance? Tragedy, whichever it was. Rowena sank to the step, gripped the cold iron rail. "This will undo her. For all she lied to me about, I canna think she feigned her love for her child. He was her everything. Her joy. Her heart."

Constable Morris stepped outside, sighing. "Your Grace, I don't know what to say. Neither of them could have done it, but it's obvious they had something to do with it, given that they're the only ones who were told where the gems were stashed. But now . . ."

"Leave it." Brice had settled beside her, wrapped an arm around her waist. "No diamonds are more important than a child's life. Do what you must do. Look into the boy's death."

"But the gems—"

"Forget them. It's not worth it."

Rowena gripped his knee. "I wish . . . I almost wish she would let me comfort her, that I could be a friend."

Morris shook his head. "Don't try it, Your Grace. She was crying to her brother about how it's your fault they're here, that you asked her to come. That if they hadn't . . ."

The ache in her heart matched the one in her stomach. Would

it have happened anywhere? At Delmore? Or had it been tied somehow to coming here? Because they *had* come because of her, because she'd promised to help them.

"Don't." Brice put a hand on her elbow and used it to pull her up alongside him as he stood. "Don't blame yourself, darling. You didn't do this. I daresay no one did. But we should go."

The constable nodded. "I'll find out anything I can, but . . ."

"Don't make it worse for them than it is. Please." Looking near to heartbreak himself, Brice tucked her hand into the crook of his arm. "There is pain enough for us all to deal with."

He led her down the steps to where he'd parked the Austin. She knew well they would head to hospital now, to see if new pain awaited. And she could find nothing to say. She could do nothing but clutch her hands together and let the scenery roll by, much like her first ride in this car. Except that now they shared the pain, shared the circumstances.

She reached out and rested her hand on his, on the gearshift.

When they arrived at hospital, they found Ella outside, rushing to meet them. For a moment, too familiar panic nipped . . . but her face was clear.

"I saw you coming. He blinked! He's unconscious again now, but he blinked. The doctor is bursting with hope." Tossing herself at the car, Ella embraced her brother and then reached over to embrace Rowena too. Her smile was pure sunshine. "I knew it! He'll recover. He will. I am certain of it—down to my very bones. Just like Phin—"

"If you launch into that story again . . ." Brice loosed a long exhale. "Praise God."

"Indeed. And we saw Stella. I know you didn't want us going there, but we did—so that's that." Ella squirmed her way back onto her feet and lifted her chin. "And she swears she didn't send a telegram to that laird. Said she wished she had, but she didn't."

Catherine, then. They'd thought it the threat she needed, but she must have decided the distraction would work even better. Rowena shook her head. Scare her, get her to tell her where the diamonds were, and then sic Malcolm on them anyway, to direct the attention away from whomever she'd sent to fetch them.

They'd underestimated her. And yet . . . Rowena could feel no anger now. Not now. Only that soul-deep pity.

Brice opened his door, slid out, gave her a hand so she could slide out behind him. Leaning into her husband's side, Rowena turned with him and Ella toward the building's doors. Maybe it was the curse that had wrought this new pain. Maybe it was merely consequences of the actions all had taken. Maybe it was sheer coincidence, unrelated.

No. She knew what it was. She knew, as surely as Ella had known that a miracle would happen for their friend. Some things were beyond their human understanding. Like that blackest of hatred, that strongest of greed.

The purest of love. She soaked in the beautiful planes of her husband's face, the earnest light in his sister's eyes. Perhaps the curse had not yet been completely broken. But they had dealt it a blow, hadn't they? They had found something bright and light and holy.

They had found love. Family. Hope. If anything would break the tiger's curse, it was that, when paired with faith.

And faith was one thing this family had in spades. She smiled as she stepped with Brice and Ella into the cool halls of the hospital. There would yet be clouds in their life. But there was sunshine too. And it shone all the brighter against the shadows.

EPILOGUE

DECEMBER 1912

Never in her life had Rowena believed she would scowl at Annie, but if the girl didn't stop laughing . . . "I'll send you back to your room. I will—dinna doubt me."

Her sister fell back on Rowena's bed in a fit of giggles. "But, Wena, ye just burst into tears over *napkins*."

Aye, and now she was as likely to burst into laughter—she couldn't, it seemed, stick to one emotion for more than five minutes at a clip these days. Wagging a finger at Annie, she shook her head. "Ye're to have patience with me in my state. Not make fun."

"I canna help it, Wena. *Napkins*?"

Her lips twitched, but Rowena didn't let the laughter out. If she did, it might just turn back to more crying. And she hadn't time to get the puffiness from her eyes as it was. Turning back to the mirror, she patted at her face with a handkerchief and adjusted her gown. Her stomach was beyond hiding, but it earned her smiles and stories about their pregnancies from all the other ladies. Common ground. Comradery. New friends.

And Brice, every night, would set his hand upon the growing flesh and try to feel the wee one move. They ought to be able to soon, the doctor said. It would be a grand day—as grand as the one when she'd woken up without having to rush to the lavatory.

Annie's giggles subsided, and she rolled onto her stomach, resting her chin on her hands. "I like that dress. So festive, especially with your plaid brooch."

Rowena smiled and touched a finger to it, then smoothed her hand over the evergreen satin. The exact shade of the wreaths upon the doors, the garlands on every rail and mantel. "Well, I want to look my best tonight. Brice's first birthday as a married man." She had been planning this fête with his mother for two months—and had done equal amounts of crying and laughing over it.

But it would go off without a hitch. All Brice's friends had come for the occasion, even the Staffords from the Cotswolds . . . and Mr. Abbott had promised to attend, though he'd warned them he might not make it through the meal. He still suffered from headaches most every evening—but he was alive, walking, talking, and still determined to accept his post in Bristol in a few short weeks. And to speak on miracles and believing in the unseen in his first sermon.

"Ye'll be the most beautiful woman there." Annie gave a happy little sigh and bent her legs, letting her feet dangle over her back. "I wish I could go."

Rowena chuckled. "Sorry, *a leanbh*. Eight is a bit young for a coming out, even in this enlightened age."

Annie grinned. "Perhaps I'll sneak down during the dancing. Just to see the gowns."

"And perhaps, if I see you doing so . . ." Rowena moved to the bed and bent down to put her nose on a level with her sister's. And grinned. "I'd nod my head to the most beautiful dress to be found."

"But that's yours! Or perhaps," she added with a thoughtful purse of her lips, "the Duchess of Stafford's. Did you see what she wore to dinner last night?"

How was she to help but chuckle? "Aye, I did—though how *you* managed to when you were supposed to have been dining up here . . ."

Annie was saved the need to respond by a quick rap on the door connecting her room to Brice's. He entered without awaiting a response, flashing a grin as he did so. "There are two of my four favorite ladies. About ready, darling?"

"Almost."

"Good, I . . . Have you been crying again?"

He'd long ago given up being concerned over her tears. Rowena waved the question away and turned back to her dressing table. "It was only that the napkins weren't folded in the shape I'd wanted them to be and . . ." Seeing the way he pressed his lips against laughter, she swatted at him as she passed. "Dinna laugh at me, Brice."

"No, no. Never. Wouldn't dream of it." But he winked at Annie.

Which she pretended not to see. "What necklace, do ye think, *mo muirnín*? Emeralds?"

"Emeralds? Nonsense. Let's be fully festive." He appeared beside her and drew out the ornate wooden box. "Rubies."

"Perfect." She presented her back to him so he could drape the beloved necklace around her throat and fasten it for her. As she had each of the three times she'd donned it since September, she touched a finger to the gold and jewels and said a prayer for Catherine. Remembered the glee in little Byron's eyes when he'd shoved it into his mouth.

Poor baby. Poor mother. Catherine and Rushworth had gone back to Yorkshire as quickly as they could after the wee one's passing, and no one had heard a peep from them since. Not Rowena or the Staffords or, so far as she could tell, any of Catherine's friends. But everyone knew that Catherine had lost Delmore, what with no heir to keep it for. She'd moved back to her childhood home with her brother, and the crown had reabsorbed the Pratt estate, the title. Everything but the few funds unattached to it.

"There." Necklace fastened, Brice rested his hands on her shoulders and pressed a kiss to her neck . . . which lingered a second too long, given their company. She gave him a soft elbow to the stomach, and he chuckled into her ear. "Don't I have a wager to settle with you, Duchess? Something about a holiday, just the two of us? A delayed honeymoon, as it were?"

She grinned at their reflection in the mirror. He so handsome and looking at her with such longing. She so content to have his heart, and his arms about her every night. "Technically, *mo muirnín*, the wager was that ye'd fall in love before I did. And if memory serves, we were rather equally matched in that."

"Mm." He slid his arms around her waist, resting his palm against her stomach. "In that case, *you* owe *me* a holiday in the destination of *my* choice. I hear Monaco is pleasant this time of year."

"You know," Annie said too loudly, "if you need to kiss you can just ask me to go to my room."

It wouldn't have done any good, given the frantic knocking now upon her door to the hall, and the redhead who let herself in with panic in her eyes. "I can't find my garnet earbobs! Have you seen them, Rowena?"

"Ella." Brice pulled away with a laugh. "Can you not keep track of *anything*?"

"It's the fairies Annie was telling me about, it must be. Thieving little beasties." She tousled the girl's curls but then joined them at the dressing table. "Didn't I take them off in here the other night? I did, I put them right here." She tapped the marble top. "I remember."

"Aye, and Lilias ran them back over to yer room the next morning."

"Drat." Screwing up her mouth, Ella glanced around the room. "Is she here? Perhaps she remembers what I did with them when she handed them back."

"I sent her off to help Mr. Child with last-minute preparations."

Brice snorted. "Brilliant. They'll just stare with moon-eyes at each other and get in the way of everyone else."

Rowena treated him to another elbow . . . but had to laugh. "They willna. And it's adorable that they're courting. Lil deserves happiness."

"As does Mr. Child. Even so."

"Yes, yes, it's wonderful. But let's focus." Ella tapped a finger to her bare earlobes. "Jewelry. I beg you. Or perhaps I should go and beg Mother. Surely someone has another pair of garnets I can borrow, or rubies, or—"

"Oh! I have rubies." Rowena spun back to the tabletop and the carved wooden box. "I canna wear them, so you might as well. Here." She pulled out the lovely dangling earrings that had nearly tempted her to let Lilias come at her with a needle.

Nearly.

"Ah . . ." Brice reached as if to snatch them before Ella could.

Rowena lifted a brow.

Ella pouted. "I won't lose them, Brice, I promise. I'll not even touch them. Lewis will be the one to take them out."

Brice looked from one of them to the other. "They're the Nottingham rubies."

Ella rolled her eyes. "They are not. They're the ones you commissioned to *look* like part of the set, you dolt. You're not believing your own stories now, are you?"

"Ye had them made?" Rowena held them up next to the bracelet she still needed to put on. "But they're a perfect match. And yer mother's wedding portrait . . ."

"Yes, the originals were lost or stolen when I was a girl. Macnab made the replacements for him while we were up in Lochaber in August." Ella batted her lashes. "And it's a shame to keep his creation locked away in a box all the time, isn't it?"

Sighing, Brice shoved his hands in his pockets. "Fine. But if you lose them, Ella . . ."

With a squeal, she snatched them from Rowena's palm and made quick work of putting them in her ears—and then made a show of peering into the mirror. "Oh, they're gorgeous. Absolutely gorgeous."

They were, at that, the way they dangled against the ivory column of her throat, nearly matching the deep red curls she'd had piled high tonight. The light caught them, dancing round the gold, toying with the rubies, setting them alight with a fire that almost . . .

Sucking in a breath, Rowena spun to face Brice, who still stood with his hands in his pockets, innocent as could be. At her open mouth, he grinned. Shrugged.

Blasted man. She'd had the Fire Eyes the whole time, right there in her dressing table. And oh, how he must have had a fit when his mother gave them to her on their wedding day, when they scarcely knew each other.

Laughter bubbled up, spilled out. She slid over to him and wrapped her arms around him. "Happy birthday, *mo muirnín*. May this year coming be filled with blessings—even more than the last."

He held her close, a chuckle rumbling in his chest beneath her ear. "A difficult task, given that this past year gave me you."

"Aye." She tipped up her face to gaze at his, which she knew so well. Loved even better.

And wondered how love did it. How could it take two people, unite them . . . and somehow make each one more? More than they'd ever been on their own.

AUTHOR'S NOTE

One thing I love about this series is the chance to be swept away to someplace new. In *The Lost Heiress*, I soaked up YouTube videos and photos of Monaco and the Riviera. I tapped the knowledge of my French-speaking friend to make sure every phrase was just right. In *The Reluctant Duchess*, I dove headlong into the Highlands. I studied other successful novels set there, scribbling frantic notes on how to handle the dialect. (There is Scots—the unique words and way of speaking that they have mixed into English—and there is Gaelic, which is a different language entirely.) I took a virtual train trip into the Lochaber region, pausing the video every few minutes to take notes on speech patterns and references. I read up on the tales of Bonny Prince Charlie, who led an ill-fated revolt against the English king.

One thing the narrator in this documentary noted was that the Scots are more proud and fond of the tragedies in their history than of their victories. Those are the stories they still tell around the fires, that they sing about, that they built statues to honor. They are a people who sprang up in a harsh place and carved a world for themselves from strength and determination . . . and more than a little bit of what most of us call superstition.

But where is the line between superstition and the unseen things of God? That's a question I have great fun asking, and hopefully you have great fun reading as my characters ponder the same.

When I first conceived this series as an eighth grader (so long ago!), I wanted the heroine of this second novel in the series to have suffered abuse that I knew absolutely nothing about firsthand. I wanted to watch her grow and change and find love—and I failed miserably back then, never finishing the story. But I revisited it seven years ago and, in rewriting it, and revising it again under the direction of Bethany House's amazing editorial staff, I finally plumbed the depths of Rowena and Brice and what it really means to feel those empty places inside . . . and then learn to trust again. I don't pretend to be well acquainted with the pain that abuse victims suffer, but I do know the power of God . . . and that He never forgets us, even when we feel He has.

Rowena's father was an especial challenge for me. I wanted him to be multi-dimensional and realistic, and yet how does one humanize a man who has hurt his child so deeply? I pray that I found a way to do so that makes him an understandable character, even if we never like him.

I hope you'll travel with me into the conclusion of the Fire Eyes's story, as optimistic Ella conveniently forgets to give back those earrings and carries the diamonds to the Staffords' home in the Cotswolds. There will, as always, be villains and true love and curse and blessing . . . and Ella's story will also have a taste of Mother Russia as the buyer sends a broken ballerina into England as a spy on his behalf.

As you leave the world of the LADIES OF THE MANOR series now, I pray you'll do so with George Müller's insights hovering in your thoughts—that we all have empty plates, empty places. But they are not a lack. They are just an opportunity for God to provide for us in ways we can't foresee.

Roseanna M. White pens her novels beneath her Betsy Ross flag, with her Jane Austen action figure watching over her. When not writing fiction, she's homeschooling her two small children, editing and designing, and pretending her house will clean itself. Roseanna is the author of ten historical novels and novellas, ranging from biblical fiction to American-set romances to her new British series. She makes her home in the breathtaking mountains of West Virginia. You can learn more about her and her stories at www.RoseannaMWhite.com.

If you enjoyed *The Reluctant Duchess*, you may also like...

When Brook Eden's friend Justin, a future duke, discovers she may be an English heiress, she travels to meet her alleged father. Once she arrives in Yorkshire, Brook undergoes a trial of the heart—and faces the same danger that led to her mother's mysterious death.

The Lost Heiress by Roseanna M. White
Ladies of the Manor
roseannamwhite.com

Lady Miranda Hawthorne secretly longs to be bold. But she is mortified when her brother's new valet accidentally mails her private thoughts to a duke she's never met—until he responds. As Miranda tries to sort out her growing feelings for two men, she uncovers secrets that will put more than her heart at risk.

A Noble Masquerade by Kristi Ann Hunter
Hawthorne House
kristiannhunter.com

More Historical Fiction From Bethany House

After the man she loves abruptly sails for Italy, Sophie Dupont's future is in jeopardy. Wesley left her in dire straits, and she has nowhere to turn—until Captain Stephen Overtree comes looking for his wayward brother. He offers her a solution . . . but can it truly be that simple?

The Painter's Daughter by Julie Klassen
julieklassen.com

Maggie Montgomery has come to America to visit her brother Rylan and his wife but secretly plans to stay for good. Rylan warns her to keep away from Adam O'Leary, yet her heart pulls her toward him. Will Adam's past—and other obstacles—prove too much for Maggie to overcome?

A Worthy Heart by Susan Anne Mason
COURAGE TO DREAM #2
susanannemason.com

When a suffragette hands a white feather of cowardice to an English spy who is masquerading as a conscientious objector, she never imagines the chain of events—and the danger—her actions will unleash.

Not by Sight by Kate Breslin
katebreslin.com

BETHANYHOUSE

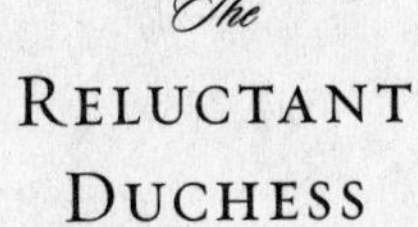
The
Reluctant
Duchess

Books by Roseanna White

Ladies of the Manor

The Lost Heiress

The Reluctant Duchess

A Lady Unrivaled